MARK
OF THE
CROSS

Books by Judith Pella

Beloved Stranger
*The Stonewycke Trilogy**
*The Stonewycke Legacy**
Texas Angel / *Heaven's Road*

DAUGHTERS OF FORTUNE
Written on the Wind
Somewhere a Song
Toward the Sunrise
Homeward My Heart

RIBBONS OF STEEL†
Distant Dreams
A Promise for Tomorrow

RIBBONS WEST†
Westward the Dream
Separate Roads
Ties That Bind

THE RUSSIANS
*The Crown and the Crucible**
*A House Divided**
*Travail and Triumph**
Heirs of the Motherland
Dawning of Deliverance
White Nights, Red Morning

*with Michael Phillips   †with Tracie Peterson

JUDITH PELLA

MARK OF THE CROSS

BethanyHouse
MINNEAPOLIS, MINNESOTA

Mark of the Cross
Copyright © 2006
Judith Pella

Cover design by Lookout Design Group, Inc.

Published by Bethany House Publishers
11400 Hampshire Avenue South
Bloomington, Minnesota 55438

Bethany House Publishers is a division of
Baker Publishing Group, Grand Rapids, Michigan.

Printed in the United States of America

ISBN-13:   978-0-7642-0132-5
ISBN-10:   0-7642-0132-8

Library of Congress Cataloging-in-Publication Data

Pella, Judith.
    Mark of the cross / Judith Pella.
        p. cm.
    ISBN 0-7642-0132-8 (pbk.)
    1. Crusades—Fiction. 2. Fathers and sons—Fiction. I. Title.
    PS3566.E415M37   2006
    813'.54—dc22

                                                                    2005032595

To my husband, Paul.
Whom else would I dedicate a book
about love and devotion to?

JUDITH PELLA is the author of several historical fiction series, both on her own and in collaboration with Michael Phillips and Tracie Peterson. The extraordinary series THE RUSSIANS, the first three written with Phillips, show-cases her creativity and skill as a historian as well as a fiction writer. A bach-elor of arts degree in social studies, along with a career in nursing and teach-ing, lends depth to her writing, providing readers with memorable novels in a variety of genres. She and her family make their home in Oregon.

PART ONE

The South of England
Spring 1263

At the foot of a sprawling elm slumped a boy, barely into his majority of age. Tears tracked through the dust of travel on his smooth young face.

He'd tried to be a man about it all, but how much could even a battle-scarred knight be expected to take? Philip de Tollard was only eighteen, after all. Forced from his only home in shame was galling enough, besides being penniless and constrained by more failures than he wished to count to take the lowliest of positions. And now this latest humiliation.

He was neither a knight nor could he ever hope to be one! Another miserable fate for him to bemoan.

Nevertheless, he hated himself for his present weakness. Tossed out like spoiled meat, he would surely be vanquished—as they all no doubt wished— if he didn't gather back the raveled threads of his wits. Sniffing loudly, he dragged a sleeve of coarse homespun across his nose. Then, as if to mock his paltry attempt at manliness, he felt a moist, hairy pressure against his left ear.

"Oh, you miserable beast!" He turned a sour look at the white face of his erstwhile companion. "Don't try to make it up to me now," he railed at the horse. "'Tis your fault I am in my present fix."

Dumpling nuzzled him again, and this time, with a wan smile, Philip ran a hand over the white patch set in the midst of the animal's silver gray nose. I am low indeed, Philip thought, if I dare blame my troubles on this fine beast, the only true friend I have, the only thing I can claim as my very own. Would that I could thrash those truly at blame! His fists balled at his sides, but no ready target presented itself, and he would not harm an innocent beast.

Nay, only I am the cause of my woes, myself and—no, not even can I blame him! Myself and myself alone.

Wiping his hands over his face, hoping to obliterate the traces of his childish emotion, he lurched to his feet. Lame horse or not, he still had to get to his destination before nightfall. This was his last chance for any semblance of a life, low and mean though it promised to be. He'd hoped to ride to his new position perched proudly upon his fine mount. Now, after walking the remaining miles in his journey, both he and his horse would limp into Cassley Manor in a most unspectacular display.

What would it matter anyway? Who but the servants would give a second glance at a mere groom?

Feeling emotion once more knotting up inside him, he turned his attention to Dumpling. His thoughts had reminded him that now he was indeed a groom, and not by mere chance but because he'd always had a way with horses. He examined each of Dumpling's hooves until he found the faulty one. With his belt knife, he gently probed until the tiny pebble, no larger than a pea, popped out from under the shoe.

"You spoiled beast!" He held out his palm, containing the pebble, before the animal's eyes, as if Dumpling could truly perceive it or, if he could, give a farthing about the sight. "I have heard of destriers riding in battle with arrows and sword gashes in their flanks. Yet you, a mere palfrey, are felled by a pebble."

Reaching into his saddlebag, he withdrew a jar of salve. The head groom at his father's estate swore by this ointment, containing ragwort, for all manner of skin irritations. The fellow even rubbed it on his own rheumatic joints. Philip applied it sparingly on the offended hoof. No sense wasting it on such a minor abrasion.

"There," he murmured. "You are treated like a war-horse in any case. But now you owe me, beast. I will ride you the last miles to the manor."

The animal snorted, as if to say, "Ha! You are lucky to possess a horse at all. And I am a fine mount for a palfrey."

"And I must be half crazy talking to a horse and imagining answers. If I hadn't been dismissed from the university for disrupting the general tranquillity, they would have soon declared me demon possessed."

Unwittingly, his thought dredged up more unpleasant memories. His last day at Oxford, though weeks ago, still curdled up inside him like milk left in the sun. But were Father Dumbarton's words prophecy?

Philip, along with Colbert Laughton, son of Lord Haliford, had been fairly dragged before the priest by the scruff of his collar. Still feeling the heat of his fury, Philip had struggled and kept trying to wring his classmate's neck even as they were hustled before the headmaster.

Laughton had started it . . . more or less. Philip hadn't been watching where he was going as he hurried down a cloister, late for his Latin lecture. The two young students had inevitably collided, with Colbert sprawling indecorously upon the stones and bringing scattered laughter from several passersby. This, of course, fired up the young lordling more than the fall itself. When Philip extended a hand to help him to his feet, Colbert had glared at it as if it were a sword poised to vivisect him. Crashing into Laughton was a pure accident, but his classmates, most of them at any rate, never lost an opportunity to deride Philip's tenuous position in society. Colbert was no different, especially now spurred on by his perceived humiliation.

"You clumsy misbegotten whoreson!" the young lord had sputtered.

Laughton had chosen just the right insult. Had he merely called him clumsy, Philip could have been reasonable about it. But after almost two years the boys knew just the right things to say to goad Philip into violence. Even then, however, Philip tried mightily to ignore them. The last fight, less than a week ago, had put him perilously close to expulsion.

"I'd stop now, Laughton," Philip warned, "while you are merely fallen upon the floor rather than made part of it!"

Colbert Laughton laughed as he lumbered to his feet. "I'd like to see you try, bastard! Prove once and for all that you do not belong among decent society."

Philip's fingers twitched, and he felt his cheeks go as red as his hair. "Leave me alone!" He started to turn away.

"Bastard and coward! Now I know why even your father won't claim you."

White-hot fury replacing the red in his face, Philip spun back round with fists flying.

By the time two teachers had rushed in to break up the melee, both young men were bruised and bloodied. There had not been time to declare a definite winner, but for Philip these brawls had little to do with winning. Father Dumbarton seemed to agree.

Philip finally calmed when standing before the headmaster. Dumbarton was strict and stern, and most of the boys feared him more than they feared God. Why he had put up with Philip's discordant behavior for so long was a mystery, but Philip was certain it wasn't out of a benevolent spirit. More than likely Philip's father had paid off the priest to keep the boy in school, though his father doing such a thing was harder to perceive than a kindly headmaster. No doubt it was merely a means of keeping Philip out of Lord Hawken's hair.

Dumbarton grilled the boys at length before ferreting out the cause of the squabble. Then he sent Laughton away with a mere week's detention. Philip remained standing before the priest, awaiting his doom.

"You have disrupted this institution for the last time, Philip de Tollard!" the priest stated.

"I don't start these fights." Philip tried to defend himself.

"I don't care about that. You prove your base birth every time you succumb to idle words."

"Idle! But—"

"Quiet!" boomed the priest. "In two years you still have not learned that words are not weapons. If you were a true man, a true gentleman, you would know that by now. You are not the only bastard I have seen within these walls, but I have never seen one with so much of the devil in him. I believe you are truly possessed with the demon of anger. You are proof that it is possible for evil to be spawned from wicked liaisons. Well, I am through with you! It is time I purge these sacred halls of your wickedness."

In a way, leaving Oxford would be a relief. Despite what Father Dumbarton might think, Philip hated the fights and the discord. Though he would have liked to continue his studies, for he enjoyed them greatly, he questioned if it was worth it. And if he truly was an evil spawn, was the Church really the best place for him? Dumbarton's words frightened him. Could they be true?

In complete disarray of mind, he had stumbled from the headmaster's chamber and encountered his second mishap of the day, one nearly as disconcerting if not as violent.

"Friar Bacon!" Philip exclaimed. "I am sorry."

The friar in question caught his balance and kept to his feet. "'Tis nothing, lad."

Philip thrust out a hand to help steady the man. Philip would rather have been smashed to pieces by Colbert Laughton than to be the cause of the great Roger Bacon's bruising himself upon the cobbles.

"Are you sure?" sputtered Philip. "I am clumsy and probably an evil spawn, as well."

"What's that?" Bacon peered at him. At forty-nine the friar had the squinted appearance of one who had spent a lifetime reading and copying many manuscripts. His robes, brown for the Franciscan order, were faded and a bit unkempt.

"Nothing," said Philip, not wanting to trouble the great man. "I was just in to see Father Dumbarton."

"Ah, I see." Bacon frowned for a moment, chewing his lip, then added, "Have you a moment, de Tollard? You appear as if you could use some refreshment."

Bacon normally kept to himself in his tower room near Folly Bridge, a room where many of the man's naysayers whispered that he practiced the black arts. He had a few loyal friends, and there were a few students whom he had taken under his wing. For some reason Philip was one of these—perhaps the friar did worship Satan in his tower and liked to be surrounded by "evil spawn."

"I should be packing my things, Father."

"Packing, you say?"

"I have been expelled."

"It is not often I have a student of your caliber. I regret that you must leave."

"As do I."

"At least walk with me as far as the common."

"I would be honored, sir."

The day was blustery and gray. Rain came in fits and starts, but at the moment the clouds were retaining their moisture.

"You mustn't place too much credence in all Dumbarton says," Bacon said. With a wry snort he added, "Truth be told, I wouldn't place credence in *anything* he says! The man would see evil in an innocent baby with a harelip."

"Then why do I sometimes burn inside?" entreated Philip. "Why do my fists often itch to smash the faces of my detractors? If not evil in my heart, then what?"

"I'll not deny you've a lion's share of anger, lad."

"Isn't anger evil?"

"If so, then we are all evil, for what man hasn't entertained anger?"

Surely Bacon knew of what he spoke, for he had never been one to restrain his own ire. It was said he had once even lashed out at the pious Thomas Aquinas. But despite the accusations of his enemies, Bacon did not seem evil to Philip. In fact, Bacon was one of a mere handful to have ever shown Philip compassion.

"I wish I could be at peace," Philip confessed.

"Peace is over-flaunted. Isn't it just the other side of complacency? Perhaps you should embrace your anger as that which drives you, motivates you. Would you have excelled in your studies if you did not have something to prove?"

Philip had tried to cling to that wisdom and to eschew Dumbarton's words when he departed Oxford. He knew he would need some positive interpretation on the matter to get him through what lay ahead once he got home. And still, several weeks later, he continued to need it, for it seemed that woe was determined to dog his every step, even to the point of his horse going lame just when he was trying to open a new chapter in his life.

He wrapped Dumpling's reins around a low branch and, in spite of himself, said, "I will rest you a bit longer, and then we must be off."

For himself, Philip was too restless to take his ease, and he was more anxious to be at his new home than he'd thought he'd be. He began pacing about the small knoll dominated by the huge elm where he'd paused. All around and slightly below him spread meadows fresh and verdant with the new growth of spring. Green shoots of leaves were evident on the scattered trees, and on his ride he had noted a few colorful blossoms of primroses in the grass. This was pretty country, the back reaches of his father's estate— Hawken, it was called.

Of course the boundary between the Hawken and Cassley estates had been in dispute since the Conquest. But the Marlowes of Cassley were of Saxon blood and should be content to have any land at all. It was said that two hundred years ago, the daughter of the then Lord of Cassley forestalled William's conquering armies by offering herself to Durand d'Aubernon, the first Norman lord of what was now Hawken. She had been, the story went, a maid whose beauty was praised in songs of the era, but regardless of her countenance there was no doubt her courageous actions saved Cassley Manor from sure destruction. True, d'Aubernon could have taken both the maid and her father's estate at will, for he had already established himself as a ruthless warrior. But at the time the Marlowes were quite powerful, and d'Aubernon, also a crafty politician, saw more advantage in allying with the Marlowes than in fighting them. It turned out to be a wise move, for over the years he managed to gain much of the Cassley holdings anyway, but by craft rather than war.

Shading his eyes from the midday sun, Philip thought he saw a rider in the distance. Yes, and approaching at great speed. In a few moments he could make out details and, to his surprise, noted it was a female. A lone female, and racing over the meadow as if chased by the demons of hell. Yet he saw no other riders in her wake.

He thought she must be in trouble to be riding at such speed. Perhaps she had lost control of her horse. Yet before he could think of any action, he was mesmerized by the picture she presented. If there had been demons chasing her, she would indeed have been an angel in full flight. The wind lifted her golden locks straight out from her head, and rather than fear on her face, he was certain he detected glee. He was further shocked when he saw her strike the magnificent ebony beast's rump with her crop. She appeared to be in perfect control of the situation!

She giggled with delight, despite knowing she would pay later if her father found out she was riding astride like a man and racing over the hilly meadow. But she would worry about that later.

"Faster, Raven!" she cried to her mount, lightly tapping its sleek black rump with her crop.

Beatrice Marlowe might be a daughter of nobility, rigidly trained in the demure strictures of ladyhood, but she was in no way prisoner to them. She loved nothing more than to ride fast and free, even if it meant eventually facing her father's ire. But why should he be angry when it was his fault that she craved such activity? Had he not placed her on the back of a horse when she was barely a year old? Had he not taught her to ride astride as well as sidesaddle? Had he not indulged her wild spirit nearly all her life? That is, until the cursed blossoming of womanhood had begun to take hold of her. Only then did Edmond Marlowe, Lord of Cassley Manor, begin to regret his toleration.

At nearly sixteen Beatrice was causing her father to fear it was too late to repair the damage.

With hardly a contrite laugh, she murmured, "Poor Papa."

Her father likely feared he would never marry her off. Already she had been passed over by his two prime candidates, both of whom had found wives of more sedate nature. Because Edmond was a minor baron, choices were limited. And, unfortunately, eligible men—or rather, their parents—were less interested in beauty than in the more practical considerations of prospective wives. Secretly Beatrice believed her father was not pursuing his daughter's marriage with total enthusiasm. They were close. It had been just the two of them for most of the time since her mother died ten years ago giving birth to a baby who also died. Her father had remarried, but his second wife gave birth to a stillborn son, and then the woman died a year later while giving birth to a second son, who died a few hours after his birth. These deaths, especially of his sons, had greatly demoralized her father, and he resigned himself from then on to being alone.

Except for Beatrice, of course. He took special delight in her, accepting the fact that the spirited girl, who was almost as good as a son, would be his only progeny. For that reason, and somewhat because of economy, he had not sent her off to another noble estate to be raised, as was the common practice among the nobility. Her departure from their home, the inevitable result of marriage, would not be easy for either of them when that time came.

Suddenly Raven stumbled. Beatrice lurched forward, but skillfully gripping the reins, she managed to keep her seat as the horse tottered dangerously. Her skill as a rider surely saved both their necks when the mare finally went down, pitching Beatrice from the saddle. The soft grass helped to break her fall.

Rolling twice, skirts askew, she came to an ungraceful stop within inches of a large rock. Shaken and fully cognizant that she could have broken her neck or split open her head on the sharp rock, she was, however, concerned foremost about her horse. Springing to her feet, she winced and, feeling woozy, nearly crumbled back to the ground. Gulping in several breaths and forcing herself to stand straight while favoring a painful hip, she hobbled over to where Raven was already attempting to gain her feet.

"Are you all right?" came a voice from nearby.

Jerking around and then groaning at the sudden movement, Beatrice saw a young man jog toward her. Dressed simply in woolen breeches, homespun shirt, and leather jerkin, he was not much older than she. His brow was creased with concern.

"I'm fine," she replied. "It is my horse that worries me."

"'Tis a shame you did not worry earlier while you rode her near to death." A slight sneer curling his lips, he gave Beatrice a cursory look, presumably to be certain that she was not hurt, and then he hurried past her toward the horse.

"Why, you—you have your nerve!" Beatrice sputtered, scurrying at his heels as fast as her bruised body would allow.

During the course of this exchange, Raven had risen to her feet. After taking a moment to let the horse grow accustomed to him, the fellow gently rubbed the animal's sleek neck, murmuring softly in the horse's ear.

"There, there, fine beast." He then carefully slid his hands from Raven's neck down the expanse of her shoulder to her right forearm and then down the entire leg. He palpated the leg, as if he knew what he was doing, then repeated the examination with the other legs. His slim hands were sure in their touch, his fingers probing with confidence yet with gentleness, as well, sliding over Raven's sleek black coat as if handling the finest Cathay silk.

Beatrice watched in silence. Oh, she'd see that this insolent fellow regretted his earlier rudeness to her soon enough, but not before she was assured that Raven was unhurt. Observing the young man's perusal of the horse, she gave no thought to interfering. She could have taken care of Raven just as well herself, for she was as skilled as her father's stable lackeys in the care of horses, but she had never seen the animal submit so placidly to the touch of a stranger before. Even the stable hands had difficulty with Raven. And no one had ever ridden the mare besides Beatrice.

Raven was standing quietly now, passively submitting to the lad's ministrations. Why, the animal even nuzzled the young man's head when he was close!

Apparently satisfied with his inspection, the fellow straightened up, turning toward Beatrice. "She seems to be unscathed except for a stone in her hoof. I assume that must have been the cause of her mishap."

Beatrice quickly shook away her awe, her ire flashing alive once more. "Assume? Of course that was the cause—"

"Driving her as you were . . . who knows what might have happened!"

"I was not 'driving' her! Raven adores racing and needs little encouragement from me to do so." Beatrice recalled using her riding crop, but she made no such admission to this stranger.

He shrugged. "At least you are both unhurt." He must have belatedly realized the error in debating with his betters.

"You can be on your way, good sir." Her tone was more smug than grateful.

He briefly cocked a brow, perhaps expecting some thanks. Well, he had done absolutely nothing, really. Why should she thank him?

"Are you far from home?" he asked.

She arched her brow. "Why do you inquire?" It suddenly occurred to her that this man, young and green though he appeared, might be some brigand just looking for a lone woman, far from home, to rob and molest.

"The stone is too deeply imbedded for me to remove without proper tools," he replied. "And I could not condone your riding this animal any distance."

"I can walk, thank you very much!" In truth it was a good four miles to Cassley, and she did not relish the idea of walking that distance, even on so fine a spring afternoon.

However, as if to prove her declaration, she started toward Raven. But she had stood still too long, and her bruised limbs had begun to stiffen. As she stepped forward, her leg, the one with the sore hip, began to buckle. She would have had a second spill had the stranger not responded so swiftly. Jumping forward, he caught her neatly in his arms. She could do little else but throw her own arms around his neck.

"Goodness!" she cried.

"I've got you." His voice was as soothing as when he had spoken to Raven.

"Really, I don't need—"

But he was already hoisting her fully into his arms. She was somewhat surprised that he lifted her so easily, because, though he was tall, he was hardly a mature, well-muscled man. He was, in fact, rather slim. But she was petite and light of figure, so he staggered only slightly under her weight. Once he steadied himself, he carried her up a low knoll to a large elm, which would provide a good resting place for her. As he set her down against the tree, she noted a dappled gray horse tied to one of the branches.

Smiling—a kind smile really, with less acerbity and more gentleness than she probably deserved—he said, "My lady, mayhap I should ascertain if *you* have any broken bones?"

"What? Oh no. Goodness no!" The very thought of his hands touching her body as he had her horse sent a shiver through her. She tried to convince herself that the sensation was one of disgust. In truth, she suddenly envied Raven.

"My lady, though it is obviously difficult for you, I would suggest you tolerate my assistance, for a short time, at least. I assure you, I mean you no harm."

"And I assure you, I have no broken bones!"

He grinned. "I shall defer to your judgment in the matter then."

"Thank you."

She took a moment to study this peculiar young man. Though dressed coarsely, his speech and bearing indicated he was not of peasant stock. From his accented English she thought he was of Norman lineage, perhaps even fresh from across the Channel. Supporting that theory was the fact that she knew most of the local noblemen and their sons. She would surely have remembered this one. In spite of the way he had perturbed her, she found him to be rather nice to look upon. His hair, darkly red like the roan coat of a horse, was clipped shorter than the current style, perhaps in an attempt to tame unruly curls. His wide-set green eyes could be filled with wry humor, and she'd already seen them flash like sunlight striking emerald. Yet, conversely, they held a gentle aspect, as well, and softened the long, straight formidability of his nose. His well-sculpted cheeks bore only peach fuzz, as did his rounded chin with its intriguing cleft. His features were clearly conflicted between boy and man. At present, "boy" was dominant, only briefly revealing "man" in a glint of the eye or a twist of his lips.

"Is something wrong?" he asked suddenly.

Beatrice's cheeks flamed at being caught staring so boldly. "Nay, 'tis nothing."

"I promise I won't touch you."

"You most certainly won't!" she exclaimed, but she tingled once more at the thought. Taking a steadying breath, she changed tack. "Is that your horse?" She nodded toward the gray.

"It is."

"You must have a generous master to allow you to ride such a fine mount." Though hardly a war-horse with its short legs and less than regal nose, it was still more than most peasants had.

He bristled, then defensively bit out, as if gnawing old meat, "Dumpling is my own horse! I am no horse thief!"

"Dumpling?" A little snicker escaped her lips before she could stop it.

"You degrade me *and* my horse?" he demanded, his fists curled, white knuckled, at his sides.

She had a feeling that had she been a man, she would have found herself taking her third spill of the day, and this no accident. The earnestness of his tone forbade any further jests the animal's ridiculous name might have prompted.

With equal solemnity she said, "I do no such thing, nor do I accuse you of thievery. I was merely curious."

"That is not what your words imply." For a moment it looked as if he regretted coming to her aid.

She quickly added, "I'm sorry. I meant no offense." She was not accustomed to making apologies, but she felt vulnerable, alone, and far from home. She did not wish to antagonize this stranger, yet she realized that was not her only reason for her words. She had sensed almost immediately that he was no thief, no peasant, not even a mean knave. What *was* he, then? Her curiosity grew intense.

Sweetly she asked, "May I inquire who you are, good sir, that I may put a name to my rescuer?"

As though he understood how difficult the contrite, almost placating, tone was for her, he smiled wryly. "I am Philip de Tollard. And you, my lady?"

"Lady Beatrice Marlowe."

"Ah yes, the daughter of Lord Cassley." He bowed gallantly, unlike any peasant.

"You appear to be familiar with my family, but I do not recognize the name de Tollard. You are not from these parts?"

It seemed as if a shadow passed briefly over Philip. His features, thus far fairly pleasant and friendly except when she raised his ire, tensed again. Then he seemed to shake away the gloom. "I am of Hawken Castle."

She shook her head. "I'm sorry, I still don't—"

"I thought perhaps you might recognize my name because I am on my way to take up a position as groom on your father's estate."

Hiding her surprise at his revelation that he was a mere groom, she said, "It is odd that my father said nothing, especially with regard to the stables. You see, I consider them my special domain."

"The stables, m'lady?" he said in astonishment.

"I suppose you think a woman should be relegated solely to the hall?"

"I have no particular opinion on the matter, but 'tis the usual way of things."

"I happen to like horses far more than kitchens and kettles and such." Tilting her head back to give him the full effect, she dared him with her eyes to dispute her.

"We have something in common then, m'lady."

Deflated that he did not take up her challenge yet pleased, too, she finally let her lips relax into a smile. "I suppose so. And because of that I shall forgive you for your earlier rude words."

"Perhaps I was more harsh than I should have been. But I cannot bear the mistreatment of animals."

"I was not—!" she began hotly, then stopped, reminded once again of her previous guilt in using the crop. "I guess I could have gone easier on Raven, especially over uneven ground but . . . Excuse me, Philip, could you please sit? My neck is getting a crick from looking up."

"Forgive me, m'lady!" he replied with the earnestness of a peasant, then dropped quickly to his knees beside her.

She found it extremely peculiar that his bearing seemed so conflicted between nobility and commonness.

"You were saying, m'lady?"

She glanced at the animal grazing placidly, as if the whole afternoon hadn't just taken a dramatic and unexpected detour.

"I am afraid I simply lost myself in the unfettered sensation of racing across the earth," she explained with sudden seriousness. "It is the only time I feel truly free. But you can't possibly know what it is like to be bound by rules and expectations. Sometimes a woman's skin is nothing more than a dungeon to imprison her."

"But such a lovely prison."

"Oh, you—!"

Quickly he added, "I am sorry again, m'lady. It was wrong of me to make light of your feelings." Pausing, his gaze wandered off toward Raven. When he drew his eyes back to Beatrice, they were filled with such a depth of understanding, almost of empathy, that it made her tremble a bit. "I have an idea of prisons, m'lady, prisons not made of walls."

Impulsively she reached up and touched his arm. "I am sorry I have been so cross with you, Philip. I believe you do understand, though I don't know why."

He glanced down at her hand, then moved his own hand as if he would touch hers in return. But he stopped it midair and hurriedly tucked it back at his side. It made her aware of the disparity of their social stations. Yet she had never felt such camaraderie with the grooms or servants at home. Whatever he was, Philip de Tollard was no common servant.

"We best get you home before your father starts to worry," he said. "We can ride my horse and walk Raven behind."

Sitting in front of Philip, snuggled close to his warm chest, made for a disquieting ride home. Beatrice did not want it to end yet reminded herself that Philip would be a regular fixture at Cassley now. She could find him any time she visited the stables, which for her was often. A most pleasant thought.

B eatrice took particular care as she dressed a week later. She had her maid plait her hair in braids and wrap them around her head like a crown. Her peach-colored kirtle made of fine linen was her best everyday garment, as was the full circular mantle of wool she now swung over her head. The blue of the mantle suited her well, bringing out the full depth of blue in her eyes. Perhaps the girdle of leather decorated with brass crosses was a bit much, as was the wreath-shaped brooch of gold with which she fastened her mantle. But since she hadn't been out riding since the mishap with Raven, she wanted to make this outing special.

It had nothing at all to do with that new groom. Though, in truth, when he had last seen her, she'd not been at her best, and it was her place as lady of the manor to repair what might have been a damaging first impression. For the *manor's* sake. She had no more interest than this in one of such a lowly station.

"My lady, are you sure you want to wear your best mantle for riding?" asked Leticia, Beatrice's maid.

"Do you buy my clothes, Leticia, that you should be concerned?" Instantly Beatrice regretted her snide tone, but who could blame her for a sour temper after being confined for a whole week, relegated to tending the kitchens and other loathsome household tasks. Such was her punishment when her father learned of the mishap. She had not even been permitted to go to the stables to give Raven a bit of turnip. She was sick of being ordered about.

She didn't blame Philip for her plight even though he had been the one to impart the story of the mishap to Lord Cassley. The information had been forced from the new groom by her father, who had been quite curious as to why Raven was being led riderless to the stable upon her return that day.

Nor was it Leticia's fault. Hadn't the maid, only four years older than Beatrice, even tried to help her slip away two days ago? True, they had been caught by Roland, her father's vassal and attendant, but for that alone, dear Leticia should be allotted special favor.

Beatrice flung herself upon her bed, an apologetic pout on her face. "Oh, I am sorry, Leticia. It's just that . . ." Should she tell the maid about the groom? Even the idea of interest in a mere groom was scandalous. But Leticia would understand. "Have you seen the new groom?" she finally asked.

"When have I time to seek the stables, my lady?" Then the maid smiled mischievously. "Oh, now I remember. I did, as you requested, go to inquire of Raven's health after the mishap. Seems I did note a new face in the stables."

"And?"

"He was a bit young . . . for me, you know. But not an entirely unsightly lad."

"Quite handsome, I would say."

Leticia cocked her head as if in deep thought. "Hardly a knight. And I have seen pages who were more fit of limb."

Beatrice thought of the brief conversation she'd had with de Tollard on their ride home the day of the accident. "He is a man of intelligence, though. He has spent two years studying in Oxford."

The amusement withered from Leticia's eyes, and she became serious. "My lady, I am told great dangers lurk in such places. Apostasy and even—" pausing, she quickly crossed herself before finishing—"the black arts!"

"Leticia! I never imagined you to harbor superstition. Education is a good thing."

"Then why is Philip de Tollard now serving as a groom?" Leticia focused a superior look down her nose at Beatrice. "Why has he not followed his education into the clergy, as is proper?"

Beatrice shrugged, perturbed with the maid's questions, insightful though they might be. Beatrice had subtly tried to ferret out the answer to these and other questions about the new groom during her week of confinement. With great subtlety, since it would have been unseemly to show too great an interest in a groom, she'd approached her father and even Roland. Both, in the stoic way of men, were not forthcoming with information. It was, they had implied, the groom's business, not hers.

Defensively, she answered her maid's questions. "I'm sure there is a very good reason!"

"And for this you wear your best mantle?"

"Of course not!" Beatrice's creamy cheeks reddened, saying far more than even she was willing to admit. "My first day riding deserves something special. That is all." She jumped up from the bed, pausing only a moment to smooth out her clothes; then she strode to the door of her chamber. She flung it open. "You may remain here and do my laundry!" she tossed over her shoulder as she exited.

"But . . . but . . ."

"You don't like to ride anyway."

"Just take your care, my lady," Leticia called after Beatrice's departing figure. "You'll be in sore trouble if there be a repeat of last time."

"I plan to follow my father's instructions implicitly." Leticia did not see the impish twinkle in Beatrice's eyes as the words were spoken nor the cunning grin she wore.

In a way that surprised him, Philip's new world did not offend him as much as he'd feared. Instead he found it rather pleasant breathing the clean fragrance of hay. Even the ripe odor of manure, mingled as it was with a tinge of leather and oil along with the sweat of hard work, was not very offensive. At least they were pure sensations, unlike the pervading reek of fear and decay he'd often imagined at Hawken.

Odd, too, that was, for Cassley Manor was older than Hawken by a good hundred years. Unlike the staunch Norman fortifications of Hawken, Cassley was, as its name implied, more of a manor house than a fortification. The Saxons, for whatever reasons, be it laziness or lack of fear, were not prone to building structures in stone to withstand armies—no doubt much to their regret when William of Normandy crossed the Channel. Some of the oldest extant parts of Cassley were constructed of wood, though a newer wing, to replace a section destroyed by fire fifty years ago, was of stone. Philip had not yet been inside the main house, but he'd heard it was light and airy compared to the austere ramparts of Hawken. It had a rambling, unaffected quality that was felt even in the attitude of the residents. Upon occasion he'd see the baron himself interact with servants in a rather jocular fashion. They did not appear to fear him in the least.

He recalled his own arrival a week ago. Lord Cassley had chanced upon

Philip and Beatrice as they were heading toward the stable. Of course, the man was curious as to why Raven was being led and not ridden by her mistress. Philip was loath to lie to his master on his first day of employment. Beatrice tried to play down the incident, coming just short of an outright lie. Like the servants, she seemed to have no fear of her father, if her boldness was any indication. Philip suspected she respected the man enough to wish to protect him from worry, especially if that would also protect her from punishment.

In any case, Edmond Marlowe directly confronted Philip, who feared the man without knowing him, simply because he held Philip's future, such as it was, in his hands. Philip had no choice but to tell the truth of the situation. Besides, he felt Miss Beatrice Marlowe ought to receive some censure for her unseemly behavior. Lord Cassley's response was mild, in Philip's estimation. She was to be confined to the grounds for a week and was forbidden to go near the stables. But then again, a week cooped up in the castle would no doubt be a great strain for one such as Lady Beatrice.

All things considered, Philip now saw the punishment as more upon himself than the girl. He found himself wondering if he would ever see Lady Beatrice again, in the stables or anywhere. He'd surprised himself with how much he thought about her and how he constantly looked for her to appear like an angelic apparition among the straw and grit of what was now his world. He had never known a woman like her.

Of course he was not yet nineteen, so he knew precious few women—or even girls, for that matter. There were the serving maids at Hawken Castle, and more than one had indicated she'd be willing to help expand his knowledge of the fairer sex. His half brother, Gareth, was frequently dallying with the female servants. As heir of the estate Gareth considered this to be his born prerogative, but Philip had no such birthright. Besides, he found it difficult to convince himself that bedding the servants, willing though they might appear, was chivalrous. He might indulge in a few kisses now and then, but his conscience would not permit more.

Who was he jesting? There was more than chivalry prompting his actions, or lack thereof. When he finally did take a female to his bed, it would be only within the bonds of matrimony. He would not be responsible for bringing upon an innocent child the awful fate he had known all his life. For a surety, it would be different for his children! They would know two parents and would find security in the affection they held for each other. Philip was determined to find not only a wife but one he could cherish eternally. And with that his thoughts came full circle back to Lady Beatrice. Yes, she could be such a woman to whom he would gladly bestow his manly favors—

"Enough of that!" he muttered, feeling heat rush up his neck and into his cheeks. With a vengeance he returned his attention to oiling the leather saddle before him.

"You are going to wear a hole right through that fine saddle."

Philip jerked his head around at the sound of the sweet voice of the very one who had so filled his thoughts.

"M'lady Beatrice!"

"Did I startle you?" The amusement glimmering in her rich blue eyes indicated that she felt no regret at all.

"You walk with the step of a fairy."

"What do you know of how a fairy walks? Have you seen one?" She focused a critical yet mocking eye upon him. "I think you have, and it has turned you red."

This served to make the heat in his face pulse all the more. "D-did you want something, m'lady?" he asked tightly. "I have work to do."

"Mayhap you have too much work to accompany me riding?" Her tone both taunted and enticed.

"Accompany you?" His heart raced at the very thought.

"I am finally permitted to venture from the grounds, but I must do so with a chaperone."

"Your father is letting you go with only one attendant?" Philip asked, astonished at Lord Cassley's liberality.

"You do not feel up to the task?" She still taunted.

He had been made the object of her amusement once too often. He gave her a derisive snort. "I would have no problem protecting you against danger, m'lady. But who would there be to protect you from *me*?"

She giggled merrily. "Oh, Philip, how you amuse me! You are only our groom, you know."

Intuitively he knew it hadn't been her intent, but nevertheless the words stung. He'd been the brunt of such comments all his life.

"Is that so?" His eyes narrowed and he stepped toward her. "So a groom is incapable of this?" He reached out his arm, pulled her to him, and before she could protest, he covered her mouth with his lips.

He had expected anything but the eager response he received. Her lips were soft and inviting as she melted into him. His arms, at first uncertain, found their way around her, encircling her firmly so that he could feel her soft curves through the cloth of his tunic. His pulse raced at the feel of her—so warm, so supple, so willing and giving. None of the servant girls had ever felt like this!

He wanted to stop. He knew he should stop, but the gesture that had begun as a jest took on a life of its own. It didn't help his weak resolve that she so readily responded to his advances. It was heady and intoxicating.

He wanted more . . . so much more! He was innocent of such matters, yet his body seemed to know the way and was leading him as if on a journey. A journey that Beatrice appeared quite eager to accompany him upon.

Neither of them would know the completion of that journey.

A creaking sound made them both freeze, then jump guiltily apart. Philip glanced around, certain his life was about to be ended by an outraged father. But they were still alone in the alcove where the saddles were stored. A moment later Tom, the head groom, appeared around a corner of the wall.

"Morning, m'lady," Tom said.

Philip breathed a sigh of relief that they had not been caught.

Tom went on, "How's them saddles coming, lad?"

"F-fine, Tom, just fine." Philip's voice squeaked an octave higher than normal as he tried to regain his composure.

"We better get that door hinge oiled," Beatrice muttered under her breath, appearing to be far less disturbed than Philip.

"I think not, Lady Beatrice," Philip said. He was most grateful for that squeaky hinge because he did not know what would have happened had they not been interrupted.

Shrugging, with a wicked smile on her face she said, "Tom, I shall be requiring Philip's attendance for a while."

"As you wish, my lady."

"You—you still want to go riding?" said Philip.

"More than ever."

"But—"

"Papa said I should take you as a chaperone, and I would not want to disobey my father, would I?"

3

There was no racing that crisp spring morning. Beatrice was content to ride sedately, sidesaddle and at a gentle cantor. Just as well it was, because her mind was only vaguely focused on riding. She simply couldn't get that kiss out of her mind.

For certain it hadn't been her first kiss. She'd exchanged kisses with the sons of neighboring gentry at parties and such—after the adults were well into their cups and had forgotten to notice that two of their young people had slipped off. But none of those had equaled what she had just shared with Philip.

In her mind that kiss must have been a truly grown-up kiss, the kind that young girls whispered about to one another.

Thanks to Leticia, motherless Beatrice was not as innocent of these matters as her father presumed and no doubt hoped that she remain. Leticia had once had a love who was killed in an awful accident. For this lost love Leticia had eschewed marriage and taken up, instead, the position of a lady's maid. She did not often speak of the matter, but since she was *experienced* and the only older woman in Beatrice's life, she felt it her responsibility to teach her charge something of the relations between the sexes.

And that kiss . . . well, Beatrice would have to ask her maid about it. However, it was possible Leticia would not approve. She often said that she only taught Beatrice about intimate matters so that the younger woman would be better equipped to guard her chastity. If the maid thought Beatrice was flirting with such intimacy, she might feel duty bound to report it to her father. That would mean trouble.

Beatrice glanced surreptitiously at her companion. He was at that moment gazing ahead, seemingly unaware of her. Suddenly her lips tingled. Even they yearned for a repeat of that moment in the stable.

But Philip de Tollard was behaving like a perfect gentleman, as chivalrous and chaste as a Knight Templar. He had made no further advances toward her. He rode stiff and alert in his saddle as though fearing attack by thieves and marauders at any moment. Scratching her chin thoughtfully, she decided she had to have one more kiss, just to see if the previous experience was not simply a fluke.

"Philip," she called with sweet innocence, "I am fatigued. Might we dismount for a few minutes? I am sure the horses would like the rest as well."

"As you wish, m'lady."

This day they had ridden east of Cassley, away from Hawken lands. Here a wood grew up around the banks of the Cassley River, which amounted to little more than a babbling brook. During Roman times and before this had been a sizable waterway, but one thing and another had reduced it to what it was today, not unlike the Cassley possessions themselves.

"Let's find a place to stop by the river," Beatrice suggested.

Nodding, Philip scanned the area as they drew close to the sparkling waterway. He selected a place where a substantial oak stood among the reedy willows and tall white alders that populated the banks of the river. Stopping, Philip dismounted quickly, then held Raven's reins and helped Beatrice to the ground. She continued grasping his steadying hand for a long moment as his eyes lingered on hers.

With sudden briskness he dropped her hand and took up Raven's reins, along with his gray's.

"I will tend the animals if you wish to sit by yon tree, m'lady."

Beatrice looked over the spot with approval. The new shoots of green on the oak lent a dappled shade, like delicate lace, over the grassy area beneath the branches of the tree. This would be the perfect setting for what she planned.

Philip hobbled the horses in a nearby grassy area so they could graze, then brought a blanket and laid it out close to the tree. With a hand sweeping toward the blanket, he said gallantly, "Your throne, my lady!"

She dropped gracefully down upon the woolen coverlet, arranging her skirts fastidiously around her. Glancing up at him with her most beguiling smile, she said, "Good sir, will you not join me?" She patted the blanket.

"I think not, m'lady. I am your chaperone, not your companion."

"Pshaw! You are what I say you are." His narrowing eyes quickly told her she had said the wrong thing. "I meant . . . oh, please sit with me!"

"I . . . uh . . . fear to, Lady Beatrice."

"Why is that?" she inquired with feigned guilelessness.

"Methinks you know very well why."

"'Twas only a kiss, Philip." She patted the blanket once again. "Come now, sit."

He shook his head. "I have stepped leagues beyond propriety. I will not do so again."

"Never again?" She could not hide her dismay.

He gaped at her. "You were not—?" He shook his head. "You, by rights, should have been scandalized."

"You know well that I was not."

"B-but . . ." he stammered, his befuddlement endearing to her in spite of everything. He bumbled on, "You *should* have been. What I did was . . . you . . . I—"

"I want you to kiss me again," she burst out with conviction.

With equal conviction he replied, "I will not."

At once a new slant on the matter occurred to her. "Did it . . . disgust you, Philip?"

"No, it did not, m'lady. But—"

"Please sit, Philip. Again my neck gets a crick in it."

He hesitated, then just as she began to believe she had lost this battle of wills, he dropped down beside her—a safe arm's distance away. He was silent for a long while, and sensing she had perhaps pushed matters too far, she also remained silent. They both stared straight ahead. She wondered what he was thinking. She thought about his declaration, "No, it did not . . ." What, then, could be the problem? Would he bore her with that stale argument about their differing stations?

Still staring straight ahead, he finally spoke. "Lady Beatrice, I will not dally with your affections. I kissed you because I wanted you to think of me as more than merely a groom. But that is, in truth, what I am."

Because it was a poor argument, she opted for a different approach. "What of your education, Philip? Of a surety, you are fit for more than a position in a stable. Why, then, are you here?"

"What do you know of my family?" he asked, eyes still facing forward so that she could not read them without twisting around.

"I have told you I have not heard the name de Tollard."

"What of the name Aubernon?"

"Ralph Aubernon is Lord of Hawken Castle. Everyone knows of him. It is a powerful estate."

"Lord Hawken is my father."

Beatrice's mouth fell ajar. As far as she knew, Ralph Aubernon had only one son—Gareth. She thought he was about her own age, but she did not know him well, for he had been away for years serving as squire in London at the court of King Henry. She had never heard of a second son. If there was one, why the different surname? It made no sense.

As if reading her confusion, he went on, "I bear my mother's name. Lord Hawken would not give me his name." This last was added with no pains to hide his bitterness. "If you had spent time on the Continent in Anjou in France, you would have known the de Tollard name. It is not the most important family in the area but is of some standing still. Although I am sure they are not well pleased that I have usurped their name, I took it anyway. Even a bastard must have a name!"

Her throat was dry and she could barely speak. She could almost feel his pain as if it were her own. She finally spoke only so he wouldn't think her appalled by his revelation.

"How came you here then, Philip?" All thoughts of a passionate kiss fled her mind, but oddly, she wanted to hold him, though more as a mother comforts a child. Despite the bitterness in his voice, he seemed to her as guileless as a lamb just then.

"Five years ago my mother, with whom I lived, died," he replied stoically, though there was a slight tremor to his voice. "She was a noblewoman. Her sin shamed her family, and they had every right to disown her or to force her to take the veil and become a nun. Even so, they were fond of her and were basically decent people. They gave her and her baseborn child a home. Then the family fortune declined over the years, and some said it was God's retribution for her sin. When she died, they sent me away, saying, 'Let your miscreant father who sullied our daughter's virtue care for his misbegotten offspring!'"

He smirked with grim irony. Beatrice wondered if he was thinking what he could have done to her in the stable, how a single kiss could indeed lead to eternal ruination.

"Philip, I—"

"You understand now, don't you?"

"You are different from your father" was all she could think to respond.

"Not so," he murmured. "My father is not such a monster."

She wondered about that, for she'd heard stories about Lord Hawken. Whether tales of ruthlessness and cunning were true, it was a sure wager he was no saint.

Philip seemed to see the doubt in her eyes and said, "He took me in, didn't he? By law he didn't have to."

"Only to thrust you into the lowly position of a groom?"

"I lived for three of the last five years at Hawken. Not the happiest of years, I will tell you. Times were better when my brother was away, but even then . . ." His features twisted. "I had no place there. I was not claimed as the son of the baron. My origin was supposedly a huge secret, one that everyone knew about though none spoke of it. Neither lord nor servant, I fit in nowhere. No one knew how to treat me, so I was ignored by most. Except . . ." With a shrug he paused and then added, "It doesn't matter. For everyone's good, I was finally sent to the university. A position as a clerk would have been far better than many in my circumstances could have expected."

"I suppose many second sons enter the Church," she said. "Few lords can afford to support more than their eldest son into the knighthood."

Nodding grimly, he replied, "But I *was* the firstborn son." Shaking his head sharply, he added, "My father can't be blamed entirely. He had his wife and legitimate son to consider. No matter. There is honor in the clergy."

She did not know Philip well, it was true, but she found it hard to imagine him in a monastery, bent over a table copying the Holy Scriptures, or even keeping some lord's accounts.

"What happened at the university?" she asked.

He let a small smile invade his forlorn expression. "I was expelled."

"I expect the study was most difficult," she commiserated. "I have learned to read, although it near burst my brain to do so. And forget doing ciphers."

"I rather enjoyed many of the courses." His eyes brightened with enthusiasm as he spoke. "They said I excelled at my studies. I especially liked science. Have you heard of Roger Bacon, the Franciscan? He said mathematics is the gateway to science. Oh, the mysteries of the universe he opened to me!" His eyes glowed with excitement, and she smiled. With a sudden scowl he demanded, "Do you mock me again, m'lady?"

"No, Philip!" she replied sincerely. "I like seeing you so enthralled about something. I would not have taken you for a scholar. But how could they expel you if you excelled so?"

"It was my fault, and my fault alone," he said dismally. "Even in the cloistered halls of Oxford one must constantly confront one's betters. Unfortu-nately I have never been able to weather such confrontations peacefully. All a bastard has are his wits and his fists. I am afraid I made too liberal use of the latter."

"I am sorry, Philip, that people were cruel to you—"

"Don't feel sorry for me!" he said sharply.

"What else am I to feel? You have been used unfairly."

"Anything except pity." He jumped up and strode a few steps away, his back to her.

"I don't feel pity," she insisted, "rather outrage. You are the son of a great baron, yet you must clean my father's stables. How came you to be here?"

Turning, he gazed down at her then swiftly slipped to his knees near her, nearer in fact than he had been before—disconcertingly near. "I chose this position," he said intensely. "I knew I was not suited to the life of a church-man, but I have always had a good way with animals. When I was sent back home to Hawken, I knew I could not endure long there. This seemed by far the more preferable route."

"I am sorry—" Seeing the error of her words when he opened his mouth to rebuke her, she quickly added, "I am only sorry that I have been insensitive toward you. That first day when we spoke of prisons, my words must have sounded glib to you. I know so little about life, don't I? I do wish I could understand it all better. For you, Philip."

He reached out, lightly touching her cheek. "You understand enough, m'lady. I appreciate it."

She laid her hand on his then gently nudged him toward her. They fell as easily into each other's arms as before, but this time their lips touched only briefly before he jerked away and scrambled to his feet. She jumped up, too, and, grabbing his shoulder, forced him to face her.

"Philip, if I promise not to try to kiss you again, can we be friends?"

"I don't know if that is possible."

"Do you have any friends?" she asked. "I have few myself and would greatly value one."

"All right," he replied. "Friends. I will not be responsible for the Lady Beatrice Marlowe losing herself to a landless bastard."

"Indeed you won't be!" But her tone was only half in jest, for if the violent racing of her heart was any indication, it was probably too late. She was already completely lost.

P hilip forked hay into the vacant stalls, realizing he would finish none too soon. Already he could hear the creak of wheels, the snorts of horses, and the barking of the estate dogs announcing the arrival of the first guests attending Edmond Marlowe's birthday celebration.

Tom came up to him to inspect the progress of his work. "You're doing a fine job, lad."

"Thank you, Tom. What else have you for me?"

"Oh, there'll be plenty to do before long. I'll take charge of the wains. You take care of the mounts. We only have room in the stable for the lords' horses, you know."

"I'll see they are well cared for." Philip knew Tom was affording him an honor of sorts to take responsibility for the far more precious destriers of the lords.

"I know you will, lad," Tom said. "I may as well tell you, you have been working out fine. I've told Lord Cassley as much."

"Thank you again, Tom."

Tom started to turn then paused. "Lad?" He shifted from foot to foot with seeming uncertainty, then plunged ahead. "Philip, ye are a good lad. I can see that. And you've a way with the horses that I can't say I have seen in the other grooms, not even my own son. I . . . I wouldn't want to lose you, lad."

"If you are well pleased with my work, then—?"

"You know of what I speak, boy. Don't make me speak more plainly."

Tom was a kindly man, and the last thing on earth he'd want was to become entangled in romantic intrigues, especially if they were to force him to deceive his master. So far he'd kept quiet about such matters, and Philip hated that he was the cause of making this good man go against his lord by his silence. Yet if honor meant that he give up the joy he'd been experiencing with Beatrice, he wasn't certain he had the strength of character to do so.

"I understand, Tom," he said. "I won't be the cause of—"

"Say no more. Just don't persist upon your present path."

"I will try." Philip had to be honest, and he simply could not swear never to see Beatrice again.

Sadly, Tom shook his head. "'Tis the road to ruin you are upon." Then he walked away.

If the road led to ruin, it was still such a sweet road. These last two months with Beatrice had been the greatest of his life, and there had not been even a hint of impropriety in their activities. After that first ride by the river, Philip had made sure they were never alone together. He'd recruited Tom's twelve-year-old son to accompany them each time since, which was nearly every day. Sometimes even Beatrice's maid joined them. They had not touched each other again, except for when Philip would extend a hand to help the lady from her mount.

But even the mere thought of that chaste and completely necessary contact made him burn inside. It might be only a quick brush of fingers, yet he saw the smoldering of her eyes every time they touched, and he felt the same.

Friends?

Oh, what liars they both were! Yet he truly believed that the passion building within them was founded on more than youthful lust. On those daily rides they talked much.

Snorting, he lunged a forkful of hay into a stall. They could do naught *but* talk! At least at times the maid feigned concentration on her needlework, and young Tom often fished in the river nearby or busied himself looking for snakes and bugs, thus giving Philip and Lady Beatrice opportunity for conversing. And Philip enjoyed their talks. It wasn't merely a distraction. Beatrice had an endearing way about her conversation. She could chatter pleasantly about the household, recounting amusing stories about the servants or even of her own mishaps. He recalled the story she told of befriending one of the household chickens when she was six years old.

"A chicken?" he'd asked with amazement, himself having never found those beasties good for much besides eggs or stew.

"She was a chick when I first made her acquaintance," Beatrice said with a defensive pout. "A dear fluffy thing, too. A small creature, though, and the other chickens were unkind to her. I first grew attached to her when the tiny thing got a broken wing from one of her nasty brothers. I nursed her and fixed it all by myself—with a little help from a scullery maid. But quickly the chick grew into a pretty, fat creature. Then came time for the Christmas feast."

"Oh no!" he had groaned, attempting to get into the spirit of the story.

"I refused to accept the inevitable, and I snatched her from the butcher's grasp. Quite literally, I did! And I ran with her out the gates, the ungrateful beast flapping her wings and squawking worse than if I'd let the axe fall upon her neck. Feathers were flying everywhere. But I led a merry chase, the butcher, the cook, a half dozen kitchen scullions all after me as if I'd taken the gold vestments from the chapel."

Even now as he worked in the stable, a smile played upon his lips as he pictured little Beatrice racing through the yard, yellow braids flying, skirts askew, fervently clutching her prize.

"What happened then?" he'd asked.

"They finally caught me. I would have made it, except one of the men was bringing in a wagonload of hay, and all the clamor of the chase made his horse rear. The wagon toppled, barely missing me and Miss Hen, but the hay didn't miss us. We were buried in the stuff. Miss Hen didn't like that at all. Odd, too, don't you think, since she lived on a bed of hay? She pecked me fiercely, trying to escape my 'rescue.'"

"Did she escape?"

Beatrice ran a hand through her golden hair. Her sapphire eyes glittered with sudden moisture. "No. But I ate lamb for dinner that Christmas, not chicken. In truth, I hardly ate at all. I wept so hard that day. I know now that I wasn't just crying for Miss Hen. That was the first Christmas without my mother. I guess the hen gave me good reason."

"I didn't know females needed reason for tears," he said.

"Papa was so sad that I felt I needed to be strong."

They both shared then about the deaths of their mothers. Beatrice proved she could not only tell a funny story, but she could be sympathetic and caring. She was intelligent, as well, and listened with fascination when he explained to her about Roger Bacon's experiments with convex lenses.

"You can actually start a fire with a piece of glass?" she asked, astonished.

"Yes, I will show you when we get home. Bacon has also figured a way to use lenses to make viewing the heavens possible."

"Why would you want to do that?"

"Don't you wonder what is up there? What makes the stars shine? And the moon?"

After a moment's thought, she said, "It seems . . . almost sinful."

"Bacon has been criticized to be sure, yet didn't God create the heavens and the Earth? Should it not all be of interest to us?"

A spiritual discussion followed, and she fairly held her own, though he'd taken a philosophy course or two at Oxford. He thought it interesting that their discussions could range over such a vast spectrum of subjects, from a maid's faux pas in the kitchen to the meaning of life. And with her he even was able to share the deepest parts of his heart, those things others would surely have mocked him for.

"I also learned from Friar Bacon about the wonders of the rest of the world, beyond England, beyond France, places even Crusaders have not seen. Have you heard of Cathay, Beatrice?" When she shook her head, her eyes sparkling with interest, he went on, "It's a land of fabulous wealth, where merchants decorate their shop fronts with strings of pearls. They guide their elephants with goads made of gold. Everyone, even the lowest peasant, wears garments of silk. It is another world, where a man like me could go and find enough gold, just lying about, so that he could live like a king in England."

"You sound as though you would go to this place if you could," she said with a touch of peevishness.

"Imagine how exciting to see a world so unlike ours that there are not even words to describe the wonders there!"

"I thought your dream was to have a fief in England and—"

"That dream is more impossible than traveling across the earth," he replied bitterly. "I would go to Cathay if I could, and I would brush the dust of England, and of Hawken, from my cloak."

"Then I would go with you, Philip!"

He gazed at her with wonder. "You would? It would be a dangerous trip and hard on a woman."

"Do you think I would let you go off to the far ends of the earth alone?"

"It is much for a friend to do."

"But that is what true friendship is."

Now that he pondered it, beyond all else, he and Beatrice were friends, insofar as he knew how to define that elusive concept. Friendship to him was as alien as true love. He'd never had a friend. There had been the occasional adult who, taking pity on his miserable estate, had been kind to him. Never, though, had he had anyone of his own age to hunt with or to make merry within a tavern. He'd been shunned at the university. No one seemed to remember or care that the Conqueror himself had been a bastard. At least William had been accepted by his father. But it was a risk for anyone to befriend Philip, considering that his powerful father had rejected him, had not even given him his name.

The only way Philip had had any social contact with his peers at Oxford had been to fight them. He'd engaged in at least one such fight a week. Some he won; some he lost. When the elders finally expelled him, they said he was too impulsive, a hothead. They had put up with him for as long as they had because of Lord Hawken, but enough was enough. Oddly, Philip didn't see himself as a warrior. Though he would have given anything to be a knight for the prestige of it, he much preferred scholarly pursuits. He enjoyed the challenge of mathematics, and the mysteries of science and geography fascinated him. Perhaps he was indeed more suited to the Church. Perhaps he could join the Franciscan Order like Roger Bacon.

He laughed harshly, fiercely stabbing the final pile of hay with the pitchfork.

He knew he didn't fit there, either. A monastery! Hah! He barely believed in God. Truth be told, he had rather enjoyed those fights. He'd felt a release of something inside him every time his fist smashed into an opponent's face. Father Dumbarton had called it a demon of anger. Oh yes! He was angry. No denying that. But he longed for peace, in his heart and in his world. Yet it was as elusive as his father's love and acceptance.

"Philip, come quickly!" Tom's shout broke into Philip's thoughts.

Philip hung the pitchfork on its hook and hurried to the front of the stable, where the first horses were being led in.

"You be sure to rub the animal down good," instructed Lord Edbury's vassal. "My master will know if you shirk the task."

"I will care for him as if he were my own," said Philip, taking the reins.

The vassal gave him a narrow look of warning, as though he were the lord himself, and then strode arrogantly away. Now, there was a face Philip would have loved to smash a little. He was no better than Philip—well, perhaps some better. He was a vassal, not a lowly groom. Still, Philip's fist itched, but not more than when, a short time later, another servant came in leading a black stallion with white "socks" on all except one foot.

This was Lord Hawken's mount. Philip knew it well.

The servant pointedly looked down his nose at Philip as he handed over the reins.

"There you go, *boy*," the fellow said, with emphasis on the final word.

Philip rankled but bit his lip. He would not start a fight and ruin the party. "The lord wants his destrier fed an oat mash in the morning," said the servant, Boyle, with whom Philip had already had several unpleasant encounters at his father's stables. "Do you remember the formula for the mash?"

"Yes, I do." Philip bit out each word. This man had deserved a thrashing long before this, but he held his ire in check.

Boyle glanced at Tom, busily fixing a wagon harness. "I hope Cassley's new groom isn't as incompetent as most of his other servants. He'll pay dearly if anything happens to this horse."

"Ye need not worry, good sir," said Tom obsequiously.

Philip cringed at the man's servile tone, hoping he'd not be expected to use the same himself. He could be respectful to these lordly vassals and servants, but never would he grovel before them. They might look down upon him and call him *boy*, yet the fact remained, he was still the son of a lord— the firstborn son. The blood of lords flowed in him from his father and his mother. He was a groom by choice not by default, and by all that was pure, he'd only be pushed so far!

Luckily, Boyle walked away, and Philip unclenched his fists. But before he turned toward one of the stalls with the stallion, he paused a moment to glance toward the manor house where the guests were being welcomed inside. He caught a brief glimpse of a black wool cloak as its wearer swept through the great oaken doors. He knew that cloak as well as he had known the white-socked stallion. His heart clenched as his fists had only a moment ago. Oddly, his hands remained slack, not balling up in perpetual anger. He did not hate the man in that cloak.

God help him! He did not hate Lord Hawken.

5

Besides nearly all the local gentry, some guests had come from as far away as London, forty miles north of Cassley. All to bid Edmond Marlowe congratulations on his fortieth birthday. The hall of Cassley Manor was decked out almost regally. Beatrice had seen that the best tapestries were hung on the walls and that the high table was set with the best linen and the fine pewter, whereas the earthenware cups and trenchers of stale bread were laid out on the lower tables. The silver saltcellar was placed prominently to Lord Cassley's right hand.

Beatrice's distaste for household tasks did not extend to preparing for feasts. Rather, she took special pride in her ability to organize an affair as well as any matron in the community. Of course, Leticia, at the ripe age of nineteen, had lent ample guidance and some level of expertise. But it was Beatrice's own special flair that had caused the decorative greenery to be laid out in such a fetching way. And it was her idea to mix rosemary with the rushes spread out upon the floor to sweeten the stale air of the manor hall.

Yes, she had definitely enjoyed planning her father's birthday celebration. And as the last of the fifty or sixty guests arrived, she determined to enjoy the affair itself. However, some of the luster had decidedly dimmed because of Philip's absence. It was not customary for the servants to attend manor festivities, but Beatrice could not think of Philip as just a groom. He was the son of one of the honored guests! Still, she understood his shock when she had invited him, and she understood his refusal. Even if he hadn't been a groom, it would have been immensely awkward for him to mingle with his estranged family.

Lord and Lady Hawken were in attendance with their son, Gareth, and a retinue of Hawken knights and their ladies. Beatrice had made sure that she herself had greeted them at the door, and she tried to be careful in her perusal of them—her dear Philip's family. It had been some time since she had seen them, and now she had quite a different perspective of them.

Lord Hawken especially piqued her interest. He was tall and rather gaunt of frame. All his features, from jutting chin to beak nose to small, sharp brown eyes and shining black hair gave a decidedly hawklike impression, as if his fortress had been named solely for him. In truth, the Hawken Castle name predated him by two hundred years.

When Beatrice welcomed him to her home, he bowed politely, then did something so un-hawklike it momentarily threw her off balance. He smiled, and to her great surprise, it was a nice smile, emitting a certain warmth. Until that moment she'd been thinking how little he resembled his elder son. But that smile looked hauntingly like Philip's smile—that of the son he refused to claim.

"My lady Beatrice," said Ralph Aubernon, Lord of Hawken, still wearing that disconcerting smile, "you have grown much since last I saw you."

"Yes, my lord. And in truth it has been far too long." Silently she thought that if their families had been more neighborly, she might have met Philip long ago.

"Had I known of the beauty sprouting at Cassley, I would surely not have denied my son the pleasure of knowing you."

Beatrice noted from the corner of her eye that young Gareth, of whom Lord Hawken must be speaking, was about to make his presence known. But another figure stepped forward instead.

"However, our Gareth has until recently been happily detained at court. He is squire to Prince Edward." This was spoken by Lady Hawken, and even before Beatrice lifted her gaze to the woman's cold gray eyes, she knew she did not like her.

"My lady Hawken." Beatrice curtsied and offered her hand in welcome.

Clarise Aubernon, styled Lady Hawken, took Beatrice's hand briefly between two cold fingers before dropping it as if it were a slimy fish. Beatrice was happy enough that the contact had been brief, for in that short span she'd felt as if she had been grasped within the talons of not a hawk, but a far less regal bird of prey. Perhaps a vulture.

The woman was beautiful, no doubt about that. Beautiful in the way of ice forming on the eaves in winter. However, Beatrice had the feeling this ice would not melt beneath spring's warmth. Lady Hawken's features were sculpted perfectly, her hair the color of shimmering sable. Her clothing was expensive and had a decidedly French look. Indeed, the Aubernons were quite close to King Henry III, of whom it was often said he was more French in his sympathies than the Conqueror himself.

Just as Beatrice was wondering what else she could possibly say to this woman, Lord Hawken stepped forward, sparing her for the moment.

"Lady Beatrice, may I present my son Gareth." He gestured toward the lad, but the expression focused on the young man was unfathomable. No warmth, no pride, nothing to indicate what he thought of this son he deemed to claim as his.

As Gareth Aubernon bowed, Beatrice saw that he was as perfectly formed as his mother. She could find absolutely no physical flaw in the young man, who, by her calculations, was about seventeen. What truly amazed her, however, was that she was so ready to search out flaws in him.

"Lady Beatrice, I am charmed," the young man said, gazing over her form in a manner no seventeen-year-old should have displayed. His eyes, black like his father's and cold like his mother's, seemed to brag, "I know what lies beneath that silken kirtle you are wearing, and I well know what to do with your womanly attributes."

Beatrice shivered and, only by great strength of will, kept the blood from rising into her face.

Just then Edmond Marlowe appeared to greet his guests. With him was another couple Beatrice had met only once before in London—Eleanor and Simon de Montfort, styled Lord and Lady Leicester.

"Lord Hawken," said Edmond, "do you remember Lord and Lady Leicester?"

"Of course I do." Hawken bowed formally. "But you have been away on the Continent for nearly two years, have you not?"

"I am back now," de Montfort said.

"I am glad of it," said Hawken.

"Are you, Lord Hawken?" asked de Montfort.

"Many of the barons are."

"That surprises me," de Montfort replied, "since two years ago all were quick to negotiate with the king, who was stomping on their rights by having his oath regarding the Provisions of Oxford absolved by the Pope."

Beatrice noted an ominous undertone to his words and tried to recall what she knew about the tall and darkly handsome son of Norman nobles. As the fifth son, he'd been given no inheritance but had been told to go to England to try to claim some disputed family lands there. In short order he had befriended the young king Henry, won a peerage in the realm by claiming the Leicester estates, among the largest in England, and perhaps his greatest victory, had married the king's sister. That had been over thirty years ago. In more recent years, Lord Leicester's relations with the king had ebbed and flowed like the Channel tides. But Beatrice paid too little attention to the affairs of state to know what the disputes were about.

"It was difficult to go against the will of the Pope," Lord Hawken said defensively.

Edmond interjected, "But much has happened in two years, has it not, Lord Hawken?"

"Enough so that I have removed my son from Henry's court," Hawken replied.

Beatrice thought she detected a snort from Lady Hawken, but when she took a surreptitious look in the woman's direction, she appeared as placid as a frosty pond.

"Then you are with us?" Edmond asked the lord of Hawken.

Beatrice wondered at her father's meaning. Though she had heard her father criticizing the king's strongly foreign sympathies, he now made it sound as if there was some more formal protest brewing.

Lady Leicester cut in smoothly. "Please, my dear gentlemen. Let us not spoil this festive occasion with politics."

Beatrice admired the woman's nerve in cutting off the men. But she was still the king's sister, even if she opposed him along with her husband.

Beatrice took Eleanor's words as a cue and wasted not another moment in quickly shuttling the guests to their seats.

The Aubernons were seated at the high table along with Beatrice, her father, Lord and Lady Edbert of Chichester, and their most exalted guests, Simon de Montfort and his wife, Eleanor, of Leicester.

Beatrice thought her father was an oddly matched crony of Simon de Montfort. Edmond, though he prided himself on the fact that he was vassal to no man but the king, was one of the lesser nobility, whereas Leicester, a relation of the king, was at the far opposite end of the social spectrum. Edmond was also proud of his Saxon lineage, though his deceased wife had been distantly related to King Henry II, the present king's grandfather. But

Edmond had ill used the extensive lands brought to the marriage by his wife. The death of Alice, along with the dwindling prosperity of the land, had greatly reduced Edmond's influence and esteem. Yet he and the Norman, de Montfort, were oft in the same company, and Beatrice wondered at the wisdom of that, given the earl's royal conflicts.

The complexities of politics were of little interest to Beatrice and were the last thing on her mind that evening. Gareth Aubernon, seated at her right, tried to ensure that by monopolizing conversation with her. Given the fact that Lady Hawken was on her opposite side, this monopoly wasn't entirely unwelcome. Nevertheless, Gareth was a dull companion. He knew how to converse only about himself and had little of personal interest to recount besides dull stories of his knighthood training. Somehow he even made dull his recitals of Henry's court.

"I was certain to have been knighted before I turned twenty-one," he said, holding a shank of lamb midair, "had my father not called me home."

"And why did he do that?" Beatrice asked, hoping to liven the conversation with a bit of gossip.

But all Gareth did was drone on about the Provisions of Oxford and other boring matters of politics.

Beatrice stifled a yawn. Unconsciously she glanced about the hall.

"Do you expect more guests?" inquired Gareth.

"No." Beatrice had secretly hoped that Philip would at least visit the hall for a moment in order to look upon her decorations. What would Gareth say if he knew her thoughts were on his bastard half brother?

Then, much to her astonishment, a thread of conversation drifted down to her from midtable.

"Your new groom? Is he working out?"

That was Lord Hawken. Asking about Philip! Was he actually interested in his son?

Beatrice strained to hear more.

"He is doing quite well," Edmond replied. "Although it is my daughter who would know best, since she nearly lives in the stables."

"Truly!"

"I fear I have been too lenient with her since her mother's passing. But she so loves to ride and has great affection for the horses, as well."

Nothing further was said about Philip. The conversation turned to horse-flesh, a subject Beatrice would have desired to hear had Gareth not drawn her attention away.

"You enjoy riding?" he asked.

Beatrice blinked, surprised he had also been eavesdropping on the conversation several seats away. "Yes, I do."

"Perhaps we can go together sometime."

"Well . . . yes . . . of course." Suddenly it occurred to Beatrice that Gareth's presence tonight was no accident. Her father was making yet another attempt to find her a husband.

"What about tomorrow?" he persisted.

"Ah . . ." What could she say? I'd already planned to ride with your brother? She had a strong feeling that would not be well received. Philip spoke little of his family, much less of his brother, but she sensed they were not exactly friendly. Regardless, her flat refusal of his invitation would be construed as a slight, especially if Gareth had been given to believe by her father that his daughter was available. The idea infuriated Beatrice, yet she had to keep in mind that a slight to a powerful family like the Aubernons could be disastrous.

What would a mere ride hurt anyway? At least they would be riding and she wouldn't have to listen to Gareth's dull prattle.

"Yes," she said sweetly, "that would be nice, Gareth."

"As you know, I will be biding the night here, so why don't we meet in the stables shortly after we break our fast in the morning?"

Nodding absently, she wondered what she would tell Philip. In the time since his disclosure about his father, they had become close, though only as friends. They had seen each other almost daily. Mostly they rode together, always with either Tom's son or Leticia along. Often she visited the stables and followed him as he went about his daily work. They talked about everything. There was probably not a thing Philip did not know about her, and though he was more reticent, Beatrice felt he had revealed more of himself to her than he ever had to anyone else.

He had never so much as touched her since that first, and last, kiss. She determined to be patient. Soon he would get over his silly notions about their stations. But it wouldn't help if she came prancing into the stable on Gareth's arm. The irony that she could openly pursue a relationship with Gareth but do so only in secret with Philip would sting his masculine sensibilities.

For the rest of the evening Beatrice pondered what she would do. She hardly tasted the tender kid, which the cook had, for once, roasted to savory perfection. By the time the dessert of wafers, cake, and spiced mead was served, she had determined to talk to Philip that very night and was ready to fly to the stables to find him. She could not just show up in the morning with Gareth without preparing Philip first.

As hostess, however, she had to sit through the entertainment. There was a sloppy juggler who, she decided, had earned only half his pay. The troupe of dancers was better and engaged her attention for a short time. Yet the evening droned on as if for an eternity. For her father's sake she was more enthusiastic than anyone when lovely decorated pastries were served in his honor and everyone wished him the best regards of the day. Still, she was never more happy than when the guests finally began to go their own ways— the few honored villagers back to their homes, household members to their respective rooms, and those who would stay the night to their chambers. As lady of the house, it fell to Beatrice to see that these last were all settled in for the night before she could consider her own plans.

6

At last Beatrice was free to retire to her own room. Quickly she found her mantle but barely had it fastened when Leticia came in.

"Where would you be going so late, m'lady?" the maid asked.

"Really, Leticia, I shouldn't have to explain my every move to you!" Beatrice snapped.

"With so many strangers about, even the manor grounds are not safe so late at night," Leticia replied evenly.

Beatrice answered glibly, "Pah! Strangers? Whatever can you mean? These are our friends and neighbors." To emphasize her words, she gave a firm tug to the neck of her mantle as she secured it with a brooch.

"Then I will accompany you to the stables."

"The stables? What makes you think I am going there?"

Leticia gave a superior nod to her head. "It is a logical assumption. Philip de Tollard will want a report of the festivities—news, mayhap, of his family."

"His family . . ." Beatrice eyed her maid with a mix of admiration and ire. Then she sighed resignedly. "So you know of the Aubernons' relationship to Philip."

"It is no great secret, no matter how Lord Hawken would wish it so. And I do not condone the man's actions, but Lady Beatrice, it is not a matter in which you should become involved."

"I am involved, Leticia. Philip is my friend."

"And what of your father?" To Beatrice's blank stare, the maid added, "Your father chooses to keep you blind to his affairs, and you apparently choose to accept this. It may be the natural way of things, but I think in this case, a lady's ignorance could well spell trouble."

"Speak plainly, Leticia!" Beatrice urged impatiently. Philip might be asleep by now, thereby foiling her attempt to smooth matters over with him.

"Your father and Lord Hawken have never been on the best of terms. Hawken looks down on your father but at the same time covets his lands, which, though smaller than the Hawken estate, are by far the richer tract of land. Lord Cassley fears Hawken's power, especially now that your father is flirting dangerously with that party of rebels calling themselves English for the English. He has been trying to curry Hawken's favor—"

"Is Lord Hawken one of these English for the English people?" Beatrice often found politics not only boring but confusing, as well.

Leticia shook her head. "Hawken seems to be the kind of man who will go where the wind blows strongest."

"Gareth said tonight that he is Prince Edward's squire," Beatrice said, impatient to be gone yet knowing Leticia well enough to realize she was not spouting politics merely for the sake of showing off her knowledge. She had a point, and it was well to take the time to hear it.

"Rumor has it that Hawken called Gareth home, a move that can be construed as a means to distance himself from the king. Though there was a time not long ago when Prince Edward himself was rather friendly with de Montfort, the leader of the rebels."

"You mean Edward allied himself against his own father?"

"I have heard that de Montfort is a very charismatic person and a skillful warrior, one to make a strong impression on a young man. At the moment Edward seems to have repented of his disloyalty toward his father. But loyalties shift as easily as the winds on the Channel."

"How do you know this?" Beatrice had always admired her maid, but this was above the woman's usual wisdom. This was information relegated to the realm of men.

"I listen, m'lady. I pay attention." The maid's words carried an obvious edge of censure. Then her tone softened. "Dear Lady Beatrice, you are young and perhaps should remain so for as long as possible—"

"No, you are right. I mustn't claim to be a woman only when it is convenient. Tell me, Leticia, tell me what this is all about. What have these things to do with Philip and me?"

"As far as I can see, your father and Lord Leicester wish to win Hawken as an ally against the king. De Montfort has a daughter who is not yet ten years old. Your father, on the other hand, has—"

"Of course! I should have known. Isn't marriage always where men's politics end up? Marriage or war." Beatrice found herself suddenly trembling despite the warmth of her mantle. Her fears about Gareth Aubernon were more real than she'd imagined.

"You well know your father believes you should have been betrothed long ere now, m'lady. But he has been loath to force the issue."

Beatrice walked to the chamber window. The quarter moon cast a little light on the courtyard below. She could see a distant candle burning in the stable loft. Turning back to her maid, her lip quivered as she asked, "Until now?"

Tenderly the maid answered, "I think your father will soon make an arrangement with Lord Hawken, betrothing you to his son." She added in a more buoyant tone, "It is not so bad, dear one. Gareth is a comely lad with a promising future."

"Leticia," Beatrice replied desperately, "I cannot marry Philip's brother!"

"Do not think you have a choice in the matter, child."

"I won't! I just won't! I'll flee to the convent first. I'll take the veil."

With that she spun around and ran from the room, ignoring her maid's plaintive calls for her to come back. She flew down the corridor, glancing back only once to see that Leticia was not following. No doubt the maid thought letting her go would do less damage than chasing her through the house, stirring the guests and perhaps the guards, as well. A few heads raised as Beatrice hurried past the servants still clearing away the remains of the feast.

She did pause a moment to tell the doorkeeper that she was just going out for a few moments to take a breath of air. He lifted the bar on the great doors for her. Her heart was still pounding in her throat when she reached the stables. By now she didn't care if Philip was already retired. Entering the stables, quiet now except for the sounds of the horses—a snort, a soft whinny, a crunch of hay—she decided what she must do.

Philip had taken a room built into the stable loft instead of one in the servants' wing of the manor house. This was a small, rough-hewn room that even Tom had eschewed. But Philip said it suited him, that he liked the stable smells better than those in the house. He especially liked falling asleep to the gentle sounds of the animals. Beatrice thought he also liked the privacy the loft room afforded. That solitude, however, was about to be shattered.

Thankfully, the light she had seen from her room was coming from Philip's chamber. She climbed the coarse steps leading up to the room and paused only a moment to suck in a calming breath before she tapped the door with her fist.

"Who is it?" came Philip's voice.

"It's me. Beatrice. Please, I must see you."

"You can't come in here! Go away."

"Let me in or . . ." She paused, swallowed, then continued with as much menace as she could muster, "or I shall come in without your leave."

There were sounds of scrambling about inside. Finally the door opened and Philip greeted her, a rather sour look on his face. He was fully clothed, at least in his braies, without chausses. His linen chemise, with its open neck, had obviously been hastily donned.

"I was nearly asleep," he grumbled.

"With a candle burning?" Peering around his shoulder, she saw a book lying by his bed. He was quite proud of this costly possession, though he said he'd copied and bound it himself. Geoffrey Monmouth's *History of the Kings of Britain* was a tale of the King Arthur legend. On several occasions Philip had read her passages from the book, and she thought it a good omen that his head would be so recently full of the chivalric romance.

"What do you want, m'lady?" he demanded in a most unchivalrous tone. "It is late. Are we under attack, or has some other equal disaster befallen us?"

"Will you let me in?" Without awaiting an answer, she brushed past him.

"Beatrice!" he exclaimed, completely forgetting to use her proper title as he was always so careful to do. "You can't come in here."

Ignoring him, she took a moment to give the chamber a quick perusal. It had no furnishings save the bed, which was little more than a frame filled with straw and covered with an old blanket. Beside the bed was an upturned pail on which sat the candle, its small flickering flame providing precious little light to the damp, dingy room. The sight of the place wrenched Beatrice's heart. Philip was the son of a lord. The eldest son. He should be surrounded by finery.

She plopped unceremoniously upon the bed, sinking so far into the straw that her feet dangled like a child's over the side. She wrinkled her nose. "This bed is uncomfortable and it smells."

"No one invited you to use it!" After closing the chamber door, he came to stand towering over her, his arms crossed over his chest.

"Sit down, Philip."

"No!" He added with a smirk, "And I don't care if your neck does get a strain!"

Softly she said, "I met your family."

"Ah, now would be the time to mention them," he said dryly. "Talk sweetly to me now and I may not murder you."

"But, Philip, you are so much better than they. Your brother is a bore, and you are far better looking."

"That is what you came to tell me? Placing my future and perhaps my very life at risk, you have come merely to inform me that I am better looking than my brother?" He gave her a withering look, then suddenly his lips parted, softening into a smile. "Ah, Beatrice, what am I going to do with you?"

"Sit next to me," she entreated with a smile, patting the frayed coverlet.

"I dare not."

"You would not sit beside a friend?"

"Do you taunt me, Beatrice?"

"I like when you call me just Beatrice." Lifting her eyes so as to look squarely into his, she confessed, "Philip, I have deceived you these last weeks."

His brow arched with curiosity, but he said nothing.

"All that talk of being friends?" she continued. "It was a lie. I cannot be your friend, Philip, because I love you—"

"Bea—Lady Beatrice—"

"Don't try to tell me I cannot love you because of who you are. It is too late. I love you!" She grabbed his hand and tugged hard on his arm, but he tensed, resisting her.

Jerking his gaze from hers, he closed his eyes. The muscles in his neck bunched spasmodically. She thought she detected a strong hint of pain in his visage, and it so filled her with an ache of her own that she knew, even if she hadn't when she'd spoken the words, that she did indeed love him. She knew because she wanted to take his pain on herself; she wanted to protect him from those who would hurt him. It never occurred to her that she could cause him pain, also.

"Say something, Philip," she breathed.

He pulled his hand from hers and, turning, paced across the room, as if putting a mere span between them would help. "We are courting disaster, you and I," he said. "But I don't blame you. I knew from the first moment I saw you . . ." He turned back to face her, a tiny smile quirking his lips. "I saw you from a distance, riding astride like some goddess come down from the heavens with no one to answer to but herself. I loved you then, even before you stamped your foot at me and gave me that regal little smirk of yours. That only made me love you more. So you see, Beatrice, I, too, have been deceptive."

Jumping up, she strode to him. "We love each other, then. It is a time to rejoice, not to mourn. I have heard the troubadours sing of this love but never thought to experience it for myself."

"What they sing about has nothing to do with marriage, you know," he said with a superior air.

"What do I care!" Reaching out, she put her arms around him, hoping, praying he would return the embrace. But he did not. His arms remained stiffly at his sides.

"This cannot be," he said as if chewing tough meat.

"Why?" she asked. Then, with a throaty breath, she tilted back her head, parting her lips and licking them demurely. She'd once seen a serving girl do this in an inn where she and her father had bided a night on the way to London. The man in whose lap the woman sat had responded quite amorously.

"Do you seek to seduce me, m'lady?"

"Answer my question first," she replied tartly. "Why? We would not be the first lovers to break with tradition—"

"You speak like a child with no notion at all of reality," he said harshly. "I am landless. I have nothing to offer you, not even the promise of a knighthood whereby I might have a hope of winning a boon from the king or my liege lord. I am nothing, nobody. I could give you a life little better than one of your father's serfs."

"I don't care!"

"You are a child!" He fingered the fine wool of her mantle with its richly embroidered trim. "You would wear rags and grub a few vegetables from the dirt to feed your family? I think not."

"Don't tell me what I would do!" she railed. "I'll go ahead and marry whom my father chooses, then take you for a lover. So there!"

"Like in the songs?" he sneered.

But she saw his ire was more from frustration than anger toward her.

"The songs never tell about the bastard spawn of those liaisons, do they?"

She gasped at the sharp reality of his words. She should have known what lay at the root of his reserve. Yet still she could not let go. She was not his mother, and he was not his father.

"It would be different for us, Philip."

"I would be no man if I allowed such to become of us." But even as he spoke of manhood, he looked more than ever the forlorn boy, lost and confused. He started to take his hand from where he still held the collar of her mantle, but she quickly took his hand and tugged his arm around her.

"Don't," he pleaded, wrenching his hand from her grasp and taking a step away from her.

Full of conviction that they were indeed different from other ill-fated lovers and desperate to force his hand and that of her father, as well, she reached up to unclasp the brooch on her mantle. Letting the garment slip from her shoulders to the floor, she began to untie the laces of her surcote.

"I think you are crazy," he murmured.

"Stop me if you will, Philip."

He stood as if frozen on the spot, the expression on his face tumbling so quickly from shock to awe and then to longing, she wasn't certain at all what he was truly thinking.

"Methinks we are both crazy," he whispered as he clumsily pulled her to him, lifting his hands, threading them through her golden hair, his lips plying her with fervent kisses.

"I am yours," she breathed.

From what she knew of such matters, she realized it would not be long now before he would claim her and she would be his and they would be united in the flesh. Then no one would deny them.

"Take me," she urged. "The world be hanged!"

With a groan he took a step away from her, she thought in order to lead her to the bed. She shivered and closed her eyes in expectation of what was to come but was confused when she heard a shuffling and felt the caress of the soft wool of her mantle against her skin. Her eyes flew open.

"No, Philip!"

Tenderly he wrapped the mantle around her shoulders. "This must not happen." His voice held little conviction, and she felt his hands tremble as they held the garment against her.

"Yes, it will!" she cried and gave her foot a childish stamp.

"Not this night, my dear sweet Beatrice." He stepped away and turned his back to her. "Tie your kirtle."

"And if I don't?"

"Will you force me to throw open my door and raise a hue and cry?"

"I hate you, Philip!" Angrily she gave the cord of her kirtle a hard yank, nearly tearing it. "Maybe I will marry your brother after all!"

"My brother?"

"It's all but arranged. How do you like that?" she dared.

She saw his hands curl into fists, but with his back to her she could not read his face. Would there be fury there or more pain? She wished for the former, that he would become so angry he would take her just to spite his brother.

"Beatrice . . ." His voice seemed to crack and break. "I don't know what to do." His tone sounded like a dirge. Then he turned, facing her, revealing his torment.

She wished she could take back her cruel words. She'd had no idea how they would hurt him.

He went on, "I could not live if my brother were to have you. But neither could I live knowing I had destroyed your life."

Her own heart near to breaking, she tried to embrace him once more, but he shook her away.

"Please go," he said.

"I can't leave like this."

Gently he touched her cheek. It was far from the kind of touch she had hoped for earlier, yet in a peculiar way that touch seemed to hold more love than anything she had imagined before.

"I will find a way for us," he assured.

"How?"

"I don't know, but one way or another, I will!"

I n the morning the guests decided to go hunting. Beatrice was relieved, for this meant she would not have to bear Gareth's company alone. All of the guests who had spent the night, about a dozen in all, mounted up after the morning meal and headed toward the wood, a royal preserve bordering the river.

Philip had been nowhere to be seen when Beatrice had gone to the stable to fetch her horse. In a way, she was relieved. She wasn't certain she'd have been able to keep her feelings in check were she and Philip to cross paths just then. She still wanted him desperately. His words last night had held her off, but she continued to believe there would be a way for their love.

Upon the back of Raven she was able to lose herself for a time, until Gareth made his presence known. A short distance out of the manor gates he rode at her side and did not leave until they reached the woods. There, he was distracted briefly with the preparations for the hunt.

The hounds had been penned up far too long and now strained at their leads, innately sensing that the hunt for which they lived was at hand. Lord Cassley was proud of his dogs. For the task of tracking he had two limers, roan bloodhounds of impeccable lineage, and two tan harriers. His two sleek greyhounds of a reddish gray color that Cassley liked to describe as a rusted sword were the swiftest in the county and seldom failed to bring down their prey.

Lord Cassley employed one of the best huntsmen in the county, to whom he paid the kingly sum of eight pence a day. Leticia disdained this extravagance, considering the lord's oft-low coffers, but Beatrice did not begrudge her father this pleasure, for it was one area where he excelled over the Hawken estate. Hawken might own more hounds and employ more huntsmen, but none came close to Lord Cassley's in quality.

Beatrice could not help a surge of pride when Lord Hawken commented—with some envy, Beatrice thought—on the braw quality of her father's dogs.

The preserve, which had been opened for use by local nobles in the early years of Henry the Third's reign by the Forest Charter, a postscript to the Magna Carta, was plenteous with game even in late spring. While the hunting party waited in a small glade, the huntsmen and handlers went forth with the limers and harriers to set upon the tracking. The sun had risen high overhead and begun its descent before they finally returned to the party with their report.

While the party of guests had waited, a meal of dried fish, fresh bread, and warm ale was served. Beatrice had little to do as hostess, so she occupied herself by visiting with the women, all of whom were older than she because their daughters her age were being raised in other noble houses. It wasn't often Beatrice socialized with any in the community. Most of the more well-off lords and their ladies were constantly on the move, traveling every few weeks or so between their estates. Lord Cassley had only one estate, so there was no place for them to travel to, but regardless, Beatrice had always been too young to go to many of the festivities in the county. Now that her father was anxious to marry her off, that situation would surely change.

Nevertheless, she tried to enjoy the camaraderie with the women, eager to glean gossip and other useful bits of information from them that a girl with no mother must find a way to learn. Eleanor de Montfort was pleasant but somewhat aloof, even to the other ladies. Or perhaps the other ladies deferred so to her social superiority that she could not breach the subtle social line separating them. Clarise Aubernon was also aloof, almost brooding. She looked down on everyone as if it were she who was sister to the king, not Eleanor. Beatrice thought that getting close to Clarise would be more dangerous than nuzzling a porcupine.

When Lady Edbert mentioned quietly to the women that she was with child, Beatrice decided to focus her attention toward that woman for a time. Who knew what she might learn? And . . . who knew how soon she'd need such knowledge? She tingled all over again as an image of Philip popped into her mind.

No wonder her cheeks flamed when Gareth Aubernon came up to her and, bowing gallantly, requested leave to sit beside her.

"No . . . I mean yes . . . of course," she stammered.

"I did not mean to cause you distress, m'lady," he said as he dropped down next to her.

"Well . . . no . . . you didn't." She quickly glanced at Lady Edbert, hoping he'd think her discomfort had something to do with that conversation, which halted immediately upon Gareth's arrival.

"I thought perhaps you would enjoy the company of one near your own age."

"How thoughtful of you."

"I confess I was also considering myself in the matter."

He spoke quite smoothly for someone so young. She thought of Philip's sometimes artless speech, then condemned herself for comparing the two brothers again.

Gareth was saying, "You are not only the youngest female here but the most beautiful." His gaze roved over her, as it had last night at the feast, a scrutiny that made her squirm beneath its lusty fervor.

She wanted to flee and cast about in search of some task that would draw her away.

"Do my words unhinge you, Lady Beatrice?"

"You are quite forward, sir."

"Surely I am not the first man to so flatter you."

A giggled escaped her at the idea of this seventeen-year-old calling himself a man.

His gaze darkened. "I have said something to amuse you, m'lady?"

She thought of the frequently tart repartee she had exchanged with Philip. Usually these interchanges had culminated in mutual laughter. Philip had even said he loved this part of her character. She didn't want Gareth to love her, but perhaps she did want to test him.

So she responded, "I have *yet* to have a man so flatter me, Gareth, unless I am to consider a smooth-cheeked, tender-eyed boy as such." Her smile mocked just a little.

"I see the beauty hides a sharp, uncomely wit."

And though she looked for it, there was not even a smile in his eyes as he spoke. "I must check the level of the casks of ale," she said, not caring if it was a lame excuse. When she jumped up, she saw Lady Hawken staring at her, and she shivered, as if she had been touched by an icicle.

It was then that the huntsman and his assistants returned to the glade. The male contingent of the party listened to the huntsman describe the tracks he'd found, indicating their size with his hands. He also described other signs, such as marks on trees made by antlers. Finally he opened a cloth that held the droppings of the stag.

The men held forth in lengthy discussion whether this would be a worthy animal to pursue, though Beatrice suspected it was sheer boredom that finally decided them. They hadn't come hunting just to sit in a glade conversing with one another. While the huntsman, on foot with the dogs and their handlers, went off in a roundabout direction with the intent of cutting off the stag's line of retreat, the men mounted up. Lord Cassley blew his horn to signal the greyhounds to begin the chase, and the horsemen followed.

Beatrice wanted to join the riders, for she'd always thought the hunt to be exciting. She found it hard to content herself with the company of the women. Yet, because Gareth had gone with the men, she decided to stay behind. If his boorish behavior wasn't bad enough, she was almost certain his mother hated her and could not bear her to be near Gareth. That was just as well for Beatrice. Yet it troubled her that this woman should feel such antagonism toward her. No doubt the reason lay in the fact that she hoped for a better match for her son.

Finally restlessness and boredom overcame all else. She instructed the groom—sadly not Philip—to ready Raven for riding. The other women raised mild protests about her going alone after the men, and the groom offered his services. Beatrice insisted, though, that he was needed to guard the horses, and she assured everyone else that she knew the country well and the men were not far ahead.

In truth, they were farther ahead than she had judged, but she didn't mind. She really preferred to be alone just now. She wanted to think about Philip. She wanted to figure out a way for them to be together. He had such high ideals about honor and chivalry. He simply could not fathom that she could be willing to eschew all her noble finery, such as it was, in order to be with him. A peasant hut where no one knew them, coarse homespun dresses, a passel of babies with smudged faces and bare feet—it sounded like heaven to her if such a life included Philip.

She was not completely sheltered. She'd seen how her father's serfs lived. It was a hard life. But she thought they were happy in their way, perhaps even more so than one such as she, bound by the strictures of society. At least none of their women were pawns in the political machinery of kings and lords.

A breeze gently ruffled the leaves on the trees overhanging the bridle path. It was like riding beneath nature's lace. The sound made her think of a flight of birds, and she looked upward but saw only stippled patches of blue sky overhead. She remembered the last time she and Philip had ridden together on this very path. Leticia had been sewing in the very glade where the women now were, letting Philip and Beatrice have a few moments to ride alone.

Beatrice had started teasing him by racing ahead while he called after to her to take care.

"In this light you'll not see a low branch!" he had warned. "Your head is too hard for it to be harmed, but what of Raven?"

She had giggled, taunting him to chase after her. Oh, how piqued he became when he believed she was mistreating Raven!

"Sometimes you are worse than an old woman!" she laughed.

"Don't think your insolence will make me chase you!"

"It is your slow little Dumpling that will keep you from that," she dared.

After mistreating horses—or what he perceived as such—he next hated any to belittle his horse's silly name.

"Why, you—!" Laughter accompanied his words as he nudged Dumpling into a trot.

The chase was on, but it only lasted a few moments until, behind her, she heard a loud thud.

"Philip!" she gasped. Turning, she saw Dumpling several paces behind, now riderless.

She raced back to where the animal stood beneath a low branch about the size of a man's arm. Philip was lying on the ground, eyes shut, arm flung over his head. She nearly catapulted off Raven in her haste to reach him.

"Oh, what have I done?" she groaned, dropping to her knees beside him. "I'm so sorry. I—"

His hand moved away from his face, and to her utter astonishment, he was grinning!

"What?" she exclaimed. Then, "Oh, you! I will put a real gash in your head!"

He was laughing so hard he could hardly sit up, and when he did he was grasping his side. Between bursts of mirth he said, "There's a lesson for you, m'lady."

Now she saw he must have struck the branch with his hands to make the sound she'd taken for his head cracking against it.

"So scaring a lady half to death is what you call a lesson, groom?" she railed. But now that her initial scare and immediate anger were over, she did think it a good jest, if only it hadn't been on her. She offered a reluctant smile.

"No, m'lady." He was trying to be serious, but laughter still danced about his countenance.

"You!" She gave him a playful shove as she scrambled to her feet.

"Did I really scare you that much, m'lady?" He rose, dusting bits of dirt and twigs from his clothes.

"Good grooms are hard to come by, you know," she replied smugly.

"So are good mistresses," he said more solemnly.

Then followed one of those moments that occurred all too often with them. A silent look passed between them, holding a power—dare she call it passion?—that fairly sizzled like kindling on the hearth. A look that must culminate in a longed-for kiss. Always in their case, however, it didn't. And always it was Philip who would break the moment, turning or busying himself with some task or other.

With a sigh Beatrice forced her thoughts back to the present. If last night did not ignite the passion they both felt, would anything? Philip was simply too strong for her, too strong in his resolve. A lesser man would have been hers, she was certain. But Philip was not a lesser man, and that was why she loved him.

A snap of a twig some distance ahead on the path caught her attention. She nudged Raven forward.

"Hello, up there!" she called, not wanting to come upon anyone unawares. No doubt it was one of the hunters who had fallen behind.

When she drew nearer, she saw a figure kneeling upon the grass, head bowed as if in prayer. He glanced up quickly upon hearing her approach. It was Gareth. Scrambling to his feet, he bowed.

"M'lady, this is a surprise." His tone was cool and showed no surprise.

"I thought to join the hunters." With a smirk, she asked, "Are you lost, Gareth?"

"Of course not! My medallion fell from my neck, and I turned back to search for it."

She wondered how rude it would be for her to merely nod her sympathy and then ride on. But he forestalled her with his next words.

"Mayhap, m'lady, you would lend me a hand, or should I say an eye?" He smiled and she saw that it was a gesture full of charm, no denying that. He was very handsome, dark and striking, telling of his Norman ancestors. The smile, though, lacked something she could not quite define. Perhaps she was just too critical of Philip's brother.

"I suppose I could," she said, dismounting.

"Many thanks. I have noted that women seem to have a special knack of finding things."

"I don't know about that, but I'll try."

Loosely tying Raven to a low branch near Gareth's mount, she set to a search of the grass, but after a moment she turned. "Pray tell, Gareth, what am I looking for?"

"A round golden medallion about so big." He circled his fingers to make a shape about the size of an egg. "It was given me by Prince Edward and is very valuable."

She was impressed in spite of herself. "Gold, you say? I should say it is precious."

"Well, it is only plated with gold, but its worth lies with the giver, my liege lord." He actually appeared to swell with pride. "All his squires are not gifted thus."

"Then we best give a thorough search. Are you sure it fell here?"

"We paused here because Lord Sardwick had a mild attack of vapors. I don't know why such an old coot insisted upon coming on the hunt in the first place and slowing us down so."

She knew Sardwick well and thought him a kindly man, though indeed ancient. She guessed he was twenty years older than her father. She called him Uncle Sardie, though he was no blood relation, only a close friend of her father's. He always had a smile for her and a twinkle in his eyes, and when she had been younger, he would perform little magic tricks for her. She thus took umbrage at Gareth's disrespect. She threw herself more intently into the search, all the faster to be done and off to join Lord Sardwick's far more pleasant company.

Several minutes later she saw a sparkle half buried in the grass at the foot of an elm.

"There!" she announced and, kneeling, pulled the item out.

"Indeed it is! I looked in this spot twice." He took the medallion from her and fastened it back around his neck on the chain from which it had escaped. "I was right about a woman's eyes." He now focused another unsettling gaze upon her. "And such eyes!" he murmured. He was so close his breath was hot upon her cheek. "How shall I thank you, my lady?"

She tried to scoot away from him, an awkward procedure with her skirts tangling around her legs. He laid a restraining hand on her shoulder, then clutched her to him suddenly and covered her lips with his. He plied her with a "grown-up" kiss. But unlike the one with Philip, he gave her no chance to respond, not that she wanted to. She felt as if she were suffocating, especially when he pushed her back against the trunk of the elm. In one sense the kiss was far more artless than Philip's had been, at least lacking in subtly, while at the same time far more practiced. Hardly able to breathe, she tried to squirm away, but he held her fast. He was very strong, his muscles well developed, no doubt from his knighthood training.

While his body pressed her like a vise against the tree, his hands were free to . . . do other things. Never had a man touched her like this, and though she had dreamed of Philip's touches, she was appalled by Gareth's to the point of nausea. She struggled harder to free herself.

"Beatrice," he murmured, "how I have longed to get you alone."

Her mouth momentarily freed as he spoke, she cried, "Stop this!"

"Why should I?"

"Please!" She had never felt so helpless.

"Please? You want more?" He fumbled at the laces of her kirtle.

"N-no!"

As her neck was bared, he lowered his lips to ply more kisses. She tried to wiggle away, pushing at him with her hands. As she did so, one hand touched the hilt of his belt knife. Intent upon his dastardly deed, he did not feel her quietly slip the knife from its sheath. In order to get a better grasp on the hilt, however, she had to wrap her arms around him, a gesture that seemed only to incense his passion further. Light-headed, she wanted to scream and swoon together. It took all her resolve to grasp the knife and position it with its point against his leather jerkin. She wondered if she would have the strength to penetrate it. She knew she had the will.

"Gareth, I have your belt knife pointed at your back," she said shakily. "If you don't stop now, I will kill you."

He did stop, but when he lifted his head, he was chuckling and smiling. In that moment she saw what was missing from his charming smile—an elemental warmth, even humanity.

"I like a woman with spirit," he smirked.

She pressed the blade, nicking the leather.

He moved away, but with crossed arms, he continued to scrutinize her with open lust. Quickly, still holding the knife in one hand, she clasped her bodice more securely together.

"Go now," she demanded, "and I will tell no one what you tried to do."

Still smiling, he said, "My dear lady, mayhap the Hawken and Cassley houses will one day be united. Why should we not have a little taste of that union beforehand?"

"Take your leave, now!" Her voice shook and her knuckles whitened as they circled the blade. How she wanted to use it! Perhaps then Philip would be made heir and they could be together.

But she dropped the knife at his feet. Murder was not the way.

He picked up the knife and slipped it back into its sheath. "Mayhap we try this again on our wedding night."

To her eyes his grin was leering, lecherous.

He untied his horse and rode off. She remained where she was and wept.

8

That very night, Beatrice sought out her father. She was almost certain a betrothal had not been brokered yet. She had not seen the two fathers alone, though she hadn't been watching them constantly. Even if an agreement had been made, it was not too late to break it. But she must act quickly.

She found her father in his study, seated at his secretary, poring over household records. Unlike many nobles, Edmond could read and cipher with great expertise. He did not engage the services of the village priest but kept his own accounts. He said it spared a few pennies to purchase Beatrice ribbons for her hair. Beatrice thought he enjoyed doing the work.

But upon seeing him thus, with guests still in the house, she panicked. Could he be assessing his accounts in order to determine a proper dowry?

He welcomed her into the small, plainly furnished room. She perched upon a high stool, the only seat other than his in the room. She forced herself to remain calm. She would defeat her purpose if she came off as a desperate ninny. She would save tears and pleading for a last resort.

"Did you enjoy your birthday, Papa?"

"Yes. I am proud of you, Bea." He took her hand in his. "You are becoming a true lady. I could not imagine even Lady Leicester performing better."

She studied him closely, as a woman would, not as a child who adored her father. A large, robust man, he had been crusading in his youth and had performed courageously. Beatrice had heard the stories, not only from her father but from the knights who had fought with him. Yet Beatrice could not imagine her father on a battlefield wielding a sword and lance. He had always been so tender with her. He had never beaten her, not even once, though she had deserved it many times. She knew in her heart he would never harm her in any way. If he would offer her into marriage to seal a political end, then it must be something he believed in passionately. But he would never do so if he believed she'd be miserable. Would he?

"What is it, Bea? I don't think I have ever seen you so pensive." He set down his pen and fully faced her.

"Papa, is it . . . true, that you want to betroth me to Lord Hawken's son?"

"I am considering it, dear," he said. "You know it is well past time that we find you a husband."

"He's a bore, Papa." She dared not tell him anything else, for she didn't want to see the negotiations broken by her father killing Gareth.

"Perhaps he has other qualities—"

"Please, don't toy with me! I am not a child. Are you going to betroth me to Gareth or are you not?" she demanded far less circumspectly than before.

A sad smile bent his lips. "You mince no words, my dear."

"Well?"

He let out a reluctant sigh. "I have discussed it with Lord Hawken. I thought it would please you, dear one. Gareth Aubernon is a handsome lad."

"Do you know him, Papa?"

"Not really. Yesterday was the first I had seen him in many years. Mayhap if you gave him half a chance . . . ?"

"And if I said no?" she challenged.

"Let's not make this a battle of wills, my sweet daughter." He crossed his arms, scowling. Times like these it wasn't so hard to picture him facing off a swarthy Saracen. Then he grinned. "It would greatly please me, Bea."

"Because it would get Aubernon's support for your English for the English—?"

"How do you know of that?" he asked sharply, all amusement faded from his countenance.

"I listen. I pay attention," she replied smugly.

He leaned back, the chair creaking beneath his weight. He looked at her as if for the first time. "Yes, you are growing up. But I do not want you to clutter your pretty head with such matters."

"Is it a rebellion, Papa?" When he started to shake his head, obviously intending not to tell her anything, she added more emphatically, "Please tell me. I want to know."

"You were never interested in such matters before."

"I am now that they seem to directly involve me."

He appeared to consider her reply for some time before responding. "All right, perhaps you should know why it is so important that you marry Gareth. You have heard me speak before of our king's decidedly French loyalties. Well, there is a growing contingent in this country that is tired of our taxes and such going to finance the king's foreign interests. We tried to rein him in a few years ago with the Provisions of Oxford, which required him to have a council of fifteen, including barons and clergy, to participate in his rule."

"Has it helped?"

"Not by much. Two years ago Henry flaunted the Provisions completely by enlisting the pope's absolution of the oath the king made to uphold them." Morosely, Edmond shook his head. "My grandfather was at Runnymede. His name is on the Great Charter made there with King John. Now, though, it seems we have regressed to those chaotic times of John's reign. Maybe it would have been different if John had lived longer than two years beyond the signing of the Magna Carta. But as it was, he died leaving a child heir who is easily swayed by all of John's foreign friends."

"And by his own wife's?" Beatrice added so as to show her father she wasn't completely ignorant of courtly matters.

"Ah, his French queen, Eleanor, so unlike his sister of the same name," he said with disdain. "A passel of the queen's French uncles and relatives have attached themselves to the king. The people might have forgiven the king for squandering the country's coffers on his wife, which he has done recklessly. But to so lavishly gift all her foreign relatives!" Edmond's lip curled with ire. "And after the famine and floods of 1258, even the common people are becoming disgruntled. There must be a change in this country, and it must begin with the lifting of the heavy burden of taxes the king has laid upon his people!" His voice rose, and Beatrice clearly saw the passion that would induce a father to use his daughter as a pawn. "The English for the English Party has tried to peacefully make the king adhere to the Provisions. But . . ."

"Will there be a rebellion?" She swallowed because she did not like the sound of that final word.

"If we must. Lord Leicester's return from his French exile is no coincidence. He will find no dearth of supporters now. With Hawken—"

"And you will have his support if I marry his son," she said with an incisive edge. Inside she quaked, for besides her dread of this happening, a disquieting part of her understood her father's motives.

"I don't enjoy placing my only daughter in such a position," he replied. "But, Beatrice, it is an honorable thing for you to do for your country." A smile somewhat softened his intensity. "However, child, do not worry just yet. Lord Hawken would prefer to broker a marriage to de Montfort's daughter."

"But she is not even ten years old." Against her will, Beatrice felt a little affronted that she was not the first choice. Still, hope also rose within her, though she was not convinced that she would be spared. "I thought Lord Hawken had an eye for our lands."

"He has coveted them for years, but the de Montfort holdings are far more vast. Of course, Gareth would have to vie with de Montfort's sons for his share. Still, there is greater prestige in a link to the de Montforts than in one with us lowly Marlowes."

"What does Lord Leicester think of a bond between his daughter and Gareth?"

She didn't like her father's slight hesitation before answering. "He would not be brokenhearted if you went to Gareth. It would create a much speedier alliance for our cause."

"It could go either way?" she asked with the hopefulness of the child she suddenly felt so very like.

"We must wait and see."

Not mollified by this discussion, she headed directly to the stables afterward.

Philip was forking fresh hay into the stalls. He set down the pitchfork and listened as she recounted her conversation with her father.

"I know how much my father wants Cassley lands," he told her with a sigh that lacked hope. "I am surprised he would want such a close link to de Montfort, who has been at odds with the king for years. My father is many things, but he is no rebel. He must see some advantage in courting de Montfort's party, but he will not place himself at too great a risk, of that I am certain. If there ever is a successful rebellion, he will be one of those who will show up on its coattails saying he was with them all along. But he will also make sure he is in a position to go the other way if it becomes needful."

Beatrice's stomach twisted. In a small, near hopeless voice she said, "Then he won't want to mix himself up with my father, either."

"I'm afraid your father, Beatrice, does not pose as great a risk. If it came to it, Hawken could make a case for the union of the two houses aside from political issues."

A sob escaping her lips, she pounded a fist against the rough wood of the stall door. "Ouch!" she cried, rubbing her hand.

Taking her hand and kissing the reddened marks forming on the knuckles, he said, "I have thought much since you visited me last."

"You have! Then you and I—?"

"Beatrice, I can make no promises."

"You must!" Tears spilled from her eyes. "Please, Philip, I cannot marry Gareth. I would die first. I would . . . oh, dear God, please no!" she groaned.

"Has something happened?" he asked, his eyes suddenly flashing.

She couldn't tell him. He'd never said anything directly, but she had always sensed there was bad blood between Philip and his brother. She remembered what he'd said the other night, that he'd die before he would let his brother have her. She feared what he would do if he knew what Gareth had attempted in the woods.

She gulped some air, trying to calm herself. "No . . . it's just . . ."

"Did he touch you, Beatrice?" He grasped her shoulder, forcing her to look into his eyes.

She stared back mutely, her lips trembling.

"I'll kill him!"

Hearing what she feared most shook the sense back into her. "No, Philip. He was forward, that's all." But the reminder of Gareth's advances, his cold, lustful touch, made her shudder.

"I know my brother," seethed Philip. "I know of what he is capable."

"He did not compromise me, Philip. He tried, no more."

Stumbling back against the stable wall, Philip let his head fall against the wood. "It is my fault," he groaned.

"How is that?"

"I leave you with no hope. I am a miserable cur!"

"Don't say that. I love you, Philip. You are the best man I have ever known, save for my father. I will not give up hope." She brushed his lips with hers, but he did not respond to the kiss.

"An irony, is it not," he said bitterly. "One brother would take you against your will. The other, whom you want, refuses you."

"I understand you a little better now," she said. "Gareth took the taste of unwedded lust from me. He befouled it. I want to offer myself to you on our wedding day, as a pure gift."

"Oh, my love! It is what I want, as well. I want it more than life. I want you more than life, and if—"

She laid her fingers against his lips. "Shh! We will have our dream. I know it."

"I so want to hold you, but I dare not."

"I understand."

"I have decided upon a course of action," he said.

"What will you do?"

"I will speak to my father."

"They have already departed for Hawken."

"That is for the best. I dare not confront him here under your father's roof or upon the road, especially with Gareth near at hand." Again his eyes flashed.

She hoped she never saw the two brothers together, for only death would come of it.

"I'll go to Hawken in the morning," he said.

"Good! Your father seemed like a reasonable man."

Philip smiled grimly. "Have I told you that my father has spoken to me only once since I went to live with him five years ago?" His gaze seemed to draw inward, becoming sad, almost tortured. "Even when I was rebuked for being expelled from Oxford, our conversation was through a go-between. That was how we discussed this position as groom. Only once . . ." He bit his lip but said no more. "I don't exist to my father. And you may as well know, I was banished from Hawken for something I didn't do. Nevertheless . . ." He finished with a deep sigh.

"How awful, Philip." She suddenly realized what he was suggesting. "It won't be easy, then, will it?"

Laughing dryly, he replied, "Hardly. But a second conversation with my father is well overdue."

The Cassley chapel was not much used these days. Only twice a year, at Christmas and Easter, could the estate coffers afford to have a priest come to the manor to minister to the residents. All other times the lord and his family went to St. Bartholomew's to worship, in the village of Cranswick, situated between Hawken and Cassley. Of course Beatrice had no way of knowing how often the chapel was used for private vespers, as she now was about to do. She believed the pious Leticia came here frequently, and that is why she asked her maid to accompany her this time.

Kneeling at the altar beside her maid, Beatrice felt a bit nervous. Duty compelled her to attend Mass on a regular basis, but seldom was her heart in the religious acts she performed. As often as she threatened to "take the veil," she knew the cloistered life of a nun would have driven her mad. But Beatrice feared God as much as the next person did and well knew that a prayer or two could not do harm in times of need.

This was most certainly a time of need.

She glanced at Leticia, whose hands were folded on the altar rail.

"Leticia, we must pray that God will soften Lord Hawken's heart and that he will grant Philip his request." Though her words were a statement, she paused to wait for her maid's agreement.

"I will pray God's will be done," said the maid.

Beatrice's brow wrinkled. "If it is what *I* want," she said stubbornly, "which is that Philip be given land and his place in society, there is no reason God should not want the same thing."

"As you wish, m'lady." Leticia's words were contrite, but something like amusement tugged at the corners of her lips.

"You mock me?"

"Nay, Lady Beatrice, but . . ." The older woman paused in an attempt at earnestness. "Dear lady, you must know that regardless of what we pray, God's will inevitably *will* be done."

"Then why bother to pray at all?" Beatrice asked rather petulantly. Maybe it didn't matter after all if she was pious.

"I believe the more you speak to God, the more likely it is that your will meshes with His."

Beatrice sighed. "Then it is useless for me to try at all. I seldom pray, so my words now will fall on deaf ears."

"Ah, but it is seemly to make our requests known to God. True, the outcome is His to determine, but know that He will always act with your best interests at heart."

Beatrice thought about that for a moment and could only think that the interests of her father were probably closer to God's will, and her father would never want her to be with Philip. Yet, there were times when her father, out of love, let her have her way. Perhaps this was one of those times.

She reached over and clasped Leticia's hand. "Will you start, Leticia?"

"Yes, m'lady, and I will ask God what you wish, but we will abide by His will."

Beatrice nodded, all the while thinking that if things did not work out between Philip and his father, she would find another way to be with her love.

9

I did not see the harm in suggesting a simple ride!" Gareth Aubernon stood before his parents in their solar, his hands clenched at his sides. He resented having to defend his actions.

"Nothing is simple in matters of marriage." Lady Hawken reclined on her settee, a piece of needlework in her hands. "Fortunately I spared any damage by suggesting the entire group of guests go hunting."

It was now three days since the feast at Cassley Manor, and Lord and Lady Hawken had only just heard of Gareth's intent, however foiled, of taking Lady Beatrice out alone. At least his manservant hadn't told all, for Gareth had been unable to keep from bragging a little of his advances toward the beautiful girl. If his parents ever learned of how he'd attempted to compromise her in the woods . . . he didn't want to even think of the consequence of that. Nevertheless, his no-account servant would pay.

"It is years before I'll want to marry," Gareth said, standing tall, squaring his shoulders. His fine embroidered surcote over his mail hauberk was belted with a chain of elegantly wrought metal from which hung his sword, a richly decorated gift from his father on his last birthday. He looked as much like a man as a seventeen-year-old could, further enhanced by the fact that he was *trying* to look even more so as he confronted his parents.

"Bah!" Lord Hawken snorted derisively. "You'll marry when I say you will."

He sat on a stool by the hearth and had been in the process of putting on his shoes when his son burst into the solar intending to defend his actions.

"An unchaperoned ride with another female could ruin your chances of a proper match," added Lady Hawken. "We will soon enter into negotiations with the de Montforts for their daughter's hand—"

"What!" Gareth exclaimed. There was so much about this statement that infuriated him, he hardly knew where to begin. He blurted out the first thing that came to mind. "She is a child. Hardly ten years old!"

"When she comes of age," Lady Hawken replied coolly, "you will be ready for the responsibilities of marriage."

"If God is gracious," put in Lord Hawken.

"What do you mean by that?" Gareth demanded, gripping the hilt of his sword. The gesture, with its implied menace, steadied him, gave him a sense of control. "I would have been knighted soon if you hadn't pulled me from Court." Gareth still deeply resented this latest affront from his father.

"You got as far as you did only because I greased the path of your promotion with a generous bribe!" Ralph Aubernon lifted his shoe and directed the pointed toe at his son, waving it in the boy's face for emphasis as he spoke. "How do you think you have succeeded thus far? Surely not by your talents."

"That's a lie!" Gareth yelled. His knuckles whitened, still gripping the hilt. "You have always despised me and tried to hold me back."

"Ha! I have given you everything—"

"But respect!"

"That, you fool, is something you must earn!" Aubernon dropped the shoe and rose to his feet. He towered over his son by several inches. "You tread a thin line, boy. At this moment the last thing you deserve is respect. You deserve that even less than all the money and boons I have squandered upon you. And believe me, I don't have to give you a single—"

"Stop immediately!" broke in Lady Hawken. The look of rancor in her eyes that she directed at her husband hardly touted her as a mediator, and when she spoke, her words held warning, not conciliation. "I'll not have you threaten my son."

"Your son, indeed," sneered Aubernon. "You have turned him into a lazy no-account. He only shows vigor with the serving maids and tavern wenches."

"He is a good lad." She raised a limp hand. "Come, Gareth, sit and let us discuss this reasonably." As she gazed at her son, her chilly eyes gave a vague hint of warmth.

"How can we discuss anything reasonably when my own father hates me?" Gareth resisted his mother's entreaty and kept standing.

"I don't hate you"—Aubernon made an attempt at moderating his tone—"else I would not have worked so hard to make the best possible marriage arrangement for you. You have two excellent candidates, though young Eleanor de Montfort is by far the best, being the king's niece. Such an alliance would place you in the king's own family. This is a coup any young man would covet."

"Simon de Montfort isn't the king's favorite person at the moment," argued Gareth, though he, too, made an attempt at moderation.

"Ah, those two. Their affections change from day to day. In any case, I have made no firm commitments. Beatrice Marlowe may be a viable candidate, as well."

"I never said I wanted to *marry* Beatrice Marlowe." Gareth could still taste the sweet taste of her and feel her supple form, and longing stirred in his own body. But an arrangement with her would likely mean a marriage within the year. He was not ready to be thus tied down.

He regretted sneering at the de Montfort arrangement. That did have its advantages. No one expected him to remain celibate until the child came of age. Nevertheless, he was tired of serving wenches who were too often plain of countenance and dull of wit. His blood boiled when he thought of bedding a beauty like Lady Beatrice, one who had vitality and fire. The serving girls and even the tavern strumpets were far too passive, no matter that they were willing.

Of course he couldn't impart all this to his parents. His mother would faint. His father would call him not only a lazy fool but a cruel womanizer, as well. Best that he play both sides against the middle for a time, appease his parents in this matter until he was ready to shoulder the burdens they wished to impose upon him.

So he merely shrugged. "You will make me a good marriage, considering, I am sure, my tender youth."

Not two moments after the door slammed shut behind Gareth, Ralph Aubernon sat back on his stool and began to tug on his shoe. Snorting with loud disdain, he said, "'Tender youth' indeed! That boy is about as tender as a wild boar in the kitchen. The mere sight of a female makes him preen like a cock—"

"Please, husband! Your language!" Clarise Aubernon tried to affect shock, but it would have been difficult for anyone, least of all her husband, to believe anything could ruffle her icy demeanor.

Aubernon tugged at his shoe. "This cursed leather has shrunk!"

"Why don't you wait for your valet?"

"Bah! I refuse to be so helpless that I cannot even put on my own shoe when I am of a mind. Too bad I cannot say as much for your son—"

"Stop speaking ill of him. He is your son, also!"

Aubernon's eyes narrowed momentarily, then he grunted, "Not my only son, I'll warrant!"

"You swore you would never speak of this." Her hands tightened around her embroidery hoop as she glared at him.

"An oath I have never ceased to regret."

"You have made that quite clear on several occasions."

Aubernon marveled at her rare restraint in not touting her superiority in property over him.

Husband and wife stared silently at each other for a long time. Years of strife and unhappiness passed between them in that brief moment. After eighteen years of marriage Aubernon could hardly recall an instance when there had been anything but strife in their relationship. They both well knew she had been his second choice.

Ralph Aubernon might have made a far different choice had he known before his marriage to Clarise that the woman he loved had borne him a child.

Ah, Gillian de Tollard. The green-eyed, redheaded beauty who had captured his heart when he had been visiting relatives on the Continent upon his return from the Crusades in the Holy Lands. Fiery and tender, sweet and tart at the same time. With her he'd always felt as if he were walking on the edge of a cliff, and the feeling had been exhilarating!

With her he had simply *felt,* as he certainly had never felt since.

But while tarrying in France, word had reached him from England that the fortunes of Hawken had seriously declined. His father had been ailing, and the estate had been run into the ground by an unscrupulous retainer. Ralph was ordered to return home immediately and to marry the girl to whom he had been betrothed while away. Clarise would bring into the marriage sizable holdings that would keep Hawken afloat.

The de Tollards had no real wealth, so Ralph's duty was clear. He well knew that marriage was about duty not passion. Would he have acted differently had he known that the woman he adored was with child when he bid her adieu? Gillian was a proud woman, willing to face scandal rather than grovel before her child's father. And even if she had groveled, he could not have acted differently. Land was life. The loss of Hawken could well have been his death. Of course the situation with Gillian could also have been his death—by the hand of her father's retribution. However, she staunchly refused to identify her child's father until she lay on her deathbed and feared for her son's future.

Ralph retained Hawken, and because of Clarise's rich dowry, his estate's fortunes soared. He did not like to think of what those fortunes had cost him.

But he did, tallying them now as if chiseling words on his crypt.

The affections of a good woman.

Self-respect.

And most costly of all, the loss of his son.

Five years ago when the boy Philip had sought his father's door, Clarise had forced Ralph to swear an oath that Gareth's place would never be usurped by the bastard child. It seemed a reasonable request, since Hawken existed because of Clarise's money and she continued to retain control over her holdings. Moreover, she had insisted that he completely deny Philip. This he could not do and maintain a shred of honor. Thus, a compromise was struck. Aubernon would provide for Philip without endangering Gareth's position and without directly claiming blood relation to Philip. Ralph hated that his detestable wife held such sway over him.

Angrily Ralph returned his attention to his stubborn shoe. He jammed his foot into the soft leather with such vehemence that the seam began to tear.

"You foolish man!" railed Lady Hawken. "Your feet have swelled again."

"Well, then, perhaps I shall die and spare myself from seeing our son destroy that which I have spent a lifetime to build." He tossed the shoe aside. "Or better still, I might ensure he will never have the opportunity to do so."

"And what do you mean by that?" Clarise looked down her lovely nose at her husband, a useless ploy considering that even with him on the stool and her on the settee, he was still taller than she.

Ralph muttered a curse before saying clearly, "Maybe it is not too late to instruct that boy properly."

"He is young. There is time." Lady Hawken rose. "I must see to some household matters."

"If you see my valet, send him in," Aubernon called after his wife.

Alone, Ralph bent over and, removing his chausses, studied his bare feet. They were indeed quite swollen, not to mention mottled and bluish. Though he was no physician, even he knew the condition was a bad sign. They were in worse shape than ever. If it were merely the feet, he would not overly concern himself. But there were also the frequent flutters in his chest and the difficulty in breathing, especially when he woke in the morning. Last year when the symptoms had begun, his physician told him he had a weakness of the heart and prescribed medicinal herbs. Ralph had kept this information from his wife, especially the man's more recent prognosis of less than a month ago. Ralph was dying.

He did not know how much longer he could keep it from his family. And he wondered if he could die at peace knowing his good-for-nothing son would gain control of Hawken. Clarise's holdings were vast enough—let the boy have them and squander them and good riddance! But Hawken—that was heart and soul to Aubernon. He himself had sacrificed too much for it, not to mention all the sacrifices his ancestors had made from the time of the Conquest. For him to be the one to lose it, or his son—better to plunge a knife into his heart!

What irony Clarise's glib words about there being time! Yet, might there yet be a small possibility that Gareth, upon reaching his majority, could change? Aubernon doubted it. There was something at the core of that boy, some pernicious angst that could be almost frightening to consider. Ralph could not describe it any better than that, and he felt certain it would not change with maturity.

In recent days Ralph's thoughts had turned more and more toward his other son. How he desired to change his will and give Philip de Tollard his rightful portion, especially because he knew that with his demise, his wife would cast Philip adrift, penniless. But acknowledging his eldest son was no easy matter. And altruism was not his only driving motive. The truth was, he had in large part spared his own shame by bringing shame upon an innocent child.

Every lord had his share of bastard offspring, though that made it no more morally tolerated. It took a man to claim one as his heir. Aubernon had long accepted the hard truth that he was not such a man.

It galled him to admit it, but he knew he was a coward.

Lately, however, the situation was pushing him into a corner. He had hoped that through the Church, by way of an education at Oxford, Philip might have obtained the opportunity to claim an honorable future. That hope had failed miserably. Stubborn, hardheaded, of independent spirit like his mother, Philip had been unable to fit into the life of a scholarly cleric.

Ralph let a proud smile quirk his lips. He wanted no monk for a son anyway. From afar Ralph had watched the boy perform on the training field— mostly in secret with one of Ralph's vassals as instructor. The boy had promise as a knight, though such would never be his fortune.

What future was there for the boy? That of a groom? If Philip had wanted to wound his father, that was the way. But what else was left for him? Ralph groaned out loud. He was pulled in too many different directions.

"No wonder my heart is giving out," he muttered.

10

Gareth made his way across the courtyard to the stable. His father's knights were training in the far meadow, and he was off to join them. He'd prove his father's vicious words untrue. Why he cared to do so, he did not know. The man had never given him credit for his abilities. At Court, his liege lord, Edward, often praised his skills. He'd been gifted with the medallion bearing the royal crest, had he not?

Only in Henry's court had Gareth felt he was accounted to be the man he was. And his father had ruined that by ordering him home. He hoped Edward believed the excuse of Aubernon's ill health as reason for the departure. Perhaps his place could be restored when this foolish alliance with de Montfort's party was eschewed.

But worse was his father's suggestion that he'd been accepted because of bribes. It made his blood boil! Edward, the twenty-three-year-old prince, called Gareth "friend." They had drunk and chased women together until more recently when the prince began taking his marital duties more seriously. That this coincided with the coming of age of his wife, Donya Eleanora of Castile, who had been ten years old when they married, was of no consequence to Gareth. He thought the man addled for settling down to only one woman. Despite that, they were still comrades-in-arms, and often Gareth stood for the prince in tournaments abroad. This camaraderie could not have been bought with money. Could it?

He shook away the seed of doubt. Curse his father for placing it there! Gareth wondered why he even bothered to come home on visits. For his mother's sake, he supposed. It was for her he took Lord Hawken's vile abuse. And for the promise of his inheritance.

As he passed the brewing hut, a small figure darted out. Gareth saw who it was from the corner of his eye but did not pause until the girl rushed up to him and tugged at his sleeve.

"My lord! Please, I wish to speak with you." She was little Mabel, one of the scullery maids. A pretty thing as peasants went, if one looked beneath the soot and grime on her face. At fourteen she was quite buxom, an attribute she made no attempt to hide. Gareth found her a most willing strumpet in his bed.

Distastefully Gareth shook away her hand. "Must you touch me?" he growled.

"You little mind my touch under your covers, m'lord," she replied tartly.

"Hold your tongue and mind your place, wench! What do you want?"

"How can I tell you if I hold my tongue?" she groused, but when he glared at her in reply, she forced a respectful tone into her voice. "Do you remember the matter I spoke to you about a week past? You gave me a penny and told me to . . . uh . . . rid myself of the problem?"

"I also told you I wanted to hear no more of it, did I not?"

At the time she had delivered her news, he'd been just a little proud that his seed had finally produced offspring. At seventeen he'd been with many females and had worried that none had yet come to him with Mabel's problem. Relieved but still worried. So her news had eased him on that behalf, though he'd naturally told her to dispose of the thing. She'd whined about such an act being a sin, but he'd convinced her it was more of a sin how it got there in the first place. In any event, he wasn't about to have any bastard spawn running about to ruin his life. There were quite enough bastards in the family already. Should such a fate ever befall him, he'd never be stupid enough to claim it or to even welcome it into his home.

"I would not bother you, m'lord," Agnes said, "if my mother had not told me I must return the penny you gave me to take care of the problem—"

"You didn't do it!" he railed. "You foolish girl!"

"No, m'lord, I didn't have to. It was an untimely alarm, because my . . . you know, my curse came to me afterward." She dug a grimy hand into the sash of her dress. "Here is your penny."

He was truly shocked she was returning the silver penny he'd given her. He had long forgotten about the matter, and she could have kept the money with him none the wiser. Instead of admiring her for her honesty, though, he thought her more foolish still. That didn't prevent his loins from burning at the sight of her wide eyes, her full parted lips, and the bodice of her dress straining over the roundness of her breasts. Briefly he thought of taking her then and there behind the brewhouse. She was a delectable morsel.

But for the moment, training was more important than appeasing his lust. The wench would always be there for him. Before turning away from her, he plucked the penny from her hand. That would teach her to be honest.

————————

Philip had taken his time traversing the distance between Cassley and Hawken. He took just over two hours to do it and slowed his dapple gray gelding when his father's towering stone fortress came into view.

Standing on a stout defensible hill with the River Stowe at its back, Hawken was far more a fortress, in the Norman style, than a home. The imposing gray walls gave no pretense of elegance. It had been built two hundred years ago by William the Conqueror to defend his claim on Saxon England and had been awarded to Durand d'Aubernon, one of his knights from Normandy. By the time he gained Hawken, Durand had already acquired an even more austere distinction, the sobriquet of Bloody Durand. The death count attributed to him rose into the hundreds if one included, in addition to Saxon warriors, all the peasants—men, women, and children—who got in the way of his conquest. The death toll was so high, he had left himself few serfs to work the land finally bestowed upon him by William. Thus it was oft said that Hawken was built upon a foundation of blood.

For that reason, Durand had made the deal with the Cassley woman—he was simply getting too low on resources to conquer the powerful Cassley army, making a peaceful approach desirable.

Philip thought it was probably just as well he could not claim such a grim place as his. Yet land was land. Some might even argue that it was more precious than blood. A man was nothing if he had no land. A knight would risk his life for the opportunity of receiving a boon of land from his liege lord. Yet without a knighthood it was next to impossible to attain even a small patch of dirt.

Philip intended to defy those odds. If he and Beatrice had any hope of being together, it would only be if he had land of his own. Lord Cassley would never give his daughter to a landless groom. To increase his chances, Philip had waited an extra day to depart Cassley. Waiting had been torture, but wisdom convinced him it would have been disastrous to approach his father while his own anger toward Gareth's actions was still hot. Now, if ever in his life, he must subdue that so-called demon of anger within.

As Philip viewed the castle, he noted a horse and rider exit the castle gates. Immediately he recognized the bay stallion as belonging to Gareth. Philip groaned. He did not relish having his brother be the first person to greet him, but neither would he turn aside on his path to avoid him. His temper had cooled somewhat—he thought he could face him now without killing him.

Philip urged Dumpling forward until he came within a couple lengths of Gareth. He reined his mount.

"Good morning to you, m'lord," Philip said tightly but respectfully.

Gareth's brow arched and his lips made a smirk. "So have you failed in yet another pursuit?"

"I am here for only a brief sojourn." Dumpling skittered nervously, and Philip tightened his fist on the rein. He had forgotten that his gray was shy of Gareth.

Philip had received the animal from his father shortly before he departed for Oxford—it was, in matter of fact, passed to Philip by a third party, since Lord Hawken refused to acknowledge Philip. Apparently Hawken felt he was getting off too cheaply in so easily disposing of his son and felt Philip ought to have at least one possession of value, a possession that could also serve to carry him away from Hawken. A fine beast, yes, but with a nose too long, legs too short, and a silly name to boot. Philip had stubbornly kept the name because he thought it fitting for a bastard's mount to be called Dumpling.

Still, despite Dumpling's shortcomings, Gareth had apparently been jealous of the gift and had sneaked the animal from the stable one day while home during a holiday, taking it racing over fen and field. When he had returned to the stable, the gray's flanks had been scored with whip marks. Even now, more than a year later, the gray had not forgotten the cruel treatment inflicted upon it.

"I see you still have not learned how to handle that beast," Gareth said.

Philip swallowed rising bile and choked back an angry retort, continuing to remind himself of the purpose of this visit and that venting his wrath toward Gareth would thwart his intent.

Steadily he replied, "I came here not to receive your abuse, Gareth."

"Then why have you come?"

" 'Tis not your business."

"These are my lands, so it is my business." Philip noted Gareth's hand close over his sword hilt, a habit his brother had.

"They are not your lands yet, or has someone failed to tell me of my father's demise?" He knew that in referring to Lord Hawken as his father he was deliberately goading Gareth. But how much abuse was he expected to take? After living with it for five years, he thought he must be close to his limit.

"You have no father, bastard!" The sudden venom in Gareth's tone was shocking even though Philip knew better than anyone what perfidy lurked deep in his brother's soul.

Instinctively Philip's hand jerked to his belt knife. It would do him little good against his brother's sword, but by all that was holy, he'd taken just about enough!

"Do you itch for a fight, bastard?" taunted Gareth.

"You are mailed and armed. What chance have I?"

"It would matter not were you garbed in the finest warrior's trappings. I am nearly a knight, while you are a failed clerk and a baseborn groom." Gareth laughed.

"I have heard about the kind of knight you are, Gareth." Philip tried to match his brother's derision but did so poorly. Gareth was simply too much of a master at it. "Give me mail and sword, and I will show you what I learned at the university besides letters and ciphers."

Gareth howled with mirth, pausing only to issue a challenge. "I go now to the training meadow. There will be spare equipage for you."

Philip made several practice swings with the unfamiliar practice sword. What did he think he was doing? He was no warrior. True, he'd learned some swordplay but nothing close to what a knight in training would have learned. While he had heard that Gareth had no natural talent for the arts of warfare, still, pitting a clerk against a squire was no less foolhardy. Philip berated himself for allowing Gareth to goad him into this position. He should have been man enough to ignore his brother's insults. Instead, he was about to have them compounded tenfold by a physical humiliation.

Sir Jocelin Grahame, one of Hawken's older knights, held out a plain wooden shield for Philip. "So you and the young master will spar a bit, eh? Bear in mind, Philip, that he has improved some over the last years."

"A lot?" Philip squeaked, unable to control the youthful variance of his voice in his concern. Clearing his throat and pitching his voice lower, he repeated, "A lot, Sir Jocelin?"

The knight grinned. "He is liable to give ye a run for yer money. But I'd still put *me* money on you, lad!"

Philip's lips twitched into a halfhearted smile. Still, he appreciated Jocelin's encouragement. The man was a veteran of many battles and had been a crusader, as well. His body, like that of many knights, was etched with the evidence of experience. His face was mapped with scars, and beneath his chemise, his arms and chest were also heavily scored. Philip had always been in awe of the man and could never figure why the knight held a fondness for him. Before Philip had departed for the university, Sir Jocelin had given him a few instructions in the arts of warfare, often in secret, away from the dis-approving eyes of the lord and lady of the castle. Sir Jocelin had never spoken of it, but Philip was certain the man knew of his place in the household. No doubt everyone knew, though few dared to speak of it, instead accepting the vague implication that he was a distant relative and Lord Hawken's ward. Nevertheless, Jocelin had attempted to take him under his wing.

"I'll give you a bit of free counsel, lad," Jocelin went on. "The young master has not yet learned to use his shield to its best advantage. Whilst he is con-centrating on other maneuvers, he has a tendency to lower it without think-ing. Ye'd do well to make the most of those moments."

"Thank you, Sir Jocelin."

"Might I give you another bit of advice?" When Philip nodded, the knight went on in a much lower voice than before. "Give the master a good run, but stay your hand in the final round. Don't humiliate him outright, if you take my meaning."

Philip smiled ironically. "As if I could."

"Oh, you could, young Philip, but mark me, Gareth is not a man to accept humiliation lightly. You would make for yourself a vile enemy with that one."

"I think he is already my enemy."

"I'll warrant ye have only seen the half of what that lad is capable."

Philip looked across the field that had been staked off for the training drills. Gareth appeared to be discussing strategy with the two knights who had agreed to be his seconds in the match. He looked regal in his shining mail. He held a shield emblazoned with a silver hawk in full flight against a red field—the crest of Hawken Castle. Philip felt even more the misfit waif in his ill-fitting borrowed hauberk and helm.

At least they had opted to limit their contest to fighting on foot. It was the only way Sir Jocelin would agree to the exercise, for Philip's horse, though a fine beast, was not a trained destrier. Philip might have learned swordplay at the university, but he had never jousted and could hardly have learned a sport condemned by the Church in a university run by clerics.

Gareth had protested loudly about this arrangement. "A knight does not fight on foot!"

"You, m'lord, are not a knight yet," Jocelin reminded him calmly. "Even a squire would not enter a contest where the combatants are unevenly matched."

"Stripped naked, I would be a better warrior than this one," Gareth sneered.

"We shall see," growled Philip. And though his fingers itched with violence and his muscles twitched with fury, he didn't feel the confidence of his words. He tried to remind himself of the many times he had beaten his brother in their small squabbles after Philip had moved to Hawken from France. Philip was older by a year, but they were equally matched in size and probably in skill, as well. Philip hoped that would be true.

Sir Jocelin called the two combatants to the center of the field. A small crowd had gathered as word had spread that the brothers were going to spar. Jocelin bade them to bow courteously to each other before they took up battle positions. They were to fight with dull-edged training blades. The blows would hurt, but the likelihood of them being fatal was slim.

At first the two young men merely circled each other, sizing his opponent. Gareth had worn a hard, menacing scowl before donning his helm, and Philip sensed this was more than a game to him. Philip wondered what this meant to himself—a game or something more?

Before he could ponder the matter further, Gareth lunged forward with the opening offensive. The first clash of steel rang through the air with a sharp, clear resonance. Philip, taken unawares by the ferociousness of his brother's blow, blocked clumsily with his blade.

Gareth's second blow glanced lightly off the wood surface of Philip's shield, bolstering Philip's confidence. His counterblow struck Gareth's shield with such power it made splinters fly. The spectators cheered. Although Philip grinned within the dark protection of his helm, the satisfaction did not dull his focus. His next strike was swift and nearly as powerful, followed by another and another. But Gareth blocked every blow, proving himself more adept than any had given him credit for.

Parry, thrust. Thud, clang! Back and forth the two fought. The blows took more and more out of them; sweat oozed and dust rose from the ground where meadow grasses were trampled. Philip knew such a battle could last for hours. He asked himself if there was a point. His training as a scholar made him question, analyze. They would not kill each other. This *was* a game! He certainly did not want to kill Gareth. He might despise his brother for his cruel treatment, compounded by his recent unchivalrous actions toward Beatrice, but to murder? Even in a fair fight?

No. He was no killer.

Why, then, play the game? He remembered Jocelin's admonition to let Gareth win. If he did that, there seemed no point at all.

Crash!

Gareth's sword drove toward Philip, and only a last-moment desperate jerk of his shield prevented disaster. That blow would have knocked him out cold if he hadn't blocked it. Philip put aside philosophizing. He must think like a warrior not a scholar.

Lunging with his own sword, he gave Gareth a few minutes to wonder about his own intent. Thrust, thrust, he drove Gareth back. Blow after blow, he made his brother retreat. Finally, however, Gareth managed to hold fast, turning the retreat into a standoff. He raised sword instead of shield. Now the swords clanged back and forth against each other.

Intent, however, on the swordplay, Gareth let his shield slip an inch or two, then three. Philip saw the opening but held back, waiting for just the right moment to use the breach to best effect. Parrying several more blows, Philip became convinced that Gareth had indeed forgotten about his shield.

Then Philip swung hard, directly at Gareth's unprotected ribs.

Gareth gasped and stumbled back. For a moment it looked as if he was going down, ending the battle. Philip hung back, giving his brother a chance to recover. He wondered what would happen if Gareth didn't recover. Jocelin had not spoken idly about Gareth's capacity for vindictiveness. Had Philip let his anger once again ruin his chances of winning a boon from his father? Philip had never really been able to gauge Lord Hawken's feelings toward Gareth. Hawken was cold and distant toward one son as much as the other. By defeating Gareth, would he also incur his father's wrath?

You fool! he silently berated himself. Again he'd let his inner demon ruin his life.

Amazingly, the young squire regained his footing and somehow managed to steady himself. No doubt if Gareth had known the relief his action had caused in Philip, he would have toppled over for spite.

While Philip looked on, his thoughts in disarray and his sword lowered, Gareth charged.

Philip gasped with surprise. Only by some instinct his left arm shot up, his shield absorbing his brother's fierce blow. He'd avoided serious injury by a mere fraction of an inch. But that wasn't the end of it, for the force of the blow threw Philip into a panic, and he stumbled wildly backward. His large feet twisted under him, and now it was his turn to waver and wobble, the ground slanting up as if to swallow him. As a drowning man clutches at a low branch, his hands lunged out. Dropping his shield, he grasped only air and crashed to the ground, his sword also bouncing from his grip.

His helmeted head struck something hard, stunning and disorienting him. Through blurred vision he saw a shadow dart toward him. He thought it must be Gareth approaching to see to his safety. Almost too late he realized the shadow was Gareth's raised sword. In the instant his vision cleared, Philip saw such vehemence in his brother's visage, shadowed though it was by his helmet, that it froze him with shock. He'd seen every kind of meanness and hatred in Gareth before, but this . . . it was as though all of it coalesced together in a violence that had no need of a sword, for it could kill all on its own.

Somewhere, as if from a far distance, he heard a shout.

"Philip!"

It roused Philip from his dazed horror. He rolled aside, but the blow never fell.

Instead, sounds of struggle reached Philip's ears. He sat up and yanked off his helm. To his utter astonishment, he saw Sir Jocelin holding a struggling Gareth by both arms. Others were running forward to lend a hand or merely to see better.

"By the saints!" cursed Jocelin. "You would have killed him!"

"Nay!" panted Gareth. "I would have turned my sword at the last moment." He wrenched himself from the older man's fierce hold. "I only wanted to be sure he knew who was the better man."

As Gareth freed himself from Jocelin's hold and ripped off his helm, Philip jumped to his feet, gasping in great gulps of air. His whole body shook when he considered his brother's intended blow and the look on his face. Rubbing his painfully bruised arm, he sucked in several more breaths, trying to steady himself.

Finally he could speak. "I believe Gareth speaks the truth." In fact, though, Philip was positive that if Jocelin had not interceded, he would be a dead man now. Even a dull-edged blade would have penetrated with the power of Gareth's rage behind it. But Philip refused to give his brother the satisfaction of knowing he had feared the intent of that blow. He added as lightly as he could, "Gareth has always liked making his points in a big way." Removing his gauntlet, Philip held his hand out to his brother. "You put up a good fight and won fairly."

Gareth stared at Philip's hand with contempt and surely would have ignored it except he happened to glance at Jocelin, who aimed a deadly glare at the squire. Only then did Gareth take the proffered hand in a weak grip, giving it a slight shake before dropping it and stepping back.

"And don't forget that," Gareth said before turning and walking away.

It was not, Philip knew, the fair fight Gareth wanted him to remember but rather that final blow—a blow that would have easily killed.

11

P hilip removed his borrowed mail and slipped into his own surcote. "I do not know why he hates me so," he murmured.

"But he does, doesn't he?"

Philip jerked his head up at Jocelin's words. He hadn't intended that anyone hear him. "It makes no sense. He has everything. I am the one with nothing." Philip picked up his borrowed sword, carefully cleaning the blade before laying it with other spare weapons. He then fastened his girdle with his own dagger attached.

"You say he has everything, lad," mused Jocelin, "but 'tis not entirely true."

Philip snorted dubiously. "Perhaps, Sir Jocelin, you have a different standard of such things than I, or all of society, for that matter."

"Let me put it differently. Ye have the one thing Lord Gareth doesn't have that he desperately desires." Jocelin reached out to touch the hilt of Philip's dagger. "You have his father's love."

Philip laughed sourly. "If your words be true, sir knight, then Lord Hawken has a strange way of showing it."

Philip glanced toward the training field. He and Jocelin had moved some distance away while they talked so that the men could go about their drills. Gareth, mounted now, was with the others. No one would believe Gareth lacked anything. Yet here this wise knight was saying that very thing. More than that, he had said Lord Hawken *loved* his bastard son. The idea was incredible, and if Philip dwelt long upon that notion, it might well tear him to pieces. Still, he could not let it go. His father loved him? How could it be?

"Sir Jocelin, Lord Hawken has not spoken to me directly but once since I came to Hawken. I remember clearly the first, last, and only time—" Philip's hand jerked to his dagger. "It was when he gave me this dagger on my sixteenth birthday just before I went to Oxford. I remember the words he said, too."

"What did he say, lad?"

Philip swallowed, still fingering the dagger, a rather plain weapon, though the iron handle was etched artfully. He repeated slowly, the memory of his father's words both painful and consoling, "'When I was in the Holy Lands on Crusade,' he said, 'I met a Jew—the very man who gave me this dagger. He told me that when a Jewish lad reached the age of thirteen, he was considered a man, and the event was celebrated in a ceremony. We have no such custom, but I thought it was fitting you have this blade now as you set out upon your own.'"

"What did Lord Hawken do for Gareth's sixteenth birthday?" Jocelin arched a brow, causing one particularly jagged scar over that brow to stand out alarmingly.

"I don't recall. I was already gone."

"I will tell you," said the knight. "He gave the lad an expensive mantle of scarlet cloth with a diamond and ruby brooch. I recall well him sending his manservant John to London to purchase something for the boy. I accompanied John on that excursion. He went into a shop where he was known, laid down his master's purse, and told the proprietor to find a gift of that amount. I don't believe yer father even looked upon the gift before it was presented." Jocelin crossed his arms over his massive chest and aimed a smug look Philip's way.

Philip shook his head, still perplexed. He remembered seeing that cloak when he returned to Hawken once on holiday. The cost of it would have put food on a villein's table for half a year. Gareth had made a point to flaunt it before his bastard brother, not unlike Joseph of the sacred Scriptures and his coat of many colors. Philip had wondered at the time how he could sell Gareth into slavery in faraway Egypt; then he'd had to confess his sinful thoughts to the priest and do penance.

Philip slipped his dagger from its sheath. "This is not worth a fraction of the cost of that mantle. You make no sense, sir knight."

"I was with Lord Hawken, as well, when he acquired that dagger." Jocelin plucked the knife from Philip's hand and held it in his own most reverently. "The Jew Hawken spoke of . . ." The knight's lips twisted into an affectionate smile. "An infidel, he descended from the killers of our Lord Christ. But he was a man of honor, no less. He had acted as guide and servant to Hawken. This Jew saved Lord Hawken's life when assassins infiltrated our camp. He was mortally wounded doing so. As he lay dying, he presented the weapon he'd used in his heroic deed to m'lord, telling him it was precious to him because it had been given him by his father when he turned thirteen, when he'd become a man." Jocelin held up the weapon, its iron surface glinting as it caught the sunlight. "This weapon was one of Lord Hawken's most prized possessions. He would not have parted with it lightly."

Philip took back the knife, wrapping his fingers around the hilt, biting a trembling lip to forestall rising emotion. He had always worn the dagger because it had been from his father. Yet a certain bitterness had accompanied it because he had believed his father had bestowed upon him the meanest gift he could. Now all was changed. In the span of a few moments Philip's entire perception of his life had been shattered.

He opened his mouth but could manage no sound, only mouthing the word *Why?*

Jocelin shook his head. "Would that life were simpler, lad, but 'tisn't. I can neither explain nor understand the complexities that beset a man like Lord Hawken. Perhaps he would explain it himself."

Philip nodded mutely and, sheathing his dagger, strode to his horse. He had avoided it long enough. The time had come to face the master of Hawken Castle.

Gareth watched his brother ride away toward the castle, a growing disquiet quaking inside him. Why was Philip being so circumspect about this visit? Gareth could see no reason why his brother should return so soon after his departure several weeks ago. No reason save to stir up trouble.

When Philip had returned to Hawken from Oxford after Candlemas, long before his term of study was completed, Gareth had not been pleased. As long as Philip's path was set toward the Church, it seemed any threat he presented toward Gareth was dulled. His brother's rejection of the Church— or its rejection of him—did not bode well. It meant he must seek another path to fortune, a path that might well cross Gareth's own.

Gareth returned home from London immediately upon hearing with the intent of making his brother's stay as miserable as possible in hopes of forcing the bastard away. He'd finally succeeded with an inspired coup to soundly dispose of his half brother, or so he'd thought. Gareth stole his father's favorite silver goblet and let it be discovered hidden among Philip's things. A lesser culprit would have been flogged and pilloried for such a crime against the lord. It indicated Lord Hawken's softness for the bastard when Philip was only banished from Hawken. Even the bite of that was diminished because their father had found a position for Philip at Cassley. Gareth might have taken comfort that it was a humiliating position for the son of a lord if he had not heard Philip himself had chosen it.

Nevertheless, the incident had strengthened Gareth's position. He wasn't about to have it threatened now that Philip had returned boldly in defiance of the banishment.

The moment he could do so, Gareth excused himself from the rest of the drills, saying he had forgotten a duty back at the castle. He took the back way so as not to risk another encounter with Philip. Leaving his horse and his mail with the stableboy, he hurried inside and went directly up to his mother's solar. The maid let him in, and he found Lady Hawken lounging upon a chaise with needlework in hand.

"Gareth, my dear." She held out a limp hand to him. "What a pleasant surprise. Come and sit with me."

"Mother, did you know we have a visitor?" He pulled a stool adjacent to the chaise and sat but was too tense to relax.

"I have heard nothing." She twisted her head and called to her maid. "Sigge, why have I not—"

Impatiently Gareth interrupted. "Mother, he came unannounced! It is *him*!"

"Him? Who? You speak in riddles, Gareth."

"It is the bastard, de Tollard."

"Him!" Lady Hawken dropped her embroidery hoop, her eyes suddenly ablaze.

"Yes. Father banished him. Why has he returned?"

"Curse him!" she seethed. "I thought we were finally rid of him."

"Then you are worried, also?" He hated the plaintive look he cast toward his mother, hated his dependence upon her judgments, yet needed them, as well. His friends would think him a fop if they guessed how important his mother was to him.

Clarise picked up her needlework again. "There is nothing to worry about." After her initial reaction, she appeared calm but punched the needle though the cloth as if scoring her foe with a sword.

"Why would he come here, else to cause trouble of some kind?" In his agitation, Gareth jumped up and paced. "He made it clear he had not lost his position at Cassley. Yet there is some specific matter that causes him to come so boldly here. I would know what it is before some calamity takes me unaware."

"I see nothing wrong with that. I agree wholeheartedly." Clarise tapped her chin with the point of the tapestry needle. "The bastard most definitely bears watching."

"Mayhap he is with Father."

"Lord Hawken was resting when I last saw him, not an hour ago. You must find John. If he is not tending your father, tell him to come to me directly."

Gareth strode to the hearth, then spun around. "John? What can he do?"

"John has lately become very useful to me." Clarise's thin lips bent into a cold smile. "The old servant has come to realize that if he wishes to continue in the rather comfortable place he has in his master's household, it is imperative that he curry the heir's loyalty, which is best obtained through me, not the lord."

"Do you mean to say you have old John spying on his master for you?" Gareth regarded his mother with renewed admiration.

She nodded. "You must always remember, son, loyalty is a commodity like any other and has a price. And its price differs for different men. Now, be a dear and fetch John."

Gareth did as his mother bid. The servant was found in his own chamber mending his master's chemise. Together they returned to Lady Hawken's solar.

"No, m'lady," John answered her inquiry. "The master sleeps, so I sent young de Tollard to the kitchen to seek sustenance and await the master's rising. I do not know why the impudent lad thinks the lord will see him now, when he has never done so in the past, and when he has been banished from here. Shall I send de Tollard on his way?"

"Nay, I think not." Clarise glanced at Gareth, who had made a protesting grunt. "If we do that, we shall never know the bastard's intent."

Gareth decided he did not give his mother enough credit. "What, then, should we do, Mother?"

"John, wake the lord and tell him of his visitor," she said. "Then when the two meet—"

"How can you be certain he will receive the bastard?" asked Gareth.

The woman's eyes narrowed, and her lips pursed distastefully. "Oh, I think he will. If not, I will come up with another plan. If there is a meeting, John, you must be sure to be present."

"But he may send me away, m'lady," protested the servant.

"Should that be, you will find a way. You *must* hear the conversation." She leveled a searing gaze at the servant, who visibly quaked. Gareth realized she must have something quite damaging on the fellow. He was obviously uncomfortable with betraying his master.

"Y-yes, m'lady! I will do as you ask." John began to back out of the room, no doubt anxious to be gone before some other loathsome task might be laid upon him. "I-is that all, madam?"

"Yes. Begone with you!"

John scrambled to the door and was gone within a blink of an eye. The old man, who often shuffled and hobbled through the castle as if he were on his last legs, now showed incredible agility in his escape. Gareth hoped the man was as efficient in his spying as he had been just then in making his exit.

Gareth swung his focus back to the now reclining woman. "Mother, tell me again there is naught to fear," he entreated.

"Why should there be? You are the only legitimate son and the legal heir. Not only has your father made a solemn oath, he has put it into his will, as well."

"Wills can be changed."

"But not an oath." She rose suddenly from her chaise, strode to her son, and placed her arm around his shoulders. It was a loving, motherly gesture—shocking Gareth, for such gestures were not forthcoming from the woman. "I will not let him break his oath." The hardness of her tone contrasted chillingly with the motherly display, but that proved far more comforting to Gareth than the embrace.

"I do not want him to have any portion," Gareth declared.

"He will not. I vow it is all yours. Trust me."

Gareth kissed his mother's cool cheek and left her presence. His steps, after exiting Lady Hawken's solar, led him past his father's chamber. His parents had not shared a chamber for years. He doubted they shared a bed even occasionally. Hearing voices from within his father's room, Gareth paused. Listening was no use, for the walls were too stout to make out anything but vague tones. He hoped John was inside.

Gareth continued to his own chamber, which was in a wing adjacent to his parents' quarters. He flopped down upon his bed but was far too restless to relax. There was a jug of ale left on his table from last evening. For once he applauded the lazy servants who had carelessly failed to clean his room. Grabbing the jug, he poured a large measure into the dirty cup. His hand trembled.

Curse that bastard de Tollard!

He tossed back the entire cupful of liquid in one gulp and poured another. This, too, he imbibed quickly, and another, and another.

Just as the ale started to help convince him he was overreacting, that de Tollard posed no threat, he would recall some incident that would cause him to doubt all over again. How many times had his father held his precarious inheritance over his head in order to intimidate Gareth into submitting to the man's will? Of course, because of the lord's oath to his wife, he never directly stated that his bastard son could inherit. The implication was always present nonetheless.

Gareth wished he would have killed his brother on the field that afternoon. Curse that knight Jocelin, as well! How close he had come to ending all his fears. Now he must tremble and worry. Curse them all! And especially his father and that sniveling bastard de Tollard.

Gareth gulped down more ale in a vain attempt to ease his fears.

12

Philip had gone to the kitchen as instructed. Maude, the fat, rosy-cheeked cook, tried to get him to eat, but he declined.

"Ye need to fill out them bones, lad," she urged. "There's a meat pasty left from this morning." She'd always been nice to him, but then, she was nice to all who ventured into her kitchen.

"Thank you. Perhaps later."

Grinning, she said, "'Tis nice to see a polite lad round here for a change. I'll save it for you, then."

His father's manservant, John, returned a short time later and bid Philip to the lord's chamber. Though he'd hoped his father would receive him, he had nearly given up. Why should his father speak to him now after so long? Philip's message requesting an audience had emphasized urgency. Well, regardless of what had finally prompted the lord's actions, Philip was finally on his way. If his father would deem to speak to him, who knew what other miracles were possible?

They passed through the Great Hall, quiet now, though soon preparations for the evening meal would begin. Some knights, however, were already wandering into the hall. Philip saw Jocelin talking with some of them. He wondered what they would think when his father announced the news of Philip's portion. Jocelin had always been kind to him, while the others had merely tolerated him. He would warrant their respect as lord of his own fief.

Quit dreaming! he silently ordered himself. His father might just rail at him for his failures.

Climbing the tower stairs, Philip pitied poor old John, huffing and puffing ahead of him. The lord's chamber was on the top level, and the long climb gave him plenty of time to think and wish and dream. It might be his dreams were not so idle as they once were. His father loved him! Incredible. Yet, if so . . .

They came to the top of the stairs, and Lord Hawken's door loomed before them. In an instant, like a candle flame being snuffed out, Philip's confidence fled. What foolish quest was he upon?

Then his father's voice bade him enter.

In the chamber, drapes were pulled across the large windows of glass, a sign of status Lord Hawken had always taken pride in. The solar was dim, and Philip had the impression it had been thus all day. The covers on the bed were rumpled, as if recently occupied. It was not like John to be so neglectful of his duties. Could it be that the lord had in fact just risen from a rest? That was not like his father, who'd always been a robust man, constantly on the move, vigorously involved in all the workings of his estate.

The fire in the hearth had burned low, and a chill hung in the stale air. Again, Philip wondered at this unusual circumstance. He strode to the hearth and picked up a log from the woodbin, forestalling the inevitable.

"My lord," he said, "let me build up the fire for you."

"It is not necessary—"

Philip had already tossed in the wood. Within a few moments a flame flared up. Unable to think of any other diversion, he turned back to face his father.

Philip restrained a gasp at the first sight of Lord Hawken he'd had at close quarters in over a month. Hawken was seated before a small table upon which resided a chessboard. From the arrangement of the pieces, a game appeared to be in progress. But Philip's attention was still directed upon the man himself. Perhaps it was only a trick of the shadowed light that made the lord seem almost gray in his coloring and gaunt, as well, with deep hollows in his cheeks and dark circles around his eyes. Surely it was the light.

"I have taught John too well," Lord Hawken said, rubbing his chin as he studied the board, not once looking at his son. His tone, however, lacked its usual rough tenor. For this being only the second time in his life that he'd addressed his son, his voice and tone were disconcertingly casual.

Philip glanced around and saw the servant in question had disappeared.

He'd probably slipped into his alcove to await his master's bidding.

"Yes, he has quite stumped me. That's what I get for teaching a servant to play."

Stepping closer, Philip noted that Hawken was indeed in check. "Perhaps if you move your rook to there . . ." He gestured to indicate his meaning.

"Ah yes. I see it now." Lord Hawken moved the indicated piece. "Did you learn this at the university?"

"Among other things."

"Then my silver was not completely wasted." Still the man did not lift his eyes toward his visitor.

Philip kept reminding himself of Jocelin's words, but by all appearances the knight had misread things. To Philip it seemed as if his father was too ashamed of him to even look him in the eye.

Desperate to garner his father's pity, if nothing else, Philip said, "My lord, I did not intend to fail you."

"You failed yourself." Some of the roughness returned to the lord's voice.

Philip realized this direction was not one that would further his cause. Hopelessness settled once more over him, but some inner determination he could not identify forced him to plow ahead. "My lord, I was not meant for the Church."

"What does a boy know of such things?" A sound came from a corner of the room, and Hawken's head jerked around. "John, is that you?"

"I'm sorry, m'lord. I dropped your shoe," said the servant. "I did not mean to disturb you."

"Well, now that you have disturbed me, I realize I am parched. Bring me some ale, you lazy boots."

There followed the creaking sound of a side door opening. Philip hoped a jug was kept nearby so the old servant didn't have to trek all the way down the stairs to the kitchen. Apparently that was the case, for only a few minutes later, the servant appeared carrying a tray bearing a jug and a cup. Philip noted there was only one cup. John poured a measure into the cup and gave it to the lord. None was offered to Philip; neither was a seat offered. He thought it appropriate that he stood before his lord as a common petitioner.

John lingered at his master's shoulder. "Anything else, m'lord?"

"No." When the servant did not move, Hawken added sharply, "Begone with you, then!"

"Perhaps I should tarry, m'lord, should you have need of me?"

"Well, then, don't stand over me like a simpleton! Find some work to be about. My sword needs a polish."

John again retreated into the shadows of the chamber, and Philip thought no more of him, so intent was he in trying to think of a way to continue the discussion with his father, though in a more positive way.

"My lord," Philip finally said, "we were speaking of my future. . . ." He'd determined no more subtle approach. He hoped his father would take up the thread of his hesitant sentence, but when the lord remained silent, Philip stumbled on. "I do not think I am destined to be a groom, either, though I well like tending horses."

"It was your choice."

"I had few choices, m'lord."

"And whose fault was that?" growled Lord Hawken. "After what you did, you should be content with what you have."

"I have nothing!" Philip burst out, immediately hating himself for the display of emotion. Miserably, he added, "Nor have I ever asked for anything."

"No . . . no, you have not." Hawken's gaze wandered to the hearth and seemed to study the depths of the flames before asking in a tone oddly earnest, "Why was that?"

"Perhaps it was pride, or perhaps I merely feared refusal."

"So you stole instead?"

Philip bit his lip, forcing himself to keep calm in the face of an accusation that would not die. Tightly he said, "I did not steal, m'lord."

"So you say." Hawken took a long draught of his ale and then wiped a sleeve across his lips. He still refused to look at Philip. Even an accuser in court did that much when facing a criminal.

Anger rising and barely biting it back, Philip replied, "You would believe your own son to be a common thief?" He prepared himself to be dismissed from the lord's presence, not only for defying his judgment but also for calling himself the man's son before his face.

Philip saw the muscles in the lord's jaw flex with barely repressed anger. Philip guessed that he and his father looked very much alike at that moment. The idea fairly doused his own anger. The lord was his father—his own father! How I want to be your son! How I want you to reach out to me, to touch me . . . even just to *look* at me! All those years as a lonely bastard child rushed in upon him. Nothing, not even his doting mother's love, could replace the boy's compelling need for his father's love and approbation.

Flatly Lord Hawken said, "I have agreed to see you. What more do you want?"

Philip, feeling like a mangy stray dog lapping up crumbs beneath the master's table, knew he would get no more approbation, much less vindication for his supposed crime, than those words. He wanted to leave right then. He did not want to beg from this man who obviously despised him. Jocelin must be unhinged!

Then Philip thought of Beatrice. If he left Hawken now, he would never have her. Could he not humble himself once more? His was an existence rife with humiliation. Certainly he could lap crumbs from the floor for the girl he loved. Besides, he was never going to get from his father what he really desired. At the least he ought to attempt to wheedle a patch of dirt from him.

Obsequiousness did not come easily, and it took all his will to press on. "My lord, I want only my rightful due, and failing that, at least a portion of what should be mine. How can you begrudge me that much? You well know a man must have land to be something. I do not ask for much, just a small fief of land, enough to allow me a place in society. Such a tract would not even be missed from among your vast holdings."

"You do not understand the complexities that face me."

Was his tone actually conflicted? Or was that merely Philip's pitiful imagination?

Then for one heart-stopping moment Lord Hawken's eyes jerked up, focusing for a brief instant upon Philip. Only a man who had never in his life really looked into the eyes of his father could truly understand what a wondrous moment that was. Even that day when Lord Hawken presented the dagger to Philip, he had managed to keep his gaze averted. Now it was as if he wanted Philip to peer into his eyes and, perhaps, through them into his soul. The span of that moment was no more than a breath; even Philip's held breath lasted longer. He knew he would spend the rest of his life trying to fathom all the emotions that brief look held.

Too quickly Lord Hawken lowered his focus, then picked up his cup and concentrated on that for a good span.

Finally he spoke, and Philip thought he heard a trace of tenderness in the man's voice. "You have been a good boy since you came to me. You have never given me a single reason to regret taking you in, save for that incident two months past." He drank deeply from his cup before continuing. "Indeed, I never believed your guilt in the matter, although I thought it best that you leave Hawken before a worse charge befell you. Mayhap it was wrong that I did not absolve you completely. Add that to the heap of wrongs I have committed in this life."

"It is within your power to set matters aright," Philip said, hope soaring once more.

"What is this sudden urge you have to raise your fortunes? Is there a woman?"

Philip flushed, and his father chose that moment to take another look at his son.

A hint of a smile quirked Lord Hawken's lips. "Yes, 'tis always a woman." He rose and strode to the hearth, his gait a bit hobbled and unsteady.

The lord lifted a log to toss upon the flame, but the weight of the wood unbalanced him and he began to topple forward. Philip leaped to the man's assistance, grasping Hawken's arm, steadying him. Were he to receive no other boon from the lord, this moment, this first touch between father and son, might well have satisfied Philip. It went leagues beyond a mere look. His hand tarried on his father's elbow longer than necessary, and the contact sent a thrill though his body.

He sensed his father was as shocked by the touch as he. Was he wondering how a man could go eighteen years without once embracing his son, much less touching him? When his astonished focus skittered toward Philip and their eyes met, Philip was astounded even more by what he saw there. Hawken's eyes had softened and seemed to glisten damply in the firelight. Philip thought that if they had lingered thus for another moment, the two might indeed embrace.

But Hawken stepped away, bending to retrieve the dropped piece of wood, which, after grasping the mantel for support, he tossed on the fire. Philip also backed away, trying to ignore the awful, empty ache the brief incident left inside.

The two men stood silent for some time. The blazing fire suddenly seemed fascinating as they gazed into the bright tongues of flame. Philip considered again his childhood longings for a father. He had built up an image of the man who, until five years ago, had neither name nor face. That mysterious man of his mind was nothing less than a saint and a warrior—brave, just, and mighty.

The man Philip had finally encountered five years ago had been none of those things. Rather, he was a man of great contradictions. His prowess on the field of battle proved him a courageous knight, but he lacked the courage to accept his bastard son, his sinful mistake. He might be just in his dealings with his serfs and vassals, yet he would see his firstborn son become a common groom before giving him his due. As for sainthood? That was expecting too much of anyone. Philip sensed that his father struggled with as many demons in his soul as any man, yet that deep in his heart he desired to conquer them, even if more often than not he failed.

"Leave me now," Hawken said abruptly.

"My lord?"

"I need time to consider your words."

Philip's jaw went slack. "Do you mean . . . ?"

"I said, begone!" Lord Hawken cried harshly.

Philip forced his feet into motion. He dared not push him further. His father was going to consider his request! That was more than a few crumbs on the floor, wasn't it?

As Philip grasped the handle of the door, Lord Hawken muttered, "You deserve justice."

Philip was not sure he had been meant to hear those barely audible words, but he could not help taking comfort in them.

For several minutes after his chamber door shut, Ralph paced before the hearth. Why had fate dealt him so? That he should despise the son he must claim, while the son he desired to draw to his heart, he must deny? Why couldn't Philip de Tollard be a worthless cur like his half brother? Why could he not be grasping and greedy and self-serving? Yes, he was now asking for something, yet it was clear he did so only because he loved a woman and wanted a portion for her sake. It was love not greed that drove the boy.

And what drives me? thought Ralph Aubernon.

Angrily he kicked the hearth stone then winced because his foot was still sore and tender.

"I know what drives me," he murmured. "Fear."

His pacing brought him to the table where the chessboard was laid. "I am the worst coward imaginable!" Suddenly he slammed his fist down on the table, scattering all the ivory chess pieces. "No more! I must do what is right."

"My lord?" came John's concerned voice from the far corner. "Is something amiss?" The servant approached cautiously.

"Not anymore!" yelled Ralph. "As God is my witness, not anymore!" Spinning around and ignoring the moment of dizziness this caused, he glared at his servant. "Go fetch my clerk."

"M'lord, Friar Martel is in the village. He is to stay there for the night, giving aid to some of the villeins."

"I pay him to be here when I need him, not to— Never mind, I will go to the village."

"But it is late," John protested.

He was a loyal servant, and Ralph knew he did not appreciate him enough.

"There is only an hour or so of light left. Your way would be hazardous. Surely your business can await the morrow."

"It has waited too long already. Go see that my mount is saddled and ready."

"M'lord, you were feeling so poorly today."

Ralph gave a dismissive grunt. "I am fine. Or I will be once I have righted a grievous wrong."

13

Lady Hawken was not in her chamber, so John sought the young master. But he was asleep and defied John's attempts to wake him. The odor of strong brew hung about the boy. No doubt he was in a drunken stupor.

In truth, John wondered about the urgency of the matter. The lord would do what he willed regardless of his wife's knowledge. If he was indeed seeking the clerk to put into writing some boon for the bastard, what could the lady do about it anyway? John's master was still Lord of Hawken. Surely the lord was to be feared over the lady.

Then John remembered that the lady held a grievous deed over his own head, a deed which, if made public, could ruin his family. He still did not know how the lady had discovered that John's eldest son had been the one who had robbed the traveling merchant some months ere. John himself had only learned of it when his son, fully repentant, had confessed the matter to him. The lad had assured him there had been no witnesses, and since the merchant was long gone, leaving no way to recompense him, John felt safe in keeping the crime secret. He would give an extra tithe to the Church until the value of the stolen candlesticks was reached, thus vindicating him and his son in God's eyes.

But Lady Hawken had spies everywhere. And though she had not the power to stay her husband's hand, she could and would make life extremely miserable for John and for his family. Thus she had sealed his enslavement to her.

How he hated being her lackey, and hated even more betraying Lord Hawken. He continued his search for the lady, knowing he must at least make a show of doing her bidding. Through no fault of his own, a minor household mishap distracted him. By the time he found Lady Hawken in the brewhouse supervising the preparation of a new batch of ale, her husband was well on his way and had no doubt reached the village and found Friar Martel.

After telling the lady of the bastard's meeting with the lord, John braced himself for the barrage of abuse he knew would be forthcoming.

Lady Hawken did not disappoint. "You idiot!" she screamed.

"M'lady, I could not stop him."

"You incompetent fool! Where is my son?"

"Asleep, m'lady."

"Asleep!" Her voice was so shrill it set the servant's teeth on edge. "At this hour?"

"There was an empty jug of ale—"

"I am surrounded by fools." She pushed past John, nearly knocking him off his feet as she strode into the keep and to the tower stairs. Before she mounted them, she craned her head around and glared again at John. "Tell me the moment Lord Hawken returns. You can do that, can't you?"

"Yes, m'lady."

But John had many duties in the household and could not stand guard at the door. Certainly not even the lady expected that of him. No doubt it would be she herself who would box his ears should he be found idle from his labors. He would know soon enough when the lord returned, if not the exact instant.

———

When Gareth awoke, his head throbbed, and his tongue felt like a chausses stuck into his dry mouth. He spit out a mumbled curse as he realized he had probably passed out hours ago. Flinging back the shutter on the window, he saw it was now dark.

His next lucid thought was of his brother. Gareth had intended to keep a close watch on the bastard, and now, because of his stupidity, de Tollard had been wandering freely in the castle. What mischief might he stir?

Gareth raced from his chamber. With no definite plan of action in mind he headed in the general direction of his mother's solar, which took him through several adjacent rooms. He was hurrying so that as he barreled through what his mother liked to call the music room, he nearly collided with his father's manservant.

"You dolt!" Gareth spat. "Have a care!"

"Sorry, m'lord." John had been carrying an armload of clean linens, which now lay scattered upon the floor. He bent to gather them up.

"Is my father in his chamber?" Gareth ignored the problem of John's upset laundry. The servant's presence reminded Gareth that it would be a good idea to know the lord's whereabouts, as well.

"I don't know, m'lord."

Gareth gave a hard kick, clipping John firmly on the side of his head. "Stand and face me when you speak."

John scrambled to his feet. "Forgive me, m'lord."

"Did my father see de Tollard?"

"Yes, m'lord."

"Well?" seethed Gareth. "What transpired?"

"I reported to your mother—"

"Report to *me*, fool!"

"It was nothing unexpected, Master Gareth."

The servant paused. Gareth glared at the man to get him to offer more.

"Young de Tollard did indeed ask a boon of your father."

"And . . . ?" growled Gareth, his hands itching to strangle the information from the servant.

"Your father said he had to think on it, and then he—" John swallowed before finishing, and when he did so, averted his gaze. "Lord Hawken went to the village to find his clerk, Friar Martel, who was biding there for the night."

"Martel!" This was worse than Gareth had feared. Was the old man going to change his will, just like that? "You are certain of this?"

"I cannot say if the lord actually made it to the village, but that is where he was bound."

"Why, you witless fool!" Gareth shouted, adding a string of curses. Yelling was not enough to appease Gareth. He felt his life crumbling before him. He had to hurt someone. Now!

Grabbing the servant, he slammed the old man's slight frame up against the stone wall.

"Help!" gasped the servant.

"What goes on here?" Lord Hawken's voice penetrated the scene.

Gareth had given no thought to the fact that the music room was adjacent to his father's chamber. He spun around. "There you are!" Gareth said, his tone lacking all proper respect for his father.

"How dare you abuse my servant so!" the lord exclaimed.

"Where have you been?" Gareth demanded, ignoring all else. He did note, however, with sinking heart, that his father was garbed in his cloak and wearing his riding boots.

"Are you my keeper that I must give you account of my coming and going?" Hawken gave a derisive snort. "Bah, you are the impertinent fool, then." He strode past Gareth and somehow, despite his lame feet, managed a haughty stride.

Hawken reached the door to his chamber, opened it, and entered. But as he flung the door shut behind him, Gareth, close on his heels, caught the door and also entered the room, giving the door a firm slam himself.

Lord Hawken, already halfway across the chamber, turned and glared at his son. "I did not invite you in here."

"I want to know where you have been and what you have been up to." Gareth had as little respect for his father as the man had for him, and now all previous pretense was shed.

"You certainly have nerve!" Hawken unclasped his cloak and flung it aside.

"You have been to see your clerk," Gareth accused.

"Why ask if you know so much?"

"It is true then. You are going to give that bastard an inheritance."

"What if I am? You have proven to me, now more than ever, that you are unworthy."

"How could you?" Gareth choked the words past his incredulity.

"It is mine to do with as I wish."

"If it were not for my mother, you would have lost Hawken long ago. She saved Hawken, not that strumpet you bedded before her!"

"Why, you good-for-nothing knave!" Hawken screamed, murder flashing in his eyes.

His father, casting wildly about, yanked his sword from its scabbard. Only then did Gareth know that he had gone too far.

Gareth stumbled back and for one brief instance saw only the mighty crusading knight that his father had once been. The weapon glinted in the firelight as the lord hoisted it over his head. Gareth was too stunned, too frightened, to even cry out.

But Ralph Aubernon of Hawken was not the same man who had wielded that very sword in Palestine twenty years ago. He was a sick old man who sometimes had trouble even taking a breath. Though his face was now flushed with the fury of hell, his arm was too weak to lend much power to the sword he swung. The weight of the weapon itself nearly brought him down.

Seeing this weakness infused some courage into Gareth. He leaped forward, grasping the old man's sword arm. He gave it a twist, and the weapon clattered to the floor. The man was about as powerful as an old crone. In another moment the one-time warrior followed the sword to the floor.

Gasping and clutching his chest, the lord seethed, "Y-you . . . will not speak of . . . her in such manner. I-I c-can't . . . breathe!" Wheezing and gulping for air, Hawken held out a silently beseeching arm. "Th-the pain! God . . . help me . . ."

Gareth stared dumbly at his father. The man was lying there making horrible pathetic sounds and turning a ghastly shade of blue.

"Help me!" Hawken silently mouthed, unable to produce sound.

Gareth was paralyzed. He had never seen his father so helpless. He was sure the man had never once asked any man for help.

Then all sound, all movement, ceased. Lord Hawken's body went still while Gareth continued to stare. Even as he realized his father was surely dead, he felt fear more than any other emotion.

The door opened. "M'lord, I have brought you a tray, since you missed the evening meal." It was John, who must have gone to the kitchen after his encounter with Gareth.

For once Gareth was happy to see the servant. "John, my father fell! He . . . I don't know what happened!"

John set down the tray and hurried to his master's fallen body. His gaze took in the sword lying on the floor; then he lifted his eyes to boldly meet Gareth's, his expression filled with accusation.

"He drew his sword!" Gareth sputtered, fear clutching at him with icy fingers. "I only defended myself."

John touched the lord's body. "He is dead."

"Go get my mother," Gareth ordered. "Say nothing to anyone about this."

Left alone, Gareth paced. Feeling queasy inside, he tried to gather his wits. The timing of such a disaster could not be worse. If his father had changed his will, then it would now be binding. All was lost! The bastard had won after all.

A few moments later Lady Hawken arrived with John. She took in the scene with astounding aplomb.

"You attacked him?" she asked with more disdain than horror.

"No! I swear I did not! He drew his sword and attacked me. I only defended myself." Sweat poured down Gareth's brow. Any ground he'd gained in calming while alone was lost in the presence of his mother. He needed her now more than ever, and that was as disconcerting as any of the horrible events transpiring around him.

"It little matters." Shaking her head, she stared down her perfect nose at her dead husband. "What a time to die!"

Then a new notion sent Gareth into renewed panic. "Mother, it will be believed I killed him!" He wiped a shaking hand across his moist brow. "What will become of me? What will happen? A murderer can't inherit—but it doesn't matter. He changed his will, gave it all to the bastard. I am finished! It is over. We have lost—"

"Shut up, you dullard!" Clarise glanced at the body once more, then tapped her chin with her slim fingers. "Give me a moment to think."

Gareth watched mutely as she paced about the room for several minutes. Just when Gareth thought he could stand the silence no longer, she spun around. He sucked in a startled breath. This woman before him, his mother, was a sight to behold. Tall, regal, like a fiery Amazon queen come to life. The sight steadied Gareth, and he knew all would be well.

With a sly glint, she said, "You are right, Gareth, a murderer cannot inherit." She turned to John. "I have a job for you. Follow my instructions precisely, do you hear?"

No one in his right mind would think to do anything other than obey this woman's demands.

14

After John departed, Clarise went to a chest in the chamber, opened it, and withdrew a dagger. Gareth watched in stunned awe.

"This must be done quickly, while there is still blood flowing in his body." Tucking the knife into her sash, she returned to the body. "We must remove his clothing and lift him to the bed."

"What?"

"Help me, Gareth! We must make it appear as if he were killed in his sleep."

Though Gareth had heard her instructions to the servant, his mind was still too muddled to fully grasp her intent. He followed her orders as if in a dream. After stripping the body down to his braies, Gareth grasped his father's lifeless body beneath the arms while his mother took the feet. Lord Hawken was still a man of formidable size, despite his recent physical decline. Gareth and his mother struggled mightily with the dead weight. Before the task was done, perspiration rolled more freely than ever from Gareth's brow. Why had they not waited to send away the servant?

Panting from the exertion, he began to sink into a chair for a rest.

"We are not done yet," Lady Hawken railed. The effort had hardly ruffled her pristine countenance.

Reluctantly he approached the bed and stood next to her. A moment ago, her strength had given him confidence. Now it was starting to scare him. His stomach began to quake as he realized what must come next.

"Mother, do I have to . . . I-I don't think I could . . ." he stammered.

"No, my son. I do not want any blood on your hands." She looked at him and smiled.

The gesture gave him no reassurance. She doled her smiles out sparingly. Why now?

"I will do the deed," she said.

She took the dagger and, holding it in both hands, raised it over her head.

"Oh no! Mother, no!" he cried. His knees grew weak, not because of the deed being done, but because he knew he would let her do it. He was under her power and too feeble to do anything about it.

With a mighty thrust, she plunged the dagger into her husband's chest. Gareth's stomach twisted and convulsed.

Blood sprayed and oozed from the wound. The covers were soiled, as were Lady Hawken's hands and sleeves.

Gareth turned away just in time as the contents of his stomach exploded from his lips. He crumpled to his knees, still retching.

After cleaning the blood from her hands and disposing of the cloth in the fire, Lady Hawken put an arm around her son. "Come, son, we are finished here."

Dazed, he looked up at his mother. He knew his father had already been dead, but in his heart he still felt like a murderer.

"Mother, my father is dead," he murmured.

"Come. We will go to my chamber and await John."

She threw closed the inside latch of the door that led to the tower stairs so that no one could enter that way. Then they departed. Gareth's knees wobbled as they walked. Back in Lady Hawken's solar he sank into a chair and hoped he wouldn't have to move ever again. He doubted his legs would support him if he had to. His mother finished cleaning herself and burned the surcote with the bloodied sleeves.

A short time later her maid came to prepare her for bed.

"Later, Sigge," said Lady Hawken. "I wish to visit with my son a while longer."

"What is that odor, m'lady?" The maid twitched her nose. "Like burning cloth."

"Oh, that. I spilled water on my surcote, and while trying to dry the thing, it scorched. I tossed it into the fire."

Sigge gave her mistress a questioning look. Lady Hawken never took care of such matters herself, but the maid knew better than to dispute the lady's word.

"I'll tidy up a bit, then—"

Lady Hawken cut in smoothly. "My son and I wish to talk alone. Be off with you. I will call when I am ready for bed."

"Yes, m'lady." Sigge turned and paused at the door. "M'lady, is the master unwell? I saw John a short while ago, and he said no one is to disturb the lord until morning."

"Tired, is all," Clarise answered, still so calm. "Now, mind John and step softly as you pass the master's door."

When the maid was gone, Clarise let out a long sigh. She glanced at Gareth. "I feel almost as if I have done something wrong."

"But we haven't, have we, Mother?" he implored.

"No, of course not. The man was already dead."

"And what of the bastard? If he is hanged, will his blood be on us?" He licked his lips. He longed for a glass of strong ale.

"I never thought you so squeamish, Gareth." She deftly skirted the issue he'd raised.

"Nor did I, but this . . ." He swallowed and rubbed his still-trembling hands over his face. "I would have rather killed de Tollard in battle, as I nearly did this afternoon."

"That would only have fired your father's wrath further. This is better. The lord has conveniently accommodated us."

"What if someone finds out what we have done? I'm sure we have forgotten something important." If he could have only a small portion of her confidence!

"It matters not. We only have to fool that dolt of a sheriff, and even he will not much dispute the word of the lady of the manor."

Gareth shifted in his chair and then, too restless to remain still, jumped up. He didn't care if his legs were unsteady. He strode to the window, pulled aside the drape, and opened the shutter a crack. It was a clear, starry night. The moon had risen. Was de Tollard out there in the village tavern drinking with the knights? Was one of those knights—the one John thought could be best trusted with the task—at this moment drugging the bastard's drink? That same knight would take de Tollard to his pallet in the servants' quarters, and John would finish his tasks.

How long would it all take? Was his mother's plan too complicated? Did it truly not matter?

The two candles lighting the solar had burned quite low before John returned. He gave Lady Hawken the dagger she'd taken from the chest in the lord's chamber and used to commit her vile deed. It was now spotlessly clean. He reported that he had purloined de Tollard's dagger and had disposed of it in the manner they had discussed. He assured her that all else had been done as directed.

"I need you to take care of one more item before you retire," she instructed.

"Yes, my lady."

"You will find a mess on the floor near my husband's bed." She raised an eyebrow at Gareth. "Take care of it and see if you can mask the odor somehow." The lady then dismissed him without a single word of thanks. By then Gareth was too numb to correct the error, not that he would have done so in any case. The servant had done his duty. What thanks did he deserve?

"Gareth, why don't you retire?" Lady Hawken suggested after John left.

"I couldn't sleep." He was now back in the chair and had been dozing in fits, though these were far from any peaceful rest. Every time his eyes drooped shut, he'd see images of his father's death throes and would shudder awake.

"You must be strong," his mother said. "You are Lord of Hawken now."

Gareth gasped. In all that had transpired that simple truth had not yet occurred to him. "It's true, isn't it?"

She nodded. "What I have waited all these years for has finally come to pass. My own son is now master."

"Why did he hate me so, Mother?"

"You must never blame yourself, son." For once her voice was tender. Then it hardened. "It was the fault of that French harlot and her spawn. She bewitched him so that he had only a heart for them."

"Curse them," Gareth breathed.

Though he would have dearly loved to have plunged a dagger into de Tollard's heart, watching him hang would be nearly as satisfying.

A stabbing pain in the head woke Philip the next morning. He was not accustomed to drinking so much, though in truth he couldn't recall imbibing enough ale to cause his present discomfort. Nevertheless, his head felt as if it had swelled to twice its size, and when he moved, the room spun round and round, making his stomach do flips like acrobats at a fair.

He forced himself from his pallet. This should be a grand day. His whole life might change today! The thought took some of the misery out of movement. He wondered when his father would make his big announcement. He'd heard the lord had ridden into the village shortly before sunset. It wasn't until later that Philip had also gone to the village to visit the tavern with some knights, but by then the lord had already returned to the castle. It certainly could be no coincidence that Hawken's visit to the village had so quickly followed his talk with Philip.

Philip wished now that he hadn't let the knight, William de Cugey, talk him into going to the tavern. He wanted to be in his best frame of mind when his fortunes changed. And in honor of what lay ahead, he decided to attend morning Mass with the household. It would be the first time since departing Oxford that he'd been to Mass. He'd given up on God's providence in his life, but now he would change. God was indeed the giver of vast blessings, even to a sinful bastard.

With that in mind, he thought a clean chemise would be in order. He found his pouch where he'd put some spare clothes. Only as he reached for it did he note the filth on his hands, something dry and reddish. What was it?

Absently wiping his hands on his breeches, he reached into his pouch. He forgot all about his chemise, though, when he saw his dagger was not there. He always took it off before he slept, and he must have done so last night even if he had been drunk, because it wasn't on him now. Perhaps William, who he recalled had helped him to his pallet, had put it elsewhere.

Philip looked all around his pallet, turning over the tangled covers but finding nothing. His despair nearly tarnished even the prospect of the good fortune awaiting him. After what Jocelin had said yesterday, that dagger meant more to him than anything he possessed.

Forgetting the clean chemise, he decided to go immediately and ask questions of the household. As he was striding toward the door, it burst open, nearly smacking him in the face. In barged Gareth with the sheriff and several knights.

One of the knights, his drinking companion William, grabbed him while Gareth hurled accusations.

"Is this your dagger?" Gareth waved the knife in his face, and it was indeed the knife Lord Hawken had given Philip for his sixteenth birthday. The blade was stained with blood.

"Y-yes, it's mine." Philip's brain was still moving slowly, as if in a fog. "Where did you find it?"

"Are you saying you lost it?" asked the sheriff.

"It wasn't with my things this morning."

"You murdered my father!" yelled Gareth.

"What?" Philip looked from Gareth to the sheriff and then into the faces of the knights. What were they saying?

"You stabbed him with this knife!" Again Gareth waved the weapon in Philip's face. "You killed him!"

"M-my father is dead?" Philip rasped. This was a mistake. His father was going to give him his portion today. His life was going to change today.

"As if you didn't know!" Gareth grabbed Philip's hands. "Look, he even has blood on his hands."

Philip looked again at his stained hands, still soiled despite his clumsy attempt to wipe them. His father's blood? He shuddered as the reality of what was happening began to penetrate his mental fog.

"It's not true!" he protested.

No one listened to him. He was taken to the dungeons, too stunned to put up a struggle. He truly felt the lamb being led to slaughter.

His captors tried to get a confession from him with the customary preparatory torture. Even the painful ordeal of the rack could not exact from him what he knew to be a lie. Unlike many, he survived the torture, but rather than attribute that to luck, he thought they let him off easily because they had other plans for his demise.

His trial was swift. A royal court was convened, and twelve local freeholders were quickly recruited to pass judgment upon him.

Nearly everyone in the shire gathered in the yard of Hawken Castle on that fine early summer morning a week to the day after the murder. This was a rare event. The lord had been murdered, and even the lowliest serf was interested. The atmosphere resembled that of market day or a fair with all the noise and merrymaking. Dogs and children were running hither and thither while the adults gossiped. The litigants could hardly be heard above the racket.

Of one thing Philip was thankful—Beatrice was not at the trial. He feared the headstrong girl would learn of his arrest and, defying good sense, make an appearance. He could thank Jocelin for her absence. The knight had managed to get into his dungeon cell once to see him. Philip asked the knight to keep an eye out for Beatrice and make sure she stayed far away.

Philip watched mutely as the case was presented to the court by the coroner who had investigated the crime. He had examined the body and questioned the household.

"The lord's servant John raised a hue and cry the morning after the murder," the coroner said in a rather bored tone. He seemed to have his mind made up that Philip was guilty of the murder and the trial was merely a formality. "It appeared to me that the lord had been stabbed during the night in his sleep. The accused had motive, feeling he'd been cheated of his due by his father."

Philip groaned inwardly. He'd never been able to convince them otherwise, now with the new will, which Father Martel had produced and which had indeed granted Philip an inheritance. Obviously, said his accusers, Philip had been too impatient to wait in due course for his inheritance. Or, they suggested, more likely he had been unaware of the will and believed his father was about to ignore his request, and therefore killed him out of revenge. He was, after all, known to be a hothead. This last was given credibility by John's testimony that during the meeting between the lord and Philip, the lord had flatly denied Philip's request. Only after he was alone did the lord change his mind and decide to surprise Philip with the new will in the morning.

"This," the coroner went on, "is the murder weapon." He held up Philip's dagger. "The accused freely admits it is his weapon."

The dagger had been found buried in a hole behind the stable. Hastily hidden and apparently easily found by one of the servants, it had been covered in blood, and no one doubted it had been used to end the lord's life.

Few questions had been raised about any of the disparities in the crime. Only the obvious was perceived and accepted. And the louder Philip cried foul, the less, it seemed, anyone saw the truth. No one perceived that in light of the changed will, the younger son, Gareth, had the greatest motive for murder. No one saw; no one cared. It must be the bastard. He had more reason than any to hate the lord, who had treated him unfairly.

How could they possibly understand that he loved his father? He didn't understand it himself. His heart had nearly broken when he had learned of the lord's death. Only fear for his own life and the rapid progression of events had kept him from prostrating himself in grief the moment the news had penetrated his numb mind. Later, in his dark cell, he'd wept when he thought of that last time in the lord's chamber, of that one look, that one touch and how it would be the last. He would never see the fulfillment of his childhood dream of a father he could call his own.

Following the coroner's presentation, the jury was given the chattels of the accused to examine. Philip had few possessions, and clearly nothing further could be discovered from the contents of his pouch.

Studying the faces of the jury, all of which were pointedly averted from him, Philip guessed what their verdict would be. He decided to take one last desperate gambit.

Making his voice heard above the din of the crowd, he declared, "I claim benefit of clergy!"

He hoped that his years at Oxford might be enough for him to plausibly take on this distinction, even if he hadn't finished and formally entered the Church. It was his only chance. If his claim was accepted, he would have to be tried in the Church, where capital punishment was forbidden.

His declaration elicited a variety of responses from the crowd. A few scattered cheers were heard, but mostly he detected disappointment that they might be denied the entertainment of a hanging. Loudest of all were Gareth's protests.

"This is a travesty!" he cried. "He failed the university. He defiles the Holy Church with his blasphemous claim!"

Again, the voice of the new lord held sway. Philip hadn't expected otherwise. It had been a lame ploy, and in truth, he was glad it hadn't worked out, because down deep it galled him to call upon God. He'd been a fool to ever think God cared about a bastard.

15

On his last night on earth Philip sat in his cell watching a rat gnaw on his untouched bread. Only a few days ago he had begun to have reason to hope for his future. He had been able to believe a life with Beatrice might truly be possible. He had let himself dream about asking for her hand in marriage and taking her to the fine new house he would build on his land.

Now the dream had become a nightmare. He would not even set eyes upon Beatrice's lovely face before he was executed. But wasn't that just as well? How could he bear the shame of it?

Nor was the shame of the manner of execution lost on him. He was the first son of a great lord and, as his new will signified, had finally been accepted by him. He deserved the honor of beheading. Instead, he would hang like a commoner. Gareth had seen to that.

Why should I care how I die? It would be a fitting end, would it not? Let me die in dishonor, he silently seethed. Were I to live, I would spit at honor. It never did anything but mock my attempts to live by its precepts!

The sound of jingling keys drew his attention from his morbid thoughts. Were they coming to take him already? It was hours yet until dawn. He shrugged. That he felt no fear at his impending demise proved he was ready. He welcomed it.

The cell door creaked open, and he dragged himself to his feet to meet his doom.

Philip's eyes had grown accustomed to the darkness of his dungeon cell, yet still it took a moment for him to identify the shadowed figure that stepped into his cell.

"Philip."

He recognized the voice. "I am ready, Sir Jocelin," Philip answered with resolve.

"Ready to save yourself, lad?"

"Ready to die."

The knight responded with a deep chuckle. " 'Tis not your time to die yet, nor will it be come morning."

"But—"

"No time for explanations, lad. We must move quickly. Suffice it to say, you have a few friends here at Hawken. Not enough to demand justice but enough to keep ye from riding the cart."

Philip knew that was the mode of transport to the gallows—another means of degrading a would-be lord.

"Come quickly!"

Though Philip had been resigned to die—in some small way he'd even welcomed the release from his miserable life that death would provide—he now realized he desired to live as much as any man if the opportunity presented itself. Death still was inviting, but it was not in his nature to let it happen should there be an alternative.

Without another word he followed the knight through the passage between cells, all empty at the moment. Negotiating the narrow stairs with Jocelin now holding a torch to light the way, they came to the guardroom. Philip watched in shock as Jocelin passed by the guard, giving the man a mere nod, pausing only to return the keys. Jocelin told Philip they would have to take better care as they exited the dungeon by a Judas gate and entered the inner ward. Here, Jocelin left behind the torch. They must make the remainder of their trip in the dark of night, but they were familiar enough with the castle grounds to do so with fair ease.

In those small hours of the morning the grounds were quiet. A light rain was falling. Jocelin motioned for Philip to keep to the wall and tread softly.

The knight took Philip to the north tower. "I was unable to secure assistance from the gatekeeper," he said, "so it must be over the wall for you."

"What about the postern gate?"

"I could not procure the key. I was fortunate to find a sympathetic gaol keeper."

The risk in betraying the lord was great, making Jocelin's defiant act even more daring. If implicated in the escape, the knight could well be accused of treason.

Trying to push this unsettling information from his mind, Philip trudged up to the top of the tower behind his rescuer. At the rampart wall he looked over it and could not prevent a nervous gulp.

"Sir Jocelin," he said, his voice quivering in spite of himself, "that must be forty ells to the bottom. Surely it is not possible."

Jocelin had secreted a thick rope behind a water barrel, and this he withdrew and held up as the solution to their problem. Philip was not convinced, but torn as he was between the will to live and the contrary longing for the release of death, he gave another shrug and helped the knight secure an end of the rope to the ironwork in one of the battlements.

"That should hold," Jocelin said, giving the rope a hard tug.

Before taking the rope in hand, Philip turned to the knight. "Sir Jocelin, someday I will repay you with more than my thanks."

"I am doing no more than setting an innocent man free," Jocelin said.

"Then you believe me innocent?" Indeed, since his arrest Philip had not heard one word from this knight, his staunchest supporter, that even hinted at his innocence. He'd thought the knight was helping him out of pity.

"You would no more murder yer own father, especially in that vile manner, than I would. But since it seems impossible to prove your innocence, this will have to do. Alas, it may be a fate little better than the one awaiting you on the morrow. You will now be a fugitive and an outlaw. You will be hunted down. Not only Gareth but the greater majority of Hawken's knights will want vengeance for the lord's murder." He gave a harsh laugh. "I may soon join you, lad, if my part is discovered. We will die together, fighting honorably, eh?"

Philip nodded. "I am sorry I have brought this upon you, sir knight, but I would count it a privilege to die at your side."

"No one is dying just yet. I believe where there is life, there is hope. And before resigning yourself to one last heroic stand, there is the option of seeking sanctuary in the Church."

Philip merely snorted in response.

Jocelin shook his head. "Much as I know all appears lost in your eyes, lad, might not this chance you have been given now be attributed to God's providence?"

"Do you call yourself God's intercessor?" Philip asked, half mocking.

Jocelin laughed. "Point well taken, lad. Now be off with you."

Philip's heart lacked all hope as he grasped the rope. "I am banished forever from my home, from all that I love." With that final word he thought again of Beatrice. Even if he survived, it would still be as if he'd died on the gallows, the only difference being that he would live to grieve losing her forever.

"The irony is that it would have been yours one day," Jocelin said.

"What do you mean? The estate?"

"You knew of the lord's will?"

"I knew that he'd changed it but know not the whole of it. I assumed he'd assigned a small fief to me, as I asked."

"You poor lad. The will stipulated that you were to inherit Hawken Castle and half the estate."

"Half?" Philip gasped. Ironic was too inadequate a word to describe his hapless life. In less than a fortnight he had gained the world and lost it all. He had not even been allowed the time to revel in his joy or wallow in his grief.

"Quiet, lad!" Jocelin glanced quickly about to confirm they were still alone. He had done well his work in paving the way for the escape.

With tight resolve Philip said, "Let us be about this escape, then, for all the good it will do."

"One more thing, Philip," the knight said. "I have hidden your horse out beyond the barbican, where the ruin of the Saxon church lies. There you will find your gray, and I have put your cloak and some provisions in the bags." With a grin he added, "I also retrieved your dagger, and it, too, is in the bags."

"My dagger? You stole it?"

"I may make a good outlaw after all." With a sly grin, made all the more sinister by the scar slicing his cheek, he slapped Philip on the back. Then he reached under his mantle and withdrew a parchment. "One last thing. Your lady came to the castle earlier today."

"Beatrice came here? I thought you told her not to come."

"I did. She appears to have a mind of her own."

"The foolish wench." The dear, lovely, foolish girl. His heart clenched in his chest. But he knew that if Gareth ever got a hint of Philip and Beatrice's affections for each other . . . he did not want to consider the repercussions.

"This message is for you," Jocelin continued. "I would suggest you do not pause to read it until you are far away from here. We have dallied overly long. Time to be off, lad."

Philip tucked the parchment within his chemise, for he had no other garments. Then he took hold of the rope and swung his leg over the rampart. He tried not to think that by rights he was now lord of this castle and should be leaving by the gate, dressed in silks and scarlet, riding a regal destrier. He also tried not to think of Beatrice, who could have been lady of this fief. He forced himself to focus instead on the tricky descent rather than on the sweet face haunting his mind's eye.

16

The darkness clung to Philip like the despair in his heart. He could not accept the clouds or the dark of night as the protection they were. The dark had been his companion all his life, and he was weary of it. Yet he was a fugitive now. Darkness was his friend.

He wondered how long before his escape was discovered and a hue and cry raised. When would he hear the crashing sounds of hooves beating down upon him? With naught but a dagger for protection, he'd make easy prey. He determined he would die before letting them capture him and toss him again into Gareth's dungeons.

After finding Dumpling at the ruin as Jocelin had instructed, Philip mounted and determined to head toward the woods. Reaching them would prove dangerous, because there were several furlongs of open ground to traverse first, though that seemed the least of the road's hazards. That path would take him close to Cassley Manor, and he wasn't certain he'd have the will to ignore being near to Beatrice. For now, though, the woods offered his best hiding place.

His thoughts turned toward his prospects. Though nearly all his dreams were crushed, perhaps there might be a chance to see one fulfilled. This might be his opportunity to see the wide world. He might even go as far as mysterious Cathay. He grunted sourly. It would be a very large miracle if he could get enough money to buy passage across the Channel, much less enough to get to the far ends of the earth. Jocelin had put a few coins in Dumpling's bags, although far from enough for a lengthy journey. Knights were not rich men, and Jocelin had no doubt given more than he could spare. The only other possession of value he had was his horse, but he loved the animal and thought dying in the woods would be preferable to parting with the beast. Dumpling seemed to be his only friend.

The rain had stopped now, replaced by a biting wind that the open meadowland did little to disperse. Pulling the cloak Jocelin had left for him more closely about his shivering wet body, he wondered what might lie beyond the woods for him. Putting aside fantastical thoughts of Cathay, he simply wondered if he could find refuge in France. He doubted his mother's family would take him in. They had rid themselves of him when he was a helpless lad. Why would they now take in a fugitive and convicted murderer?

Regardless, his pursuers would surely look for him there. He had no doubt that Gareth would pursue him to the ends of the earth. No place was safe. Yet why was he thinking of safety when a short time ago he had been looking forward to a glorious last stand in the woods?

Who could think aright in straits such as his? The snap of a twig startled him. Then panic seized him. If anything proved he had a desire to live, the panic did. He dug his knees into the gray's sides, spurring him into a gallop, and rode wildly for several minutes, not daring to look back. If Gareth didn't kill him, surely this insane gallop in the night would.

Only as he crested a small hillock did he regain his wits and take a moment to survey who might be after him. Turning in his saddle, he expected to see a dozen of the sheriff's men in hot pursuit, with Gareth in the lead. Common sense should have told him that by sound alone there could not have been so many. But he had little sense functioning, much less the common kind.

Yet his fears were not entirely unfounded, for a rider was racing up the hill toward him. A lone rider. Not the fat sheriff. Not Gareth upon his bay stallion. A rider whose cloak was flying out behind a slight frame, a rider seated upon a mount as black as the night.

Even as Philip began to identify the rider, his fear did not abate.

"You lead a merry chase," she said, drawing nigh unto him.

"Had I a bow, you might have been shot, creeping up behind me in the dark."

"I was willing to take that risk." She reached up and, throwing back the hood of her cloak, revealed her fair countenance.

"What are you doing here, Beatrice?" he asked as crossly as he could. His heart pounded with the thrill of seeing her, yet fear for both of them clouded any joy there might be.

"You did not read my note?"

"I thought to wait until I was well away." Philip felt a twinge of guilt that she might think less of him for not appearing more eager.

"I wanted you to meet me at the elm where we oft sat when we rode together. Sir Jocelin knew."

Of course the knight knew, and that was surely why he had told Philip not to read the note immediately. He had meant to protect both Philip and Beatrice. He had feared Philip too weak to fight the temptation of seeing the lady. And Philip had surely proven the knight aright, for now he had, unthinking, ridden near to the elm where they had first met. Perhaps fate was urging them together.

"I would that you had not come after me, Beatrice," Philip said.

"Why?"

"Why?" he parroted, in utter astonishment at her guilelessness. "I am a fugitive now. Any who help me or become involved with me could well suffer the same punishment as I. You must leave now."

"I will not!" Unintentionally, she gave a frustrated jerk on the reins. Raven snorted and skittered. She patted the animal's neck. "Sorry, Raven." To Philip she added, "I will go with you."

"You will cast your lot with a convicted murderer, Beatrice?"

"Do you believe I think that of you, Philip?" Giving an angry toss of her head, she rushed ahead to answer her own question. "How dare you think so little of me! That my faith in you is so weak, and worse, that I would side with the likes of your accusers!"

His misery was lifted as a slight smile invaded. "I have precious few supporters," he said.

"You will always have me. That is why I will go with you now, to the far end of the world if you wish." Her chin tilted with defiance.

"You know that is impossible. It is not a life to be thrust upon a lady." He tried to match her in resolve but came just short. The very idea of not being alone in what lay ahead thrilled him beyond reason.

"Let us dismount and talk," she said. "Can you not spare me just a few moments?"

He knew he could not deny her this, nor could he deny himself. Fear, however, still gripped him—fear that he would not be strong enough, that he would let his heart overcome good sense. Nevertheless he dismounted. She did also, and they led their horses a short distance to a thicket of broom where they tied them to a couple of stout branches.

"I do owe you a proper farewell," he conceded tenderly.

"You know I want more than that."

"More than I can give—"

She flung her arms around him and pressed herself against him. He could do naught but return the embrace. Nor did he wish to resist. As he felt her nearness, smelled her sweet fragrance of lavender blossoms, he knew it would be impossible to let her go. He held her, pressing his lips against hers. Remembering the sweet kisses they had shared in the stable, he realized these now were more desperate than sweet. He desired to take her, to make her his, just as she had asked him to do in his room at Cassley. Every sinew in his body cried out for her.

She made no pains to hide her desire for the same thing. She would be one with him. And there was nobody to stop them.

Why should he not at least have that?

Why shouldn't they go off together? They could find some place to hide, to live their lives happily together. A place where they would not be known, where they would not be outlaws.

He grasped her more tightly to him, then loosed her cloak, and it fell into the grass. Her fumbling fingers worked at the clasp of Philip's cloak. Finally Philip gave the thing a hard tug, and with a sharp tearing sound, it fell free.

He would have her. He would have her now.

She tugged him toward a niche in the bushes where the ground was fairly dry, and they sank to their knees.

"Beatrice, I do love you so," he murmured.

"I know . . . I know . . ."

He cupped her face in his hands, his eyes roving over her delicate beauty. In that very instant the clouds parted and the early light of dawn cast a sudden illumination upon Beatrice's dear face. Philip did not believe in spiritual apparitions; indeed, in the last weeks he had come to question all matters spiritual, especially God. Yet that sudden stab of light seemed to force the scales from his eyes as it brought Beatrice into an entirely new relief, her countenance appearing almost angelic. In the clarity of her face he saw her innocence, her youth. For all her feisty, independent nature, he saw now stark vulnerability as she trusted herself completely to him. She was giving him not only her body and her innocence, but her life, as well.

And he would take it. He would defile it, make of her a fornicator and an outlaw, too. He would ravage her heart, her soul, her future.

Tensing, he drew away.

"No, Philip! Don't stop . . . please!" Her fingers dug into his shoulders.

"Beatrice, I can't . . . we can't." He swallowed hard, but the bitter taste of his resolve remained.

"Curse you!" she cried. "Don't do this again."

Still she clung to him, and it took all his will to pull away from her.

"I cannot draw you into the life that awaits me." His voice shook as he tried to reason with her while trying to find the sense in his noble actions himself. He knew for both of them only the harshest argument would suffice. "Beatrice, this is no lark I am set upon. Gareth will surely hunt me down and kill me. Do you understand? I have no means, no talent to withstand him long. I expect I will die ere long."

"Then why did you escape from the gaol?" She was sobbing, her words agonized.

"I could not bear the dishonor of hanging. I would rather die in battle."

She crumpled in tears and sobs. How he hated seeing the spirited girl he loved so broken! She finally realized the truth of his words, the hopelessness of his situation. The comforting stroke of his hand on her shoulder felt entirely inadequate.

Finally she lifted her tear-stained face to him. "Philip, couple with me now. Then I will go away and we will never see each other again."

Even in his despair he could not keep his lips from twitching with amusement. "You are a stubborn one, are you not?" At great risk he touched her chin. The mere brush of contact made him tremble, yet he was still able to shake his head. "I will not risk putting a bastard into your belly."

"I ask only this final gift from you," she breathed. "You know I have a penchant for loving bastards. I will love our child as I love you."

"No . . ." There was little conviction in his tone. Would his last words to her then be rejection? If only he had something of value to give her.

"Then I ask this of you," she said, reluctantly accepting the inevitable. "I ask for your life. Do not give it easily to your enemies. If I cannot have you or your child, then I want only to know you live. Will you promise me, Philip, to fight for your life, to hold it as dear to yourself as I hold it dear to me?"

This was a harder gift to give than she imagined, for he disdained life without her. Yet he managed a nod.

Earnestly he said, "On my oath I grant you this boon!" Then, because only one thing would be worse than parting from her, worse than even death, he added, "Beatrice, I have no right to ask this of you . . . please, do not marry my brother!"

"Oh, my dear Philip! That is the easiest request to fulfill."

"What if you have no choice?"

"My father would never force me into a marriage I did not want. But if it makes you feel better, I give you my solemn oath that I will never marry your brother."

Gazing deeply into her eyes, he saw her words were not frivolous. And he knew Lord Cassley was a man to indulge his daughter. For the first time in days, he felt some easing in his heart. "You will marry, though?" He was uncertain if it was question or statement. Either way, it took the greatest gall a landless bastard, and now fugitive, could have to speak the words.

She smiled. "I will always love you, Philip." He understood her circumventing the question. No sense in torturing them further.

With a last tender kiss on his cheek, she rose. He followed and they silently rearranged their clothing. As her fingers touched the brooch on her cloak, she unfastened the ornament and held it out to him.

"A remembrance of me," she said simply.

His fingers closed around the golden wreath of laurel leaves, the symbol of the Marlowe family, and he whispered, "I'll need no token to remember you, dear Beatrice." Nevertheless he tucked the brooch into his belt.

When they retrieved their mounts, he said, "I fear to let you ride home in this darkness."

"I will be all right. It will soon be light."

"Anyway, there is naught to be done about it." He turned toward his horse, but she took hold of his hand.

"I would have given everything up for you, Philip."

"I know," he replied. "I will carry that knowledge always in my heart."

"Will you ride away first," she asked, "so I can watch until you disappear?"

He hesitated, ever mindful of her safety, but the pleading in her eyes told him how important this was to her. He mounted the gray and spurred him into a gentle canter. He felt Beatrice's eyes upon him for a long time, long after he had vanished from her sight.

17

S he stayed in that place weeping until dawn lighted the sky. Only a
threat of more rain forced her to rise from her grief and leave. Mount-
ing Raven, she rode slowly despite the dark clouds traversing the sky. Nothing
was going to keep her from getting drenched before reaching home, and she
was not anxious to face the possible repercussions for her late night interlude.

She had gone only half a furlong when she heard the rumble of approaching riders. A quick glance over her shoulder revealed about a dozen knights,
the silver hawk against the bloodred field clearly visible on their equipage.
Beatrice's first impulse was to dig her heels into Raven's flanks and fly away
from them. But good sense prevailed. Nothing spoke of guilt more than a wild
flight.

She kept to an easy canter, and the riders caught up to her quickly.

"My lady," said their leader, Gareth Aubernon himself, "this is a nasty day
for you to be riding, and all alone so early in the morn."

"What business are my actions to you, my lord?" she snapped before realizing a sharp word might draw attention to her guilt. Her cross response was
in large part to serve as cover for the tears that lay at the edge of her emotions.
Seeing Gareth made it all come close to erupting once more. She had learned
from her meeting with the knight Jocelin that Gareth was the most vocal of
Philip's accusers. Although his vindictive nature did not surprise her, she

wondered if there was more to it than that. Logic told Beatrice that since Philip did not kill his father, someone else had. Even if Gareth was not a murderer, she still despised him for ruining Philip's life.

"'Tis only concern for a lady's safety," Gareth replied with such sincerity she nearly forgot he was the enemy.

"I enjoy riding in the freshness of a new day." She moderated her tone to a polite coolness.

"Even so close to your home, the byways are not without danger. You may not have heard that there is a dangerous murderer upon the loose. My knights and I are even now seeking him out."

"Oh, how unsettling!" She gave a shudder and tried to appear appropriately abashed.

"I take it then that you have seen no lone riders nor anything else to rouse your suspicions?"

"Oh no."

"I would suggest you return to your home with all haste."

"I will indeed."

Over his shoulder he called forth two of his knights. "These will accompany you home."

It would have looked too suspicious for her to refuse, so she replied, "Thank you." She saw no reason why she shouldn't have an escort as long as she convinced the knights to leave her before reaching Cassley's gates so that she could enter without causing too much of a stir.

The last thing she wanted was to face a lot of questions from guards or from her father. After dismissing Gareth's knights about a quarter of a furlong from Cassley, she hoped she could slip quietly past the gates and be alone in her chamber. If her father but glanced at her, she knew her little remaining restraint would crumble. How she hated deceiving him.

It did occur to her that her father, as a lord of the realm, might make an appeal to the king on Philip's behalf. But more than her father's lowly standing, the fact that Lord Cassley had been a prominent supporter of the rebels for years would surely hurt any chance of success. Moreover, if her father caught even a hint of her feelings for Philip, his wrath toward Philip might supersede Gareth's by far.

As Beatrice trudged up to her chamber, undetected by any except the gatekeeper, who, on his word, would keep mum about her activities, she felt alone and helpless. Recalling the only other time she had felt like this—when her mother had died—Beatrice flung herself upon her bed and wept. She did not know Leticia had quietly entered the chamber until she felt her maid's cool hand gently stroke her hair.

"There, there, my child," cooed the maid.

Beatrice had left the manor hours earlier, not telling a soul, though she suspected Leticia had known her intent. And bless her, she had not attempted to stop Beatrice. Had Leticia resigned herself to the inevitability of losing her young charge to the groom, now turned outlaw? Beatrice thought not. More likely the wise maid had believed that if Beatrice did find Philip, he would prove himself a man of honor and reject her. The maid had been right.

Sobs shook her anew. It seemed a long time before they abated.

"It's not right!" she cried, her words muffled by the pillow into which her face was buried.

"Sometimes life is like that."

Only then did Beatrice lift her head, knowing her maid's words were more than mere placation. "You know, don't you, Leticia? Is this how it was when you lost the love of your life?"

"I think perhaps it is, Beatrice, but my love is dead. Yours is not."

"W-what do you mean?"

"Only that where our Lord sustains the breath of life, there is yet hope."

Beatrice sniffed, wiping a hand across her damp eyes. "You are saying maybe Philip will come back for me?"

"I do not wish that for you, because he is a fugitive," she replied, seeming to regret her previous words. "It is in God's hands."

"Leticia, you knew I had gone after him tonight, didn't you?"

"Yes, and I was foolish beyond words not to send a search party out after you." Ever mindful of her duties, Leticia slipped her kerchief from her sleeve and gave it to her distraught charge. "I feared for your safety, m'lady, but I also feared that sending someone after you would have brought calamity upon Philip. I prayed for you every minute. I would have killed myself had any ill befallen you."

Beatrice blew her nose into the embroidered kerchief. "But . . . ?" she pressed.

The maid sighed. "There are times when a girl—a young woman—must be allowed to fulfill whatever destiny awaits her. I had some faith in the boy. He's good at heart, certainly no murderer. I counted heavily upon him to do the right thing, to release you. I also believe that justice will prevail. Your Philip de Tollard will one day be exonerated, his inheritance restored, and you and he will then be free to have each other."

"I-I fear it is a dream never to be realized." New sobs choked Beatrice.

"The only dream that will never come to pass is that I will marry my Allan—"

"But you are still alive," Beatrice argued, momentarily rising above her own distress to comfort her friend. "There is still hope you will one day find love."

With a dismissive chuckle, the maid answered, "At my age, child? I am too old, fit for no man. You, however"—she smiled tenderly—"there is hope for you."

"To be with Philip?"

"Perhaps. Or to find love with another—"

"How can you even suggest that?" Beatrice exclaimed with passion then quickly moderated her ire, realizing Leticia was trying to make her feel better. "I'll never love another. I know you may think my feelings for him are mere infatuation or girlish fancy. You think I have listened to too many songs of the troubadours. I can hardly explain it, Leticia, but what I feel for Philip goes deeper than that. There will always be a part of me bonded to him as you are with your Allan."

"Then I grieve with you, child, and I also share your joy in finding such a bond of true love. Mind, though, dear, what lies ahead for you—joy and grief, mingled like blood and myrrh. I so wish I could change it for you."

"Don't you think the grief will be easier to bear if steeped in love?"

Leticia nodded. Beatrice took a breath and tried to be strong and wise like her maid, though she found little success in it.

Her eye caught sight of something on her bedside table. The clasp from Philip's cloak. It had torn off during their frenzied and futile attempt to couple, and it had fallen unnoticed into the grass. She had found it when, after he had departed, she had crumbled to her knees in tears. It was a simple chain of linked brass rings with a clasp that bore the Hawken crest—a hawk in full flight, with three arrows in its talons. Poorly fashioned, it was probably something the common knights wore. Though tarnished and worn, it was all she had from Philip, and she would cherish it forever as she prayed he would do with the brooch she had given him.

Now the sight of it brought new waves of anguish. Her brave words of a few moments ago fell to pieces. Another sob escaped her lips, followed by several more. Leticia took her into her arms and comforted her once again.

Beatrice reached for the clasp, wrapping her fingers around it so tightly it cut into her flesh. She welcomed the pain and had a glimpse of what the mingling of joy and grief truly was.

Gareth felt an odd disquiet as he watched the lady Beatrice ride away. Perhaps it was just a stirring of desire within him as he had looked upon her beauty.

"My lord," said his knight, Sir William de Cugey, "it is peculiar that the lady should be riding upon the moor at this hour, is it not?"

"She is of free, unfettered spirit, that one." And now he felt a burning in his loins as he thought of fettering her himself, a conquest of her pale unsullied body with his own. His excitement intensified as he realized that now, as lord of Hawken, he had to answer only to the king in the choice of a bride. And the king would like nothing more than for Cassley Manor to be subdued in such a manner.

"Lord Hawken, I think we should carefully search this area," Sir William said.

For a moment, even as Gareth fantasized about the benefits of being lord, it did not register that the knight was speaking to him. He reminded himself once more that he was Lord Hawken now.

"To what avail?" he asked impatiently. Now that he had been interrupted from his reverie, he was anxious to continue the hunt.

"I know not exactly. Only I have a feeling of disquiet. Also, since the earlier rain washed out signs of the fugitive's passing, we are not completely certain of his direction. Perhaps we will find a clue before it rains once again."

Gareth was about to brush off the knight's words when he remembered what he owed Sir William, who'd had a small part in the deception of his father's demise. William had not once questioned Gareth's request to drug Philip's drink at the tavern the night of Lord Hawken's death. Yet Gareth knew there was an unspoken understanding that he would show his gratitude for the knight's actions. William's silence and loyalty could be bought.

"A good idea, William."

Gareth thought his half brother must have gotten farther than this by now. The dungeon guard had admitted to dozing at his post about two or three hours before dawn, the only time when the prisoner could have made his escape. The guard would be flogged for falling asleep on duty. Those who more directly aided Philip, when they were discovered, would be executed.

Regardless of the timing, a search of the area couldn't hurt. They were heading toward the woods because that seemed the most likely place for an outlaw to hide, but they could spare a short span for seeking a more definite indication.

The men spread out over the area, and as the full light of morning pierced the clouds, Gareth heard a shout. He spurred his animal in the direction of the sound and met Sir William, also riding toward it. They reached a couple of knights who were standing by some broom.

"My lord," said one, "there are distinct tracks here. It looks like horses were tied there." He pointed toward a particularly thick branch.

"And over there," said the other knight, "are footprints."

Gareth and William dismounted and examined the area. The prints in the mud were smeared but clearly showed boots and . . . a woman's riding shoe?

"Two people met here on horseback," said William. "Then obviously tarried on foot." His brow arched suggestively.

"Is there any way to know if these prints belong to the bastard?" asked Gareth.

"Of course not," said William, who had some knowledge of such matters. "But these tracks were made since it last rained, not two hours ago. Is it a coincidence they were made on the very night of the bastard's escape?"

"And the female?" Gareth's throat tightened as he spoke.

"Another coincidence that Lady Beatrice happened to be out riding at this hour of the morning, not far from this very spot?"

Fire of a different sort than burned earlier in him flamed up inside Gareth's guts. The truth of the matter seared him with white-hot fury. Unconsciously his hand gripped the hilt of his sword. So great was his hunger for blood just then that only by great strength of will did he not lash out at his own knights.

Instead, he spun on his heel and paced a short distance away to rein in his fury. So the bastard was Lady Beatrice's lover. And by the look of the lady during their recent encounter and the sound of her lies, she had been a willing slut for him. Rising bile nearly choked him. He would ride to Cassley Manor now, drag her into the yard, and force a confession from her. She'd be condemned as an accomplice to murder and hang beside her lover!

The word *lover* brought him up short. He knew his rage came not because she had aided Philip's escape but rather because she and Philip—

Curse him again!

Though a convicted murderer and forced fugitive, Philip de Tollard had somehow still managed to win. For if the bastard had even one thing Gareth wanted, it was too much!

A single thought managed to penetrate his mind. You are still Lord of Hawken. Think like a lord! The blood of Durand d'Aubernon runs in your veins, and he would not have allowed a silly girl or a miserable bastard to defeat him.

Gulping in several breaths, Gareth began to calm. There must be a way to use this turn of events to his advantage.

"Lord Hawken, what will you do?" Sir William asked.

"Let me think a moment," snapped Gareth.

His mind was not as quick as his mother's in its deviousness, but he was young yet, and recent events were helping him to learn. He had to pace about for several minutes before a plan began to form in his mind. First, he must not reveal what he suspected to Beatrice. He would set a watch upon her, for it was possible that she and the bastard had arranged another meeting. He'd find it most pleasing to catch them unawares.

It was also possible, though, that the lovers had parted ways permanently this evening. Even a fool like Philip must know the futility of such a relationship under the circumstances. That being the case, Gareth would then be in a plum position to thrust yet another knife into his brother's back. He would take Lady Beatrice, sullied though she was, as his wife. No one need ever know of her ill-fated liaison with Philip. She certainly would not want any to learn of it. He would have revenge on both of them, and especially on Philip, by yet again taking what was his. All the better if he could catch Philip and watch him hang.

18

Philip was deep in the woods when he was finally forced to stop in order to rest Dumpling. The poor horse had begun to stumble along as if drunk. He tied the animal to a branch and then found a place beneath a leafy elm to sit and wait. He had no intention of sleeping himself, though where he thought he'd find the stamina to remain awake when he had barely slept for days, even in Hawken's dungeons, was a mystery. More than that, he was simply weary with all that had been hurled at him in the last days.

So he slept for hours and hours. The rain that fell shortly after he'd settled down did not disturb him. Even the nightmares that beset him did not rouse him. He dreamed, not surprisingly, of being chased, only the pursuers were not always those he expected. Sometimes his father or Beatrice was hotly after him. At other times the pursuers were hideous blood-thirsty monsters of his own imagination. The worst was when he chased himself in the dream; then he caught himself and slit his own throat, the blood dripping all over him. He'd heard if you died in your dreams, then you had died in reality. Mercifully, this was not the case for him. It was this dream that finally woke him, trembling, from his slumber.

He found moisture was indeed drenching his body, but it was rain not blood. The tree and forest foliage had proven a poor protection. Yet he was certain the shivering and shaking was only in part due to the soaking of the downpour and the chill it brought.

He could not tell how long he'd slept, for what he could see of the sky through the canopy of trees was gray and thick with clouds. But the leaden feel of his limbs and the dull ache in his head indicated it had been a long time. Even so it seemed to have done him no good at all. He still felt weary right to the core of his bones.

He ate a bit of bread that Jocelin had kindly packed in Dumpling's saddlebag.

"I have no breakfast for you, Dumpling," he said to his horse as he licked the last of the crumbs from his fingers. "I hope you found enough grass beneath the trees to sustain you."

The damp wool of his breeches chafed at his skin when he mounted, but there was nothing to be done about it. Rain continued to fall. Thankfully all his physical miseries sufficiently occupied his mind so that the torment of his heart's grief could be pushed from the forefront for a time.

He wondered how far the forest extended and whether he could hide here indefinitely. Not long without food, and he was not a skilled enough hunter to kill even a rabbit with his dagger. Even if he were fortunate enough to capture game, could he eat it raw? Building a fire was out of the question.

The village lay roughly on the border between Hawken and Cassley, no more than a score of furlongs from his present position, for the forest ran behind the village and he could not have traveled so far as to have bypassed it. He would have to backtrack in order to reach it, but perhaps it would be worth the risk of drawing close to Hawken if there was a chance to steal some food—he doubted any villeins would deem to give the lord's convicted murderer a morsel of sustenance.

So now he must add thievery to his long list of sins.

He rode back to the edge of the forest, thinking to wait until nightfall before making his way to the village. With a better view of the sky, though still thick with gray clouds, he judged there were a couple of hours of light left. The thought of a meal made his stomach rumble, and it made him think of poor Dumpling. The stalwart mount had carried him a long way on a few tufts of grass to nourish him. Perhaps if he kept close to the woods, he could leave its protection for a short time in order to graze the animal.

The rain was far more pervasive outside the cover of the trees. Even the horse was not anxious to eat in such conditions. Taking the reins in hand, Philip decided to return to the woods, walking Dumpling. As he turned, a rider sprang up as if from nowhere. Immediately Philip saw by the crest on his hauberk that the rider was a Hawken knight. Philip and the knight froze where they were, both taken unawares by the other.

Then the knight gave a shout. "Over here!"

Philip gathered his wits, leaped onto Dumpling's back, and spurred the horse into a gallop. He resisted the urge to look back. What need was there? He had no doubt that all of Hawken would soon be bearing down upon him. Arriving at the river, he splashed across its shallow, muddy expanse and began climbing the steep bank on the opposite side. Dumpling slowed as he struggled to keep his footing on the slippery incline.

Coaxing the animal on, Philip could hear his pursuers behind him. No doubt their horses were well fed and rested, and the bank would present no great obstacle to them.

"Come, Dumpling," he urged. "I'll steal you a lump of sugar before the day is out."

As if the bribe had been understood, the animal gave a final heave and topped the bank. Only then did Philip allow himself a backward glance. The Hawken knights had reached the river. He didn't see Gareth's bay among them. Not pausing to ponder this, Philip urged his horse into another gallop, but the moor here was rough and broken, and he could not risk a breakneck pace. Still, Dumpling made a good effort, and the distance widened while those in pursuit crossed the river.

He did not expect to outrun the knights once they reached the moor, so Philip kept an eye alert for a good defensible spot from which to make a stand. A last stand.

Then he remembered his oath to Beatrice. She wanted him to hold his life dear. She wanted him to live. Did that mean he should not fight his enemies? What else could he do? He could not hope to elude them for long. Should he surrender? Wasn't that squandering his life, as well? For surely then he would hang.

The moor began to level out, and he dug his heels hard into Dumpling's flanks. He crossed a field of rye, the horse's hooves digging into the furrows, tearing up the new sprouts of grain, sending clumps of muddy soil flying. Soon a few peasant huts came into view. The village was not far away. He raced through a yard, scattering laundry left out in the rain and nearly colliding with a dog, whose yelps brought a householder to his door yelling curses. Most of the villagers were indoors because of the weather or no telling what mayhem his mad dash would have caused. And behind him, the troop of knights chasing him was closing in.

Spurring Dumpling on faster and faster, Philip was concentrating so intently on not killing any innocent peasants that it was a miracle he saw in time the three riders who suddenly loomed up in front of him. Some of the

Hawken men had circled around in an attempt to intercept him. One was on a bay stallion.

In a perverse way Philip was glad that Gareth would be present during the last battle of his life. If he was about to die, perhaps it would be worth it if he did so fighting his brother.

At the same moment that he saw the three riders, he also saw the spire of the village church rising up just beyond Gareth's shoulder. St. Bartholomew's was hardly Westminster Abbey, but it had been constructed with an eye for beauty by both Philip's grandfather and the Lord of Cassley at the time. It was said the building of the church was the only time the two lords had ever cooperated on any endeavor, though the parish itself was administered by and was the property of St. Mary's Priory, not a far distance north of both estates.

Part of Philip rebelled against seeking out this place now in his extreme need. He'd given up his faith or close to it. Yet the words of Beatrice rang in his ears. "Promise me to fight for your life, to hold it as dear to yourself as I hold it dear to me."

Was it not fitting that her words might now become the litany to his new faith, the canon of St. Beatrice, the holy virgin, patron of worthless bastards?

For her alone, then, he charged the three riders, barreling between them as if he were an arrow shot from a bow. They had been so sure he would surrender when faced with their might that they had not even drawn their swords. He had one brief glimpse of their faces and saw they were as shocked by his bold action as he was himself. Surely Gareth had felt certain he had snared the fugitive. Instead, the new lord found himself barely able to control his own horse as all three destriers, thoroughly spooked by the charge, skittered and reared. Only by holding a tight rein did Philip keep his own mount in hand as he raced into St. Bartholomew's yard.

Father Bavent, no doubt roused from his holy pursuits by the clamor in the village, was exiting the parsonage, which was adjacent to the church. Philip leaped from Dumpling's back, barely reining the animal to a stop.

"What is this unearthly racket?" the large, barrel-chested man demanded. His robes looked more like a tent than holy vestments. It was said that he had been a Crusader and had proved himself a worthy knight. But when he'd reached the Church of the Holy Sepulcher in Jerusalem, he had laid down his sword and dedicated himself to the service of God. Knight or priest, he was one to be reckoned with, his demands not taken lightly.

Only sheer desperation restrained Philip from respectfully falling on his knees before the priest. Already Gareth and his two knights were galloping toward the churchyard.

Hurriedly Philip blurted, "Holy Father, I seek sanctuary in this church!"

The words had barely departed Philip's lips when Gareth and his men burst into the yard.

"You fool!" Gareth cried. "You are mine now!" He jumped from his horse and stalked up to where Philip and the priest stood. To the priest, Gareth continued, "I will take charge of him now, Father."

Bavent thrust his bulk between the brothers. "I think not, m'lord!"

"He murdered Lord Hawken," railed Gareth. "You saw him convicted of the crime yourself."

"And he has sought sanctuary in my church," the priest replied coolly. Not one strand of his thinning gray hair appeared ruffled. He might have been carrying a sword instead of a fistful of prayer beads.

"What!" screamed Gareth. "This is blasphemy!"

"It is the law," answered the priest. "He is under my protection now, and under the protection of God. You will not touch him."

Bavent stood firm while Gareth cursed and sputtered. Philip, suddenly feeling like a bystander, nearly smiled at the scene. But Gareth's venomous threats, before he finally spun on his heel and left the yard, wiped away any fleeting amusement. For now, the priest had managed to keep him at bay, but Philip knew his brother was capable of much mayhem.

In the middle of the churchyard, Bavent said, "I don't like that boy."

In what was surely the understatement of the age, Philip replied, "Neither do I."

19

"N ow, what to do with you, young Philip de Tollard?" Bavent exhaled a heavy sigh. Fighting infidels was one thing, but standing up against the lord of the manor was quite another. He'd become a priest because he was tired of fighting.

"I had no choice, Father."

"No, I'm certain you didn't."

During the altercation, other members of the church staff had ventured into the yard. This was the most excitement at the church since two springs past when a visiting bishop from London had collapsed and died right upon the altar while saying Mass.

"Peter!" Bavent called over his shoulder, and one of the bystanders jumped forward.

"Yes, Father?"

The young man was no more than two or three years older than Philip and apparently was the Father's suffragan, or assistant clerk.

"Take the lad's horse into the stable and see to him," Bavent said.

"Thank you, Father," said Philip, who to his shame, had all but forgotten about his faithful mount. To the suffragan he added, "If it please you, his name is Dumpling, and he has had little nourishment for some time. He is partial to oats." Again, the mere thought of food set Philip's own innards to rumbling.

"Come," said the priest. "It is almost time for Vespers, but after prayers we will see to your sustenance, as well."

Following devotions, the two made their way to Bavent's humble dwelling, and after a simple meal of bread and cheese with warm ale, Bavent constrained Philip to remain at the table so they could talk.

"Do you understand what sanctuary entails?" Bavent asked.

Feeling foolish, Philip shook his head. Of course he knew of the activity in general terms from his studies at the university, but no more than the idea itself, which he was sure Bavent meant.

"This is what will be expected of you," the priest said. "You can tarry here no longer than forty days. You must surrender your weapons—"

Philip touched the dagger in his belt. "This is all I have of my father's."

"I am sorry, lad. Is it worth your life?" After Philip handed over the weapon in its sheath, Bavent continued. "This may be the least demanded of you," he said, turning the simple knife over in his hand. "It is imperative that you confess of your crimes—"

"But, Father, I cannot confess to what I did not do!"

"Your life, not to mention your soul, depends upon confession."

"Would you have me commit the sin of lying in order to be absolved of that of which I am innocent?"

Bavent sighed and rubbed his large hand over his face. "I would have you do what is expedient."

Philip shrugged. What did a lie matter anyway? It would be his first step in eschewing the honorable way that had defeated him all his life. "Then what?" he asked with resignation.

"The royal coroner will come and hear your oath, and then you must abjure the country."

"When will that be?"

"I know the coroner left shortly after your trial to deal with business in the south. I would not expect him to return this way for at least a fortnight."

Philip glanced toward the window. Gareth was out there and would no doubt remain, so as to swoop down upon Philip should he thrust even a toe outside the church grounds.

Understanding his concern, Bavent said, "He will not touch you. Even he must respect the sanctity of God's house."

For the next week it seemed that Bavent was right. A half dozen Hawken knights encamped outside the churchyard. Often Gareth was among them, though a few times Philip saw him ride off in the direction of Hawken. There were, of course, duties for the new lord to attend to at home. In all that time,

Gareth never made any threatening advances on Philip.

Philip's days at St. Bartholomew's were hardly ones of peaceful respite. Though seemingly sympathetic to his cause, the priest was a hard taskmaster and expected Philip to honor the bounds of sanctuary by exaggerated shows of repentance. First, he was required at every meal to beg for his food from the priest, to get on his knees and utter words such as, "Please, Father, can you spare me a crust of bread?"

Bavent spared little more than bread. He occasionally allowed some cheese but never any meat. He felt it wouldn't hurt Philip to endure a monk's existence. And to that end, Philip was required to ring the church bells daily, work like a slave and, perhaps the most undesirable requirement of all, attend every Mass. If Bavent had hoped by this to win the errant lad back to the fold, he was not successful. Unlike the peasants and many of the nobles, Philip understood much of the Latin used in the services and should have benefited from the liturgy. But Philip closed himself to all matters spiritual.

One day when Philip was up to his elbows cleaning soot out of the parsonage hearth, Peter, the suffragan, came in and announced, "You have a visitor."

"Who is it?"

"A female."

Philip's heart sank and leaped all at once. The thing he had dreaded most was that Beatrice would attempt to see him. He could not bear another good-bye and was about to tell Peter to send her away when the door burst open and Bavent's hulking frame ducked in.

"Who has left this lady on the doorstep?" he demanded. Despite his godly vocation, the man always sounded like a knight shouting orders on a battle-field.

He stepped aside and the lady entered. It was Beatrice's maid. Philip started breathing again.

"I wanted to see Philip de Tollard," she said.

"I am in no fit condition to receive a lady," he replied, holding out his grimy hands as evidence.

"Please, this will only take a few moments."

With an arched brow Bavent took Peter in hand and they exited. Philip grabbed a rag and rubbed as much of the soot from his hands as he could.

"Will you have a seat, my lady?" he asked.

"I am no lady, as you well know," Leticia replied. "And I will remain standing, for this will not take long."

"Did Lady Beatrice send you?"

"Yes—"

"She cannot come here," Philip said quickly. "It would be disastrous if my brother saw her—"

"Even she realizes that." A small smile played upon the maid's lips, though otherwise she remained solemn. "She felt it important, however, that you knew why she wasn't coming here to you."

"I understand the wisdom of it," he said. "We have bid our farewells. There is no reason to torture ourselves further."

"For a time she entertained a notion that you would escape into the woods, where you would become an outlaw and she would join you."

"That will never happen," he said sadly.

"She knows it was a childish fancy. She sent me to be certain you were not entertaining . . . well, such hopes as well. She could not bear the thought of you waiting vainly for her."

Pain twisted like a knife in him. He knew that with a single word he could bring her to him and they could have a few happy days together as outlaws in the woods—before a violent death would take them both.

He resolved more firmly than ever that he must protect Beatrice at all costs.

Grimly he said, "I will soon quit this country and all within it. If I survive beyond my youth, she will become but a memory to me. Tell her that. Tell her to put aside childish fancies."

"I will, m'lord."

"You know I am no lord."

"By rights you are Lord of Hawken—"

"I curse Hawken!" he spat, his restraint pushed well beyond its limit by the maid's innocent reminder of his miserable fate. "I curse the day I ever came here! Now go before I curse her, as well!"

"Yes, good sir."

She turned to leave, but as she opened the door, he called out, "Forgive me! I didn't mean—" Sudden emotion choked off further speech.

"I understand, Philip," the maid said gently. "As does she."

The moment he was alone, he sank dejectedly onto the hard bench by the trestle table. Despair, blacker than the hearth's soot, came near to over-whelming him. The door creaked open, and a shaft of light shot into the great room, only to be immediately shadowed by the priest's large frame. Closing the door behind him, Bavent strode to the table and sat on the opposite bench.

"So this is the woman you sacrificed all for?" he asked.

His tone lacking all respect, Philip muttered, "What do you know of it?"

The priest arched a brow warningly at Philip's tone but then apparently decided there were more important matters to confront than this breach of decorum. "You forget, I was one of the last people to see your father alive. I witnessed his dealings with Friar Martel in which Lord Hawken changed his will. I not only heard him dictate his new will to his clerk but also heard him tell of your conversation with him. He was of the opinion the mystery woman was a noblewoman, not a lady's maid. He even speculated it might well be the only girl you'd had contact with in the last weeks, one Beatrice Marlowe."

Philip's head shot up. "You must never repeat that to another soul, Father!"

"I have not yet seen a reason to do so." Bavent pursed his lips together, tapping them thoughtfully with steepled fingers. "Unless . . ." Leaning forward, he leveled piercing eyes at Philip. "Have you anything to confess besides your crime, boy?" the one-time knight growled.

"No!"

"Have you dishonored the young lass?"

"Never!"

Crossing his thick arms over his broad chest, Bavent continued to scrutinize Philip as if his penetrating gaze could ferret out the truth.

With deep passion he insisted, "I swear to God, I did not despoil the girl!"

"I'd believe you better if you swore upon that which meant more to you than God," countered the priest dryly.

"If you don't think I believe in God, then why do you let me stay here?"

Bavent chuckled. "You are clever, lad, to steer the intent of the conversation astray. Let us first, though, clear the former matter. I believe you did not touch the girl. But the maid came for a reason. Planning a rendezvous perhaps?"

"No," Philip answered firmly. "I care for her too much to draw her further into my hapless life. When the opportunity arises, I will leave this country in order to protect her from any temptation."

"Very admirable, lad." The priest seemed to truly mean it. "Now we can move on to the matter of your immortal soul."

Philip groaned. For a week he had been avoiding this inevitable discussion, just as he had also avoided making the confession Bavent had requested upon his arrival.

"It is time for you to make your confession," Bavent said.

Philip shrugged.

"Do you believe in God?"

"Not very subtle, are you, Father?"

"I am never subtle in matters of the spirit." Still linking his arms before his chest, he eyed Philip with a hard gaze.

Resigned, Philip replied, "I don't know if I believe."

"Yet you came to the church for sanctuary."

"I did so to honor an oath."

Bavent nodded, his eyes now drooping sadly. "You leave me with a deep dilemma, Philip. Out there"—he swept a hand toward the window—"is a young man who is as cruel, mean-spirited, and even perverse as they come. Yet he seeks regular confession, attends Mass several times a week, holds all the religious observances, and as the new Lord of Hawken, has already contributed a large sum to the coffers of my mother church, St. Mary's."

"You know as well as I," argued Philip, "that he performs his holy duties in order to be absolved of his sins."

"He has the fear of God in him."

"And it has not changed him."

"Then there is you," mused Bavent. "You have never darkened the door of this church before you came here a week ago. Nor have you said confession. Perhaps it was different up in Oxford."

"I was required to attend Mass."

"Of course, but for all practical purposes, you have eschewed all the forms of faith, correct?"

"Yes."

"Yet all the reports I have of you indicate you are a man of honor, pure of heart. Even your father, who we would both agree was never a man to squander compliments, spoke highly of you. Observing you closely this past week, I am faced with the same conclusion."

"I am neither pure nor innocent." Now Philip folded his own arms over his chest, a look of challenge in his eyes.

"None are," said the priest. "I only meant your intent is toward purity."

"And that is why my faith fails me!" Philip declared as if he'd won a debate at the university. "I have tried to do right, yet God has repaid me with adversity. Tell me, Father, why I should honor such a God with my fealty."

"Because He asks it of you."

"That is not reason enough!"

"Can you not look upon your adversities as God's means to make a better man of you?"

"I answer that by reminding you of the man who waits outside the gates of this church," said Philip, too defeated to feel smug over making such an apt argument. "God's time would be better spent placing a bit of adversity in *his* path!"

"We will never understand God's ways."

Philip received the priest's inadequate response as his own victory—albeit a bitter one. If he did believe in God, it was a God who had no room for bastards. What else could it be? He also knew he owed this God nothing.

"I am ready to make confession, Father," he said, now unable to keep traces of smugness from his tone. He certainly did not owe this God honesty, even in the confessional.

Bavent hesitated before responding. Perhaps he understood Philip's intent. It seemed he might be wrestling with his own inner conflicts. Finally he answered, "Kneel, my son."

As much as Philip tried to harden his heart, his stomach churned as he moved from the bench to kneel before the priest. There would always be a small part of him that would fear the wrath of God. Yet he convinced himself that his oath to Beatrice superseded all.

Laying a hand on Philip's head, Bavent asked, "How long since your last confession, my son?"

"Five years, Father." No doubt the priest would see that was the exact length of time since his coming from France to Hawken.

"Go on, then."

"Father, I have entertained unkind thoughts toward my brother. I have lusted in my heart for a woman. I had intended to commit theft had I not been forced to flee here to the church. I—"

"Yes, yes, lad," Bavent said with exaggerated patience, "let us just assume you have committed many such sins in the last five years. Why don't we skip ahead to the crux of the matter, eh?"

"I have questioned God," Philip hedged.

"And?" prompted the priest.

Philip reminded himself again of his oath to Beatrice. The lie still came hard. "I confess to the mortal sin of murder!"

"Is your heart repentant, my son?"

Needing to couch his lie in truth, he decided that had he actually committed murder, he would surely be repentant. So he said with confidence, "Yes, Father."

"In the name of the Father, the Son, and the Holy Ghost, I absolve you of this sin. Go and sin no more."

Philip lifted his chin and saw Bavent make the sign of the cross over his head as he also made the sign over his own heart. He thought it was all a sham, yet something told him that Bavent would not have performed such an outright blasphemy. Maybe the priest could read his heart, and perhaps it wasn't as black as he feared.

Two days later the royal coroner arrived earlier than expected. Before him, Philip swore to leave the country forever. As a sign of his oath, the coroner branded Philip's thumb with the letter A for *abjurer*. When the pain subsided, Philip was able to consider this sign with a touch of irony. Hadn't he been branded his entire life with the sin of his birth? Thus, this exterior mark hardly fazed him.

The coroner instructed Philip to take a ship from England at Dover. Peter would accompany him on his journey to the port, about four days on foot, to guard against the possibility of foul play along the road. Though the young suffragan was hardly much protection against trained knights should Gareth attempt to attack Philip on the road, his presence alone as God's representative might prove a deterrent.

One final matter weighed on Philip—the disposition of his horse, Dumpling. Since by rights his conviction had caused all of his possessions to be forfeited to his lord, Dumpling no longer was his. But the idea of putting the animal into Gareth's hands tormented Philip almost as much as placing himself into his brother's merciless grasp. Neither could he take the horse with him. The cost of transporting him across the Channel would have been exorbitant, and he was allotted only enough coin to take the meanest passage possible. So he gave Dumpling to Bavent, who promised that he would do all within his power to keep the horse in his care.

Thus Philip left England as he had come, with only the clothes on his back and a borrowed name. Then he discovered on his first night on the road with the clerk that he had one other possession. Upon opening his pack to sup on the bread and cheese Bavent had given him, he saw his dagger tucked inside. He knew this to be the work of Bavent and took it for a sign that the priest might be more than sympathetic, that he did, in truth, believe in Philip's innocence.

Philip did not touch the dagger. He must remain unarmed until he departed England, and also he would not give reason for Gareth, who shadowed him all the way to Dover, to charge Philip with breaking his oaths to the Church.

Philip was in Dover for a week before the winds and tides became favorable for passage across the Channel. Each day he was constrained to walk into the sea up to his waist in order to confirm his intent to leave the country. Only his resolve to protect Beatrice eased the difficulty of his oath.

When the ship finally sailed out of port, his departure was more difficult than he'd imagined. Leaving Beatrice behind was painful, even though he'd been long resigned to their fate. What surprised him more was the heartache he felt at leaving England, especially leaving Hawken. He'd known nothing but misery there, the shattering of all his hopes and dreams.

Yet something drew him to Hawken.

Perhaps it was that now, by rights, Hawken was his. If justice were ever to be served, he would one day be Lord of Hawken. That alone put the mark of the land upon him, a mark seared deeper into his heart than the letter *A* burned upon his thumb.

PART TWO

20

England
Summer 1263

In a twinkling all of England changed, or so it seemed to Beatrice. The changes were not entirely because of Philip's absence, though that he was not present to witness them did add a touch of irony to it all.

It had begun with Simon de Montfort's return to England in the spring and his calling a council of barons to meet shortly after Philip's departure. Anyone with an ounce of sense—and life had begun to bestow upon Beatrice more than an ounce—realized the council's purpose was nothing less than a call to war. Had Beatrice not guessed it, she would have known for a certainty when her father rode off one fine summer morning in full armor, accompanied by an impressive contingent of Cassley knights. They were bound for Oxford, an appropriate setting for the council, as the much-contested Provisions of Oxford had first been drawn up there. The king had ignored the Provisions, which reduced his power by giving more control to the council of barons.

News trickled into Cassley over the next weeks. The barons demanded that the king abide by the Provisions, and in short order the king rejected those demands. After that there was little news, and Beatrice waited in agony to hear the outcome, of which she was certain would be war, thus placing her father in grave danger.

Vague reports arrived of plundering and of battles. Rumors reported that the queen had escaped London. Beatrice had never met Queen Eleanor but knew that many disliked her, partly because she was French and also because she held her English subjects in barely disguised contempt. Mobs in the London streets were said to have pelted the escaping queen with rotten vegetables and cursed her with angry invectives. "Down with the French witch!" they had yelled.

Near the end of July Beatrice went to St. Bartholomew's for midweek Mass. Other than for Christmas and Easter, Lord Cassley had not been able to afford to have Father Bavent come to the manor to hold services in the small chapel there. But Beatrice had always enjoyed going to the village and mingling with the manor's vassals and serfs. Not, of course, that she, as lady of the manor, mingled much, although it did give her the sense of being a part of the lives of their peasants. Also, St. Bartholomew's was a beautiful, if simple, structure, with a lovely stained-glass depiction of the Annunciation that never failed to stir Beatrice's spiritual senses.

Admittedly, this day her motivation for going into the village was more than spiritual, for she hoped Bavent would have news of events to the north. The priest, however, could only confirm that there was indeed fighting between the rebel barons and the royalists.

Returning home, she went to the garden to harvest a few herbs, an activity she found quite relaxing. The few knights who had remained behind to guard the manor needed to be fed, not to mention her father's factor and others on the staff. While bending over to pick some basil, she heard the clamor of hoofbeats in the courtyard. Thinking—hoping—it was her father, she dropped her basket and raced toward the sound.

Half a dozen knights were dismounting in the yard. Three wore the Cassley crest, and one of these was her father's most favored vassal, Sir Roland. Her father was not among them.

"Sir Roland!" she said, rushing forward. "Where is my father? Is he well?"

"Yes, quite well, m'lady," said Roland, dismounting and handing his reins to the young groom who had recently taken Philip's place.

"Where is he?"

"He remains in London with Lord Leicester, restoring order after their great victory."

"Then the barons were successful in winning the king's obedience?"

"I am instructed to give you a full report," the knight replied. "First, though, mayhap we impose upon you for some food for our empty bellies?"

"Oh, please forgive my rudeness." She took note that the retinue of men indeed looked travel worn. "Take them to wash up and see to their billeting. By then the meal should be ready."

Smiling his thanks, he did as she bid while she returned to the kitchen to expedite the meal. The cook grumbled that she must rush her stew, that the freshly picked herbs should simmer in the stock for a spell to reach their full flavor. In truth Beatrice knew the cook was glad for the guests, since there had been few around to do justice to her meals over the last weeks since the lord's departure. Beatrice was pleased, as well, since the quiet of the manor had played into her morose mood over recent events. She only wished one of those present at supper could have been her father, but at least he was well. A huge burden lifted from her shoulders.

It was not only Beatrice who was hungry for news. Everyone in the manor was anxious to hear their guests' reports, and it was a lively meal they enjoyed that day in the great hall. Though all the guests chattered about their experiences and answered questions, they seemed to think it was Roland's duty to directly inform Beatrice.

"Tell her the best first," suggested one of the younger Cassley knights.

"Yes, tell her about Hawken," said another.

Beatrice turned inquiring eyes upon Roland. "What of Hawken, Sir Roland?"

"We have just come from there, m'lady," he answered. "Your father sent me and a dozen knights south, in part to inform you of his well-being and also to garner support from any remaining royalists in the area. If they continued to hold out, we were to . . . uh . . . well, discipline them."

"And Hawken?"

"Most of the barons around here had long supported the baronial cause. One or two were undecided, however came quickly to our way when they perceived how things were going for Lord Leicester. Except for Hawken. Had the old lord still been alive, things might have gone differently for those at Hawken. But the young lord—"

"He's long had it coming!" shouted one of the Cassley men. While there had always been a natural rivalry between the knights of the two neighboring estates, Beatrice had never guessed there was a particular animosity toward Gareth. Not that it surprised her.

"Is he . . . is he dead?" Beatrice asked, a hundred different emotions assailing her. If Gareth were dead, perhaps Philip could come back and assume his rightful place as Lord of Hawken.

"Last I knew he was in the north, alive and a captive of the barons," Roland replied. "Today, though, he has truly paid for his misplaced loyalties.

His fields are burned and his castle is plundered."

Beatrice gasped. On the way to Mass that morning she had seen plumes of smoke in the distance, and several men had left the service to investigate, but she had returned home before hearing the cause.

"There was no loss of life, m'lady," Roland assured. "The castle guards surrendered quickly."

"But where are the rest of your men?"

"Half have gone to secure other areas."

"Tell her about Lady Hawken," prompted one of the knights.

Roland chuckled. "Sorry, m'lady, 'tis not in fact funny, but the scene with Lady Hawken reminds me of a cat that's been doused with water and is scared and angry and humiliated all at once. Not a pretty sight."

Beatrice could not restrain a smile at the image with Clarise Aubernon replacing the hapless feline.

"She refused to vacate the keep when we were about to set it ablaze," said Roland, trying mightily to curb his own amusement. "We had to drag her out, clawing and screaming. Why, the old hag had more fight in her than any imagined!"

Though she thought the woman was cold and arrogant, Beatrice was forced to feel some admiration for her spirit. "What will become of Hawken now?" she asked.

"I expect the lands will be forfeit if the lord does not have a dramatic change of heart. He is a fool to continue to support the king, for the king has fled to his holdings in France."

"The king has abdicated!" Beatrice had never dreamed of the rebellion going this far. Always before when pushed to such extremes, the royals had conceded.

"No, m'lady. The king has merely been temporarily moved aside. Simon de Montfort is now ruler of England, though most regard him as regent until King Henry returns," Roland explained. "Leicester has formed a provisional government, and your father is one of his closest counselors." The knight added this last with great pride.

"My father?" She was not surprised at this, though she had never thought her father so close with de Montfort.

"Many of the barons supporting Lord Leicester are young men, hardy warriors but green and inexperienced. Men with Lord Cassley's seasoned wisdom are in short supply and have been called to step forth into leadership. And that, m'lady, is what my lord wanted me to tell you. That is the reason he will be away from home longer than expected."

It took a moment for Beatrice to take it all in. Her father was helping to rule the country? The king and his heir were gone, along with Gareth Aubernon? Simon de Montfort was now regent of England? Surely he would not claim himself to be king, though since his sons were royal nephews, one of them might well claim the throne.

Then Roland handed her a letter from her father. She waited until after supper to read it alone in her chamber.

My dear Bea,

By now you should know of the propitious events that have overtaken England in the last weeks. I am still stunned at our victory. But then, Lord Leicester is a most capable military leader. He understood the necessity of a swift and decisive victory. It seemed he could do no wrong in his battle strategy. When Simon fooled all by boldly attacking toward Kent, the stronghold of the royalists, the enemy seemed to scatter before him like sand in the wind. The king fled to the Tower, and at that point many of his supporters deserted him. Simon quickly set up a provisional government. Hugh le Despenser is once again his justiciar, and Simon has honored me with the custody of the great seal.

I know you have little interest in politics, so I will proceed to the part of this missive that most affects you, my daughter. As you know, not long ago I was prepared to broker a marriage contract with Lord Hawken for his son, Gareth. Considering recent events, that is now no longer suitable. Even if the Hawken lands remain intact and in possession of Gareth, now Lord Hawken, I am loath to align my house to one who has proven his disloyalty to a cause I hold dear.

Yet I believe your marriage is long overdue. So when one of Simon's loyal supporters approached me, asking for your hand, I responded favorably. I must tell you, Bea, I believe this union to be in your best interests. And, contrary to what you may think, I have not been completely blind to all the goings-on in my own home. I did not protest your apparent interest in one so beneath your station because, knowing you as I do, I believed protest would only have spurred your rebellion. I felt time and the good sense of at least one of you would prevail. As it turned out, terrible fate intervened. I am sorry for the boy's trials, for I believed him a well-meaning lad and very likely innocent of wrongdoing. I would be remiss, however, if I did not say it was the best thing to happen for your sake. I did worry when shortly before I departed for Oxford you came to me with talk of taking the veil. I guessed your heart was broken, but I cannot fathom the depth of feelings you held for the lad. Nevertheless, I cannot bear to see my dear, spirited only child enter a convent. Perhaps it is selfish, but I would greatly enjoy grandchildren.

Of a truth, I believe this a perfect match for you. I know what it is to lose one whom you have loved, and I understand it may be too soon for you to offer your heart to another. With me now required to be in London, it is imperative that you have the covering of a husband; therefore, I have found for you a man who will require no emotional commitment from you. He is a good man and will treat you well, probably more like a daughter. He desires only that you provide him with an heir, for you see, his only son was one of the few casualties of the recent conflict. I ask only that you think before you react. The man I wish to betroth you to is Nigel Fitzjohn, Lord Sardwick. Please, Bea, remember to think! Show this letter to your maid. I trust her wisdom in guiding you to a logical decision. I would be pleased if you could come to a decision quickly so that Sir Roland can bring your reply back to London when he departs Cassley.

I love you, Bea, with all my heart!

Your beloved father

Beatrice barely perceived any of the letter after reading Lord Sardwick's name. She dropped the parchment and started screaming for Leticia.

The maid raced into the room, no doubt thinking Beatrice was in mortal danger. Unceremoniously, Beatrice tossed the parchment at her maid.

"My father has betrayed me!" she cried, flinging herself down upon her bed.

Leticia picked up the parchment from where it had landed on the floor and quickly read it. She hurried to Beatrice's bed, sat on the edge, and placed a comforting arm on the girl's shoulder.

"There, there, child."

"Leticia, pack my things immediately. I'm going to St. Mary's Priory."

"That would break your father's heart, Lady Beatrice."

"Why should I care? He doesn't give a farthing about *my* heart." Sniffing, she picked up a corner of the bed sheet and dragged it across her moist eyes.

"Perhaps you should read the letter again," said Leticia in a tone just bordering on scolding. "I have never known a man to care so tenderly for a child. Imagine, he knew about Philip all along yet did not lock you in your room, as most fathers would have done."

Beatrice had been so shaken over the news about Lord Sardwick that it had barely registered about her father knowing about Philip. Surely he was only guessing. If he had been truly concerned about her chastity, he *would* have locked her up!

"He was only afraid I'd run off with Philip to spite him," she said. "And I would have!"

"So he was right in how to handle you."

"He would have been very wrong if Lord Hawken hadn't been killed." Beatrice tried to sound smug, but the mere mention of those horrible events still humbled and dismayed her.

"He was right about one thing," the maid said gently. "You and I know, even if your father can only guess, how much you love—yes, *still* love—Philip. You have more than once threatened to take the veil rather than marry another—"

"And I mean it! I will. I will—"

"Don't be a fool, child!" The maid folded her arms across her chest and directed a near-withering gaze at her charge.

"Are you telling me you support my father's choice?" This could not have shocked Beatrice more. She had always looked upon Leticia as an ally.

"I am telling you to heed your father's words. Think!" Leticia paused, as if giving Beatrice the opportunity to do that very thing.

But Beatrice's mind was in too much turmoil for logic. Her head felt like the besieged walls of a castle, bombarded by too much at once. Surely it would crumble and fall. Marry Uncle Sardie? At sixty he was quite decrepit. She'd considered him old when she was a little girl and he had performed his magic tricks for her. When his first wife had died a few years ago, Beatrice had attended her funeral and recalled feeling sorry for the "poor old man." The very idea of becoming his wife was like a stout battering ram hitting her between the eyes. He was so old that even his son would have been too old for her. Her father had tried to soften it by telling her the man would treat her more as a daughter than a wife. Except under the covers of his bed! Beatrice shuddered at the thought.

Lifting stricken eyes toward Leticia, she groaned, "Leticia, he's so-o-o"—she drew out the word like a dirge—"old!"

"Yes, you could be a widow while you are still young," Leticia said, her brow arched cunningly. Beatrice gasped at the maid's forthrightness. But Leticia clicked her tongue censoriously. "Come now, Beatrice, don't be a child. Your father said to think, so think! This match could indeed be perfect. You can fulfill your marriage obligation. Sardwick and Cassley lands will be joined to make a formidable holding. You will have to give no more of yourself to your husband than you can. All he will want from you is an heir. And you will have a child to nurture and love."

"I just don't know!"

"Do you worry Philip would not understand?"

She shrugged. "He accepted the fact that I must marry. He asked only that I not marry his brother."

"There, you see! This arrangement will make everyone happy."

"Except me."

"You may be surprised, Beatrice."

She still was not sure about the whole thing, but two days later she sent a letter with Roland when he departed for London. In it she accepted the marriage contract.

21

T he first thing one noticed in a city the size of Paris was the stench. The pervading odor of some two hundred thousand people packed together upon narrow streets simply could not be avoided. Even the king, whose palace stood on Île de la Cité, an isle in the middle of the Seine, was not immune from the stench. King Philip Augustus, who died in 1223, one day stood upon the balcony of his palace watching the carts rattle by on the muddy road below. The stench so sickened him that he ordered the main roads to be paved with stone, a process still underway.

Noble undertaking though it was, the noxious mud on the roadways proved only a small culprit in fouling the air. No amount of paving could dispel the odors of human life mingled with the animal flesh that roamed about, especially near the markets.

Philip de Tollard had almost forgotten what a real city was like. Paris was many times larger than London, a city he had visited twice while at Oxford. He had never been to a city the size of Paris.

The heat of summer was past, slightly easing the close, airless atmosphere of the streets. Philip had been in France now a little more than a year, having been slowly making his way across Normandy for much of the time. He had no particular destination in mind; he merely headed where life led him. Life? What he really meant was survival. A penniless young man cast adrift by the world could expect little more.

Had he ever believed a new life awaited him on the Continent? Perhaps some part of him, after Father Bavent had given him a second chance at life, had thought he might actually come to France and find his fortune.

What would it take to squash once and for all that niggling sprout of optimism within him?

As he had moved about laboring at demeaning tasks, usually for no more remuneration than a crust of bread and a roof over his head, he had kept hoping that something good would finally happen to him. Perhaps he would save the life of a great lord or tend an ailing destrier, and for his noble efforts he'd be given an honored position upon the man's fief. Maybe even given a small fief of his own. But there were few, if any, lords roaming about needing their lives saved or their horses tended.

How he wished he could stay in one place for a while. Alas, he could blame his transience only on himself. Back in Oxford, Father Dumbarton had tagged Philip as being possessed with "the demon of anger." It must be true. The months at Cassley Manor had almost led him to believe it wasn't. Sweet, dear Beatrice had soothed the anger from him, but now it was back with a vengeance, and it took little to coax it to the surface. His actions had given proof to that.

At a farm near Bayeux he'd taken a job mucking out stalls and slopping the pigs. He received one meal a day and a corner of the barn to sleep in for his labors. One day, barely two days into the job, the farmer's son had thought it would be amusing to watch Philip take a "swim" in the feeding trough. It was freshly filled with a batch of an especially slimy concoction. As Philip walked past, the lad, loitering about, stuck out his foot at just the right moment, sending Philip flying headfirst into the trough. Smeared with the offensive contents, Philip had leaped to his feet and attacked the boy. Philip was throttling the boy when the farmer came and pulled him off, ending that brief work.

Moving to the next village a short distance away, he'd found work sweeping in an inn. It lasted only a day. A patron had derided Philip's red hair. "He must be the devil's spawn, that one, with the fires of hell upon his head."

Philip attacked, but this time he was the one throttled and tossed out into the street. The innkeeper told him not to come back, and if he valued his life, he should leave the village.

He took bruised body and pride on to another village, where inevitably, he found another reason to start, or finish, a fight. He didn't enjoy fighting, yet in some twisted way he derived satisfaction from it. Far more than half the time he lost these battles, but it wasn't the winning that gave him the satisfaction. He wasn't sure what it was. He only knew that when his fists were smashing something—or another's fists were smashing him!—he felt alive, or at least less dead. Maybe fighting was the only time in his life he was actually choosing for himself and not being pushed to and fro by the whims of others.

Or maybe it was the release of his private demons that eased him.

With another winter approaching he questioned the wisdom of remaining in the countryside. He'd nearly died last winter living off the rare charity of others, pleased if he found so much as a stable in which to retreat from the elements. No good had come to him in the country. To the contrary, he was half starved. The only food he'd had in a week was a few potatoes he'd pilfered from a garden and some apples, also stolen. Both "meals" had nearly cost him his life. After grabbing the potatoes, the housewife had chased him off with a broom, and her husband, seeing the ruckus, had grabbed a pitchfork. Philip escaped with a nasty gash on his hindquarters from the pitchfork. Obtaining the apples had been less exciting, since he'd only fallen from the tree he'd climbed when a rotten branch broke.

Although he'd always known land was important to a man, he now realized there was more to it than the status it provided. It meant not only owning land but also being a part of the land, belonging to the land as well as the land belonging to you. Even the meanest, lowest serf belonged to something. He had a place in society. He was known in his village and accepted. A wanderer, such as Philip had become, had no place. Wherever he went, he was a stranger. No matter where he journeyed, he was looked upon with suspicion. He well knew that even if he tarried in a village for several years, he would always be a stranger there, never truly part of the fiber of the community. Some might extend themselves enough to give him some lowly work, but if anything went awry, the first fingers of accusation would be pointed at him.

To wander eternally, to never fit in, to never feel the comforting embrace of friends or family was by far the worst of his punishment.

So what harm would it do to test his fortunes in the city? In a place like Paris he might not feel his solitude so acutely. Among the teeming thousands of souls there must be many others like him. Pausing as he crossed the Petit Pont, one of the bridges that spanned the Seine connecting the Île de la Cité with the Left Bank, he still felt no less alone. Even among thousands, he was still a stranger.

His gaze fell upon the majestic Gothic façade of Notre Dame. After a hundred years workmen were still constructing the awesome edifice. The sight made him think of Father Bavent and his homely little church of St. Bartholomew. How many times had Bavent told him that in Christ's embrace he'd never be alone again? Would he be standing here now, as isolated as ever a man could be, if he had accepted what the priest had offered? He would still have had to leave England, for no amount of religious enlightenment would have spared him his criminal conviction. Would Christ's love have clothed him and fed him these last months? Others would still have looked upon him as a stranger. Even in Notre Dame, the most magnificent symbol of Christ in all of Christendom, he would hardly find succor. With a sour grunt, he wondered if a monastery would even accept him.

Unsettled by his thoughts, he swung his focus away, seeking to look anywhere but at the symbol of all he found so elusive.

"I see you admire the steeple of Sainte-Chapelle," a male voice said, breaking into his reverie.

It startled Philip. He hadn't realized that his gaze indeed had rested upon the extraordinary structure, a stone's throw from Notre Dame, with its similarly ornate Gothic style and soaring stained-glass windows. For a moment he was struck dumb. It had been a long time since he'd had a conversation with another human being. When he saw that the man was about to continue on his way, Philip said the first thing that came to mind.

"Is the Crown of Thorns really kept in there?" he asked in French, now his primary language. "The actual crown Christ wore at His crucifixion?"

"That and a fragment of the True Cross," answered the man, who by his garb appeared to be a common man, perhaps a laborer or a street vendor. "I helped lay stone for the structure myself!" He preened as he spoke.

"You have every reason to be proud. It is a splendid building," Philip replied. "Are you sure, though, it holds the real cross of Christ?" Philip was unable to keep the skepticism from his tone.

"That is why the king had the chapel built. Do you disbelieve our king?"

"Well . . . no, of course not. But how could *he* be sure of the man from whom he received it?"

Many crusaders had returned from the Holy Lands with what they claimed were relics of Christ—pieces of the lance that had impaled Him at his crucifixion, swatches of His robe, even the chalice from which He drank at the Last Supper. Most were proven frauds, the rest highly suspect. If people understood more of science, they would know many of those items could not possibly have survived a thousand years. Though if the question of science were raised, it would simply have been brushed aside by attributing magical powers to the relics.

"King Louis is the wisest, most venerable king France has ever had," the man replied, referring to France's present king, Louis IX. His tone was haughty, as if he himself were related to the royal personage. "The man is pious enough to be a saint. He would know. It is said he paid one hundred and thirty-five thousand livres for the Crown of Thorns. More than twice what he paid to build the church that holds them."

Philip snorted. "Such blatant excess hardly seems saintly to me."

"What do you know?" huffed the fellow. "Look at you! A common street urchin, I'll warrant!" The man hurried away in great affront.

Philip shrugged and started on his way once again. He crossed the bridge and came into the Latin Quarter, so named for the profusion of Latin-speaking teachers and students attending the university located here. Philip had come purposefully in this direction, hoping to see the new school, the Sorbonne, which had been founded only a few years ago and was already gaining repute for excellence. Friar Bacon had spent many years in Paris and had extolled this center of learning. Philip had always wanted to see it.

Church bells began tolling, indicating time for Nones. Philip knew it was frivolous to waste time visiting a university he'd never attend. He should be searching out a place to bide the night. Here in the city there would be no sleeping beneath the stars. He'd hoped to find work but thus far had been unsuccessful. It might be best to leave now before the gates closed for the night. Outside the city he could sleep upon the roadside unbothered by the authorities, though there was always the threat of attack by thieves and thugs.

Just one brief look around, he told himself, so I can say I was here. He was already near Rue St. Jacques, a street that led out of the city. Just in time he saw a woman lean out a window overhead and tip a large pot. The torrent of refuse barely missed him.

"You there!" he yelled. "Watch what you're about!"

The woman only cackled with amusement. Philip sidestepped the foul matter and hurried on. Within a few blocks the odor of refuse was replaced by the more pleasant aroma of pastries and sizzling meat. Turning aside, a few more steps led him to a narrow street lined with about a dozen stalls of various vendors, mostly food sellers, though a shoemaker and a tailor were nestled there, as well. It was the smells from the baker and butcher stalls that drew Philip. His mouth watered, but he had no coin in his possession.

Sauntering up to a butcher's stall, Philip paused, watching strips of meat, impaled upon thin sticks, sizzle on a brazier. It had been weeks since he had tasted meat, and though the offerings looked as though they had reposed on the coals a bit too long, he began wondering what he could do to obtain a taste.

"They're half price now near the end of the day," said the butcher, a portly man in an apron so stained with grease and blood one could hardly tell it had once been white.

"I'll help you clean up for a couple of them," Philip offered.

"I've got two sons for that job."

"Oh." Crestfallen, Philip turned.

"Wait, lad," the man relented. "I hear the baker down the street could use some help. His wife has been ailing, and it's just the two of them."

"Thank you, sir." Philip brightened. A good hunk of bread might help, though it was hard to get the heady fragrance of roasted kid out of his head.

The street was busy with shoppers looking for bargains, especially in food goods that would not keep overnight. Philip watched a woman purchase several onions from a produce seller, laying her coins upon the counter. It seemed a fortune, and he could not help a tinge of envy.

Suddenly a figure hurrying past jostled him to and fro. "Hey!" Philip said but was speaking only to the back of the person's head, now a mere blur of blue wool.

At the same moment the produce seller yelled, "Stop, thief!"

No two words in any language could raise a more dramatic response. Instinctively Philip looked about in search of the culprit. It may have been the very person who had rushed past a moment ago. There he was! A head capped in a ragged blue wool hat was quickly threading its way through the crowd.

"Over there!" Philip cried, then took off after the fellow. He should have known better than to get involved, but in the back of his mind an annoying spark of optimism suggested that if he caught the thief he might be rewarded in some manner.

Another voice shouted, "There he is!"

Several of the bystanders took off after Philip, but he quickly lost track of the blue hat. Assuming these men had joined him in the chase, he turned to inform them of his failure. Like a swarm of angry hornets, they swooped down upon Philip, laying hands roughly upon him.

"We've got him!" someone yelled.

Philip realized his peril. "No!" he cried.

His captors were not listening to his protests, and he knew he was doomed. He fought and struggled against the restraining hands, kicking one man in the shins and another in the groin, and as another hand reached out to grab him, he bit it. All his inner rage welled up against the mob, and the half dozen or so men had little chance against it. In but a few moments he had struggled free and sprinted away.

With the mob hot on his heels, he shot down an alleyway, then another and another. Still he could not shake his pursuers. What had blue-hat stolen? Something more valuable than a pastry, judging by the tenacity of the pursuit. He was thoroughly lost in the maze of narrow streets when he turned a corner and for a few moments was out of sight of the mob. He knew he could not outrun them much longer. There were more vendor stalls on this street, but a sign over a door caught his eye.

"Lion's Paw."

Laughter and voices sounded from inside. Without a moment's hesitation he grasped the door latch and slipped inside. To his relief, none of the customers noticed his entry, though a few heads turned toward the sudden stab of light that shot into the tavern. Thirty or forty men were crowded into the very small room. Philip quickly tried to lose himself in the crowd, hoping the proprietor didn't ask him to purchase a drink. He quietly strolled among the customers, some standing, some seated on benches at coarse tables.

A shaft of light penetrated the room once more as the door opened again. Panic surged up. He felt trapped, seeing no way out until he spied the curtains at the back of the room. One was partly opened, and he saw behind it a small cubicle. He had an idea what this was, but having no other choice, he hurried through the opening, quickly pulling it completely closed behind him.

"Och! An anxious one you are, eh?" came a feminine voice.

Surprisingly, the cubicle was no dimmer than the room outside. It was even a bit lighter, for there were open slats high in the eaves of the building that bathed the curtained cubicles in a bit more light. Less surprising was what met Philip's eyes. A woman lay upon a narrow pallet, no doubt filled with straw and covered with a dirty quilt, which filled most of the cubicle. There was just enough room next to the bed for one to stand without disturbing the curtain.

"I-I don't—" Philip was at a loss for words. If he told her outright he had no coin to pay for her services, she might well cause a ruckus and bring upon him the mob he was afraid had entered the tavern looking for him. The longer he stood there, though, the more he began to think he had been mistaken about the mob. Of a surety, if they had tracked him here, they would have raised a loud hue and cry.

"A young one, too," she said coyly. "First time, lad?"

At first Philip thought he'd come upon an old woman, because her voice was hard edged and bore a certain grave maturity. A closer look told him that despite her calling him *lad*, she was no older than he and could be even younger. There were no lines of age beneath the grime on her face, and her hair, a tangled brown mop on her head, had no telltale hint of gray. Finally, there was a youthful litheness to the petite girl's figure, clad in no more than a thin gray shift. The flowering of womanhood was but a hint beneath the shift.

"No," he said. "I mean . . . that is, I've made a blunder." He thought it would be safer out in the streets with the mob on his heels than in the cubicle.

"Come on, *chéri*." She scooted over and patted the bed. "I won't bite, honest." She gave her eyelashes a coquettish flutter. She was not an especially pretty girl. Her nose was large and her chin almost nonexistent. There was a nasty-looking sore on the corner of her upper lip.

Outside he heard some snips of conversation. "Red hair, you say?"

"Yes, we've been chasing him . . ." Laughter drowned out the rest.

Philip knew he had to stay where he was. "You're right," he told the girl. "I have never—"

"You're very fortunate. I know just what to do." She grinned, revealing a missing front tooth.

"Well, I . . ."

He heard a female scream, then a string of curses. They were searching the cubicles! He threw a frantic glance at the curtain.

The girl reached up and grabbed his hand. "Hurry," she said.

For a moment he gave only a blank, uncomprehending stare until she tugged at him again.

A few moments later when the curtain was flung open, Philip's pursuers saw only two lumps under the quilt.

"Ayeee!" squealed the girl. "What's this?" She brought her head out from under the quilt and glared at the interlopers.

"We're looking for a thief," said one of the men. "He came in here not long ago."

"Couldn't be him," said the girl. "He paid me for a whole hour and has been sleeping most of that time. Want me to wake him?"

Philip groaned and stirred, careful to keep the quilt over his head. He thought it would appear too suspicious if the noise didn't disturb his "sleep" at all.

The men stumped away, and the girl quickly jumped up and pulled the curtain shut. They listened while the last of the cubicles was searched. Soon Philip was certain the pursuers had exited.

"Thank you," he said simply to the girl.

She shrugged. "You don't look like a bad thief."

"I'm not a thief!"

"Shush!" she hissed. "You want to bring 'em back? Then why did you come in here if not to hide? Not the usual reason, I'll warrant."

"Yes, they were chasing me, but do you think they were going to believe me, a stranger, with no home, no one to speak for me?"

She eyed him with such a wise look that he squirmed as he might when censured by an elder. "I was once as you, an orphaned street urchin, until Arnaud took me in." She made it sound as if she were speaking of ancient times.

"Who's Arnaud?"

"He runs this place. He's a decent fellow."

"Mayhap he'd have work for me?"

"Perhaps . . ." She gave her head a toss, her lips bending into a beguiling smile. Indeed, she had such a way about her that Philip almost forgot what a homely lass she was. She went on, "But first, you owe me something, hmm?"

"I have no coin." He braced himself for her injured cry.

"But I saved your life. At least your right hand."

Paling, he rubbed his right wrist. If he had been caught, his accusers surely might have cut off his hand as punishment, not an uncommon way to deal with thieves.

"Perhaps I can repay you when Arnaud—"

"A comely lad such as yourself does not need money—not with me." She sat down on the cot and slid her hand over his shoulder, then slipped closer to him.

What would she think if she knew he truly had never been with a woman? But why shouldn't he? Even that irrepressible optimistic part of him should know by now that he was never going to have the life of which he had once dreamed. He doubted even this grimy prostitute would have him for a husband. He had nothing to offer a wife and never would. Yet this forced him to recall why he was in his present state and why he had forborne giving up his innocence this long. Now more than ever he knew he'd be the worst kind of man to bring his fate upon an innocent child.

"I'm sorry," he said, pushing away from her. "I can't." Knowing he must offer her more, though, he added, "I will not until I can pay like any man."

"Still proud, then. That's no fault, I suppose." She wiggled from the pallet and rose. "Come, let's find Arnaud."

22

A rnaud did not need more help in his establishment, but he did need Brise, the young prostitute who had rescued Philip. She was one of his most favored girls, and he was willing to make her happy by giving Philip some work in exchange for a couple of meals and a bed. He also seemed willing to overlook the obvious fact that Philip, with his dark red hair, was likely the thief who had prompted the search of his place. Brise said that half of Arnaud's customers were thieves of some kind, so he probably thought it would be an advantage to employ one to keep an eye on the others.

Philip swept the place, carried the heavy casks of ale up from the cellar, and even served the ale on busy nights. Although he worked hard, it put no coin in his purse. He understood better than ever the plight of peasants and serfs. Even if one wished it, there was little chance of ever bettering one's station, since coin, much less profit, seldom crossed their palms. He'd always considered himself a nobleman despite having been rejected by his family, but now he must accept the fact that he was a peasant. A freeman, yes, however that status did him little good. Perhaps peasant was even too good a word to describe himself, for he worked no land and did precious little of any consequence.

Once a month the quilts on the girls' beds were given a shake behind the tavern, their only concession to cleanliness. That job fell to Philip a few days after his arrival because he was tall and strong. The girls carried them out to him.

Brise lingered a few moments when she brought hers. "What's that scar on your hand, Philip?"

He had almost forgotten the brand on his thumb. It was healed now, and the white outline of the letter *A* barely discernible.

He shrugged, responding with the lie he'd already prepared should it be mentioned. "Burned myself on a hearth."

"It almost looks like . . ." Pausing, she shrugged, as well. "'Tis none of my affair. But was that hearth in Anjou perhaps? You've an Angevin sound to your accent. I myself am from Blois."

"It's been a long time since I have been there," he answered vaguely. In his present plight he had never allowed himself to grow close to anyone, not that he was in one place long enough to do so. Still, he closely guarded all personal information. He gave the quilt a hard shake, sending dust particles all around them.

"Me too." She coughed and waved her hand back and forth in front of her face.

"This is no place for a pleasant conversation," he said. "Go on inside." He had shaken the quilt with the precise intention of ending the conversation.

But she was a sharp one. "You'll not rid yourself of me that easily!" she said tartly. Then she grinned. "You still owe me for saving your life, you know."

"And I still have no coin."

"And I said—"

He gave the quilt another vigorous shake and another. The thing was quite filthy and made Brise cough so much she finally did give up and went inside. He wondered how much longer he'd be able to put her off. Should he? What would be the harm? Brise was a pleasant girl and nice to him. No doubt it would be an enjoyable encounter.

Yet he would not. Most days he thought his life was ruined beyond repair, that he was bound to live it out a penniless wanderer. He believed he could not get much lower. And still the death knell had not rung upon his hope. What would it take? How low must he sink before he truly believed he would never regain his rightful place in society? Or marry Beatrice and have the life he dreamed of?

He had no idea. He only knew he wasn't there yet.

That night the tavern was busy. Word had circulated that Arnaud would be offering a fresh batch of ale. Since the ale, made of grains and spices, kept only two or three days, a new brew would draw many customers. The crowd on this night, as on most, was a mixed assortment of lower-class Parisians, common laborers for the most part, and many peasants from the surrounding countryside who had come into the city to hawk their produce. The Lion's Paw also drew the occasional minor baron, because Arnaud was known to be a skilled brewer. He used the finest malted barley in his brew and had a secret ingredient—a few long peppers—which Philip learned when he helped with the brewing.

Two such nobles sauntered into the tavern, their station apparent by their ankle-length surcotes of linen, one in rich green, the other in scarlet. Arnaud leaned toward Philip, who had just come up from the cellar, a cask perched on his shoulder.

"Eh, lad," the tavern keeper said in a low voice, "see to it those fellows are taken care of. Their pockets are heavy with coin, or I'm a son of a mud hen."

Philip set the cask down on a shelf and, as he filled two of Arnaud's finest pewter mugs with ale, noted that Arnaud called Brise over and gave her similar instructions, though her manner of taking care of the gentlemen would no doubt be far different than his. He disliked watching the women work their "trade" among Arnaud's customers. Though he made a concerted attempt to ignore the comings and goings around the curtained cubicles, it was hard to completely ignore the sounds that were little muffled by the woolen "walls." Brise had told him that this life was far better than she, an orphaned girl set adrift by tragic circumstances, might have otherwise expected. She made a decent living—that is, she had enough to eat and a roof over her head—and she controlled her own destiny because the only part Arnaud played in her "business" was to charge her rent for her cubicle. Still, he saw some of the men who sought her out, and they were more often than not crude and filthy and harsh with her. Philip had come close to throttling a couple, but Brise had interceded before he had gone too far.

Philip brought the tray of ale to the trestle table where the two young barons, or more likely sons of barons, were seated. By the look of their attire they were knights, though they wore no mail and were armed only with short swords on their belts. Brise and another girl sat on each of their laps, the two men plying them with kisses. The men laughed and the girls giggled, all apparently enjoying themselves. Philip placed the mugs on the table and went about his other work, returning to the table often because Arnaud told him to make sure the mugs never emptied.

The barons apparently began to think of Philip as their personal servant. When one spilled a mug, he called, "Hey, boy, clean this up."

And when they became hungry, they ordered, "Boy, run to the cookshop next door and bring us some pies." Like most taverns, food wasn't served in Arnaud's place, and if a customer wanted a meal, he usually fetched it himself. This night, Arnaud purchased the pies for the nobles, thinking he'd garner a larger fee from them in the end. Philip groused because the cookshop was not next door but rather at the far end of the street. He'd had to make two or three trips through the course of the evening.

There was never a word of appreciation. Instead, they took his compliance as reason to heap on more abuse.

"What kind of a pigsty is this? The table is sticky. Put your back into it, boy."

"These pies are tough and dry. I'll not pay a single coin for them!"

They proceeded to gobble them up anyway, and Arnaud was out his expenditure, a situation he did not take with good nature. He punished Philip by boxing his ears. The barons saw this and laughed.

Philip was gritting his teeth by the time the barons ordered him to go out and feed their horses. When he returned from this task, his new overlords were hotly involved in a dice game with several other customers.

Brise sidled up to Philip as he gathered empty mugs from the tables so they could be reused.

"They're arrogant blighters, they are!" she said. "But I've made more off them in one night than I do in a whole week bedding foul-smelling workmen."

"That's good for you, then," he said tightly. "I'm glad *you're* having a fine time." While he'd been fretting about the way they had been treating her, all along she was apparently enjoying it.

"Fine? Ha! They're perverted sons of devils. I've worked for my coin, make no mistake."

"What do you mean? Are they hurting you?" He gave her a closer inspection and saw some bruising around her left eye and a red welt on one cheek.

She shrugged. "The short one can't seem to find his manhood unless he's beating on his woman. I'll heal."

Philip had never heard anything so disgusting. "Brise, you shouldn't allow that. Let me tell him to mind his place."

"Don't you dare! The money is worth it. I just hope he doesn't call me to the back again." She shuddered.

"Tell him no."

"You are such a child, Philip. You don't tell that sort no."

For the first time in a long time Philip thought of his brother. He was surely of the same ilk, believing that anyone of a lesser social station was fair game for bullying, especially women. It made him seethe inside and determine that he would not bow to those miscreants again.

Four newcomers came into the tavern. Philip wouldn't have noticed them among the many coming and going except that one of the group was huge, a head taller than anyone in the place and built like a castle fortification.

"*Garçon,*" the big one called to Philip, who was holding a tray loaded with mugs. "Four ales, if you please."

Philip filled four of the mugs on his tray—Arnaud saw no reason to wash the receptacles between customers.

"This better be the fresh stuff," said one of the big man's companions, a wiry fellow with an ugly scar that ran down the side of his face, making his right eye droop in a menacing fashion.

"'Tis the first draw from a fresh cask," assured Philip, setting the mugs on the table.

The wiry, scarred man took a long draw from the mug. "It'll pass," he said when he finished.

The big man counted out coins from a leather purse tucked into his belt. "Since it meets with your most discerning approval, Gilly, I'll pay the bill!" He laid the coins on Philip's tray. "That'll cover another round for me and me friends, eh? And a *denier* for yourself, too, lad."

Philip had never received money from a customer before and gaped at the coin. A denier was a small fortune for him, the first time in months he'd had a coin in his possession.

"Thank you, *monsieur!*" Philip gave the man another appraisal. He didn't look a wealthy man. Nor did his three companions. Besides the wiry fellow, there was a swarthy man only a year or two older than Philip—he looked the most refined of the four—and a thickset man of middling height whose scowl set Philip's teeth on edge. All were dressed as peasants, their attire as coarse as any workman's, with drab knee-length tunics, unlike the brightly colored longer garments of the nobles. It only proved the futility of judging a man by his appearance. He just wished others would consider that philosophy regarding him!

The night wore on, the customers grew drunker, and the fresh ale supply dwindled. Arnaud began watering it, and when the watered product was gone, he brought out the older ale, believing his guests were by now too far into their cups to notice the slightly tainted flavor. Philip was run ragged and wondered that Arnaud had said he didn't need another servant. No doubt it had merely been a ploy to get him for a pittance. At least the barons were too involved in gambling to be a bother—that is, until the short baron Brise had spoken of began losing badly at dice. He nearly throttled one of the players, accusing him of substituting dishonest dice. When he was proven wrong, he turned away from the game grumbling curses.

The baron boldly grabbed Brise, who was trying to interest another customer in her services. "Come with me, wench!"

"Och! Easy then," she said, rubbing her arm. "I'm with another, as you can see."

"Yeah," said her companion. "Find yourself another one."

The baron laughed harshly. "I'll do no such a thing." His hand went to the hilt of his sword.

Quickly the other man pushed Brise away. "Have her, then," he said. "I'll just find me another wench."

The baron kept hold of Brise's arm, twisting it unnecessarily.

Brise grimaced. "Stop that now. I'm coming!"

"I'm not hurting you, am I?" the baron mocked. "Maybe I'll give my coin to another."

"M-maybe you s-should—"

He laughed. "You are the prettiest piece of flesh here—not that that's saying much!" He started to propel her toward the back.

Philip would have pounced even before seeing the look of desperate resignation on Brise's usually plucky countenance. He was halfway there, and that final look only lent a spark to the flint of his rage. He laid hands on the baron's shoulders, wrenching him away so hard the man had to let loose of Brise.

"Philip, no!" Brise cried.

But he heard none of her protests.

"Unhand me, you scurrilous dog!" shouted the baron.

"Leave the girl alone!" warned Philip.

Drawing his sword, the baron laughed. "Now see what comes of touching your betters!"

Philip jumped back from the threatening weapon, but he was so infused with fury that he was far from ready to retreat. His hand went to his belt for his own dagger before he remembered it was in the storeroom where he slept. He had ceased wearing his dagger because an armed man usually drew too much attention, especially one as ragged as he.

Frantically he looked around for a weapon—anything, even a broomstick. But few of the customers in the tavern were of the kind that went about armed. And even fewer were going to help a serving lad against a baron.

The baron had raised his sword and was about to charge when suddenly, as if out of nowhere, one of Arnaud's wooden trays seemed to leap into

Philip's hands. He had no idea who had placed it there and had no time to look around. He had only an instant to raise the tray to deflect the blow of the sword. Had the weapon been a broadsword, it would have bisected the tray and Philip's head with it. Instead, the short sword cut through half the wood and stopped.

Giving a hard twist to the tray, Philip managed to wrench the sword from the baron's hand. He flung the sword-impaled tray aside before launching a bodily attack on the baron. His opponent was shorter than Philip but far more skilled. As always, Philip's inner rage made up for his lack of weapons and skill.

His initial offensive slammed the baron back over a table, the surprise of the attack stunning the fellow. He rebounded quickly, though, and when Philip raised a fist aimed at the baron's nose, the man deflected it with his wrist, then twisted his body away from the table, leaping back to his feet.

The other customers scurried back, giving the combatants a wide girth. Arnaud was yelling but knew better than to get into the middle of a fight. Besides, when the fight was over, the winner and the spectators would be thirsty. The loser, whom he was certain would be Philip, would be no loss to him at all.

Philip and the baron battled for a few minutes, with Philip holding his own until the baron's friend leaped into the fray. As the short baron made a frontal attack, the second baron slipped to the rear of Philip and grabbed him by the arms. The short baron's fist then plowed freely into Philip's gut. After two or three of these blows, Philip greatly regretted the meal he had taken earlier, though he kept it down by great force of will.

When the short baron prepared for another assault, Philip struggled like a madman to throw off the second baron's hold. Before that had any effect, however, both he and the second baron were knocked off their feet. As they sprawled to the floor, a voice penetrated the yells and shouts of the crowd.

"Play fair, m'lord!"

Out of the corner of his bruised eye, Philip saw someone slam a fist into the second baron's face, and there was no further interference from that baron. Philip had barely risen to his feet when the short baron flew once again at him.

Before he could block the blow, the baron's fist struck him squarely in the nose. White pain shot through Philip as blood spurted everywhere. The baron followed up quickly with another blow to the side of Philip's head. Already staggering from the first blow, Philip could little defend himself. Now black spots dotted the searing white flashes in his vision. Almost blindly he swung his fists, clipping the baron on the jaw yet hardly fazing the man, who responded with another punishing blow. Philip went to his knees but forced himself up, grasping the edge of a bench. Panting, near exhaustion, and barely able to see through his battered eyes, he raised his fists for another charge.

His opponent met this with an uppercut to his chin. Philip bit his tongue, and blood sprayed from his mouth. Another blow again landed on the side of his head, and again he came into intimate contact with the boards of Arnaud's tavern.

For an instant his vision turned to blackness, and he knew he'd soon be senseless. The thought of that baron standing over him, gloating in victory, incensed him, turning the blackness to flashes of white light, not of pain but of fury. He clawed at the boards until he was on his knees yet again. The edge of a table came into view, and he reached for it to brace himself as he pulled himself to his feet. Before he could get far, the baron's foot smashed into his face and down he went again. Dimly, as if from a distance, he heard the shouts and cheers of the crowd.

What! Were they cheering this vermin of a baron instead of their own, a simple common man?

He lifted his face from the floor. He knew he would die now before giving up and letting this mob of traitors have their way. He groped his way up to his knees, and again the baron's foot shot forward. This time Philip had enough presence of mind to grab the foot.

Bang!

The baron hit the boards.

Yet that proved only a minor setback to the baron, who'd received only two or three substantial blows during the entire battle. He was back on his feet by the time Philip had struggled to his. The two opponents circled each other, both panting. Philip was easily more worse for the wear, covered in blood, his eyes nearly swollen shut; nevertheless he was the first to lunge, a great miscalculation he belatedly realized. As always, he had more verve than wits. The baron was ready for the attack, his swinging fists aimed perfectly to connect with Philip's face. Philip spun around until he was completely disoriented, but he kept on his feet, and when he stopped spinning, his fists were raised even though he could barely see. Instantly, the baron blindsided him, and he toppled to the floor again.

As he tried to claw his way up once more, he realized what a fool he was. Yet he couldn't help it. He managed to get up on all fours before his enemy's foot toppled him again.

Blackness began to engulf him, and he was just barely aware of Arnaud standing over him, cursing and yelling.

"Get out, you cursed troublemaker! I'll have you arrested!"

Blurrily, he also saw Brise's homely face.

"Oh, you foolish boy. What have you done?"

Several hands grabbed him. He was too sick and wracked with pain to struggle further against the inevitable, especially now that his fate was sealed. He managed one pathetic twist of protest and as he did so, he saw something that surely must prove he was insane and imagining things. While the men picked him up off the floor, he saw another man come up surreptitiously behind the gloating baron and crack him over the head with a pewter mug. The baron crumbled to the floor.

"Please, Arnaud," Brise cried. "Don't turn him in. They'll hang him sure!"

"He deserves to hang!"

"Then let the baron turn him in."

"The baron's out cold," someone yelled.

"I'll give you my earnings for a month if you let him go," persisted Brise.

Philip's mind was too numb to fully appreciate the exchange, and the next thing he knew, his body was hitting the dirt outside. The last thing he saw before darkness overtook him was his rucksack hitting the street next to him.

Arnaud's voice was more like a dream than reality. "If I see your cursed face again, you'll hang for sure!"

23

L et's go before those miserable lords wake up!"
    "And leave this poor sot to hang?"
"Better him than us."
"*Sí*, Theo. He'd be dead already if we hadn't lent a hand."
"'Tis just why we are now responsible for him."

The voices drifted down to Philip, lying prostrate in the street, his face buried in the mud. Rolling over he opened his eyes, but the shapes hovering above him were fuzzy and seemed to undulate, as if they were spirits instead of solid forms. He tried to rise, but the previous act of rolling had set his innards to undulating as badly as the things around him. Unwilling to further humiliate himself by vomiting, he fell helplessly back into the mud.

"Come on, he's awake. He can look out for himself."

"I hear a ruckus inside. Those blighters are awake!"

"Let's go, Theo, before they realize we helped the fool!"

Even in his woozy state, Philip grasped the gist of the voices. I'll be hanged indeed if I need any help! he thought. He struggled harder to rise, made more difficult because there was nothing upon which to brace himself and the street was muddy. When helpful hands reached for him, he brushed them aside.

"Leave me!" he spat along with a mouthful of mud.

He managed to get up on one knee, but when he attempted to bring his other leg up, it slipped in the slime and he went sprawling again. In despair he could now hear yells and shouts from inside the tavern.

Suddenly his whole world spun out from under him. The figures that a moment ago were leaning over him were now at eye level. Then, in another instant, all he could see was a huge blankness which, when his senses cleared a little, he realized was the coarse homespun cloth on the back of one of his reluctant helpers. He hated needing their help, hated being at the mercy of strangers. Hadn't that been the case since the moment he'd set foot on the Continent? Or in reality, his entire cursed life! His mother's family, his father, aiding him out of duty and pity, not because they wanted to. Probably even Beatrice had been kind to him out of pity rather than love.

What was left of his pride vanished when the man who had hoisted him over his shoulder began running. It had to be the big customer who had given him a coin earlier, for he would be the only man who could have not only lifted him with such ease but also run—not a lumbering trot but a full-out run!

This may have saved Philip, but it also proved his undoing. The jostling motion made him jerk and sway sickeningly until his stomach finally emptied itself—all over his rescuer's backside!

The big man cursed. "Oh, you'll pay for that, you scurvy worm!"

Amazingly, the fellow did not pitch Philip aside then and there.

Philip faded into oblivion once again as the man kept running. He woke briefly when the jostling ceased for a few moments. Apparently his rescuers were haggling with a gatekeeper.

"Thought you were a friend."

"*Oui,* but that looks like trouble."

"Give him the coins, Gilly—"

"Not from my portion!"

"From mine, then. Would have just gone to drink anyway."

Soon Philip's body began to bounce again against the big man's back. He was certain he would lose what was left in his stomach.

"L-let me d-down," he stammered.

"Not till we've put some distance 'tween us and those lords."

The fellow was hardly out of breath. "I c-can w-walk!"

"You've got pluck, I'll say! But you'll slow us down."

Thankfully, a few moments later Philip faded out and knew no more until he felt a painful thump as he was deposited on the hard ground. When he tried to open his eyes, the world still spun around before them. He turned aside and vomited for a second time.

"We've helped him enough, Theo. Let's slit his throat and put him out of his misery." Philip recognized the voice as belonging to the big man's wiry companion, the one he had called Gilly.

A booming laugh responded.

Philip wanted to agree with the wiry fellow. Surely he was better off dead. He must have fulfilled his oath to Beatrice by now. Yet anger was stronger than resignation. They were mocking him! Laughing at him! Let them kill him if they chose, but he would not lie back in his own vomit and accept it without a fight.

"You foul blackguards!" he cried, twisting and clawing at the ground, trying to rise. "Mock me, will you!"

He got to one knee, using the tree he'd been lying near to brace himself. Again his innards heaved and his head spun, but focusing on his anger, he pushed aside all else.

The big man knelt beside him and laid a hand on his shoulder. "Be at ease, lad—"

Philip seized the opportunity of being on a level with the man and swung his fist, striking the fellow square on the chin.

Instantly the big man's ham-sized hand grasped Philip by the neck, lifting him off the ground and slamming him up against the tree trunk.

"Why, you ungrateful muck-faced sot!" It was the first time in all that had occurred that Philip had heard the man's voiced raised. The sound of that voice was as if the oak upon which Philip's body was now pinned had cracked and fallen to the earth with an ear-shattering boom. Philip winced with the sound and with the truth of the man's words.

"You're laughing at me!" Philip said weakly, barely able to get speech past the man's grip.

"And laughable you are, you pathetic worm!"

Indeed, Philip felt like a worm pinned to a log by a mean child. Still, he could not give it up. Knowing that he was a laughingstock, pathetic, a worm, only fueled his temper. He swung his fists again, but the big man's arms were so long, Philip could not touch him.

The big man laughed once more, and Philip kept swinging.

The wiry fellow stepped forward wielding a dagger. "Come, Theo, have done wi' him before he remembers his feet and kicks you in your privates."

Now Philip felt more foolish than ever. He'd had a clear shot where he could have hurt the big man most but had not been thinking clearly enough to take advantage of it.

Immediately Theo let go of Philip, and he collapsed to the ground.

The swarthy man spoke, though Philip did not understand him, for he spoke a confusing mixture of French and another language. Spanish, Philip thought. As the man spoke Philip took more careful note of the big man's other two companions. The dark-haired Spaniard was certainly the better looking of the four men with his dark hair wavy and thick, the lines of his jaw well formed and strong. Philip was struck with the thought that he could have been a Moorish prince.

Because the fourth companion had remained silent, Philip had taken little note of him, but he was not a man to be easily ignored. When he removed his cloth cap to wipe the sweat from his brow, Philip was surprised to see that his brown hair was tonsured like a monk's. His features, though, grim and hard, were in no way monkish. He looked like he could kill without thought and enjoy it.

Theo spoke. "My friend here reminds me that we should not tarry long. Those lords will come after you, no doubt, and us, as well, for helping you."

"You keep implying that you helped me," Philip said, "but beyond carrying me from the city—an act which the barons could not know because they didn't see you do so—I saw no man fighting at my side."

The wiry man growled, the dagger in his hand twitching.

"Wait, Gilly," said Theo. "The boy makes a point despite his despicable lack of gratitude."

The one called Gilly snorted. "Do you think we were fools enough to get into the middle of a fight with two lords—mean sons of devils though they were?"

"What he means," explained Theo, "is that we lent a more subtle hand."

Philip now recalled a few instances during the fight when some assistance had been most conveniently timed. "The tray?" he asked. "The second baron . . . ?"

"*Oui*, that was us," said Theo. "But my greatest pleasure was cracking the little misbegotten devil on his head at the end—with his own mug at that! I thought if you could still walk, you'd need time while the fellow was unconscious to get away. As it turned out, you couldn't walk."

"Why?" Philip asked, bewildered.

"Why not?" countered Theo with a laugh. "We came to the city for a bit of fun, and it was the least we could do to thank you for so ably providing it."

Philip rankled once more at the mockery in the man's tone even though it was uttered in good nature. Then he remembered that they had saved him, and he had truly been ungrateful.

"Mayhap I behaved rashly toward you," Philip conceded.

Gilly grunted.

"All right!" Philip added, "If thanks you wish, then . . . my thanks you have."

The Spaniard spoke in an urgent tone. "*Vámonos!*"

"Rodrigo is getting nervous," Theo said. "'Tis time we were on our way."

Loath to accept more help from these strangers, Philip did not move.

"Do you expect me to carry you again?" demanded Theo.

"No, of course not! Neither do I expect you to help me further." What he did not admit was that his leg had been wrenched, probably when he had been tossed from the tavern, and was now cramping so that he feared he could not move it.

"Listen to him, Theo," Gilly said. "He'll only slow us down."

"You know I have always been partial to worms, Gilly." Theo reached out a hand to Philip. "I'll warrant you've no place else to go."

When Philip made no move toward the proffered hand, Theo grabbed Philip's arm and pulled him to his feet. Pain shot up his wrenched right leg and it buckled, nearly sending him back down. Theo caught him and slung him once more over his shoulder. Philip tried to protest, but the big man seemed to hear nothing as he propelled himself into an easy jog.

Their progress was not so frenzied now; nonetheless they moved quickly through the woods. After a few minutes Philip had to close his eyes because the movement began to upset his insides again. Amazingly, he fell asleep at some point. When he opened his eyes next, the forest was lightening with dawn. He guessed it must have been around midnight when the fight had begun in Arnaud's tavern. So they'd been in flight for several hours. Vaguely he recalled a few stops for rest along the way. Theo had deposited Philip upon the ground, but he had been too groggy with sleep to take note nor to care further when Theo slung him again over his shoulder to continue the journey. He had many questions to ask but could not find the will to speak during the brief rests.

Who were these men? Why did the big man seem to care what happened to him? Where were they taking him?

Even in his near-senseless state, he had a small inkling of the answer at least to the first question. Surely they were outlaws. The silent one and the wiry one named Gilly were definitely murderers. The Spaniard certainly was no farmer. Theo was harder to place. He had the power to kill at will, but

Philip could just as easily see him behind a plow or swinging a scythe at harvest.

Well, it was fitting that the only souls on Earth who saw fit to aid him were outlaws.

Before dawn fully lit the skies, or what could be seen of the sky through the thick canopy of trees overhead, they splashed across a shallow stream and then began to ascend a rocky slope. Theo started showing his first signs of fatigue on the steep climb. Philip heard great puffs of breath and felt the heaving of his huge chest.

"Let me down," Philip said. "You'll kill yourself."

"We've not much farther," Theo replied.

They reached higher ground now, rough and rocky, with a dense growth of trees. What light penetrated the woods was dim and gloomy, for the early autumn day was cloudy. Because there was no view of the sun, Philip had no idea in which direction they were headed. He could not tell if they had gone north, south, east, or west from Paris. If he had struck out on his own when they had first stopped, he would have been hopelessly lost by now. But his companions appeared to know exactly where they were going.

It wasn't long before they finally stopped, and Philip knew even before Theo said, "Home at last!" that they had reached their destination.

With a sigh of relief the big man dumped Philip onto the ground, and Philip was no less relieved to have the constant jostling ended. He thought it would take a week for his innards to right themselves. Though his eyes were mere swollen slits now, he was able to take note of his surroundings. They were in a large clearing in a thick stand of trees. Two crude lean-tos, constructed between stout tree trunks, were the only concessions to habitation, but nevertheless there was a lived-in, almost homey feel to the place. A fire pit built with a circle of stones had an iron frame over it where game might be roasted. The pit was cold now, but Philip could picture an inviting warm fire dancing in it, hissing every now and then as the juices of a roasting rabbit splashed among the flames. He could almost smell the delicious fragrance of sizzling game and realized that despite his touchy stomach, he hadn't eaten anything for hours and could well do justice to a good joint of meat.

The others must have felt the same way, for Gilly and the silent one set out immediately on a hunting expedition. Theo changed his breeches, which reeked of Philip's vomit. He took the fresh clothing from one of two chests stowed under the shelters. The Spaniard took a tinderbox from the same chest and began building a fire.

Philip stayed where he'd been dropped, watching the activities of the others with wonder. These men were indeed home, and this rustic camp was a far better home than he'd had in months. Though they were no doubt as displaced as he, they had managed to carve out a place where they belonged. In an odd way these men, doubtless killers and thieves all, had formed a sort of family. He was not as appalled as he should have been by what they surely were.

Theo came to the fire, which had begun to crackle nicely, and rubbed his hands over it.

"Well, Worm, what do you think?" he asked Philip. "'Tis not a tavern or a harlot's crib, but neither is it a ditch on the side of the road, eh?"

"What are you saying?" Philip asked suspiciously. It shook him a bit that the fellow had described his own recent existence quite well.

"You look to be an urchin without home or hearth," Theo replied. "You look like all of us have looked at one time or another. So I am saying you can bide here till you recover your strength. We don't live like kings, but we seldom go hungry."

"Even in winter?" Philip cast a sidelong glance at the flimsy buildings.

"We survive like everyone else. I doubt most peasant huts are warm in winter, either. But at least we are free, not under any lord's thumb."

"Why do you make this magnanimous offer to me?" Philip asked with a touch of sarcasm.

"How much longer do you expect to survive on your own, lad?"

Philip had already come to the conclusion he would not last much longer as he was. He could now understand the practicality for even outlaws to band together. Yet it was still hard for him to accept help from others.

"What do you want from me in return?" he asked. "I obviously have nothing with which to pay you."

"We seldom have coin to pay our way. We all pitch in. And when we must seek . . . ah . . . revenue, we all pitch in equally with that, as well, and equally share the bounty."

"You steal."

"Only from those who can well afford it."

"You steal from the rich, then? And no doubt give to the poor."

Theo barked a hearty laugh. "You've listened to too many troubadours, Worm."

"I've never taken what wasn't mine," Philip said self-righteously, well knowing he'd stolen food to survive, but that he reasoned didn't count.

Theo snatched up Philip's hand. "What's this, then?" He turned the hand so the brand showed. "What crime was it that set a green lad such as you out in the world to fend for yourself?"

"Murder," Philip sneered. Perhaps it was time, for his own security, that these outlaws did not think him a completely helpless child.

Theo guffawed so loudly the birds in the trees overhead rustled and took flight. "Rodrigo, did you hear? The worm is a murderer. Ha, ha!"

"And I am a Spanish princess," said the Spaniard sourly, now speaking tolerable French though heavily accented. He had gone off to collect wood for the fire and had returned to hear the last part of the conversation.

"So you are the leader of this outlaw band?" Philip asked the big man, adroitly changing the subject. The less they knew of his past the better.

Theo shrugged. "Rodrigo, am I the leader?"

The Spaniard dumped a pile of branches next to the fire circle. "I will go to my death for you, Theobald LeFauve!" Amazingly there was no mockery in his voice. He stood tall and proud, his dark features fell and noble.

Theo himself looked rather taken aback by the response. He cleared his throat and stammered, "Well . . . ah . . . and I'd go to my death for you, as well, my friend."

"Do the others feel the same?" Philip asked, astonished.

"You'd have to ask them," Theo said.

"Did you take the rest of them in as you have offered to do with me?"

"No. One thing and another led us together."

Rodrigo dropped a branch onto the fire and hunkered down on the ground. "Theobald saved my life many years ago in Toledo. Though by then the Christians had conquered the city, it had once been the center for the Muslim religion. My mother and I had traveled there from Granada, where the Christian Spaniards had forced all infidels to dwell. She wanted me to just once in my life look upon the fabulous mosques built there."

"You are an infidel?" asked Philip, astonished.

"My father was a Christian, but my mother was Muslim." He arched a brow slyly. "I am . . . undecided. Not so my mother. She was proud of what she was, even when some local thugs in Toledo took it into their heads to burn her at the stake, and me with her. They had only to set a torch to the dry branches at our feet when Theo came along. Ten Christian thugs were no match for his sword—"

"Though you were but a boy of twelve, you fought hard once I cut your bonds and put an enemy sword into your hand," Theo interjected.

"Ha! I knew little of the sword then and would have been quickly cut down if it hadn't been for you." Rodrigo rubbed the neatly trimmed black beard on his chin. "Thanks to you we escaped, and so it is two lives I owe to you—my mother's and my own!"

"A pity she died so soon afterward from wounds she received in the battle. What a woman she was! She fought like a lioness herself. Any debt you may have owed has been repaid many times over since then."

The Spaniard did not appear convinced, but he remained silent, focusing attention on tending the fire. Philip considered what had been said. Perhaps he could do worse than throw his lot in with these men. He was little better than an outlaw himself. Moreover, he'd tried to live his life in a moral, upright way, and where had it gotten him? Accused of crimes he did not commit, penniless, wandering alone, and starving. Maybe he had a right to devote his life to stealing from the very nobles who rejected him. He was about to inform Theo that he'd made a decision when the other two outlaws returned, each carrying a brace of rabbits. He was distracted from speaking on this matter as his companions focused on preparing a meal. First, however, there was an argument over whether to roast the game or to boil them in a stew. The silent outlaw had gathered some edible roots and savory herbs and, though wordless, made his opinion on the matter clear. The Spaniard wanted roasted meat and made his stand just as evident, lapsing into Spanish as his excitement grew. Gilly was arguing with both men, trying unsuccessfully to calm them, while Theo watched with detached amusement.

Apparently the rabbits had been found in snares set by the Spaniard, who felt that gave him the prerogative in how to cook them. The silent one, however, had expended the effort to check the snares and find the other ingredients. What Philip did not understand was why such a minor disagreement should ignite such passion.

"Why don't they cook two one way and two the other?" Philip suggested to Theo.

Theo shook his head. "This has less to do with cooking rabbits, Worm, than it does with religion."

"Religion?"

"Rodrigo is an infidel, oui?"

"He said he didn't know."

"Well, in Pippin's mind there is no question."

"Pippin is the silent one?"

"Oui. So sorry we haven't made proper introductions. We have not learned your name, either."

"Philip," he responded, his voice rising to be heard over the escalating argument of the others. "What has religion to do with it?"

"The vow of silence may be the only vow Pippin keeps these days from his years as a monk, but he still keeps his faith. He cannot help holding Rodrigo in contempt—"

Just then Philip and Theo had to duck as Pippin's brace of rabbits flew over their heads in a miscalculated launch by the silent one, who had intended them to strike the Spaniard. With a resigned sigh, Theo heaved to his feet.

"Enough!" he bellowed.

Instant silence met his words. Though he claimed no leadership of this group, his was surely the voice of authority.

"I don't want my meat bruised, whether stewed or roasted," he added more quietly. "We will let our guest make this most momentous decision." With a wink, he turned toward Philip. "What will it be, lad?"

The others swung their heads in Philip's direction, as well, and none seemed pleased. Philip rather liked the sense of power he suddenly felt, though the sensible part of him knew it was fleeting and meaningless. Still, he gave the matter careful thought before speaking, and he surprised himself by not taking the easy way of compromise.

"Stew them!" he said. It would take longer, and he was starved, but a warm broth would be soothing to his stomach. Moreover, he was far less afraid of the Spaniard than he was of the ex-monk.

24

Philip did not like playing a helpless decoy. In the several days since he'd come to the outlaw camp, he had recovered from his battering and now wanted to prove his worth to his new friends, if he could truly call them friends. The Spaniard was aloof; the wiry one had argued vehemently against his staying in the camp; the silent one was, well, silent. As for Theo, he treated Philip like a lost child, and Philip thought he might burst if he was called Worm one more time. Yet part of him did not voice his ire at this because he thought it an apt description of himself.

When, after several days, Rodrigo returned to camp from a scouting expedition with a report that a small caravan of nobles was passing through the forest, Philip had rebelled at being told he would act as a decoy to draw the nobles into a trap. He argued for a more substantial role in the attack.

"Attack!" boomed Theo with a laugh. "God preserve us if it should come to that!"

"How else will you waylay the caravan?"

Gilly grimaced and rolled his eyes. "We are doomed if we take this stupid puppy along."

Philip rose up angrily before the wiry thief. "I will not be mocked!"

He'd been itching from the start to throttle the man who had protested against Theo's offer to allow him to stay in the camp and persisted in belittling him. Unlike Theo's pet name of Worm, which seemed in good nature, Gilly's insults held a sincere edge. Of all the men, Gilly, or Gilbert de Rennes, as Philip learned was his full name, was the most annoying and unpleasant. He was as tough as an old bull and, unfortunately, had the temperament of an old bull, as well. He was not only dangerous but also meanspirited. Even Hugh Pippin, the ex-monk, had more of a rein on the seething volcano within him. Gilly had no rein, and his saving grace was that it was no volcano in him but more of a sparking flint. He spoke his mind, seemingly a foul, churlish hotbed for all the disagreeable remarks spouting from it. He no doubt reveled in having a new target for his abuse, the others having long since learned to turn a deaf ear to him.

Gilly immediately raised his fists defensively. "Come on then, ye bone-headed dolt. Show us what you've got!"

Philip prepared to swing, but his arm was caught midair in the vise of Theo's grip.

"Let me go!" Philip yelled. "He deserves a thrashing!"

"I've no argument there," Theo said, still holding back Philip's arm. "If you want to be any use to us, however, you have to learn not to go off like a spark in dry brush. I'm beginning to believe you did commit murder."

"I did not! I was falsely accused." He gave his arm a hard wrench, freeing it, then stood glowering at his companions.

Theo nodded, appearing not in the least surprised by this admission. If Philip had once hoped to instill fear into them by claiming to be a murderer, he had certainly failed. His admission now seemed to make no change in their low perception of him.

Theo said, "Methinks you and Gilly are not so different. You've both a querulous nature, only Gilly renders his with his tongue while you do so with your fists."

When Theo paused, Gilly snorted disdainfully. Philip's lip curled and he made a move toward the little thief. Theo stepped between them.

"Soon I will let you two at each other's throats, but for now we have other work." With his eyes, Theo dared them to dispute him. "And you, Worm, will be our decoy, because if I let you anywhere near a noble with that dagger of yours, there will be blood spilt. And though you may think us cutthroats and killers, we do not like to shed blood unless it is absolutely necessary. Even Pippin has some discretion in that area, right, Pip, my friend?"

The monk nodded grimly. No one, least of all Philip, believed him. Philip did, however, concede to the underlying truths of Theo's words. He also was no killer, yet there were times when it might feel good to slit a nobleman's throat. It might serve to ease the hunger in him to slit his brother's throat. He didn't want to find out.

"I don't want to hurt anyone," he conceded.

Gilly snorted again, this time with amusement. "As if you could—"

"Gilly!" warned Theo.

"What? A man can't speak freely anymore? I'd be better off a shackled serf on your father's fief—"

Theo cut in sharply. "Just show the sense God gave you, *mon ami*! Now, are we ready to do this thing?"

He turned and strode away without waiting for any response.

The Spaniard followed. Before Gilly joined him, he turned toward Philip. "When we return, I'll show you how to use that dagger of yours."

"I—" Philip was about to protest that he already knew how to use it but then realized the cantankerous thief was in his own way making a grand concession. "I would like that," Philip replied. Then they both followed the others into the woods.

The outlaws did not usually go about armed except for belt knives, so Philip was surprised that the chests in the camp held a varied assortment of weaponry—swords, bows and arrows, daggers, and short swords. Each man left the camp fully armed—except for Philip. Since he was to be the "helpless" decoy, he could wear no weapons save for his dagger tucked under his chemise at his back.

After hiking for well over a league, they came to a spot in the woods where they knew the caravan must pass and which lent itself to their plan. Everyone took his position. Gilly, Rodrigo, and Pippin shimmied up trees surrounding a small glade. Theo would have been too big for the trees, but he hid in the thick gorse, his drab clothes blending in well enough that he became nearly invisible. They all pulled hoods, with slits for their eyes, over their faces.

Philip could wear no hood, but Theo gave him a cap that would cover most of his hair, his most memorable aspect.

"Except for that smoldering fire upon your head, you look like any boy your age," Theo said. "If the hair's not showing, they'll quickly forget your face."

"Oh, thank you!" Philip replied dryly. "And I return the compliment."

"Come on, let's finish the job."

Philip rubbed dirt on his face and chemise and tore a sleeve. He thought it would look odd for him to appear so battered yet still have his cap neatly in place, but Theo insisted everything would happen so quickly no one would notice. Philip waited just off the side of the road, hardly able to breathe. He'd never robbed anyone before, though besides the murder of his father, he'd been accused of many lesser crimes, especially since returning to France. Oddly, the most fear he felt now came from not wanting to make a fool of himself in front of Theo, who had treated him decently and, despite his nefarious activities, appeared to be a good man. Philip had no great compunction about the robbery itself. With the exception of Beatrice, nearly everyone he'd ever met thought him guilty of some crime, be it only the accident of his birth. So what did it matter if he did commit a crime? Certainly he no longer cared about guarding his immortal soul. He'd given that up the day he'd lied to Father Bavent.

In a way, he was looking forward to the moment he heard the approach of horses. That moment would launch him upon a new course. Perhaps he'd fare better as a highwayman. Perhaps that was his destiny.

He heard the sounds of horses' hooves crunching over the uneven road, the snorting of horses and the jingling of harness. Rodrigo had said there was a litter borne by four horses in the caravan, along with several guards. It must be someone of import.

His heart pounding, he glanced up at the treetops to assure himself his cohorts were well hidden. He saw Pippin's bow, but only because he knew where to look. With dry mouth and sweaty palms he waited until the horses hit the precise spot Theo had indicated. It occurred to him that this could go terribly wrong and in a short span he could be dead. That still did not scare him.

The first horse hit the mark. Philip scrambled onto the road.

"Help me! Please help!" he cried, limping into view, leaning heavily on a stout tree branch.

The mounted knight at the lead of the caravan held up a hand, and the others quickly came to a stop.

"Out of the way, *bouffon!*" ordered the lead knight.

Philip quickly noted there were a half-dozen knights in rich equipage of silver and purple, all well armed. The litter was curtained in ornate red-and-gold brocade. This was a rich noble indeed!

"Please, I am injured," Philip pleaded. "I twisted my leg in a rabbit hole. My bones are surely broken."

"That is no affair of ours. Stand aside."

Just as the curtain of the litter was pulled back, Theo made his move, leaping into the path just beyond Philip. The guards immediately went for their swords, but before they could draw them, an arrow struck one of the upright beams of the litter. A woman screamed.

"No one need be hurt," Theo fired in that commanding voice he used seldom but to great effect when he did. "I've a dozen archers trained upon you, so it would be unwise to make another move."

The trees rustled and Rodrigo, Gilly, and Pippin came into view, holding bows with arrows at the ready, one pointed at the lead knight's unprotected throat, while the remaining two targeted other knights. A tense moment passed as the knights gauged their chances of success in a pitched battle. Even if there were no more than three archers, it would mean three knights would be cut down immediately, leaving the other three against at least five outlaws, perhaps more if Theo's words were to be believed.

"Do you hold your coin dearer than your lives or that of your lady?" Theo asked, surely voicing the exact debate in the knights' minds. "Remove your weapons."

The lead knight signaled for his men to stand down. As the men tossed their swords and daggers onto the ground, the knight said, "We are not foolish enough to travel in these woods with treasure under guard of such a small entourage."

"We seek not a king's ransom. What coin you have on your persons will be enough. Kindly give them to my young friend." Theo nodded toward Philip. "Go, Worm."

The knights quickly divested themselves of their purses, though it was a small booty since knights were notoriously nearly as penniless as their master's serfs. Yet these had more than most, for no doubt they were headed to Paris. Philip hesitated as he approached the litter. He found only a woman and her maid inside. The lady, in her middle years, was dressed in a luxurious wool frock with a fur collar. Around her thick waist was a silver belt and at her neck, framing a double chin, was a brooch with a large ruby circled by what looked like diamonds.

Philip didn't mind at all taking the coins from the knights, but it seemed different to steal from a lady, especially since she and her maid were trembling and appeared on the verge of tears. He glanced at Theo.

"Hurry up!" Theo said. "I'm sure these good people are anxious to be on their way."

As he had done with the knights, Philip pictured in his mind other faces, ones that he'd be happy to steal from. "Your purse, please," Philip said to the woman, trying to copy Theo's easy yet firm tone.

"Oh, we have nothing," the woman said shakily. "We've been to market and spent—"

"M'lady, methinks you are heading in the wrong direction for that," said Theo, who had come up to Philip's side. "Please, my archers are growing restless."

"Oh, dear me!" The lady seemed on the verge of swooning, but she turned toward her maid, who frantically dug among their belongings stowed in the litter.

A large leather purse, fairly bulging with coins, was produced. Philip took it and tucked it, with the booty from the knights, into a sack he'd strapped to his back. Then the lady reached for her brooch. This certainly was valuable enough for a king's ransom.

"Forbear, my lady!" Theo said. "We seek only coin. Your jewels would look a pretty sight on me, I fear."

"Thank you, sir. 'Twas my mother's, and I am loath to lose it."

Theo bowed gallantly. "I am a thief, my lady, not a villain." The lead knight grunted at that, but wisely Theo chose to ignore it. "Be off with you, then."

"I'll see that you all hang one day for this," threatened the knight.

"I'm sure you will," Theo replied in a genial tone. "But not today. Now, I would make haste if I were you. My men do not like to nock their arrows without putting them to use." He slapped the rump of the knight's mount, and the entourage lumbered into motion, making way as quickly as it could without greatly upsetting the litter.

Philip stood in the middle of the road watching the retreat, mouth slightly ajar. Even though his knees were trembling, he felt a strange exhilaration.

"Let's also be off, Philip," Theo said. "Those knights will get the lady a safe distance away and then surely a few will return for their swords and will hunt for us."

Philip shook away the strange euphoria and bent down to gather up the weapons.

"Leave them. They'll be too hard to sell without exposing us for thieves, likewise with the lady's jewels. We are not greedy, and we have enough coin to buy ale for a month."

Philip looked longingly at the swords. How he would like to wield one once again and show his new companions that he wasn't the babe they thought him to be. "May I just take one for my own use, not to sell?"

"All right. Take the plain one there. Less chance of it being identified should we ever meet those knights again. Now hurry."

Philip strapped the sword on and then sprinted into the woods after Theo.

"Where are the others?" he asked when he was close.

"They are long gone, all by different routes so we will be harder to track. You'll stay with me until you know the woods better."

Philip liked to think that was the truth and it wasn't because of the booty he carried. At least the others had enough trust of Theo to let him guard Philip!

They ran for a while, easing the pace at times, until they had gone a few furlongs. Then they slowed to a brisk walk, and Theo took care with covering their tracks. Finally, after about an hour he permitted them to pause for a rest. They hunkered down beneath some trees.

"So, Worm, did you enjoy yourself?" Theo asked.

Philip nodded. "More than I expected."

"I can tell you've been genteelly raised, so I feared you might balk at the last minute."

"All I did was picture my half-brother's face on those knights and his mother's face on the lady; then I was happy to relieve them of their gold."

"Ah, bad blood between you and your brother?"

"You could say that."

Theo arched a brow. "Was it he that you murdered?"

"I murdered no one!" Philip felt foolish for his self-righteous tone. He was a thief now, almost as bad as a murderer, so he had no right to be so sanctimonious. He added, "It was my father, who I was *accused* of murdering, my brother being the loudest voice against me."

"I can see where that might set the two of you at odds."

"He thought I threatened his inheritance. I was my father's bastard son, though he refused to claim me. I thought it was because he hated me, but I have come to believe there might be more to it. I think his wife poisoned him against me in favor of her son." Attempting to put it all into words was daunting. Philip realized even as he spoke that a complex maze of loyalties and betrayals was involved. "It still confuses me. But the worst of it is that I will never know my father's heart."

"At least there is a possibility he may have loved you." Theo threaded his fingers together and put his hands behind his head. He seemed no longer in a hurry.

Philip decided to broach a subject he'd been curious about. "What of your family? Gilly said something about your father's fief. Is your father a nobleman also?"

Theo grunted. "Gilly has a big mouth." He paused, seeming to consider whether to say more. Then he continued, "I had a brother, too. Only we were close. He was older than I, but as the fates would have it, I was bigger and stronger. If we'd been a litter of puppies, he would have been the runt. He was pale and thin and sickly. He lost his breath often and would cough and wheeze and turn blue. Nevertheless we both trained for the knighthood on a neighboring fief. Everyone told my father it was a waste of money to train Robert because he might die at any time. My father had a special fondness for him, though. I suppose it was because for five years he was his only heir, and there had been many times when he nearly died only to revive, bringing great joy to my parents."

"Surely they took joy in your birth, if for no other reason than as an assurance of the continuation of the family name?"

"As you must know from your experience, these matters are never simple. By the time I was ten, I was taller than my father and nearly every man on the land. People said God was making up for my brother's lack."

"Did he resent you for that?"

"No. Robert was a good-hearted person. He just laughed and said he was thankful he had a big brother to protect him. Deep inside he ached to be normal yet didn't hold my strength against me. My father expected me to protect him, but we tried to be subtle about it so as not to bruise his manhood unduly." He paused, rubbing his face with his big fists. "We best be on our way. I'm hungry and we won't get dinner until we reach camp."

They started on their way again, walking side by side when the woods allowed. Philip could not ignore his curiosity. "What happened to your brother, Theo?"

"I don't enjoy speaking of it, but doubtless you'll pester me until you know the whole of it."

Of all the unusual characters in the outlaw band, Theo was the greatest mystery. Philip would never have guessed him to be the son of a nobleman, a wealthy one at that if he could afford to finance two sons in knighthood training.

"All right!" Theo said with a resigned sigh. "Robert and I became knights. Everyone knew Robert's knighthood had been bought, yet still it made him happy. Soon it wasn't enough, though, and he wanted to compete with me in the tournaments. I let him come along as my second, though he did not cease begging me to let him compete. Finally, I thought if he entered a contest just once, it might satisfy him. It was a joust. I arranged it so that his opponent was a friend who agreed to take it easy."

"Something went wrong," Philip guessed.

Theo responded with a slow, sad nod. "Just as the contest was to begin, a crack of thunder caused Robert's horse to rear in a panic. He fell to the ground. Most men would have quickly rebounded from such a fall, but Robert's bones were weak. His neck snapped like a dry twig. He died instantly."

"I'm sorry, Theo."

"I could not even tell him farewell."

"It was the same with me and my father."

"Then you understand my grief and that of my father." But something in Theo's eyes said he still did not comprehend it all fully. "I blamed myself. My father blamed me, as well. He called me a murderer and banished me from his lands. I went willingly. Gilly wanted to raise a rebellion. I might have gathered enough knights to support me, but I had no heart for it."

"Gilly was with you then? Gilly was a knight?"

Theo chuckled. "Hard to believe, I know. He was a good one, too! And loyal."

They walked for a time in silence. The entire wood was silent except for the sounds of birds and the rustling of the wind in the trees and their footsteps crunching over the path. They were alone. No knights were after them. With fresh wonder, Philip was reminded that he was a thief and an outlaw. Yet he felt oddly justified.

"Theo, our fathers gave us no choice other than to take the path we have."

"Ah, Worm, we did indeed have choices. But neither you nor I are the kind of men to accept subservient poverty. We chose our way, make no mistake."

All right, Philip thought with a touch of defiance. I chose, and I will live with that choice.

England
December 1264

"L eticia, I'm frightened!"

"Please, Lady Beatrice, you mustn't be." Leticia wiped a cloth over her lady's brow. "I have often believed you were built well for this."

"My mother died in childbirth and my stepmother, as well," moaned Beatrice. "My father has lost three infant sons. And your mother, too, Leticia."

"Don't speak of such things," implored the midwife, who had been summoned some time earlier. "It will bring a bad omen."

"I can't help it! That's all I can—" Suddenly another pain gripped her. It pressed on her stomach like a vise—a vise with a knife in it! She screamed until her throat was raw.

The chamber door opened a crack. "Please! Tell me she lives."

"Lord Sardwick!" One of the maids in attendance scurried to the door. "You shouldn't be here."

"I heard the screams . . . I feared . . ." The man looked haggard beyond his sixty-one years. His skin was gray, and every line was deeper than ever.

Leticia called in a soothing voice, "M'lord, your wife is fine. I told her it would feel better if she screamed. Now you must go."

"I am praying for her," he said.

"That is exactly what you should be doing," Leticia replied.

"Beatrice, I'm . . . sorry!" he added in a pathetic-sounding tone.

The dreadful pain had passed, but Beatrice offered no encouraging word to her husband. Nigel—after a year of marriage she still felt strange using his given name, for he'd always be Uncle Sardie in her mind—deserved better treatment. He was a good man, always treating her kindly. She had hoped after the marriage that he'd be off to London, like her father, attending to the needs of Simon de Montfort's new government. But he seemed to think it a greater priority to produce an heir.

Despite his constant presence and doting attendance, she simply could not feel entirely comfortable around him. She dreaded his nightly visits to her bed. True, he was kind to her, and when they were intimate, he was tender and considerate. But she didn't feel passion for him as she had for Philip, nor did her heart race at the mere thought of seeing him.

There was not even a hint of that with her husband. Leticia admonished her that she was not giving her husband a fair chance by holding him to the standard of an eighteen-year-old youth. Maybe Nigel's whiskers were scratchy and his aged lips did tremble a bit, but he had other attributes she would do well to dwell upon instead. He made her laugh with his amusing tales and sleight-of-hand tricks. And despite their vast age difference, he never treated her like a child. He was quick with praise and admiration of her abilities. She definitely could have done worse for a husband.

After she discovered she was with child, he never touched her in an intimate way again. In fact, husband and wife then relaxed a great deal, and much to her surprise, Nigel became an amiable companion. Yet Beatrice dreaded two things. First that she'd lose the child, and second, that she would have a girl and then would have to start over again until she produced a son.

For the entire duration of her pregnancy Beatrice had slept on her right side because Leticia said this would ensure a boy. Leticia had wanted to prick Beatrice's finger and squeeze a drop of her blood into a bowl of pure spring water. "If the blood floats it will be a girl," she said. "If it sinks, then you will have a boy."

But Beatrice didn't want to make the test. She was afraid to know the truth.

During this time, civil war and general unrest continued to plague England, for as it turned out, the victory of the previous summer had been a tenuous one. The king had managed to get to France and there had enlisted the support of the French king, Louis IX, who agreed to arbitrate the English conflict. Prince Edward had remained in England and was building loyalist support. Seeing his own support wane, Simon de Montfort agreed to have Louis arbitrate. In January of 1264 Louis found in favor of Henry, shocking the country and inciting more unrest. The ferment ripened further when the new pope, Urban IV, also a Frenchman, threw his weight behind the two kings. De Montfort swore he would not abide by this unjust decision.

Inevitably, war erupted again, and Beatrice's personal problems faded when her husband was called to arms.

"But, Uncle—that is, Nigel—surely a man of your . . . ah . . . season in life would not be expected to fight in battle." She was concerned for him, but she was also afraid of being alone during the early months of her confinement, when she'd heard so many women experienced miscarriages.

"Lord Leicester needs every able man at his side, my dear. I will not abandon a cause that claimed my own son. And I am not so old that I cannot wield a sword." But he added in concession, "Do not fear. A large contingent of knights will be left here, for I fear the fighting may come close to home."

He'd been right about that. The bulk of the fighting took place less than five leagues away, near the town of Lewes. At least it was over quickly, and Simon de Montfort's forces defeated the king once and for all. Henry and Edward were captured. That had been in May. Following the victory Lord Leicester had once again taken the reins of government. But when Lord Sardwick returned home, he reported that all was not running as smoothly as they might have hoped.

"The barons in the north refuse to accept the Peace of Canterbury, which the king and the prince signed," he told his wife.

"Then it is not really over?" Beatrice asked with dismay.

"I hate to burden you with these tidings," Lord Sardwick said. "Not in your condition."

"I want to know," she said petulantly. "Will there be more war?"

He shrugged. "I believe the northern barons can be brought to heel if the king stays firm to his word. With them subdued, it will greatly weaken the young upstarts in the west."

By *young upstarts,* he was referring to a contingent of men, mostly of Prince Edward's age, who the prince had insisted be released from captivity after the rout at Lewes. These had immediately fled to the west and continued to rattle their swords, a situation that worsened when Edward escaped his captors and joined them.

"Nigel, is it true Gareth Aubernon helped the prince escape?"

"Yes, I believe so. He is certainly among those young nobles in the west. He has no place else to go, since his estate is occupied by a force loyal to Simon."

Beatrice shuddered, for she knew that had circumstances not been what they were, she very likely would now be awaiting the birth of Gareth's child. And, as always when she thought of Gareth, images of Philip filled her mind. If life had truly been kind to her, it would be Philip's child in her womb. Sometimes, though perhaps it was as wicked as adultery, she imagined that indeed she carried Philip's child, that the babe would be born with a shock of red hair and tender green eyes and a smile to melt her heart.

Dear God, what did I do to anger you so? How did I displease you so that I did not receive the desire of my heart?

Then her husband spoke, almost as if he'd been reading her thoughts. "The English clergy support the baronial cause," he was saying, "but many fear the pope will place us under an interdict for going against both Louis's and Urban's decision. This may weaken the barons' resolve and thereby shake the support we have from the common man."

An interdict would prevent the Sacraments from being performed in England, causing a huge hardship upon the people. Moreover, she would consider it God's personal judgment upon her if her child would be born without opportunity for the proper baptism.

"At least our child will be properly baptized before any such thing can happen," Lord Sardwick assured, apparently noting the look of dismay on her face. He gently patted Beatrice's arm.

She'd wondered about such an assurance. Anything could have happened between then and her expected time of confinement in December. But as time passed, the situation in the country did settle down. With the king confined at St. Paul's in London, where an eye could be kept on him, de Montfort set up a Council of Nine to oversee all the king's official actions. In reality, however, it was de Montfort who made the decisions of government. He staved off the threat of invasion from across the Channel with such lengthy negotiations with Louis that it strained Queen Eleanor's finances to the point that the troops and ships she had been holding for such a purpose had to be dispersed.

Sardwick and a contingent of his knights had been called to London once again in November when there had been a flare-up of tempers at an attempt by the pope to excommunicate de Montfort. Beatrice feared that she'd be alone when her time came. She had written to her father and implored him to come home, to which he'd replied that he would do the best he could. She knew he would not be able to get away. At the least she would have Leticia. Moreover, men were not permitted near a birth anyway.

She could not contain her joy when her husband arrived, accompanied by her father, shortly before the final days of her confinement.

"I was so certain you wouldn't make it," she said.

"And miss the birth of my first grandchild?" Her father had laughed, and she was reminded how dear he was to her. The time apart and the stresses of her marriage had conspired to make her almost forget the days when she had been young and he had been the center of her life. Not that it had been all that long ago! Less than two years since Philip had nudged her father slightly off-center. Had he felt the shifting of her focus? Was that why he stayed away, using the needs of the country to fill the emptiness left in him by the changing of her girlish affections? She supposed that's what growing up meant. If only she could tell him that with Philip's departure she had needed her father that much more. Save for that obscure mention of him in her father's letter offering Lord Sardwick as a marriage candidate, neither she nor her father ever spoke of Philip.

"How long before you must go?" Beatrice asked.

"I will not leave until the child is born," her husband responded.

Beatrice had actually intended the question for her father. She added off-handedly, "And you, Papa?"

"I must leave the moment Simon summons me. I hope it won't be for several days. The first parliament meeting of the new government will be in the middle of the month, so it will be over by Christmas. I must attend that. But regardless, you have Nigel. I thank God every day for your marriage and the protection it gives you, since I am away so much."

She offered her father a brave smile, but inside she was thinking that she cursed God for the marriage. No! It wasn't that bad. Her husband was never drunk, nor did he beat her. And he was attentive. God, forgive me. I am a fool to even think of cursing you. It's just that . . . Oh, I am being a child. This is all for the best. And soon, as Leticia so often reminds me, I will have a little child to love who will fill the emptiness inside me.

Another wrenching pain brought her abruptly back to the present.

The midwife lifted away Beatrice's bedcovers and gently rubbed ointment over her bulging belly. The gesture seemed to help, and she didn't scream as loudly when the next pain wrenched her. But it went on for hours and hours. It had begun in the small hours of the night and seemed no closer to its conclusion when she saw the light of dawn brighten the windows. The new day wore on, and the lines of worry etching Leticia's face did not soothe her. Beatrice felt like a wet rag, wrung out and tattered.

The midwife began to utter strange words in Beatrice's ear. What was she saying? They sounded like . . . incantations!

"Leticia! Leticia!" Beatrice cried out.

Her maid hurried to her bedside.

"Don't leave me!" Beatrice demanded. "Leticia, the midwife is a witch!"

"What?"

"No, m'lady," protested the midwife.

"What were you saying in my ear?"

"'Tis only words my mother taught me would help. I'm no witch. Truly!" The midwife was near to tears. "You must let me do something. This is taking overlong, m'lady."

"I-it doesn't usually take this long?"

Dismally the midwife shook her head. "Let me put this under your pillow." From her sash, she took a stone the size of a robin's egg.

"What is it?"

"Jasper, m'lady. It will help. My mama swears by it."

Beatrice was beginning to wish they'd got the girl's mother to act as midwife instead of this woman. She now seemed awfully young and green. Beatrice glanced at Leticia, who nodded.

"All right," she said shakily as another pain descended upon her.

Another hour passed. Then, to Beatrice's horror, the midwife began to press down hard upon her swollen abdomen.

"Stop!" she screamed. "You'll hurt my baby!"

"This will help speed it down the birthing canal."

"No!" Beatrice screamed. "It hurts. Stop!" Another pain shuddered through her. "Le-ti-ci-a! Make her stop!"

Beatrice hardly noticed when the woman's pressure ceased. The next pain was the worst yet. Another followed close on its heels. Then they came in rapid succession. How could she bear such agony? Screaming, she knew she was about to die.

"Blessed Virgin, save my baby!" she gasped, realizing that was all that mattered. Her own life was of little consequence compared to the baby's. It made no difference that it wasn't Philip's child. This was her baby, a life she had nurtured for the last nine months. She could not bear to live if the babe died.

For a time she was aware of little else but the pain until Leticia's voice penetrated her agony.

"You must push, Beatrice."

She wondered where she'd find the strength for any such effort, but suddenly she discovered within a need to do that very thing. And when she bore down, it was actually a relief. After a few strenuous efforts, she felt terribly weak.

"I can't . . . No more . . ."

"Once more, Bea!"

"I'm so tired."

"It'll be over soon."

From somewhere inside, she found that last shred of strength.

"His head! I see his head!" cried Leticia.

"Push again," ordered the midwife.

Amazingly it hadn't been the last shred at all. She found, if not the strength, then the will to push again.

"It's a boy!" Leticia announced.

A boy. Thank God! And, as if a responding chorus of hallelujahs, a peal of infant cries filled the room. My baby lives! And I live, as well.

She felt as though she might swoon, but she desperately wanted to see her child, so she willed herself to remain conscious. Hearing a splash of water, she turned in time to see the maids dip the baby into a small tub prepared for bathing the newborn. It seemed to take an eternity for them to clean and swaddle him, but the midwife insisted they take their time with this, for she would be responsible if the child's limbs were malformed from improper wrapping.

Finally Leticia brought the baby to her.

His hair wasn't red. He had no hair at all! He was bald and just a bit wrinkly. He looked indeed like his father!

"He won't always look like a little old man," said Leticia, as though reading her thoughts.

Beatrice smiled and took the babe in her arms. "I don't care. I thank dear Uncle Sardie for giving me this gift. I don't care what he looks like. He's mine, and I love him."

26

Edmond Alexander Fitzjohn gave Beatrice new purpose in life. He indeed helped to fill the emptiness in her left by Philip's departure. So much for such a little bit of a life. But everyone assured her he was quite large, as newborns went, thus her difficult labor. Once he was put to the breast of the wet nurse, his wrinkles filled out and he became wonderfully formed. A beautiful child with a tuft of fine, pale hair. Why, he hadn't been bald at all at birth. Beatrice had simply not looked closely enough! His eyes were as blue as the sea, as blue as his mother's.

Beatrice hated to be parted from him for even a moment. When they had taken him from her a mere hour after his birth in order to take him to the church to be baptized, she nearly became hysterical. Leticia tried to comfort her, telling her this was a good thing, for if he had been sickly, the midwife would have been compelled to baptize the child in the chamber immediately after his birth.

She also disliked the idea of another suckling her child, but all noble-women used wet nurses. Leticia had informed her that many peasant mothers nursed their own babies, and Beatrice envied them. She thought that if she and Philip had run off together, she would have lived like a peasant, and she then would have suckled Edmond herself. She often just sat and watched the nurse feed her son. The nurse would chide her for this indulgence, but she didn't care. When her own milk dried up shortly after the birth, she experienced several days of melancholy. She decided then and there that with her next child she would nurse him herself.

Her next child? Was she daft? Yet the memories of her painful travail had definitely faded. She indeed would like more children, but that would mean intimacy with Sardie again. Well, that would have to be her choice and her move since he'd already assured her he would not trouble her again.

For now, she was content with little Edmond.

A week after the birth, her father came to her. "After you are churched tomorrow, I must depart, my dear."

"I am so happy you were able to stay this long. I wish you could tarry long enough to celebrate Christmas with us." She was lounging on the chaise in her chamber, young Edmond tucked in the crook of her arm.

"I must return to London for the Parliament."

Smiling her understanding, she said, "He is so beautiful, isn't he, Papa?"

"You made me quite proud naming him for me."

"If it wasn't for your wisdom, I wouldn't have him." She gave her father's hand a tender pat.

"I thought I'd never hear those words from you. I feared you'd hate me eternally—"

"Never, Papa! I know I can be stubborn and spoiled—"

"Not you, my dear princess!" he laughed.

"Well, just a little!" She chuckled with him. Young Edmond stirred. "He makes me feel as if I have been reborn."

"I'm glad of it, Bea. All the past is forgotten, then?"

The merest crease quirked upon her brow. Then she nodded. She would not admit to him that part of her heart would always be hopelessly lost to a lowly groom. Best she not even admit it to herself, though that was all but impossible.

Lord Cassley grasped her hand. "I am proud of you, Bea. You are brave and strong. I wish your mother could be here to witness it. I wish she could see what a splendid mother you are."

"Do you truly think so?"

"Oh yes. It seems to come naturally to you."

She kissed him and he held his grandson for a time. Then he left and she didn't see him again until the next day.

Some women waited longer than a week for their churching, for it often took a considerable time to recover from the rigors of childbirth. However even they didn't wait too long because they were considered impure after giving birth and could not perform many basic tasks, such as making bread or serving food or, more importantly, touching holy water or taking the sacraments. Beatrice waited only a week so that her father could witness the ceremony and enjoy the celebration afterward.

Leticia insisted the day chosen not be a Friday, for this would make her barren. Also, she said it would bring bad luck if a wedding took place at the church on the same day. Beatrice had never realized how superstitious her maid was, but she complied with all the stipulations because she felt she needed every bit of luck she could get.

Many local noble families attended the ceremony. It was like old times, almost as if there wasn't a cauldron of civil unrest bubbling in the country. It was nearly as festive as her wedding, and she wore her wedding dress this day despite the fact that the waistline was tight and had to have a gusset inserted by the dressmaker. Leticia assured her she would lose her "baby weight" soon enough.

She entered the church holding a single candle and was met by Father Bavent. He marked her with the sign of the cross and sprinkled her with holy water. Then, with her hand on his stole, he accompanied her down the aisle. She was glad it was he who performed the rite. She had heard how he had helped Philip, and thereafter she had held a fondness for the priest.

At the altar, he said in Latin, "In the name of the Father and the Son and the Holy Ghost, enter ye into the House of God. Adore the Son of the Blessed Virgin, who has given you the gift of motherhood."

She heard the words and knew their truth, but mostly she wanted the ceremony to end so she could hold her child again.

The next morning she bid her father good-bye, not knowing when she'd see him again, and then she settled into life at Sardwick Castle. It took young Edmond to finally make the place feel like home to her. Before his birth, she'd been a brokenhearted girl in an unwelcome marriage, never feeling settled, always out of place. Now, because this was Edmond's home, his inheritance, it became her home, as well.

Sardwick was as dreary a castle as could be imagined. Apparently Nigel's first wife had been an extremely pious woman who believed any decoration beyond that of necessity was an evil extravagance. In truth, Beatrice thought the former lady was merely a miser who tried to couch it in spirituality. With Nigel's approval, Beatrice set out to make some changes, to make Sardwick her own. She ordered new tapestries from Brussels to replace the old worn ones on the walls of the great hall. She also bought new bedclothes and carpets. She chose such vivid colors that Leticia warned she might raise the disapproving specter of Lady Sardwick from the grave.

"I am Lady Sardwick now!" Beatrice laughed. "And you know what? Uncle Sardie is quite pleased with what I am doing. He said he likes the bright colors. I'll tell you something else. I always thought he was poor like my father because the castle always looked so threadbare and his knights looked like paupers. He tells me now it was because his wife kept a tight fist on the household coffers. I really should thank her, because I find that my husband is rather rich! He says that for Twelfth Night, he has ordered a tailor from London to come here and fit me for new gowns."

"So no more complaints, then, about your unlucky marriage?" Leticia asked smugly.

"What's the use?" Beatrice replied, frowning ever so slightly. She brightened suddenly. "I'll get a gown in silk. Poor Papa could never afford silk except for my wedding gown."

Winter passed and the new year of 1265 seemed filled with promise for the new wife and mother. It was not the life she desired, but it was not a bad life. Her baby filled her with exquisite joy, and her husband was a pleasant companion if nothing else. He still amused her with his magic, now lifting a silver penny from their baby's ear or making an egg disappear. When Edmond got older he would delight in his father's sleight of hand. Beatrice wondered at her contentment. Could it last forever?

Before long, though, the loyal barons were once more called to arms. Nigel informed her he must leave with his knights. She knew arguments were futile. He gave her one of his wet, scratchy kisses on her forehead. And, oddly, her heart ached with affection for the man. He kissed their son, then stiffly mounted his destrier and rode away. Something told her she would never see the dear old man again.

———

Lord Cassley rode hard with a contingent of about a dozen knights. Crossing the Severn River near the Welsh border, he hoped to reach Lord Leicester by nightfall. He further hoped his information was current and Simon was still in the Welsh stronghold in the Usk Valley. He had gone there some days ago with the intent first of obtaining the support of his Welsh ally, Llewellyn, and then of intercepting the western royalist forces in their stronghold near Worcester.

Looking back from the admittedly short vantage point of the last few months, Lord Cassley realized that the Great Parliament of December might well be counted the high point of Lord Leicester's rule of England. Not only did the majority of the most powerful English lords gather, but there were also many prosperous commoners in attendance—for the first time in history men not born of nobility were included in the high councils of the land. Of course, Simon knew that his power, unlike that of a hereditary king, depended greatly on the goodwill of the common man. Lord Cassley knew that Simon desired to throw off the bonds of feudalism altogether. The two of them had discussed the matter in private; however, for the sake of maintaining the loyalty of the barons, Simon guarded this aspiration closely.

Nevertheless, though the king was present and had his say, in the end it was Simon de Montfort's will that prevailed over all. Solemnly, King Henry and Prince Edward swore to uphold the terms of peace.

Shortly after Twelfth Night, when Edmond had sent letters to Beatrice and Nigel by the hand of a tailor hired to attend Lady Sardwick in acquiring a new wardrobe, he had written with great optimism about the direction of the new government. However, by May of 1265 it seemed the tide might be turning against the barons' cause.

After the death of Pope Urban IV the previous fall, his replacement proved an even more ardent enemy of Simon. The new pope, Cardinal Guy Fulcodi, had previously been sent as a legate to England in order to bring the rebel barons into line. A Frenchman, he was a zealous supporter of the absolute right of kings. It was he who, in a fury, had excommunicated Simon. Now, as Clement IV, he would surely bring to bear the fullness of his hostility toward the rebellious government.

In addition to having the weight of the Church against them, many of the rebel barons grew disgruntled. There were petty differences, mostly regarding money. Some felt they had been denied ransom money when royalist prisoners were ordered to be released. Others thought their share of the victory booty was too small.

Edmond grew disgusted with their greed. If it weren't for his loyalty to Simon he might have thrown up his hands and gone home so that he could enjoy bouncing his grandchild upon his knee. Instead, he was bouncing his own tired body upon the back of his horse on a warm August day in what was likely a futile mission.

But Simon must be told of this latest, and perhaps most disastrous, event.

Relieved to find Simon still at the Welsh leader's castle, he was welcomed inside. Simon and Llewellyn had just concluded their treaty. Edmond was not surprised it had taken so little time to court the support of the Welsh leader against his perpetual enemies—the royals of England.

"Come join us, Edmond, as we toast our new alliance!" Simon greeted him. It wasn't actually his place to do so because he wasn't the host, but it appeared there had already been several toasts to the occasion.

"Thank you, my lord. I would be pleased to do so. But . . ." Edmond hated to upset the celebration.

"I see you have come with ill tidings, my friend." Simon's broad grin sobered instantly. Suddenly Edmond was impressed by how the last two years had aged the man. Simon had always been a vigorous and handsome man, but now he looked all of his fifty-seven years and more besides. He'd lost weight, which was most evident in his thin face. His eyes, rimmed with dark circles, seemed to have sunk deep.

"Come, sit," he added.

"Thank you, my lord. And if you don't mind, perhaps I will have a measure of that ale, for I am parched from the ride."

A servant brought a pewter cup brimming with warm ale. Edmond brought it to his lips and drained it by half before he began. "I am sorry to report, my lord, that Prince Edward has escaped yet again."

Before Simon left London he'd placed a careful watch over the prince, leaving Simon's eldest son, Henry, in charge of the watch. The news was thus a double-edged blow. Simon's features tightened as he obviously considered his son's failure.

"How long ago?" Simon asked.

"I am afraid long enough to make mischief. I know for a certainty that he met with several lords at Ludlow." Edmond paused for another bracing swallow of ale before delivering the worst of his news. "Lord Gloucester was there."

"You warned me against taking him into our cause," lamented Simon. "You told me he was mercurial and could not be trusted."

"And you told me we had no choice but to trust him, that we needed every lord we could get, especially one as influential as Gloucester. I agreed."

"And now Edward has usurped all his influence to his side." Simon shrugged with resignation. "It matters not. We are set upon our course. There is no turning back. At least we still have the king in our custody."

"I fear Edward is far more dangerous than Henry."

Simon sighed, staring blankly into his cup. "Edward and I were close once," he said sadly. "I taught him much about warfare. I suppose we are fated to see if the student has outgrown the master."

"Simon, don't forget you defeated him at Lewes."

"Edward is an intelligent and cunning man. Far more so than his father. He will have learned from his mistakes last year, and he will also be chafing beneath the weight of his humiliation. I fear it will be a far different man I will meet in battle this time." He paused for a long while, deep in his musings. Finally he asked in a brisk tone, "What do you know of my wife, Edmond?"

"She has been very successful in the tasks with which you entrusted her," Edmond replied. "The Cinque Ports are secured. There will be no invasion force coming from France. Also, the support of the southern lords has been rallied. Your son Simon has already begun marching north with them."

"If all goes well, we will meet him before we meet Edward." De Montfort turned toward his host. "Lord Llewellyn, I must march in the morning."

The Welsh leader nodded. "I can commit to you a few hundred archers."

This paltry offering stunned Edmond, and he thought Simon, also, though the man maintained a stoic expression. Edmond wondered what exactly their treaty had accomplished. Nothing more was said on the subject. They drank together once more, and then Simon and Edmond departed in order to review their troops. When they were out of Llewellyn's hearing, Simon elaborated.

"The archers were the most I could get out of him, at least in direct aid," Simon said. "He also agreed to make annual payments, but the money won't be forthcoming for a while."

"Do we set out for Hereford in the morning?" Edmond asked. This northern route, in his estimation, would be the best course for Simon's army to take in order to meet his son's forces coming from the east.

"I've been thinking about that, and I am of a mind to take a risk. Edward will expect me to go north, but I believe surprise will be our best ally, as it was at Lewes. I have four thousand men in addition to Llewellyn's archers, a considerably smaller force than Edward's. Therefore, I believe our success will come from audaciousness rather than caution. I doubt Edward will be looking for me to cross the Severn as far south as the juncture with the Wye and the Usk. By doing so I can take them unaware and cut down their rear flank, perhaps even break through his forces and meet my son."

Edmond tried to push for the safer northern route, but Simon prevailed. He sent riders off to secure boats for the crossing. The next morning his army began its march. Without enough money to purchase food on the way, their rations ran short. They were hungry and tired by the time they reached the crossing, only to find Edward had arrived first and had captured and destroyed the boats. With the river crossing impossible, they were forced to turn around and retrace their steps, heading north. Nevertheless, they still had hope of meeting up with young Simon's army from the east. But they crossed mile after arduous mile, and the eastern forces were never seen.

Unknown to Lord Leicester, Prince Edward had made a tactical gambit that had yielded him one of the first victories in the conflict. Realizing that Simon's forces were trapped on the wrong side of the Severn, Edward used the additional time this gave him to seek out the eastern forces of Lord Leicester's younger son, Simon. A spy informed him this army was encamped in the region around the de Montfort holdings in Kenilworth.

Edward led his forces in an incredible forced march of thirteen hours to reach the rebels. Then he made an unprecedented night attack, catching the rebels completely off guard. A few, including Simon, managed to get to safety behind the castle walls, but thousands were routed and scattered over the countryside.

Lord Sardwick also tried to retreat to the castle, but his horse stumbled and broke a leg, forcing him to run the distance on foot. Nigel's mail weighted down his tired old bones. He tripped over the uneven ground and fell twice, each time barely able to claw his way back to his feet. The last time, with the castle moat a short sprint away, a searing pain gripped his chest. Gasping for breath, he crumpled to his knees and crawled another few feet until his arms and legs gave way. Sprawled in the dirt, he took his last breath. No sleight-of-hand in the world could have saved him.

———

Lord Leicester's army got off to a slow start the day they finally crossed the Severn, about fifteen miles south of Edward's stronghold in Worcester. The king, who was accompanying Simon's forces, had insisted upon morning prayers and holding a Mass.

"My lord," Edmond suggested to Leicester when they finally were mounted and on the move, "I know you needed the king with you to lend his validation to your rule, but now that we are engaged in a civil war, what use is he to us? Why don't we send the king south with a small guard of knights? He will only encumber us."

Simon snorted harshly. "I know that would be the practical move. Curse us all if he is mistakenly cut down in battle by his own men. Yet I am loath to send him into safe seclusion. Let him see the carnage his stubborn incompetence has wrought!"

Then scouts, sent to survey the situation in Worcester, returned with disquieting though not entirely unexpected news. "The royalist forces have left the stronghold and are marching east."

So that was why there had been no opposition to their crossing the river. Edward had set off to engage young Simon's army.

"It is possible now to trap Edward between our two armies," mused Simon.

When they crossed the path that led to London, where they could have turned aside and greatly augmented their forces, thereby offering a stronger opposition to Edward, Edmond prayed that Simon had made the right decision. Their only hope was in young Simon's army. Lord Leicester veered more southerly toward Evesham, located in a crook of the Avon River, hoping to circumvent Edward's army and link forces with his son.

At daybreak the following day the enemy was sighted. Seeing them approach, still at a distance, Simon nodded his approval. "By the arm of St. James! They make a fine advance. He learned this from me!" Perhaps he had a right to be proud. He was, after all, Edward's godfather and one-time mentor.

Then a breeze caught hold of the approaching army's banners. They were not Edward's banners but de Montfort's! Had they finally caught up with young Simon's army? It seemed too good to be true. Edmond felt an odd disquiet. Rather than flying the banners, could they be *flaunting* them instead? He was glad when de Montfort dispatched one of his men to climb the bell tower of the local church. Dismayed, the man returned and informed his commander that it was after all Edward's army.

They could not turn back now even if they had wished to. Their hearts sank, knowing there would be no linking up with young Simon's reinforcements, no rescue at all. The captured banners meant that young Simon had met defeat. But it mattered not, for the rebel army was set upon a course, one that had been inevitable as long as two years ago when they had first raised their voice against their king.

De Montfort ordered the charge. From that moment on there was no more time for thinking, for strategies, for regrets. Edmond knew he would die that day along with his friend and leader.

The royalist army came on like a vicious bull. They fought as men on a sacred mission. Edmond had seen this kind of single-minded indomitableness among the Knights Templar while on Crusade. Edward's forces were fighting a holy cause, stamping out traitors, even heretics. Nevertheless, when the spearhead of de Montfort's army rammed the enemy's line, it gave, but it did not break.

The baronial army had its own cause, true, but by then it had to be clear to most that it was a lost cause. Edmond knew this for a certainty when he saw that Prince Edward had divided his army into three units. As the baronial army charged, the two flanks of Edward's army appeared, hemming in de

Montfort's force. Edmond Marlowe fought now for honor more than for victory. Still, when history told of this day, at least it would recount how the forces fighting for liberty had fallen heroically.

Edmond raised his shield in time to deflect a battle-ax, then instantly slashed with his sword, the blow knocking his assailant from his horse. As he turned to meet another opponent, he saw the only sight that day that came close to bringing a smile to his soiled and sweaty face.

The king had been accoutered for battle—without crest or identifying banner—mounted, and led into the fray. Now Edmond saw him frantically turning this way and that upon his mount, crying miserably, "I am your king! Don't kill me! I am King Henry."

Finally several riders reached him and formed a protective circle about him as they led him from the field of battle. Henry would live to rule another day.

The August day had started with sunshine, but shortly after the confrontation of the armies, a dark cloud slipped across the sky. Claps of thunder joined the clash of steel. No rain came, but the heavy air felt like the weight of a shroud upon them. Fitting it was, for all around him Edmond watched his comrades fall, given no quarter by the rampaging enemy. Two of Simon's sons were cut down, and Edmond in those moments was truly thankful he had no sons to watch die.

The worst moment came when Simon himself was knocked from his horse. The attackers moved in on this most prized quarry, and Simon slashed desperately at them, but it was obvious his sword arm was weakened. He could not break through and was finally cut down. Yet the blood of the royalist army was hot that day and the mere death of the despised rebel leader was not enough to appease their bloodlust. They hacked at de Montfort's body, dismembering it brutally.

Even the vicious acts of Saracen infidels had not horrified Edmond so. His own blood rose, and lifting his sword, he charged into the wall of Simon's attackers. He cut down one before his own sword was slashed from his hand. Grabbing his short sword, he turned and found himself face-to-face with his old adversary's son—Gareth Aubernon. With a snarl of rage, Edmond lunged with his short sword, but it was no match for Gareth's broadsword. One-handed, Gareth thrust once with his weapon, needing little more than that to penetrate the old warrior's mail and impale him.

Edmond toppled from his horse as Gareth withdrew his blade. Still Edmond fought against death. Something other than the wrenching pain in his mangled gut told him that if Gareth Aubernon did not die here, he would bring terror and grief upon Edmond's lands and his family. Hawken lords had been waiting for generations for a moment such as this. Feeling within the depths of his dying heart that he was striking a blow for his daughter, he reached for his broadsword lying on the ground nearby. Scrambling to his feet he slashed at Gareth's horse. As expected, the animal reared in pain, throwing its rider to the ground.

Barely able to stand, much less hold his weighty sword, Edmond waited for his young adversary to rise. He must kill Aubernon before he himself died of his wounds.

Gareth quickly recovered from the fall and jumped to his feet. "You old fool!" he panted. "You've injured my horse. For this you will pay!"

He raised his sword. Edmond did the same, but it felt heavy as an anvil. He swayed with the weight of it, then crumbled to the ground.

Gareth spit on the old man, then slashed with his sword, killing Edmond Marlowe with a final quick blow.

27

B eatrice's eyes popped open. Moonlight poured in through her chamber window. Since becoming a mother she never slept soundly, always attuned to her baby's cries. But it was not young Edmond who woke her this night. Out in the courtyard the sound of horses rose to her window.

Slipping from her bed, she padded barefoot to the window. She pushed open the shutter and leaned out, the cool night air wafting over her. Still she could see nothing. Her chamber was situated so that the courtyard was just out of view. Turning, she headed toward the door and then paused. If there were late-night guests, she could not greet them in her sleeping shift. But before she could retrieve her wrapper from the wardrobe, her chamber door burst open.

"My lady, you are awake," Leticia said. She, too, was dressed in her wrapper.

"Who is out there, Leticia?"

"It is your father's vassal, Roland."

"My father! He's here!"

"No, my lady. But there is no time for explanations. We must hurry." Without awaiting a response, Leticia began rushing around the room, first to the wardrobe, where she took out a cloak and gown.

Beatrice strode to her maid and grasped her by the arm. "What is going on, Leticia?"

Leticia thrust the clothing at Beatrice. "I will tell you as much as I know, my lady, but please, will you dress as I talk?"

Beatrice wanted to protest but saw a deadly earnestness in her maid's eyes. Something awful had happened. She took the clothing, then went to a chest to get undergarments.

"Go on, Leticia," Beatrice ordered as she slipped her chemise over her head.

"All Sir Roland told me," said the maid, "was that the baronial army has been defeated."

Beatrice gasped and forgot the hose she now held in her hands. In the time since her father and Nigel had departed she had hardly given a thought to the conflict in the country. There had been no news, and she had assumed the dispute would merely involve a few skirmishes, as there had been in the last year, but mostly just a series of verbal debates between the royalists and the barons, with perhaps the French king and the pope lending their voices.

"How?" she asked, befuddled. "We have heard of no war."

"It was far to the north, m'lady."

"Tell me truly, Leticia, are my father and Lord Sardwick dead?"

"I do not know. Sir Roland insisted he would give only you the details. It is very possible they are only captives. Still, their lands would be forfeit."

"Yes, of course. But they may yet appeal to the king." Beatrice sat on a stool by the hearth and put on her hose. "Where are we going?"

"To St. Mary's priory."

"Surely he doesn't think the situation warrants vacating our home?" Leticia bent to help with the hose, but Beatrice brushed her away. "See to Edmond. I will pack my things while you dress yourself."

A smile twitched Leticia's lips. She had apparently forgotten about that detail. "I will be back in a few moments." She hurried to her small chamber next to Beatrice's.

When Leticia returned, Beatrice had piled the bed high with gowns and other personal items and was in the process of carefully folding one of her new gowns and placing it into a traveling chest she had dragged from a corner of the room.

"My lady, Roland said we must hurry and take only the barest necessities." Beatrice noted her maid was carrying a tapestry bag that could have only held a single change of clothes.

"When does he mean for us to leave?"

"Immediately. He didn't even want me to pack a bag for you, but I insisted."

"This is ridiculous. Surely there cannot be a need for such haste—"

"There was no mistaking his urgency, m'lady," Leticia said, already filling the bag with Beatrice's things.

Beatrice felt like a fool. She should have guessed the utter urgency with horses racing into the courtyard at this late hour, then being roused and urged to dress for travel. Perhaps her wits were still slow from sleep—no, it wasn't that. She simply did not want to imagine the real meaning of it all. So instead, she threw herself into the preparations for departure. She would put off facing reality as long as possible.

Soon enough both hers and Leticia's bags were packed and they were hastily exiting the chamber. They went to the nursery, but it had already been vacated, so they hurried down the narrow castle stairs, dimly lit by candles in wall sconces. In the great hall Beatrice first was relieved to see that young Edmond was well and safely in the care of his nurse. Then she turned to Roland. His appearance shocked her. He was normally a fastidious man, but now he was as ragged as a beggar. His mail hauberk was scored and tattered, and his left arm was in a dirty sling. A bandage, soaked with filth and blood, was bound around his head, and countless bruises and cuts marked his face.

Before she could speak, he held up a hand, a rudeness he would never have committed except under extreme duress.

"My lady, your horses are saddled and ready. We must fly!"

"Fly? But—" Though it simply was not in her nature to blandly accept her fate, she forced down her questions. Roland was no fool. He never spoke frivolously.

However he did seem to understand what she was asking, so he paused and, speaking quite calmly, said, "I have ridden hard for a week to get here, fearing pursuit at every turn. Perhaps the urgency I feel is unwarranted, but I would die if all my efforts were for naught and I failed to get you to safety. There is little else I can do."

Nodding, she knew to brace herself for the worst. She said no more as the small retinue exited to the courtyard, where horses were waiting. Three more of her father's knights were also mounted and ready. She recognized their mounts as Sardwick's, so they must have exchanged their tired horses for fresh ones.

St. Mary's Priory was several leagues away, and regardless of urgency three women and a baby could be pushed only so much. Besides, they must proceed carefully with only a three-quarter moon to light their way. When they reached the steep trail leading to the priory atop a forested ridge, the party was forced to proceed in single file because the path was narrow, rocky, and winding. All was quiet when the party finally reached the priory gate.

Roland rang the bell. Beatrice noted dew-covered cobwebs crossing the ornamental iron gate. This place seldom had visitors. Would she be welcome here? How much were they touched by the political unrest in the country? She well knew that the pope opposed the rebellion. Now that it had failed, would the daughter and wife of two of its leaders be given succor in the Church?

A woman in black habit and white wimple and veil came to the gate, her face in a shadow. "Who breaks our peace at such an hour?" she asked breathlessly.

"I am Sir Roland Leyburn, vassal to Lord Cassley. I come with Lady Sardwick, her son, Lord Sardwick, and their retainers."

Beatrice was so weary she almost didn't catch Roland's specific naming of her son as Lord Sardwick. When she realized what he had said, her fatigue fell away, replaced by sick tension. Though Roland had promised to tell her what had happened on their way, the journey had been too intense for conversation. She still knew nothing and wasn't sure she wanted to find out the details.

The nun was saying, "What do you want with us?"

"I seek shelter for my lady, her son, and her retainers. They have had to vacate their home in haste."

"These are troubled times—"

Roland cut in sharply, "Too troubled for the homeless to find refuge in the house of God? Is this what the Church has come to, then?"

"Bah!" the woman grated. "Hold your tongue before you speak blasphemy." She turned the key in the lock. It grated, as her voice had, with age and disuse.

Creaking, the gate swung open, and the riders entered. The nun closed the gate behind them and followed the party on foot. They rode slowly so that she did not lag too far behind. Beatrice saw why the nun had been panting when she reached the gate, for it was another hundred paces before the abbey came into view, mostly shadowy forms of buildings.

While two stable boys, with the help of the three knights, took charge of the horses, the rest of the company was ushered inside. It was quite dark, with only a few wall candles lit along the corridor. No doubt the entire convent had woken twice during the night at Matins and again at Laudes for prayer, but now they were back in their beds, and the place would not stir again until sunrise. Beatrice wished they would have arrived in time for Laudes. She felt she could use some prayer. She knew her husband was dead, but she clung to the hope her father had survived. Yes, it would go hard on him. He would surely lose everything and perhaps be banished, since he was such a close confederate of de Montfort's. Perchance they would go to France. Maybe they could find Philip. He would not appear such a bad match now! They could start a new life together.

As her thoughts ranged over a future filled with promise, she and her companions were led to the prioress's chambers.

The prioress of St. Mary's, a Benedictine order, was a tall, stately woman in her middle years. She'd been a noblewoman and had taken the veil when she became widowed at the age of sixteen. She was childless and apparently had no desire to remarry. She was quite beautiful, too, even at her age, and likely would have been sought after as a marriage candidate. Beatrice wondered why then she had traded the life of a pampered noblewoman for this. Many times Beatrice had declared, or threatened, that she would take the veil. She'd done so thinking it was the closest thing to death. Yet Prioress Agnes Thomasia gave the appearance of such serenity, such ease with herself and all around her, that Beatrice almost envied her.

The Holy Mother spoke to the nun who had escorted the visitors to her chamber. "Sister Elueua, please take the nurse and the child to a guest chamber so that the baby can be fed and cared for."

As they had entered the prioress's chamber, Edmond, who had slept during the entire midnight flight, chose that moment to wake, demanding with a hearty bellow to break his fast.

"Please, Holy Mother, don't make him leave," Beatrice begged. "I . . . I fear to be parted from him."

"He will not be far away, and I promise you that while he is in this place he will be safe."

There was something in the woman's voice that stilled Beatrice's fears. Nevertheless, she beckoned the nurse to her and gave Edmond a kiss on the forehead before he was taken away. The boy did not cease his lusty cries even for his mother.

"Please sit," the prioress said.

There were only two chairs for visitors in the room. Roland refused to sit despite his utter fatigue. Leticia also would not sit in the presence of her mistress. Beatrice thought this odd since she and Leticia usually received one another more as friends than as servant and mistress. Perhaps her sudden sense of formality had to do with the presence of the prioress, whose regal bearing made even Beatrice conscious of minding her manners. Mother Agnes turned to her own chair, a richly upholstered high-backed seat that resembled a throne. Before she sat, a fluff of fur, which Beatrice had at first taken to be a pillow on the table beside the chair, came to life and jumped into the prioress's arms.

"There, there, Fou Fou. Did you miss me?" The prioress patted the fluffy tan head of a small dog. Beatrice knew only the breeds of hunting dogs and had no idea what breed this was. It was as small as a cat, with short brown fur and floppy ears. With the dog nestled in her arms, the woman took her seat, then said, "Since the hour is late and your knight here, though he refuses to sit, appears about to fall over in a heap, I will try to make this interview brief. First, if you will, explain what has taken you from your home in the middle of the night."

"Holy Mother, you must know of the civil war—"

"Some call it a rebellion," the prioress said, brow arched incisively. "But, yes, I am aware of what has been transpiring beyond the walls of this priory. How does this involve you, Lady Sardwick?"

"My husband and my father have actively supported the baronial cause."

"And?"

Beatrice glanced at Roland. "The tide of war has gone against the barons. My father's vassal, Sir Roland, has had opportunity to impart to me only the briefest of details."

"Then it might be best if he answered the question," Prioress Agnes said. "What is the latest news of the . . . rebellion, Sir Roland?"

Roland blinked a couple of times, as if he had been dozing on his feet. Then he replied, "There was a decisive battle in the north some days ago. The army of the barons under command of Lord Leicester was defeated." He paused and swallowed. Beatrice saw for the first time that besides fatigue, his eyes resonated with the hollow emptiness of the bereft. Grief clung to him, which perhaps was only noticeable now because he was so tired. "I have not had the heart to tell all the details to my lord's daughter." He offered Beatrice an apologetic look.

"Please tell me now, Sir Roland. Are they dead?" implored Beatrice.

"Telling you is like watching your father die all over again, m'lady," he said.

Unexpectedly a sob escaped her lips. She could not cry now. She *must* be strong, but it did not help her resolve when she felt Leticia's hand press down gently upon her shoulder. She was silent for a long time as she dragged her emotions under submission. Later she would cry for the loss of the only other man she had ever loved. Later she would weep for the loss of her world . . . her life . . . her son's life. A lady did not air her emotions in public. There would be time for that later.

"I might suggest we wait until morning to speak further," said Prioress Agnes, no doubt noting Beatrice's inner struggle.

"No," Beatrice said firmly. "I have waited too long already. I want to know the fate of my father. And my husband, too." She looked again toward Roland.

He licked his lips. Though he swayed slightly on his feet, he, too, was working furiously to steel himself against the moment. "I was not present when Lord Sardwick fell. I know that he was with young Simon de Montfort's army, which was coming from the south to meet his father's army. I know he died on the field of battle, for I was told so by one of his knights who survived the fighting. As for your father—" his voice wavered a bit before he continued—"I myself saw him fall at Evesham on the fourth day of August in the year of our Lord 1265. My lady Beatrice, he died as bravely as any man can. With my own eyes I saw him fall. Please believe me when I say I desperately tried to aid him, but I was cut off from him by the battle. I saw . . . I saw him die. I am so sorry, Lady Beatrice!" He fell to his knees before her, succumbing, she feared, to his fatigue. Then she saw his bowed head and the tears oozing from his eyes. He drew his short sword and, balancing it in both hands, held it out to her. "I would that you would end my life this instant, for I have failed my master!"

For a moment she just stared in shock at the weapon. It did cross her mind to take it but only because she feared he might turn the blade and impale himself upon it.

Softly, because she could barely find her voice, she said, "There has been enough killing, Sir Roland."

Agnes nodded. "Stand, knight. Your mistress needs you alive."

Roland obeyed, but he did not appear relieved. Beatrice thought only death would have brought him relief. Well, brave knight, you, like the rest of us, must sacrifice the blessed peace of death. 'Tis life for us unlucky souls. Beatrice offered him what she hoped was a look of understanding before she spoke.

"Sir Roland, what was the cause of your urgency this night?" she asked.

"The royal army is full of vengeance and violence," he answered. "If the king gives them full rein, they will surely go rampaging through the country and unleash punishment upon the rebel supporters."

As the rebels themselves did last year when *they* were victorious? she thought grimly. Yes, she knew the Hawken forces would dearly love to repay Cassley knights for what they did to Hawken lands. And she had no doubt they would repay tenfold, for they were known to be as vicious and ruthless as their lord.

"Our king is no fool," said the prioress. "He will not condone the destroying of lands from which he hopes to make an income. And after all this warring, the royal coffers will be in desperate need of replenishing."

"I could not trust the wisdom of a man who had balked at granting even the most basic rights to his people," Roland rejoined, his fatigue making him forget respect toward his betters.

"This is not the time nor place for political debates." Agnes swung her gaze upon Beatrice. "You, my lady, should have some time to yourself, to contemplate and pray. You and yours shall be safe in this refuge until these matters can be sorted out."

Beatrice didn't like the sound of that final phrase. It was easy to see the prioress was a royalist at heart, but would that supersede her duty to God? On the other hand the pope was also a royalist, and he surely dictated her duty to God. Yet Beatrice had no other choice. She would accept the offered protection, however tenuous. So she nodded toward the prioress. She really did need to be alone. She wasn't certain how much longer she could maintain her stoicism. Let her fate be in this woman's hands. If in the end it meant succumbing to the will of the king or even the pope, what did it matter? What more could they do to her?

28

I n the priory garden Beatrice could hear the approach of horsemen. The fact that the sound carried over the walls and into the secluded garden indicated there were more than a few riders. Could it be that the king's men had finally come for her?

She had hoped they would leave her alone behind these holy walls, at least for longer than a week. She was only a woman, of little account in their political machinations, though the prioress, Mother Agnes, had hinted it might not be so simple.

"You have a son, Lady Beatrice," she'd reminded Beatrice during one of their talks. "He is heir to Sardwick and Cassley."

"But if our lands are forfeit to the king because of the rebellion—"

"Nevertheless, his claim could be contested at a future date. When the bitter fires of rebellion have quieted, it may be that the king—or his heir—might by that time look more favorably upon your son. Who knows what the future may bring?"

"Then all is not lost for Edmond?"

"The chances of this happening are, it is true, quite small, but as long as there is a chance . . ." The prioress shrugged her shoulders and gave Beatrice a knowing look.

Beatrice did not know what it meant. She'd questioned Leticia, but even her maid could not perceive all the ramifications involved. Or mayhap the maid was just sparing Beatrice the truth?

So with stark honesty she said to the prioress, "Mother Agnes, I have no idea what you mean. I thought I'd be safe here, but if that is not the case, then please tell me what I must look forward to."

Agnes studied Beatrice for a long moment, seeming to assess the sincerity of her words. Finally the nun answered, "Beatrice, I have heard, though it should come as no surprise to you, that Lord Hawken has received both Sardwick and Cassley as a reward for his loyalty."

Grimly Beatrice nodded. She had heard the same, and though it wrenched her heart, she had no choice but to accept it.

"You poor child," Agnes murmured, reaching out a hand to caress the little dog that seemed always to be in her lap when she was seated. "The fact of the matter is, Lady Sardwick, that Lord Hawken's claim on the two estates would be far stronger if no heirs existed. Do you understand—"

The prioress stopped abruptly when Beatrice gasped, finally perceiving what all had been reluctant to tell her.

"Hawken would never kill my son!" Beatrice cried. Even as she spoke, though, she knew the truth to be otherwise.

Now hearing horsemen approach, she sprang up from the bench upon which she'd been sitting, enjoying the warm afternoon and the sweet fragrance of roses. Her heart clenched in fear, she raced into the building and nearly collided with one of the nuns. She stammered a hurried apology then continued to her rooms.

The scene that greeted her when she threw open the nursery door was so serene she almost laughed at the fear rising like bile in her throat. The nurse was seated beside the cradle, rocking it gently and humming a soothing tune.

"M'lady!" said the nurse, abruptly ending her song.

Edmond stirred and whimpered.

"I'm sorry," said Beatrice. "I've woken him."

"He was not yet asleep, m'lady."

Beatrice strode to the cradle and looked down at her son. His blue eyes were open, and he was making little cooing sounds. Beatrice laid a hand on his head, his pale locks feeling like silk beneath her fingers. His eyes seemed to focus on her, and she was certain he recognized her as his mother. She smiled down at the chubby baby. He was nearly too big for the cradle the priory had provided for him. Beatrice let out a relieved breath. He was safe and would remain so in God's house. No one could touch him here.

The door opened once again. This time Leticia came in.

"M'lady, horsemen are at the gates."

"I know." Beatrice smiled. Both she and her maid had the same intent, to see to the protection of the child.

Since Roland had departed the priory two days earlier in order to ascertain, and perhaps secure, the safety of Cassley and Sardwick knights, Beatrice had felt far less secure. When she voiced the prioress's suggestion that Lord Hawken posed a danger to Edmond, Roland had been even more insistent about making contact with the other knights. He felt confident he could rally every Cassley and Sardwick knight to defend the infant lord if need be. But Beatrice wondered how many knights were left after the decimation at Evesham.

"Leticia, do you know who they are?"

"No, let us just stay here. It might be nothing to worry ourselves about." The maid's trembling voice betrayed her deepest fear. Though Beatrice had shuddered to consider Roland and his men waging some sort of pitched battle to protect Edmond, she now desperately wished the man was here with his knights.

Beatrice lifted Edmond from his cradle, needing his comfort more than he needed hers. She sat on the window seat that looked down on the very garden where she had recently strolled. Over and over she told herself she was safe in this place. Besides, these were civilized times, not like the days of William the Conqueror, when hordes of knights swooped down upon innocents and took what they wanted. There were laws now, laws that the Conqueror himself had established so that the land and those who dwelt upon it could live in peace. Yet she could not forget that the peace of the land had just been broken. There had been a war, lives lost—the lives of those dearest to her. Violence was again upon the land. Maybe she was fooling herself to think it had ever really left. Hadn't violence taken Philip from her? This latest rebellion was not the only war since the days of William the Conqueror.

Through the window Beatrice watched as the afternoon shadows lengthened. Leticia saw that a meal was brought to the nursery, but Beatrice could eat little. Who were the riders? Why had they not yet departed? Perhaps they had merely stopped by the priory for their evening sustenance and had no other intent.

Finally Beatrice could stand it no longer. She would send Leticia to find out what was happening. Before she could do so, a soft knock came on the nursery door. It was one of the nuns requesting that Beatrice go to Mother Agnes's apartment. Reluctantly Beatrice gave Edmond back to her maid. He'd fallen asleep in her arms by this time, and his soft baby snores had given her some comfort.

"Shall I attend you, m'lady?" Leticia asked.

Beatrice considered this a moment. She hated going alone, but she could not think only of herself. "Stay with Edmond, Leticia."

Leticia nodded with grim determination, her eyes saying what neither of them wished to voice, that she would guard the child with her life.

As Beatrice and the nun passed the chapel, Beatrice had a strong urge to run inside. Being in a priory these last days had not stimulated her godly sensibilities as one might have expected. Attending Mass three times a day, as the prioress required of her, caused her to consider spiritual matters more than ever before, but she knew her heart lacked a strong resolve toward God. Perhaps it was only that by comparison she fell far short of the devotion the holy sisters practiced—even Leticia. She simply was not much motivated toward things of the Spirit.

There were many times when she wished to pray, but her mind wandered easily. Once she even fell asleep while praying in the chapel. So it was rather easy to fight that sudden urge to pray now. First, she would see what the prioress wanted.

The sister let Beatrice into Agnes's waiting room, and a few moments later the prioress herself came for Beatrice and took her into the chamber where she received guests.

When they were seated, the prioress said, "I have just had a long consultation with Lord Hawken."

Beatrice's mouth went dry as the blood drained from her head, but she said nothing.

"He is now in the chapel purifying himself before God," the prioress continued.

Beatrice knew not how to respond, though her mind was in a furor. Was Edmond safe if the prioress gave Hawken free rein of the priory? Was Leticia even at that very moment fending off Hawken knights? She gripped the arm of her chair and started to rise.

"Be at peace, Lady Beatrice," the prioress said in a calm voice.

Beatrice had to force words past her dry, constricted throat. "How can I be so, Mother? My enemy roams free in the place where I sought refuge."

"None will come to harm within these walls."

"How can I believe that?" Words came now, but they were balanced upon the edge of a sharp blade. "I know where your sympathies lie. You say he might wish my son dead, yet you let him loose—"

"I said you are safe here," Mother Agnes said, her own tone sharp. "All who enter here are safe."

"Even my enemy?"

"Even your supposed enemy."

"Supposed!"

"Calm your tone, my lady. Do not forget to whom you are speaking. Not only am I prioress, but I have sheltered you and yours. I demand your respect."

"My papa used to say that true respect was given as a gift." She could not help the haughty sneer in her tone, though she knew she was wrong and would regret it.

"Your father was a wise man."

Sudden tears rose to Beatrice's eyes with the remembrance of her father. She had wept for two days after she'd heard of his death, but tears were still close to the surface of her emotions. As they spilled from her eyes, she dashed them away with the back of her hand. The gesture also seemed to wipe away her ire.

"Forgive me, Mother," she said contritely. "Fear has wrought poorly upon my emotions."

"I understand, child," soothed the older woman. "But I do believe you have naught to fear from Lord Hawken."

"But you yourself said—"

"I was merely stating possibilities because you have seemed so innocent of the realities of life. Yes, it is true Hawken holds a certain power over you. After my talk with him, however, I now realize you hold some power over him, as well. If you keep a cool head about you, you may come out of this quite well."

"I don't understand."

"Hawken will be here in a few moments, and he will make it all clear to you. Listen to him and be wise, as I know you were taught to be." Mother Agnes folded her hands in her lap, which for once did not contain her fluffy little dog.

"Can you not tell me what he wishes?"

"He asked me not to." Agnes smiled slightly and chuckled. "I do believe he thought you'd bolt and he'd never see you if you knew beforehand. I will say this: when you consider what he has to say, think of your son and what he has to gain."

A brisk knock at the door made Beatrice jump. Indeed, she did want nothing more than to bolt like a spooked colt. She made herself sit still and calm as the door opened and Gareth Aubernon entered the prioress's chamber.

The last time she had seen him, save for that brief early morning encounter the day of Philip's escape, was at her father's birthday party two years ago. He was now only nineteen, but while before he'd tried to put on an air of authority, now there was a true air of it about him. A swagger in his gait, a tautness around his mouth. He even sported a neatly trimmed beard, which was black like his hair. As lord of Hawken, he'd been a nobleman of means, but with Cassley and Sardwick, also, he was surely one of the most formidable lords in the realm. He definitely carried himself as if he knew this. Further, he was now also a battle-seasoned knight, and the image he presented to Beatrice was that of a mature man not a callow youth.

"My lady Beatrice," he said smoothly with a gallant bow. His tunic of blue linen with gold trim was impeccably neat for a man who had journeyed some distance. His leather riding boots were spotless. Of course, he wore neither mail nor sword, for these he would have been required to leave at the priory door.

"Lord Hawken," she replied tightly.

"I wish our meeting could be under better circumstances," he said. "The last truly happy time I remember was at your father's birthday celebration. Do you remember, m'lady?"

"I do, m'lord." He'd obviously forgotten she had escaped his advances by nearly plunging a dagger into his heart.

He turned to the prioress. "Mother Agnes, is there someplace where the lady and I could converse alone?"

Before Agnes could answer, Beatrice quickly cut in, "I would rather the prioress remain."

"You have naught to fear from me, my lady," said Gareth.

"Nevertheless . . ."

Agnes interjected, "I will retire to the anteroom. I will be close should you have need of me, Lady Beatrice."

Beatrice thought the prioress was too trusting of Lord Hawken. Yet she could hardly protest. Gareth was the picture of decorum and charm. Mother Agnes would no doubt think Beatrice unhinged if she tried to cast the lord in an evil light.

When they were alone, Beatrice fought the inclination to tremble. She forced from her mind the fact that he held her life and that of her son in his hands. Instead, she haughtily strode to the prioress's thronelike chair and sat upon it as if she belonged there.

"Well, Lord Hawken, be quick about your business. I have pressing matters to attend to."

He grinned!

She wished there was something close at hand to throw at him and his condescending expression, but the only thing that would have done damage was the prioress's crucifix, and even Beatrice was not about to throw that. What made her most angry about Gareth's mocking response, besides its infuriating arrogance, was the brief hint she saw there of Philip's own grin. It made her heart skip a beat, then clench in pain. Before this she hadn't believed there was any resemblance between the two half brothers. Now she realized she had seen that same grin worn also by their father.

"I will not be mocked," she said as evenly as her distraught emotions would permit.

"I am not mocking you, Lady Beatrice," he replied, seeming to make a true attempt at earnestness. "I must say, though, I am pleased that the tragic reverses of late have not tempered that most beguiling fire within you." Pausing, he added even more soberly, "First let me offer my deepest condolences at the loss of your husband and father. They were good men, if only a bit misguided."

"Thank you." She chose to overlook the end of his remark. At least he was making an attempt at civility. How could she do less? "If you wish, you may sit," she added politely.

"What I have to say is best said standing, or perhaps upon one knee." He smiled again, and indeed it held a good deal of charm. She almost forgot what a knave he was and all the ire Philip held against him.

"Say on, m'lord."

"As I am sure you know, the king has granted to me, unworthy vassal that I am, the forfeited estates of Cassley and Sardwick. But it saddens me to reap benefit from your loss."

"Does it?"

"Truly it does. I would that you continue as mistress of your family trust."

"Then you will return control of the estates to their rightful lord—my son?" She tried to temper the hope in her tone. She knew that could not be his intent.

"Alas, that would not please the king, or I might be tempted to do just that. There is another way, though, at least for you to remain as you were regarding the estates. Have you considered that possibility?"

"What possibility is that?" Her heart sank as she spoke. She had tried hard *not* to consider what he implied. Her oath to Philip weighed heavily upon her soul.

"Let me be plain, m'lady. I would ask for your hand in marriage. Let us together administer these estates as they were always meant to be."

She wanted to scream, "No! Never!" But she could not forget the prioress's words, "When you consider what he has to say, think of your son and what he has to gain." Yet clearly Gareth was not including Edmond in his proposal. He had said, "There is a way *at least for you* to remain as you were. . . ." Not for her son. How, then, could Edmond gain from Gareth's proposal? The only way would be if Gareth would agree to grant Edmond his rightful inheritance. But why should he? Beatrice had no hold over him. Did she? Mother Agnes had implied so. Well, it wouldn't hurt to test him out.

"Lord Hawken, I am sorry to say that I have decided to take the veil. I cannot bear to marry again."

For a brief moment a shadow seemed to pass over his visage. His lips tightened; his eyes narrowed.

"Lady Beatrice, I would have you for my wife." A fearsome edge accompanied his words; at least Beatrice thought she should fear them. But she refused to show him trepidation of any sort.

"A lord of your prowess can have any maid in the realm."

"Truly, m'lady, I can have any maid I choose. I choose you."

"But—"

"The king has granted his blessing upon our union."

"He hopes it will help appease the rebels."

"And why would that be wrong, m'lady? We all wish to heal the wounds of rebellion. This would go a long way toward that. All would gain."

"All?" Then she understood the prioress's words. There was a chance for Edmond if indeed Gareth wanted her above all else. She went on, "There is only one whose benefit I would desire above all. Give my son his rightful inheritance, and I will marry you."

"Sardwick?"

"Sardwick and Cassley."

His lips slanted, the grin this time more sly than before, holding no likeness at all to Philip. "My lady, would you use my ardor to strip me bare?" He held out his arms, and now there was a leering quality in his eyes, almost as if he was daring her to do just that.

"Ardor, Lord Hawken?"

"You must know I have hungered after you since that day in the woods when you turned my dagger upon me." His brow arched suggestively, and she recalled that he had been enticed rather than angered by the dagger. "You are the most beautiful, desirable woman I have ever known. Even now I ache to take you and make you mine."

"You are the victor, Lord Hawken. You could force me—"

"You well know the Church would not recognize a forced union."

She had to smile ironically at this. Many were the maids forced into marriage—not at sword point as in ancient times, yet just as surely against their will. She hadn't wanted her marriage to Sardwick, but circumstances, if not a sword, had forced her. Women had no choices. Rare and very fortunate was the woman who fell into a marriage of mutual affection. Beatrice knew she was not fated to be one of the fortunate ones.

Coolly, she said, "So, my lord, what say you? What is the price for quenching your ardor?"

"I will give him Sardwick for an inheritance."

"He will have Sardwick now, or that is, from the moment we marry, Edmond will be the Lord of Sardwick." She knew she would never wrench Cassley from Gareth, whose family had lusted after it for so many generations. She had only thrown it in as a bargaining point.

She hated her intense relief when he smiled. She hated the control he had over her. "You will make a canny mistress of our lands, m'lady. You and I together will make my estates great."

No time was wasted after that. Gareth had brought a priest with him to the priory. Beatrice insisted upon only one thing before they took their vows— that Gareth put his promise regarding Edmond into writing, making two copies, one to be put into the church records and the other for Beatrice to keep. He didn't want to wait another moment to consummate his marriage. He well knew the winds of victory were fickle, and if the last few years were any gauge, tomorrow the rebels might somehow gain the upper hand once more.

The next morning as Beatrice walked down the aisle of the church, she could not help hoping to hear other horsemen approach the priory—Roland and his loyal knights—to rescue her. But what good would rescue do? She was not being forced—not in the strictest sense of the word—into this marriage. She was making a choice, a choice for her son.

Even as she uttered the holy vows taking Gareth Aubernon as her husband, she thought of his brother. Philip, of all people, ought to understand why she must do this. He knew how hopeless it was for a young man without land or position. She prayed he would understand why she had to break her solemn oath to him and that he would forgive her.

Gareth took her immediately after the ceremony back to Hawken to consummate their marriage. She thought she might put him off for a while with excuses of fatigue, for it had been a long ride. Such excuses had always worked with Uncle Sardie. Even a mild case of flutters had been enough to give her a day or two reprieve from his intimate attentions.

She said to Gareth as he led her to the chamber they would share, "I am so tired after the ride. Can it not wait till the morrow?"

He laughed. "I will not be put off, wife."

"But we are both travel-stained—"

He pushed her onto the bed and tore at her clothing, ripping open the finely stitched seams of her gown. "You have your paper, wench. I own you now."

For the next hour as her body was ravished, she silently bemoaned her foolishness. Was her son's future worth this? She'd never thought Philip's life had been as miserable as he had believed. Surely she and Edmond could have been happy to live out their lives in a priory cell, or even a peasant hut.

Instead, she had sold herself for a piece of land. She tried to find the nobility in what she had done, in what she had sacrificed for her child. Instead, she felt as vile as her husband's passions. In truth, she was worse even than that, for she had broken a solemn oath, a vow made to the man she truly loved.

29

France
October 1265

The lone traveler was tall and probably brawny under his wool cloak, but with the element of surprise on his side, Philip thought he could take him. Crouched upon a ledge at the side of the road, hidden by shrubbery, Philip waited for his intended victim to reach the ideal spot for an ambush. Obviously the traveler was unfamiliar with this part of the woods, or he would have avoided this particular stretch of the road, where thieves were known to lie in wait for the unsuspecting.

Would Theo be furious that Philip had gone off on his own to stage a robbery? What did he or the others expect when they still, even after a year of camaraderie, persisted in treating Philip like a helpless child? He just wanted a chance to prove to them that he could do more than act as bait or hold their cloaks while they attacked. He'd learned a lot in his time with the robbers. He was sure he could do this, and when he returned to camp with a fistful of coins, they would start to think differently of him.

His victim drew nearer. Philip palmed a fist-sized rock in one hand and the hilt of his dagger in the other. His heart thudded wildly inside his chest, but his hands were amazingly steady.

At just the right moment Philip leaped and fell upon the traveler. In an instant the dagger was at the man's throat, quickly stilling his struggles as the man felt the edge of the blade press against his skin. For once Philip was grateful for Gilly's lessons, even if they were often harsh.

"I want only your purse, and your life is yours," Philip demanded, speaking French.

"I am but a poor wanderer," the man replied in English, and there was a familiar quality to it, no doubt because Philip had heard the language so seldom since leaving England.

But Philip was most disturbed that the man's voice, though slightly shaken, held no fear. Instinctively he sensed this was a man who knew how to handle himself in a circumstance such as this, and the only reason Philip had overcome him was because he'd surprised him. Wasting no further time in deliberations, Philip raised the arm that held the rock and slammed it against the traveler's head. The fellow grunted and then went limp. His chest still rose and fell as Philip quickly went through his clothing, finding beneath the leather jerkin a purse containing several coins. Philip slipped this inside his own jerkin, then turned his attention to the knapsack the man had slung over his shoulder. In this he found a mail hauberk wrapped in cloth, confirming Philip's suspicion that the man was a knight. With the mail there was also some food and a few more coins. Philip took the coins and tucked them away with the others.

The traveler began to stir. Philip jumped up, but before he raced off, he took a last glance at his victim to assess how close to waking up he was and to determine if the fellow needed another blow to allow Philip a better chance of escape. Philip gasped. The traveler had been hooded before, his face shadowed. Now the hood had fallen back, revealing a face he knew well.

Cursing, Philip fell to his knees beside the man. "Wake up! Wake up!" He shook the man and slapped his face.

The man did wake, and as quickly as the heart beats one time, he flung his hands around Philip's throat.

Gagging, barely able to emit sound, Philip croaked, this time in English to be certain the man understood, "P-please . . . Sir Jocelin . . . s-t-o-p . . ."

It was another agonizing moment before the knight perceived Philip's words and loosened his grip.

"How do you know me, thief?"

"Let me remove my hood, and you will see."

"Your voice is familiar."

"I am Philip de Tollard."

The hands now fell completely away from Philip's throat, then reached up and pulled off the hood that he wore to cover his distinctive red hair.

"It is you!" exclaimed Jocelin. Rubbing the rising lump on the side of his head, he added with a perplexed scowl, "What are ye about, lad?"

Philip thought he had completely accepted and justified his present occupation, but now, before one of the few men in this world he truly respected,
he felt ashamed. Lowering his eyes, he felt heat rise up his neck and face.

"I-I am surviving," he answered with more defense than conviction.

To his surprise the knight nodded. "I understand, lad. I have been but a
few weeks on my own in a strange land, and it has not been easy, though I
had some coin and the benefit of experience to aid me. I know you had
naught but coin for the Channel crossing when you left Father Bavent. Why,
though, did you not return to your family in Anjou?"

"Why would they help me now as a man when they had already turned
me out as a helpless child?" Philip said bitterly, but he did not want to appear
piteous before this man, so he swiftly changed the subject. "What brings you
to France, Sir Jocelin?"

"It would seem, lad, that I am now an outlaw like you."

Philip gaped in shock. "How? Because of me?"

"We have much to talk about, Philip. Let's not do so in the middle of the
road, lest other travelers come along."

"Come with me to my camp. It's a bit of a trek, but we can talk as we
walk."

Both men rose, brushing the dust of the road from their clothing. Jocelin
slung his pack over his shoulder, and then Philip remembered the ill-gotten
coin in his jerkin. He handed it back to his friend with an apologetic smile.
The knight laughed.

"For me to be so easily taken, you should keep it. A lesson for me," said
Jocelin, though he took the purse in hand regardless.

Momentarily forgetting himself, Philip started to take umbrage at the
man's statement. After all, he *had* taken the knight down and felt some skill
besides surprise had done the job.

Noting the flash in Philip's eyes, Jocelin added, "You've learned a lot since
leaving England, eh?"

"I've had to." Philip quickly tempered his ire. This was not an enemy. Sir
Jocelin had saved Philip's life at a huge risk to his own. That reminded Philip
of his previous query. "So, Sir Jocelin," he repeated as they started hiking
through the woods, "how came you to be in France?"

"How much news have ye heard from England?"

"Little enough. I heard there was a rebellion and Lord Leicester reportedly
deposed the king."

"That was some time ago. Leicester ruled England for more than a year, though more as regent than king. However, he made the mistake of leaving the king and his heir alive. Eventually they rallied support, and nearly two months ago the rebels were defeated. Leicester was killed, along with others of his closest allies."

With a sinking feeling Philip recalled that before he left England, Lord Cassley, Beatrice's father, had supported Leicester. Hawken, Philip's father, had been undecided. Where did the loyalties of the new Lord Hawken lie? And how had all this affected Beatrice? He could not bring himself to make a direct inquiry, for he feared what even hearing her name might do to him. In all this time she still haunted his memory. He often dreamed of her, both while awake and sleeping.

"Sir Jocelin, was my . . . that is, was Lord Hawken with the rebels or with the king?"

"Gareth was solidly with the king. For a time when Lord Leicester ruled, Hawken lands were forfeited, and Gareth was something of a fugitive himself. Cassley knights burned part of Hawken Castle and its fields."

"And you were forced to flee to France?"

"Not at that time. I had been left to protect the castle while Gareth went off to fight the rebels. I did not mind this, for my loyalties regarding the rebellion were torn. Had your father still been alive, I would have fought to the death at his side. But my fealty toward the new lord was clouded. I would have done my duty toward my new liege lord, though my heart would not have been in it; thus I was glad to remain behind. During the occupation the Hawken Castle guards were imprisoned in the dungeon." Jocelin paused, taking several deep breaths. "Lad, I have been walking all morning. Mayhap we might find a place to pause for some rest and sustenance while we talk?"

"Not far ahead is a good spot."

"You know this wood well?"

Philip nodded. He'd had to learn his way well to make quick escapes but made no mention of this. He did not wish to draw undue attention to his questionable means of survival.

Just before they came to a bend in the road, Philip motioned his companion to follow him as he left the road. They trekked through a thicket of gorse and came to the bank of a sluggish creek. There was soft grass on the slopes of the bank and several rocks to lean against. The two men settled themselves in a comfortable spot, and then Jocelin took some bread and apples from his pack. Philip had retrieved his own pack after he attacked Jocelin. In it he had some dried meat and bread. Together they made a meal.

Jocelin returned to his account of events in England. "After the defeat of the rebels at Evesham in August, Gareth reclaimed his lands. He returned to Hawken, and his knights were freed, but we were looked upon with disdain because we failed to guard Hawken from the rebels. It hardly mattered that we were only a handful against twenty or thirty of the enemy. Nevertheless, when rescue came, some of the knights did what they could to regain the good graces of the lord. One who had discovered my part in your escape secured his place with the lord by exposing me and others who had helped. Lord Hawken had always suspected you'd had help, and because I had in the past shown sympathy toward you, he believed I was involved. But the rebellion kept him too occupied to prove these suspicions. With the fighting over and his lands reinstated, he was finally free to turn his attentions to this matter. Some of us got wind of our impending danger and we fled. I decided to take yer way and quit England altogether rather than live there as a hunted fugitive."

"I hope you fare better than I, Sir Jocelin," Philip said. "What will you do here? You are a trained knight and would be fit to hire yourself out as a mercenary." Theo and the others had often discussed this prospect for themselves. They were all trained soldiers except for the monk, but he had all the natural instincts of a warrior. Several months back they had taken the coin from a recent robbery and gone to Paris to buy horses for that purpose. But one thing had led to another, and before they had even found horses for sale, they had drunk and gambled away their money. No one liked the prospect of becoming foot soldiers, so the idea was put aside.

Then something occurred to Philip. "Sir Jocelin, where is your horse?"

"I could not afford to bring him across the Channel with me, and even if I could, I have little enough means to support myself, much less a horse. I have considered what ye suggest, but what I truly wish is to go to the Holy Land. There I could fight for something in which I deeply believe."

"Has the pope called a new Crusade, then?"

"Nay, but there are always skirmishes there, with the Christian knights trying to hang on to their territory. I miss the purpose I had when I was a crusader."

"Surely it would cost a king's ransom to finance your way there."

Jocelin shrugged and nodded. "Truly, it is so."

"In the last year," Philip said a bit boastfully, "I have seen enough coin to pay for a passage to Palestine." With a sour sigh he added, "Alas, every bit of it has been frittered away meaninglessly. There is no point in saving a fortune. I will never have what I truly desire."

"In all this time, Philip, nigh on to two years, your heart has not changed?"

Philip did not want to answer. It seemed sad and pathetic that he still yearned for the impossible. He looked down at the crust of bread he held in his hand, unable to meet this man's eyes and reveal the hopeless void within him.

"Oh, poor lad! I wish it was not so."

Jocelin's tone was full of pity, and Philip knew he should not pursue the matter further. He was silent for a long time as he fought a battle between his heart and his head. His head argued that it was indeed best for him to forget, to let go of useless longings, to face the reality of his life, despicable as it was. His heart, on the other hand, cried out against logic and practicality. His heart longed to hear her name, to know of her life, and to still be a part of her.

Finally he lifted his eyes toward his friend. "Though I know I will regret it, I must know, Jocelin. Please tell me about her."

The knight's lips grew taut, and he looked as if he might refuse. "You will not like what you hear."

"Did she marry, then? I knew she must." He tried to sound brave.

"Following Lord Leicester's victory, shortly after you left England, Lady Beatrice married Lord Sardwick—"

"Sardwick? His estate is to the south of Cassley, isn't it? I recall the lord was quite old. He must have died, then, and it was his son she—"

"No, Philip, Beatrice married the old lord, a man of some sixty years."

Philip let out a relieved breath. He knew then that it was a marriage purely for the political convenience of uniting the two houses. There would be no passion in such a marriage. Beatrice knew the man as "Uncle Sardie."

"I understand that she had no other choice in this marriage. We knew it must happen. I do not blame her." He meant his words, though the very idea of Beatrice belonging to another, even in a chaste manner, made his heart ache.

Jocelin continued, "I'm afraid the marriage did not last. Shortly after Beatrice bore Sardwick a son, the rebel's rule was challenged by the king. During the battle that ended a mere two months ago, Sardwick was killed."

"She is a widow, then, back in her father's house?"

"Philip, Lord Cassley was also killed." Jocelin paused, perhaps to allow the deeper meaning of his words to penetrate Philip's wildly careening thoughts. "You understand, don't you?" Jocelin tried to speak gently. "The rebels were soundly defeated. The lands of the leading rebels were forfeited to the king. Lady Beatrice was forced to flee to the priory for the safety of herself and her son."

"Did she take the veil?"

"No."

"What has become of her, then?" Philip's thoughts spun in new directions. She was free! She could flee to France now. He could get word to her on where to find him. They could be together at last!

"The king awarded both Cassley and Sardwick to your brother," Jocelin said with an element of caution in his tone.

"I don't care about that," Philip exclaimed. "I must get a message to her. There is a chance for us here—"

Jocelin sighed deeply. "She will not come to France."

"But—"

"I am loath to go on, Philip; however, I must. It is time these pointless hopes of yours be dispelled. Before I do so, you must understand that a woman in Lady Beatrice's position has few choices. Keep in mind she has a son she must consider."

What did she do? Fear clutched at Philip's throat, stilling any speech.

"Lady Beatrice married yer brother."

"No!" Philip's head fell back against the rock where he sat, making a loud thud. He banged his head again and again in anguish. "How could she?" he moaned.

"She had to consider her son," Jocelin answered.

"She made an oath to me."

"Would you expect her to keep an oath to you, a man she thought likely to be dead, over the future of her own son? Are you so selfish and cruel that you would hold her to it at the cost of her son?"

"An oath is an oath!"

Jocelin shook his head. "On my honor, I have never seen you look more like your father. He kept an oath, too, at the cost of *his* son, and you have hated him for it—"

"For good reason!"

"Nay, only because you are as stubborn as he."

"I care not what say you," Philip retorted. "I will not believe she had no other choices. She could have come here. I would have cared for her."

"As you have cared for yourself these past two years? Would you have embroiled her in a company of thieves? I have always believed you to be a decent man, a man of honor."

"Curse honor! Why should I be any different from all the other spawn of Hawken blood? Or even different from that faithless wench whose love was as false as her oath-making?" Shaking with his fury, Philip jumped up. Never had he been so possessed by his anger without anyone to vent it on. His hands ached to throttle someone, and he even glanced fleetingly at Jocelin. Instead, he paced over the grass like a caged wild bear he had once seen at a menagerie in Paris.

"You must not speak so," Jocelin said quietly.

"Don't tell me how to speak!" Philip cried. "I thought you were my friend, but I see you are still a Hawken knight at heart. Tell me, did you stand up for the happy couple?" He spun around and glared at his companion.

Jocelin jumped up, as well, and met Philip's glare eye-to-eye. "Take back those words!" he demanded.

"Why? I'll wager you held my brother's cloak as he and his bride consummated their union."

Philip did not even see the fist that smashed into his face. He tottered as black and white spots flashed in his eyes, then he crumbled to the ground. Dazed but not unconscious, he clawed back to his feet and charged the waiting knight. Philip flung his fists at the man, first left, then right, slamming into Jocelin's chest, into his jaw. Back and forth he pummeled the knight. Jocelin made no defense. Philip kept hitting until his knuckles were raw, and only then did the oddity of the situation finally penetrate.

The knight was *allowing* Philip to hit him!

The realization drained all the vitality from him. Panting, he let his arms fall limply at his sides.

"Do you feel better?" Jocelin asked calmly.

"No," Philip rasped, feeling only shame and disgust with himself.

Jocelin rubbed his bruised chin. "Nor do I."

"I'm sorry. You should have struck back. I deserved it."

"I saw that you needed the release of violence, not punishment."

Philip sank back down to the ground and dropped his head dejectedly into his hands. "I am a fool," he muttered.

"It was wrong of me to blame you for how you felt," said the knight. "But now you understand how it was with her."

Philip lifted his head. With a suddenness he could not fathom, the heat of anger was replaced with an icy chill. Coldly, he said, "No, I don't understand, and I will never forgive her. This I declare—nay, I make a solemn oath. I will never let such a thing happen to me again. I will never be vulnerable to another; I will never be naive; I will never be such a fool again!"

Then, as if to seal his oath, he reached into his tunic to where he had always kept Beatrice's brooch safely tucked. He yanked it out and, with a mighty toss, flung it into the woods. It felt as though he were ripping away a part of him, perhaps the last good part that had remained.

30

Philip was glad Jocelin decided not to return to the thieves' camp with him. The knight said he had heard of a lord who was looking for mercenaries and did not want to miss out on that opportunity by tarrying too long. But Philip knew the real reason was that Jocelin had no taste for mingling with thieves. Part of Philip felt shamed by his friend's disdain, albeit silent. Yet a greater part squashed that small vestige of nobility still within his soul. That part convinced him that he *favored* the company of thieves. Too many so-called law-abiding people were more deceptive and dishonest and mean-spirited than any thief he had ever known.

He reached camp in a markedly foul mood. His attack on Jocelin had not appeased his longing for violence. Immediately Gilly seemed willing to accommodate him.

"Where have you been?" the wiry thief demanded.

"I'm touched by the depth of your concern," sneered Philip in reply. Indeed, Gilly was the last person he expected to care about him. The peace between him and Gilly was tenuous at best. They were the two most apt to disagree on a matter and had come to blows more than once. True, they often fought side by side, defending each other's lives when a robbery went sour, but that did not prevent them from constantly bickering when they were safe in camp.

"Believe me," Gilly said dryly, "I barely noticed you were gone, but Theo, good fellow that he is, grew worried when the sun arched toward evening and you had not returned from your stroll in the woods. He left some time ago, taking Rodrigo with him, to look for you. I expected he would be dragging your lifeless body back any time now."

"Hoped, you mean!" retorted Philip.

"Think what you will. You are a man, though a pathetic imitation of one. You don't need a nursemaid."

"Pathetic! Why, you dried-up old piece of dung!" Philip rounded on Gilly, fists raised.

Gilly jumped up. He was always ready for a fight. "Come on, then. If it's a thrashing you want—"

A loud rustling of branches drew his attention. Philip turned in time to see Theo and Rodrigo burst through the bushes surrounding the camp.

"It's a good thing I'm not the constable," bellowed Theo. "We heard you two shouting a furlong away."

"Very good timing, Theo," Gilly said. "You got here before I pummeled your precious Worm."

"Ha!" grunted Philip. "'Tis you who will be—"

"Go ahead, Gilly, have at him," yelled Rodrigo. "Because of him I stumbled into a bush of poison ivy. A rash is already rising upon my hands."

"No one asked you to go searching for me," Philip said. "I can take care of myself. I am not a child."

"Any of us would have done the same for the other," Theo replied reasonably enough.

And it was true, Philip knew, but he was in no mood to admit this. "I'll have you know," he said, "I felled a knight today and would have had a fine purse of coin had it not turned out the man was a friend of mine from England."

Gilly grunted a dry laugh. "You felled an English knight, but you let him go because he was a friend? Sounds like a line of a ballad—and just as fanciful."

"Do you call me a liar?" Philip did not wait for a reply and charged Gilly, who quickly reached out and had his arm around Philip's head before the blink of an eye.

Philip struggled a moment before Gilly flung him down on the ground. He would have jumped up and engaged a counterattack, but Theo, as usual, stepped between them.

"This friend of yours must have put you in a foul mood," Theo said.

"Imaginary friend," interjected Gilly.

"There you are wrong," Theo said as Philip tensed to defend himself once more. "Rodrigo and I saw a travel-stained knight not far from here. At least his fell appearance marked him as a knight. We considered waylaying him but decided he looked too poor to be worth the effort. Was this your friend, Worm?"

"Perhaps."

"Did he bring you bad news?"

"I'm hungry," Philip said. "Isn't it Pippin's day to get supper?"

Theo looked for a moment as if he might press his inquiry, then shrugged and said, "The pickings must be slim or he'd be back by now."

"No mind." Philip grabbed his knapsack from the ground and slung it over his shoulder. "I'm going into town for some real food and a bit of fun."

"You'll never get there before the gates close," Rodrigo said.

"I will if I hurry."

"He's right," said Theo. "There's plenty of time. I'm up for a little fun myself."

Philip was about to argue again that he didn't need a protector but realized that he didn't relish the idea of being alone, either.

"I'll join you," said Rodrigo.

"Well, I'm not going to race through the woods for a glass of stale ale," groused Gilly. "Besides, someone should stay to tell Pip why no one is here to partake of his efforts." He said this with a pointed look at Philip.

Philip and his two companions hurried off to their destination of Rouen, a distance of more than two leagues. In the last year the thieves had moved their camp several times, so this city was now closer than Paris. Though smaller than Paris, Rouen was still a thriving town of some fifty thousand souls.

As the three men came to the town, it seemed as if a good number of these souls were now exiting the city. Evening was approaching, and the gates were about to close on the country folk who had come for market and could not afford the price of an inn. For once in his life Philip had enough coin for a cheap inn. He had ferreted away some of his bounty in the last year, for he usually abstained from the kind of overindulgence the others enjoyed when they came to town. Always in the back of his mind Philip hoped one day to improve his lot. He thought he really might one day have enough saved to visit faraway Cathay and there make his fortune. Now he realized his dreams were folly, the addled whimsy of a foolish boy. All he wanted now was as much ale as he could buy and an evening of forgetfulness.

Though many were leaving, a fair number were also hurrying into the town before the Gates closed. Philip and his companions fell in with this throng and were carried along the Rue de la Grosse Horloge toward the city center. As darkness descended, the crowds quickly thinned out, though the reek of sheep—the town's main trade—remained. Perhaps Philip would double his coin gambling, visit the market in the morning, and spend his money lavishly. Or, if the dice did not favor him, he might find other ways to increase his wealth in the morning when the people crowded the streets. He had become quite adept at picking pockets, thanks to Rodrigo's instructions. As a boy before Theo had rescued him, the Spaniard had been forced to do whatever he could to feed himself and his mother.

Soon Philip and his friends veered from the main thoroughfare and made their way to the street of taverns. Now that darkness had fallen, noise, laughter, bits of conversation, and even an occasional song filtered out to the street. The little group had no preference for a particular establishment. They decided to start at the first one and work their way down the street as the evening progressed.

Ale began to flow as Philip freely divested himself of his coin. There was no more point in hording his money. He'd never go anywhere or be anything but a bastard—a thieving bastard at that! When he was deep enough into his cups he also visited one of the curtained rooms at the back of one tavern. He cared less about his seed than he did his money, for he knew now he would never have the perfect family he'd always dreamed of.

By the time they reached the fourth tavern—or was it the fifth?—Philip had a hankering for dice. A circle of men crouched upon the floor in the corner of the common room were hot into a game, and they welcomed Philip when he threw down a coin. Theo also joined, but Rodrigo only watched, for he had already spent most of his money on women. The current game in play, similar to one Philip had played in the taverns of Oxford, was called raffle. The men threw three dice, hoping for the highest pair or, even better, three alike.

From the moment Philip got hold of the dice, it seemed he was charmed. He kept rolling and winning—he couldn't seem to lose. Inwardly he groaned. He knew now he was cursed above all men. His winning only proved that if there was a God, He held a special malice toward Philip. Had Philip *wanted* to win, he probably would have been stripped of even his shirt!

After he pocketed several large winnings, some of the players began to grumble.

"No man is that lucky!" one man accused.

"Let me see those dice!" demanded another.

"You dare call me a cheater?" Philip rejoined, fists balling until the edges of the dice bit into his flesh.

Theo, seeing the familiar flash of violence in Philip's eyes, quickly interjected, "How can he cheat? These are house dice."

"Sleight of hand. I'll warrant he palmed the original dice and replaced them with his own."

"That's ridiculous!" Philip shot back, rising and daring each man with his eyes to accuse him again.

Theo jumped up. "We've had enough of the game." He grabbed Philip's arm and began tugging him away.

The tavern keeper interceded. "Let me see those dice."

With a grudging scowl, Philip handed them over, and the man examined them carefully beneath the glow of a candle.

"These are my dice," the proprietor declared. "He won fairly." But to Philip he said under his breath, "You may have won honestly, but you need to find a new alehouse. You have the look of trouble about you."

Philip was still tense, but he let Theo nudge him outside. After Rodrigo joined them Theo suggested they find a place to bide the night. It was past Matins. The church bells had chimed the midnight hour about the time the altercation at the dice game had begun. But Philip felt the bulge of the coin-filled purse in his shirt and could not bear the thought of going to sleep a rich man.

"A drink first," he said. "I'm parched."

He saw Theo and Rodrigo exchange a concerned glance. They knew this behavior was unusual for Philip. Well, he wasn't going to let Theo treat him like a child anymore! He strode ahead of them and fairly ran into the next tavern. As they followed, Theo said, "One drink."

"Why are you so prudent tonight, Theo?" Philip asked. It was usually Philip urging his friends to moderation, and Theo was the worst of the lot when gambling and drinking were involved.

"Someone must be," Theo replied dryly.

A dice game was going on in this tavern, as well, and Philip veered toward it, but Theo caught his arm. "Don't tempt your luck, Worm."

"Cursed luck," groused Philip.

"Come, you wanted a drink. Wench," Theo called to a passing barmaid, "bring three cups of ale."

They found an empty table, and Philip slumped down upon a bench. The leather pouch in his shirt felt like a millstone around his neck. He took it out and dropped it onto the table. Rodrigo quickly pushed it back toward Philip and out of sight.

"Don't show your money to the world," he hissed. "There are other thieves besides us, sí?"

"Let them have it," Philip spat. "'Tis wasted on me."

"Since I have known you," Theo said, "you have hoarded your money like a miser, telling us how you dream of seeing the wonders of Cathay."

"Dreams change, don't they?" Their ale arrived, and Philip brought the cup to his lips and swallowed half of it in one gulp. Wiping a sleeve across his lips, he added, "My dreams were squashed beneath the cruel heel of life. I am weary of dreams." He downed the rest of his ale and grabbed a passing maid, demanding more. She scowled at him but took the mug anyway.

"Has this to do with that English knight you saw today?" asked Theo.

"I don't want to talk about it." Before he realized it, though, he contradicted his own words and blurted out his troubles. "My eyes were opened today, so I should rejoice! The pity would be if I'd spent my life pining for a faithless shrew. I am free now . . . free." His gaze wandered to the leather pouch on the table. He fingered it thoughtfully. "Maybe you are right. I need no land anymore, nor title, nor position. I can go where I will. Come with me, Theo, Rodrigo! Together we will discover wonders few eyes have ever beheld. And we'll have riches, too. That will show her! They say there is so much gold in Cathay it just lies about waiting to be gathered by any who will. It is also said the women of Cathay are as delicate as flowers, and they live to serve men and to please them."

"Truly?" said Rodrigo with wonder. "How far away is this wondrous place?"

"Twice as far as Jerusalem, I'll wager," put in Theo with a voice of reason. "I am sorry, Worm, but even that bulging pouch won't get you that far."

"Of course. You are right," lamented Philip. "What was I thinking to even try to hope? Will I never learn?"

They were all silent, nursing their ale as if it were a sick friend. Finally Philip pushed back his bench and started to rise.

"Curse it, then!" he growled. "Let the dice have my future."

Theo grasped his arm, restraining him. "Wait, Worm! Don't give up so easily."

"Easily!" he spat. "For twenty years, since I pushed my way from my mother's womb, I have been fighting. Why should I continue? Give me one good reason, Theo."

Theo's hesitation before speaking was answer enough for Philip, even when his friend finally said, "I have no good reason. Take that dagger you prize so highly and plunge it into your heart!"

Philip took his father's dagger from his belt, slowly, with uncertainty, not strong intent. Studying it, he wondered if he could truly do it. He'd never been that low before. With the bond between him and Beatrice broken, he had no reason not to.

Then Theo said, "Or . . ."

Philip's head snapped up, eyes eager for a reason, any reason. Hope still clung to him like the dirt on his unwashed skin, like the vermin in his clothing. Hope was not a good thing, but it was there anyway. "Or what?" he rasped.

"I have heard the king's brother, Charles of Anjou, is raising an army to go capture Sicily. You can practically swim from there to the land of the infidels. You'd be halfway to Cathay then, I'll warrant, and Charles would be paying you to get there. You would need no money for the journey. Together, we probably have enough coin to buy horses and armor."

"We?"

"Why not? I tire of our present existence. Maybe it is harder to justify, or perhaps it is only that the thrill of parting the rich from their wealth has dulled. I am a soldier, and since I have heard of this Sicilian war, I have had an urge to return to that occupation."

Was it worth the sacrifice? Philip wondered. To risk his life in order to make one last attempt to fulfill his dream? What did he care? What did it matter? It was better than spending the rest of his life as he was, a pathetic wretch with a broken heart and no hope of it being mended. With not even the will or courage to end this cursed existence by his own hand.

"Yes, let's do this thing," he declared.

"And you, Rodrigo?" asked Theo.

"Of course. We fight together, no?"

"Even if it means fighting infidels?"

"What does a mercenary care who he fights?" Rodrigo turned to Philip. "You are sure about this place Cathay? The riches and the women?"

"It is what I've heard."

The Spaniard shrugged. "I must find out for myself. Do you think Gilly and the monk will come, as well?"

"Gilly would rather fight in a war than continue in his present living," said Theo. "And Pippin—need you ask? He will fight, always."

The three men were silent and they looked at one another, all a bit bemused over the decision they had come to. But they were no less resolved, even excited. Though Philip knew some swordplay, he had never fought in a real battle. It was very possible he'd get no farther than Sicily before being cut down by an enemy sword. He shrugged. If Beatrice could break her oath to him, then it was only fitting that he break his to her. He was certain that she no longer cared how he spent his life.

PART THREE

Hawken Castle
Spring 1268

T he rich brown earth was of a perfect consistency for planting after a week of fair weather. Beatrice worked her trowel into the dirt to make an even furrow. She wanted to give the seedlings the best possible chance of survival, for she had already put much time into nurturing the St.-John's-wort seeds given her by Father Bavent. She'd kept them in a sunlit nook of the kitchen for two months, waiting for the weather to be just right for transplanting, and she was pleased with the results. Lifting one of the seedlings from its pot, she carefully placed it in the furrow.

She smiled fondly as she recalled her many discussions with Father Bavent about gardening and about healing herbs. Had she thanked him properly for giving her the gift of this interest? Surely it had helped her to survive the harsh realities of her life, and it had certainly helped her endure all his talk about faith.

Well, that was not entirely true, was it? She did not endure it silently. Often she debated with him about spiritual matters, about her deep doubts, about her simmering anger. The priest always listened patiently, offering words of wisdom when they seemed appropriate, though never in a heavy-handed way. He said she must work out her faith in her own time and manner. She was not so sure she wanted to work it out at all.

What had God ever done for her? The list of His wrongs toward her was beginning to read like the story of Job. But she had not Job's forbearance. There were many times when she thought she would just "curse God and die," as Job might have been tempted to do. Never had she been closer than on that darkest of days last winter when fever had struck the community. Many became ill, and she had worked tirelessly to care for the sick, though she knew little of how to do so. Though she herself had fallen ill, most of the deaths were among the very old and the very young. Thus, her dear young Edmond, only three years old, had passed from this life, from the tender arms of his mother.

She'd been disconsolate for weeks afterward. For three days she had locked herself in her chamber, refusing to eat or bathe, barely sleeping. She would not even allow Leticia in. Finally Gareth had axed down the door, find-ing her nearly wasted away, close to death herself. And what had he said?

"Cleanse yourself and take food! I will not be married to a wraith. Maybe now you will do your duty and bear *me* a son."

Only the hope of holding another babe in her arms induced her to rise from her bed and determine to live. Even if she bore Gareth a child, it would be hers, as well, to love and nurture. Of a truth, she did not wish to die. As long as there was life, there was a chance that her life might take a turn for the good.

So she made herself continue to plod through each day. It had been shortly thereafter that she had gone to St. Bartholomew's on business and had chanced upon Father Bavent preparing some medicinal herbs in a little shed at the back of the property. She spoke to him of her frustration in helping the sick during the fever plague, of not having the ability to save her own child. He described a few of the herbs he was working with and how they were used to treat the sick. It sparked an interest in her, and he had taken her under his wing to teach her this herbal healing.

Suddenly she started, trowel in midair, and glanced over her shoulder. What was that? A horse in the courtyard? She waited with held breath. It must have been her imagination, though her husband was due back from London at any time. She focused her attention back on the task at hand. Not a task, really. She had come to enjoy working in the herb garden, taking plea-sure in watching things grow and partaking of the harvest of her handiwork. There were servants to help with the work, of course, for the garden was too large for one person to tend. But she tried to do as much herself as she could. It was one of her few pleasures.

Too few pleasures indeed!

If only after Edmond's death she'd had a husband to support her, to comfort her. Her assessment of Gareth when they had been teenagers had not been far off the mark—except that she had underestimated his cruelty by far. She could never understand the great pleasure he appeared to take in beating her. But once, when he was very drunk, he had mumbled Philip's name, or at least made reference to him.

"I'll show the bastard for trying to take what's mine!"

Had Gareth somehow discovered her and Philip's relationship? But why such high dudgeon toward her, or even Philip? Gareth was the victor. Yet the hatred in his expression was unmistakable. She'd realized then that the animosity between the brothers was mutual. It was not merely Philip's despising Gareth for taking his place in his father's house and heart.

Another sound caused Beatrice to flinch, and she directed her focus at the courtyard just beyond the hedge surrounding the garden. But the sound had not come from there. Footsteps crunched over the stones that made a footpath between the garden rows. Beatrice quickly averted her eyes. It wasn't the one she feared most—her husband. It was her mother-in-law. Perhaps if she pretended not to notice the woman, she would go away.

The footsteps came nearer and stopped. Beatrice took a breath and then lifted her head.

"Lady Clarise," she said.

"I thought I'd find you out here," Clarise replied in the guarded monotone she usually used when addressing Beatrice. Her voice lacked all feeling and indicated to Beatrice a loathing so deep she dare not let her voice betray the emotion. Beatrice wasn't sure why the woman hated her so.

"The Saint-John's-wort Father Bavent gave me are ready to be transplanted." Beatrice tried to inject polite civility into her tone, belying her own emotions—confusion, dislike, and more fear than she cared to admit—toward the woman.

"We have servants for that work," Clarise said. "It is unseemly for you to be on your knees digging in the dirt like a peasant."

"I enjoy it."

"I could not expect better from one raised at Cassley, little more than a peasant hovel itself. But you are a lady of Hawken now, and you are expected to behave in a respectable manner."

Beatrice bit her tongue and forced her tone to remain civil. "Many ladies tend to the health of their vassals and servants. I feel it is a respectable endeavor."

Clarise sniffed her disapproval. "People will take you for a witch if you are not careful."

"I see not why. Father Bavent himself has been teaching me the art of using medicinal herbs."

"Well, I did not come out here to debate theology with you. I came to inform you that your husband has returned from London. You should make yourself presentable."

Beatrice wanted to tell her that she didn't need the dowager to tell her what to do! She wanted to emphasize the fact that *she* was Lady Hawken now and would appreciate it if the old woman would remember that. She wanted to use the word *dowager* because Lady Clarise hated the term, as it implied age. Instead she swallowed all the scathing retorts she had thought but refrained from using over the years. She'd learned early in her marriage that insulting the dowager only brought painful repercussions upon herself from the lord.

"Yes," said Beatrice, "that is a good suggestion." She placed some emphasis on the final word; then she rose, brushed the soil from her hands and gown, and headed toward the castle, being careful to remain a pace or two behind Clarise in order to avoid further conversation.

Beatrice was certain that half of Gareth's cruelty was encouraged by his mother. She had once actually overheard Lady Clarise tell Gareth that he should beat Beatrice for an egregious wrong committed. That had been early in their marriage when Beatrice had gone out riding alone without asking permission. She'd paid for that "crime" not only with a beating but with a kind of imprisonment, as well. She was never allowed to leave the castle unattended by two or more knights, and she must always have permission from her husband first. In truth, she was assigned a guard of sorts—more like a watchdog!—to ensure she never tried to slip away. That was why the herb garden became so important to her—it helped to take the place of her first love—riding.

She simply did not understand why her husband and mother-in-law wished to make her life miserable. Leticia thought it just came naturally to them. They were unkind to everyone.

Inside the castle Beatrice went immediately to the great hall. The lord was nowhere to be seen, though several of the men who had traveled to London with him were milling around. Beatrice inquired of them, but Gareth's exit seemed to have slipped their notice.

"He is likely already retired to his solar, freshening up after his long journey," suggested the dowager.

"Then I shall see to an early meal for them," said Beatrice, turning toward the kitchen.

"They can wait to sup. Mayhap your lord will wish your . . . ah . . . attentions after being away so many days." The woman's brow was arched in a coy manner. All Beatrice saw was an evil glint. But then, her ability to produce an heir was doubtless the only worth the woman saw in her. If she didn't do so soon, Beatrice would not be surprised to find her marriage annulled and herself banished to St. Mary's Priory. Such a prospect held great appeal to Beatrice, at least in her fantasies. Reality, however, was a harsher mistress than her mother-in-law. She was still young, barely twenty-one years old. Anything might yet happen to ease the burdens of her life. Of course having both her husband and her mother-in-law struck by the same bolt of lightning might be too perfect to hope for, but Gareth *could* die. Hadn't every other man in her life died? Why not him? Would it not be ironic if he, of them all, should live forever?

It would not be the first irony of her marriage. Most grievous was that about two years ago the king, in a gesture to bring goodwill back to the land, had begun to repatriate lands forfeited by the rebels. She had wept when she heard of this, but Leticia had comforted her with the suggestion that even had she not married Gareth, she might not have benefited from the repatriation because she was a woman, and neither would have young Edmond because he was an infant at the time. She must continue to believe that her marriage was necessary—or else die inside. Then Edmond had died, leaving her bound to a useless agreement. She had spoken to Father Bavent, hoping that Edmond's death could give her grounds for an annulment, but the priest had sadly informed her that it wouldn't. Gareth had upheld his end of the bargain and could not be slighted because of an act of God.

Without saying a word, Beatrice walked toward the narrow stairway leading to the upper floor. She met Leticia on the landing.

"The lord is back," Beatrice said flatly, even though she didn't want to think about it.

"Well, you had a week," Leticia said with understanding.

Beatrice shrugged. They could speak no more freely in such an open place. The dowager had spies everywhere. "Leticia, would you come with me to my solar so I can make myself presentable for him?" Beatrice had to accept the inevitable. She'd had a week of relative freedom. A week for her bruises to heal. A week not to dread each night when he came to her solar. A week to briefly feel human and not like a worthless piece of chattel.

When they were alone in Beatrice's chamber, Leticia began to lay out a fresh gown and undergarments.

"Never mind that," said Beatrice. "I didn't really want to freshen up. He doesn't care if I'm clean or dirty. I could smell like dung, and he'd still take me."

"Well, he's used to it, isn't he? Some of the tavern wenches he takes smell worse than dung."

"Leticia!" Beatrice gasped. It wasn't like her prim maid to speak so crudely. Then she giggled and added gamely, "What do you mean? They *are* dung!"

Leticia glanced around. "No spies about."

"I don't care. I'm due for a beating anyway. I started my monthly flux today."

"Oh, my poor Bea." Leticia rubbed her shoulder sympathetically. Beatrice did not flinch from the gesture as she once might have. She no longer cared enough to balk at the pity of others.

"At least it may spare me his attentions tonight." With a sigh she sat on the chaise at the foot of her bed. "Every time he goes away, I pray he will meet with an accident. I am that evil. But sometimes I simply don't care."

"You must care, Beatrice," Leticia said emphatically. "You must not bring God's wrath upon you with a careless thought."

Beatrice laughed dryly. "If my life isn't already evidence of God's wrath, then perhaps I should be afraid that worse might come!" Listlessly, she picked up the hoop of needlework by the side of the chaise. She used to hate sewing but now found she appreciated the shield it provided. She could absorb herself in sewing and pretend the unpleasantness around her did not exist, just as she did in her garden. "In any case, the penance Father Bavent gives when I confess my evil thoughts is light. I think even he understands. He has little love for Lord Hawken, either. I honestly try not to think bad things."

"Well, then, maybe you'll be all right."

"The truly terrible thoughts I think are the ones I think when Gareth comes into my bed at night. I imagine—"

"Say no more, m'lady!" Leticia implored. "Thinking is one thing—speaking is another."

"I can't help if I still think of . . . him." Tears welled up in Beatrice's eyes, and she could barely see where to insert the needle into the linen cloth.

"You must not."

"I tell you, I cannot stop it. I've asked God to expunge thoughts of him from my mind. I've begged Him to! Do you think I want to conjure the pain of what is lost while I am immersed in current pain?" Absently she reached a hand to the chain she wore always around her neck. On it was Philip's brooch, the one she'd found in the grass after his departure. She fingered the plain lines that signified the Hawken crest. When Gareth asked about it, she told him she wore it to remind her that her loyalties lay with Hawken now. Maybe he believed her. It was true in a way—her loyalties lay with the true Lord of Hawken.

"It has been five years, Bea. Why torture yourself?"

"Because I have truly loved only one man in my life, and only one man has truly loved me. True love, Leticia. How often does anyone find that? I cannot forget."

The solar door burst open. A thrill of fear shot through Beatrice. Had her words been heard? The fear was no less when she saw the intruder was her husband. He would surely kill her if he knew about Philip—but there was no murder in his dark eyes.

"There you are," he said with an accusatory tone. "A husband expects to be greeted by his wife after a long absence."

"I-I . . . ah, came to clean up a bit first," she lied, though she was hardly cleaning up while lying upon her chaise with sewing in hand.

He snorted his disbelief. "Leave, maid. I want to be alone with my wife." When Leticia hesitated and glanced at Beatrice, he said more forcefully, "I said *leave*! Don't look to her for approval. I am lord of this house. Do as I say!"

Quickly Leticia rose and hurried from the room. Beatrice did not blame her, for it was not unknown for Gareth to beat the servants, as well. She knew that Leticia had received one or two cuffs upon the head for slow responses to orders. Leticia purposely left the door open, but Gareth slammed it shut.

"Put your sewing down and get on your bed," he ordered.

She wondered why he was so anxious. Surely he had not denied himself while away, for his many faults included rampant unfaithfulness to their marriage vows. She did, however, lay aside her sewing and rise from the chaise, but she did not go to the bed.

"M'lord, you may as well know my monthly flux is upon me," she said dispassionately.

"Is it?" He strode closer to her. "So once again you have betrayed me."

She tensed. "I don't know how you can call it betrayal—"

She barely saw his hand move. The sting of his slap upon her cheek quickly brought tears to her eyes.

"God only knows what goes on when I am not looking," he said. "I would not put it past that maid of yours to have the talent for getting rid of an unborn child."

"She would never! I would never! Believe it or not, I want a baby as much as you do. I don't know what prevents it."

"You bore a brat to that shriveled-up old Sardwick," he rejoined.

"Yes, I did," Beatrice said archly. She was past caring if he struck her. She had been expecting it the moment she'd heard he returned.

"What are you implying?"

"Only that *my* equipment has proven itself functional."

His only response to that most slanderous of all accusations was another slap and another. He pushed her until she was backed up against the bed. It wasn't long before he shoved her onto the bed and the abuse continued.

Later, he rose and clothed himself. Before he exited her solar, he turned and said, "There is news you should know about."

She lay listlessly upon the bed with the covers pulled up tightly about her chin.

Gareth continued, "Edward has taken the Cross."

"Another Crusade?" she asked, and something sparked within her.

"Yes. I and several of his close comrades have taken the Cross with him."

The spark in Beatrice turned into a wild surge of hope. Gareth was going on Crusade! That could mean he'd be gone for two years and more. Two years of freedom for her! She became practically giddy with the thought of it.

She did not realize her reaction was so transparent until Gareth spoke. "Don't get your hopes up, woman. You will be going with me."

Her ecstasy plummeted as quickly as a bubble collapsing after being poked. But she couldn't give it up easily.

"I do not wish to go. It isn't a woman's place."

"You will go whether you wish it or not. Do you think I would trust you here alone, left to your own devious devices?" He buckled on his sword as he spoke. It seemed to give him a sense of power in her presence. He often lovingly stroked it, as he never did her.

"Besides, Princess Eleanora will accompany Prince Edward, and she fancies the company of a few women of her station. She has especially requested your attendance. Don't ask me why, but she has taken a liking to you."

"What about her children?"

"Richard of Cornwall has been appointed to look after the prince's affairs while he is gone, and his children, as well. Luckily, you no longer have any such concerns. You are free to take this journey, and you shall take it. I could be away for two years and more. We wouldn't want to waste perfectly good years for getting you with child. The only thing that could possibly save you is if you conceived a child while we are preparing to leave."

"How long until then?"

"It could take as much as a year or more to raise men and finances."

She said no more, and he turned and took his leave. If she argued further, he'd only beat her again. Besides, she comforted herself that a lot could happen in a year. Her husband could fall from his horse and break his neck.

Immediately she chided herself for the wicked thought, offering up a silent prayer instead. Oh, God, I wish no ill upon anyone, even he who would so misuse me. But please, God, somehow deliver me from this onerous duty.

Perhaps she would conceive a child before they left. Even Gareth would not drag a pregnant wife, or one with a newborn infant, to the Holy Lands. But she was beginning to hold little hope of conceiving. For all the philandering Gareth did, she had never heard of any bastards he'd fathered. However, as she well knew, to even hint that he was to blame for the lack of offspring was dangerous indeed.

She was trying to think of other ways to get out of the trip when Leticia returned. Beatrice told her the news.

"Why don't you wish to go, Bea?" asked the maid as she fetched a fresh gown from a trunk for Beatrice to wear for supper.

"Why do you even have to ask? Two years free of him, why else?"

"Yes, I can see that, but . . ." Leticia paused as she laid a clean blue surcote on the chaise.

"What are you thinking, Leticia?"

"Only that it would be a marvelous adventure. Imagine seeing foreign lands, the very lands where Christ walked!"

"That has not the appeal for me as it has for you." She hoped Leticia did not start preaching to her now, for if the maid had one fault it was her religious prattling. She was convinced Beatrice's soul was veering dangerously away from heaven and felt it her responsibility to put it back on the right path.

"When you were younger, you were quite taken with your father's tales of his Crusade with the good king Louis of France. Your eyes would light up, and you would tell me that one day you would be a knight and go crusading."

"I am older now." Beatrice noted that her tone *was* that of an old lady, brittle and sad.

"Do you think you'll be happier left here, even with the lord gone? *She* will still be here. There will still be guards watching you, perhaps even more so with him out of the country. And think of this, Bea. If you are in the company of the prince and his party, in a situation where privacy will be at a premium, won't the lord treat you better? It is common knowledge that Prince Edward adores his Eleanora. I doubt he would abide Gareth's treatment of you. You could easily have more freedom there than you ever dreamed of."

"I had not thought of that."

Beatrice slipped off her wrapper and began dressing. Her hands trembled a little with the laces of her cote. Excitement began to bubble up as she thought of foreign lands, strange adventures, new companions. As usual, her maid had brought forth some interesting points.

Leticia smiled. "My lady, I have not seen such a light in your eyes since . . . in a very long time."

"Mayhap I will find my old self in Outremer."

Still smiling, Leticia added, "Mayhap you will find more."

Beatrice wondered what she meant but didn't ask, for she was probably making some spiritual reference. Although she was not going to be looking for God, the Holy Lands were no doubt the best place to seek Him . . . if one *were* looking.

Quickly Beatrice finished dressing. Supper was still to be served. As she left her solar, she felt a lightness in her step she hadn't felt for years.

32

Tuscany
Summer 1268

War was a disappointment to Philip, though not in the way it was for most men. For one thing, he had thus far survived.

Though he placed himself in the fore of every skirmish, though he took every risk, though he volunteered for every dangerous task, he stood, at the end of nearly two years of soldiering, unscathed. Gilly was furious with him, fiercely declaring that in the next battle he would not fight beside such a madman. Philip certainly hadn't asked the man to do so, but what else did he expect? His friends would not think to do otherwise than fight side by side.

"Leave the worm be," Theo said. "He's quite the hero, and I'm proud of him."

"Nay, Theo, I am no hero," Philip protested, and the answering look Theo gave him seemed to say that he understood.

The fact that Philip's first battle had been victorious was quite lost on him. In that first battle at Benevento in the early winter of 1266, the army of Charles of Anjou, now King Charles of Sicily, had met the enemy and beaten them in a single day. Philip pondered the use of the word *enemy*. He had no particular animosity toward the opposing army and hardly even understood the politics behind the campaign. The pope had termed the king's adventure a "Crusade." Manfred, the leader of the opposing army and claimant for the throne of Sicily, did employ some Muslims in his army. It was even said he had converted to the religion of the infidels himself. That may have been why the pope wanted him defeated and had supported Charles in claiming the leadership of the Sicilian kingdom. Philip cared not who ruled this region. But since Charles was paying him, he owed him his fealty. Perhaps it helped that the king's roots were in Anjou, as were Philip's.

Thus Philip found himself not only alive but a victor in a strange land. He also had honed his battle skills and was now adept in the art of warfare. Which meant his chances of survival were that much better. Well, then, he would survive. He might still get to Cathay and find his fortune. At the least he might gain a knighthood from this, though that was an unlikely prospect since his superiors already thought him a knight. They had not questioned it when he had lied about the matter while enlisting in Lyon two years ago.

After that first battle there had been a few minor skirmishes, but since Manfred had been killed at Benevento, the opposition had waned. Talk of a more major Crusade to the Holy Land held Philip and his friends to Charles's army—that and the hope of being paid. Charles's finances were uncertain and pay was not forthcoming, so the soldiers stayed in hope of remuneration. As rumors of a Crusade grew, Gilly took it in his head to go on a real Crusade before he died. Philip and Rodrigo had no argument with this, for it would bring them closer to Cathay. Pippin was eager, as well, but mostly because the lull after the first battle was making him restless. Theo was the only one who showed ambivalence. While the army was occupying Tuscany, he had met a woman, a widow with two children, and had grown smitten with the little family. He didn't often speak of it, but Philip thought the man was weary of the unsettled life he'd lived for so many years. After all, in France he was the son of a lord, and when his father died, there was still a chance he would inherit the fief and title.

Tuscany was a pleasant enough place to abide. "Mayhap I'll find myself a voluptuous Tuscan woman and live out my days here," Philip told himself more than once. "It would be a peasant's life, but I could do worse. I *have* done worse!"

But he knew he would not stay, though he wasn't certain why. In truth, he wasn't ready to admit the reason. How could he admit that the anger and bitterness inside him were too deeply imbedded to allow him to embrace happiness?

Waiting became his chief occupation as a mercenary. Charles may have subdued Sicily and moved his authority as far north as Tuscany, but unrest in the area continued, so the army simply existed between flare-ups. And there was also the wait for the Crusade to begin in earnest. In May of 1267, King

Louis IX officially "took the Cross." But making the Crusade an official entity only delayed the start of it further, for with the support of the king, the army grew, making it that much more difficult to organize.

On a warm spring afternoon, Theo sauntered over to where Philip was sitting beneath a fig tree, cleaning his gear.

"I've some news," he said, hunkering down on the ground next to Philip. "Word has come of an uprising in Lucera, and because it is largely Muslim, the pope is insisting that Charles take an army there to subdue it. It is believed that Conradin's agents are stirring up trouble."

Conradin was Manfred's half brother, who now that he had reached his majority, or close enough to it, was vying for his brother's lost crown.

"Good," said Philip. "We've tarried too long in one place. I'll be glad to be on the move again."

"I've decided to stay behind. I've already told our commander."

"So you're going to become a family man?"

Theo shrugged. "I've tried everything else. Why not that? I'm not a young man anymore. It is time I had a few children of my own before it is too late."

Philip hated the idea of parting ways with Theo. The man had become like an older brother to him, maybe even at times like a father. He'd never had a friend like this, and certainly never for so long. But he should have known at the start that it could not last. No good thing ever did.

"What of the others?"

"Gilly will stay with me," Theo replied. "He swore an oath of loyalty to me the day we parted from my father's land, and he will not break it. Not even his desire to go crusading will supersede it. Pippin and Rodrigo will go with you. Like you, they are weary of the inactivity. And Rodrigo thinks only you know the way to Cathay, so he won't let you out of his sight."

"I don't know anything. He's a fool to follow me."

"Ah, Worm, you don't perceive your own power."

"What do you mean?"

Theo nodded sagely. "You truly have no idea, do you? Don't you know how you have changed since I dragged you away from that Parisian tavern four years ago? You were a sallow-eyed lad then. Look in the pond yon. You now fill out your mail, which you certainly didn't the day we stole it for you. Don't you remember how it hung limply from your shoulders? You've got hair on your chest and a beard on your chin. You are a man now, Worm, seasoned like a good sword."

Philip didn't need to see his reflection in the water. He knew what his friend said was true, at least regarding the physical manifestations. And he was glad the innocent boy of the past was gone. His hide was tough now, too tough to be hurt by others. Unconsciously he lifted his hand and touched the scar over his left brow, the scar he had earned at the battle of Benevento. Though it was healed, it was still not a pretty sight. He had other scars on his body, as most soldiers did, but none were as painful as the scars that didn't show, the ones inflicted upon him by those who were supposed to have loved him. He would never be hurt like that again.

"Then why do you persist on calling me Worm?" Philip asked, wishing to divert his thoughts from such a morose path. He tried to sound perturbed, but he knew the nickname was used fondly.

"Probably because I often miss Robert, my dead brother. I don't know if I ever told you that I called him Worm, too."

"No, you never told me." Philip felt an unexpected lump rise in his throat. That bit of information only affirmed the mutual bond between him and Theo, something between brothers or between fathers and sons—only those were brothers and fathers of an ilk that Philip had never known. Uncomfortable with the niggling emotion this evoked, he said roughly, "Well, they are still fools to follow me. I don't wish to lead them."

"Sometimes what you wish matters not. You have the gift. I saw hints of it from the beginning, and these years of warfare have emphasized it more than ever. You are a leader at heart, Worm. I have seen you in battle, and men other than your friends have oft looked to you for direction. And you have provided it."

"I've only done what I have had to do."

"Unlike many, you have *known* what you had to do, and you have done it." When Philip tried to protest, Theo hurried on. "I know. You think your aggression, even your brashness, springs from a sense of carelessness for your own life. But it would not come so naturally to you if that were the only reason for it. Men would follow you if you let them. And when I am gone, you, Philip, will be the leader of our little band—whether you wish it or not. They will look to you, especially Rodrigo."

"That's ridiculous. They are both older than me."

"It won't matter. Just lead them well, Worm."

"What if I desert them as you are deserting us?" Philip couldn't keep his bitterness from escaping. He added quickly, "I'm sorry, Theo. You've a right to your own life. It's just—" He could not finish. He couldn't say what Theo's friendship had meant to him. What if it hadn't meant as much to Theo? What if such a verbal gesture was rejected? Philip knew he couldn't stand to be scorned yet again.

"I love her, Worm. Imagine that!" mused Theo. "And even more wondrous, Aletta loves me. I must hold on to this as long as I can."

It was hard, but Philip gave Theo a reassuring pat on the shoulder. "I understand," he said.

Charles's army departed a week later, leaving behind a contingent, of which Theo was part, to hold Tuscany. The mountainous terrain east of Rome hampered the departing army's progress. They had no sooner arrived at their destination and laid siege on Lucera when word reached them that Conradin had defeated the forces Charles had left in Tuscany and was moving to intercept the Angevin army. Philip worried about Theo and Gilly but convinced himself that they were too tough to die.

Charles quickly abandoned the siege of Lucera, and his army marched to a more defensible position, commanding the Mount Bove pass where the southern Italian town of Tagliacozzo lay at its foot. Philip volunteered to scout out the enemy position, taking a party of a hundred horsemen. He discovered that Conradin's army had moved surprisingly fast and was closer than expected. The enemy force numbered about six thousand, larger than Charles's army of four thousand.

The scouting party was making its way back when it stumbled into the vanguard of Conradin's army, a smaller force but not by much. Philip charged eagerly into the first clash of the battle. The enemy gave the Angevin force a good run. Rodrigo was unscathed, but Philip's arm was slashed and Pippin lost his horse before the enemy retreated. There were only six Angevin deaths and substantially more of the enemy. Philip wrapped a cloth around his wound to stanch the bleeding, and then, with Pippin mounted behind him on his destrier, they returned to the main force. Only when he made his report to his commander did he fully understand the significance of his victory in that small skirmish.

"You've done well, Sir Philip," said the commander. "By your report, Conradin must have wanted to enter the plain on the east side of the Salto River. You have kept them west of the river and slowed their progress so that we will reach the bridge first, thus forcing them to make a river crossing. You deserve a reward for this valor."

Philip was quick to disclose the request weighing most on his mind. "I would that you'd give my comrade Hugh Pippin a horse to replace the one lost in the skirmish."

The commander eyed him with some admiration. Holding one's comrade above oneself was the essence of chivalry. "As you wish," he replied. "Tell Pippin to look over the stock of spares and choose one."

How often Philip had dreamed of performing some valorous deed in battle and winning a boon from his lord, a reward that would make him worthy to take Beatrice as his wife. Now it hardly fazed him to trade such an opportunity to aid a friend, even the stoical ex-monk.

The two armies camped on opposite sides of the river that night. The battle would be engaged the next day. It was a warm, sultry August night, but the energy was high in the Angevin camp, as it must also have been in the enemy camp. The night before a battle was different from any other night because with it came the knowledge that it might be a man's last night on earth. Groups of men played at dice while others polished their weapons. Some found the priest who accompanied the army and made their peace with God. If they were to die, they knew they had done their utmost for Christendom.

Philip had no such delusions.

He knew he would never be a partaker in God's blessings. God's eye was definitely turned away from him—if indeed there was a God. And if there was, it must be true that the sins of the fathers were visited upon the sons. Philip could think of no other reason for his luckless life.

Philip ran a brush over his destrier's tan coat. He thought fondly of the last horse he had possessed, the stout palfrey Dumpling. He had been at heart a better mount, though Topaz, named for the golden hue of his coat, was not without merit. He'd been quite scrawny when Philip had bought him two years ago, but he'd been able to afford no better. He'd been able to buy only two horses with his dice winnings—the others for his friends had to be stolen. Under Philip's care the animal had filled out, and now his silky coat truly warranted the grand name the previous owner had given him. He'd carried Philip well in previous battles. They had both been properly blooded.

Unlike many of his comrades Philip felt no fear of tomorrow's battle. That was for those who feared death. He no longer welcomed death as he once had. He simply felt nothing.

Ah, you fool! he berated himself. Then he shook away his morose thoughts, laid aside the brush, and joined a knot of men gambling with dice.

33

That summer morning in August dawned warm and hazy. Two divisions of King Charles's army drew up on the east side of the Salto bridge. They did not expect the audacious charge of the enemy force on the west side of the bridge, led by Henry of Castile. But they fought fiercely to hold them back.

Philip saw Rodrigo knocked from his horse into the water. He couldn't tell how badly he was injured. Maybe he would survive. Pippin was slashing away at the enemy as if cutting apples from a tree. One glimpse of his friends was all Philip could manage before he was engaged in a struggle with a German mercenary. He cut and slashed and met each counterblow adroitly with his shield. Topaz kept a steady head and responded well to Philip's movements. In such close quarters on the bridge, though, the German was not Philip's only worry. Unintentional blows from his comrades also had to be guarded against.

Philip had no sooner cut down the German when another enemy knight was upon him, this one an Italian Ghibelline by his crest. Conradin's army was an allied effort consisting of Sicilians, Italians of several regions, and a small corps of stout German knights from Conradin's home. Philip hoped this diversity would prove their undoing.

At the moment, however, they were far from being undone, especially when part of the enemy force found a shallow crossing of the river and turned on the Angevin army's flank. Soon they were unable to hold their position as their numbers were steadily decimated by the enemy. Finally, the Angevins broke and ran.

Philip looked around for Pippin. It seemed he had but one friend left in the world, even if it was the silent, implacable monk. Philip had not the heart to leave him behind if he still lived. Relief washed over him as he saw the monk mounted and no more battered than the rest of the army. They exchanged a brief look before they wheeled about and made their retreat.

Philip wondered where the third division of the Angevin army was, the one under command of Charles himself. This would be an opportune time for it to appear and offer the retreating troops support. But they did not. The retreating Angevins raced southeast up the valley. They hadn't gone far when Philip noted there was no pursuit. At the same moment he realized no one seemed to be in command of the routed army.

He slowed Topaz and took a moment to scan the horizon. He wasn't sure what he was looking for, but something kept niggling at the back of his mind.

Then he saw it. On a rise to the west of the road to Avezzano, he saw Charles's division. Perhaps they had been in hiding so as to ambush the pursuing enemy. More likely they were merely being held in reserve. For what, though, Philip could not guess. Surely they must have seen the retreating Angevins. If the retreat could be halted before it scattered too far, the two forces could join and present a good front for a renewed assault. But no one else appeared to have seen Charles's force. It was up to Philip.

Without further consideration he sprang into action. Shouting and waving his arms, he tried to signal the retreating men, but none perceived his intent. He saw the standard bearer still clutching the tattered Angevin standard and headed his mount toward him. Philip tried to get him to raise the standard, but either he didn't understand or was unwilling, so Philip grabbed it and thrust it into the air himself, waving it wildly about.

That was not enough, so he dug his spurs into Topaz's flank and raced to the fore of the troops to be better seen. The animal proved his mettle beyond doubt as Philip put a handful of lengths between him and the Angevins. Riding across the vanguard, waving the standard, he finally induced the men to slow and eventually stop. He pointed out the reserve division, now riding down the ridge to join them.

He tried not to feel proud when Charles rewarded his initiative by giving him command over what was left of the retreating divisions. It was only because he'd held the banner that the men had rallied. He'd not done anything so impressive. In truth, he would have refused the commission, but there was no time for arguments. If they were to have any success, they must stage a counterattack while the Italian forces were regrouping after their minor victory.

Much to Philip's surprise, the men raised no question at all to his leadership. Had Theo been right after all? But how would it ever benefit him, a landless bastard? He would never have a fief to rule and vassals to command. Yet he did not refuse the responsibility thrust upon him.

When they met Conradin's army again, they were still outnumbered, but Alard of St. Valery, a seasoned crusader and one of Charles's close advisors, took a small force of men and lured part of the enemy army away from the main force. Philip knew an important axiom of battle was "divide and conquer," and it worked beautifully for the Angevins. Final success was theirs.

The Angevin victory at Tagliacozzo not only gave Charles solid control of Sicily and much of southern Italy, but it also established the Capetians, the French royal family, now with two crowned heads in the family, as a dynasty to be reckoned with in Europe. This paved the way for Louis IX to plow ahead with his plans for an Eighth Crusade to the Holy Land.

———————

Being part of an occupying army held no allure for Philip. The battles he had fought in had been short, though the time between long and tedious. Over the next weeks he often wondered what to do next. Choices were few because money was always in short supply. He knew Pippin and Rodrigo would follow his lead, so not wanting to lead them astray, he dragged his feet making any decision, which turned out to be fortuitous.

He was currying Topaz's sleek golden coat when, glancing up, he saw two familiar figures approach—one as big as a mountain, the other short and wiry. Dropping his brush he hurried toward them. Without thought he flung his arms around the burly figure as he would greet a brother—a beloved brother.

"We took you for dead," Philip said, dropping his arms, a little embarrassed when he realized what he had done.

"We are alive," said Theo. Though he grinned, his tone lacked essential enthusiasm.

Philip glanced covertly at Gilly, who shrugged and gave a slight shake of the head as if to say, "Don't press the matter."

"Come, let's find Rodrigo and Pip, and you can tell us what you've been up to," said Philip. "Rodrigo will be beside himself. He has felt terrible parting company with you."

"At least you have all survived the fighting," Theo said.

"Incredibly, yes. Rodrigo nearly drowned when he took a fall from the Salto bridge, but we found him washed up on the bank. When we realized his arm was broken, Pip revealed some hidden medical talents and set the bone so that it is nearly back to normal."

They had been walking over a meadow as they talked and now came to the camp of soldiers. Soon they were reunited with their other friends, and there was much laughter and hearty greetings. Rodrigo also could not control his emotion, and he grasped Theo in a fond embrace. None would dare, regardless of their affection, to thus engage Gilly. But Philip was just as pleased to see the cantankerous little man, too. He'd missed their frequent sparring.

Theo and Gilly gave a sketchy account of their activities in the several months since their separation in Tuscany. As Philip had heard, Conradin's army had attacked and defeated the Angevins left to guard the Tuscan region. The French had scattered in their retreat, and though many had been hunted down and killed, some, including Theo and Gilly, had managed to escape.

"It appears you have been cured of the desire to be a family man," Rodrigo said.

Gilly was making frantic silencing hand motions, but Theo cut in, "Never mind, Gilly. They would know eventually." To the others he went on glumly, "You might say I have been cured." For a moment it seemed as if he would say no more, then he forged ahead. "You may as well know. My Aletta was killed in the aftermath of Conradin's attack. The louts burned and pillaged her village, and she died protecting her children. I was not there for her—"

"You nearly were killed yourself trying to get back to her," put in Gilly. To the others he explained, "When our army knew the battle was a lost cause, everyone retreated, for we knew the enemy would give us no quarter. All except Theo. He fought to get back to the village, but it was too late. Only then did we go into hiding—after he got the children to the safety of a local monastery." Facing Theo, he added firmly, "You did all you could."

Theo looked unconvinced. With resignation, he said, "What is done is done."

"Theo," Philip asked after a few moments of silence, "what should we do now?" He was quite willing to give up any semblance of leadership he might have acquired. It was rightfully Theo's anyway.

"I came because I heard Charles's army was encamped here. Gilly and I hoped to find you three," Theo replied. "It took all my will to get this far. What were you planning to do before I came?"

Rodrigo and Pippin cast questioning glances at Philip. It had become their habit to look to him for direction.

Reluctantly he answered, "We were waiting to see where the wind blew."

"There's still talk of another Crusade," Gilly said. "King Louis is getting ships assembled and collecting a tithe from the towns and villages of France. I've even heard King Henry of England has authorized Prince Edward to join forces with Louis."

"But Charles seems reluctant to support his brother," said Philip. "Now that he has his Sicilian crown, he doesn't want to endanger his position by a lengthy absence. If we had the coin, we might try to join up with Louis's army." It was obvious from their ragged and half-starved look that Theo and Gilly had no money.

Theo sighed and everyone glanced in his direction, but he only responded with a shrug and a mumbled, "As you wish."

————————

When a year passed and King Charles still had not made a solid commitment to the Crusade, Gilly grew impatient. "I have heard Louis's fleet will assemble at the port of Cagliari in Sardinia. We could take a ship from Palermo and meet them."

"We could get to Tunisia faster if we left directly from here," said Philip.

"There are no ships from here. And even if there were, the cost would be exorbitant. I know of a fishing vessel that would take us there for only the cost of our labor."

"What of our horses?"

"We would have to sell them and get new mounts at Cagliari."

Philip resisted the urge to look to Theo for input. Had the big man been a king, it would have been said that he had abdicated. He had lost his old zest for life, and that worried Philip more than his lack of leadership. In truth, Philip had fallen into that role comfortably. More often than not his friends looked to him for guidance rather than to Theo, and Philip had finally come to terms with it.

"It sounds better than sitting around here doing nothing," Philip said. "Does everyone agree?"

There were no protests. Pippin gave a very vigorous nod of his tonsured head. He had come to Gilly's way of thinking, and also was determined to go on a Crusade. Rodrigo was still mostly interested in getting to Palestine as a steppingstone to the Far East. And since it appeared as if Charles was taking his time in making a commitment, Gilly's suggestion seemed the most logical.

By the time they reached Sardinia, Philip swore he never wanted to see another fish. He had done many things in his life, but working on a fishing boat had been the worst job yet. Moreover, it had been a rough winter crossing. One of the vessel's crew had gone overboard and drowned. No sooner had they set foot on land than word reached them, in February of 1270, that Charles had finally taken the Cross. But now they were committed in their path, and Gilly insisted that crusading with the pious King Louis would bring them better fortune.

34

The would-be crusaders were beset with one misfortune after another. The death of Pope Clement IV in 1268 sounded the first blow, and the fact that the cardinals were slow to replace him meant that the Crusade must proceed without a spiritual head. The contingent from Aragon, which set sail in September of 1269, met with heavy storms and was forced to turn back. The English were having difficulty raising money because the royal coffers had been decimated by the civil war.

King Louis departed France on July 2, 1270. The fleet met with storms and was scattered. By the time they reached Sardinia several men and horses had been lost, and over a hundred men were so sick they had to be put ashore. Thus they were happy to find new recruits awaiting them there. Philip learned then that, contrary to what most believed, the expedition was headed for Tunis rather than Egypt.

Talking with some of the knights in the crusader camp, Philip heard many opinions about the objectives of the expedition.

"The king's brother Charles put him up to it," said one man. "The Tunisian caliph is a threat to Charles's Sicilian throne."

"Nay," said another. "The king has learned that the caliph supplies the sultan of Egypt with many arms and provisions. Cutting these off will weaken Egypt."

"Then the expedition will turn to Egypt once we have defeated the Tunisians?" Philip asked. He hoped they would not return to Europe after only one campaign. Being a soldier was the one occupation at which he'd found some success, and he hated for it to cease.

"Of course. The threat to the Holy Lands centers in Egypt."

"You are all mistaken," said another knight. "I happen to know that our sainted king heard that Emir Mohammed of Tunisia has expressed a desire to become Christian. Louis seeks a most important Christian conversion."

"We came to fight infidels!"

"Yes," said Philip dryly. "Converting them will spoil all our fun."

He was pleased that his jest brought a response of laughter from the men. The last thing on earth he wanted was to dwell on the spiritual ramifications of the expedition. Most of the men were of his mind—that the spiritual element of the Crusade was only a thin veil for their real passion, which was simply to fight. But on such an enterprise it was hard to avoid enlisting a good number of zealots. Gilly had become one of the latter, spouting off constantly about the holy cause and how his participation would assure his place in heaven. He and Rodrigo had nearly come to blows on several occasions when Gilly denigrated evil infidels. Rodrigo's spiritual ambivalence kept him rather pragmatic about his crusading commitment as long as the black and white of it wasn't forced down his throat. He would have deserted had not Philip talked him into staying, reminding him of what lay behind it all—their dream of reaching Cathay.

The fleet landed on the Tunisian coast two days after departing Sardinia. They easily captured the harbor, then disembarked onto a tongue of marshy land near the village of Carthage, where they set up camp. They held off enemy attacks but quickly realized their position was less than ideal. It lacked fresh water, especially enough for a force of ten thousand men, and food sources were limited. The humid summer heat only added to the general misery. Fever and stomach flux swept through the camp. Louis's second son, only twenty years old, died. The heir, Philip, also became ill, as did Louis himself. There were several other deaths among the nobles.

Rodrigo and Gilly also became sick, along with scores of the common soldiers. But Pippin was hit hardest. Philip and Theo were untouched by illness, though Philip received a nasty cut on his cheek during one of the skirmishes. It festered a long time before finally healing. The two tended their sick friends until the army was mustered for an attack on the little fortified town of Carthage. But, after taking the town, King Louis decided that the main force should continue to camp in the open, sheltering only the sick in the town. Gilly and Rodrigo were carried away to the town, but before they could take away Pippin, he died.

Philip and Theo had been by the silent monk's side at the moment of death. For the first and last time in six years the monk spoke.

"Seek ye first the kingdom of God, and all these things shall be added unto you!" the man rasped.

Philip squirmed. He told himself that it was mere chance that the monk happened to be looking directly at him when he spoke.

Later, after they buried Pippin, Philip and Theo were cleaning and repairing their battle gear when Theo said to Philip, "I always knew the monk thought highly of you."

"What do you mean?"

"He offered his last words to you, didn't he?"

"We were both there, Theo." Philip's hand wavered over repairing a rent in his mail hauberk.

"But he was looking at you—"

"He was fevered and probably didn't know what he was looking at, much less what he was saying." But Philip's growing discomfort indicated that even he didn't fully believe that. "Why would he speak so of God anyway?" Philip wondered aloud. "I thought he'd spurned God."

"Just because he spurned his holy orders doesn't mean he rejected God," Theo said. "That he kept his vow of silence all these years surely was a sign of his faith."

"Why break it at the end?"

"I don't know. Sounds like he had a message for you."

"Or you . . . or the wind."

They returned their attention to their work for a time. The blade of Philip's sword was scored in several places from years of battles, and it was telling of his skill that he still used the same sword he had long ago taken from the booty of his first robbery. It had been stained with his enemy's blood many times over. As he wiped off fresh soil, he tried to remember his first kill—and could not. His adversaries seldom had faces discernible beneath their helms, but only Philip knew that when he faced an enemy, he found the will to do violence only by picturing his brother's face on that of his opponent. After all this time, the ire remained. While he might be fighting Saracens now, they were not his real enemy.

He thought of Pippin's last words: "Seek ye first the kingdom of God . . ."

Could the words have been inspired by God? A heavenly insight at the moment of death? Had they really been directed at Philip? Who was Pippin to be spouting Scripture anyway? There was far more blood on his hands than on Philip's.

If there was a God, was He keeping a tally of these things?

It might be different if, like Gilly, Philip was on a holy mission. That wasn't what he sought at all. Could the monk have known?

All his life Philip had been seeking various things. First, it was his father's love and acceptance; then a place in noble society; then Beatrice's love. He might have given the monk's words some thought if just one of his desires had been granted. Sorry, Pip, your first and final words have fallen on fallow ground.

He lifted his blade, turning it to catch the rays of afternoon sun. The metal gleamed despite the nicks of use on its surface. He must accept it as it was, for repair would be too costly. He was much like his blade, he supposed. He would never be perfect—not as he was on the day he had been forged. The scars he had accumulated over the years were forever etched in his flesh. He could not pay the price to remove them, nor was he willing to do so.

As Philip came to terms with the monk's unsettling words, King Louis, growing more and more ill with fever, turned his thoughts toward the conversion of the Tunisian infidels. But with the papal legate recently expired from the fever, the king could find no one to serve as missionary. He hoped the emir would declare his faith before the French army moved to attack Tunis.

But on August 25, the saintly King Louis died, uttering the same words spoken by Christ on the cross: "Father, into thy hands I commend my spirit." With him also departed the driving spirit of the Crusade.

The fleet of King Charles of Sicily arrived within hours of the king's death. Charles rushed to his brother's tent, hoping to find him still alive, but he was too late. The grief of the brother was great and so was that of the French army, which had lost its guiding light. Though Charles was a strong, capable man, his crusading zeal had never been as great as his brother's. For days the army wavered in uncertainty while the Saracens continued to launch attacks. But the Muslim army was suffering from the heat and fever as greatly as were the French, and finally the emir declared his desire to come to terms. Charles prevailed over the new king, young Philip III, to accept the terms of peace. It was important for the new king to return to France as soon as possible. Moreover, the army's will to fight had dulled with Louis's death.

Philip and Theo discussed how all these events would affect their personal plans. Neither was inclined to return to France, and when they visited

Gilly and Rodrigo in the barracks in Carthage, they, too, had no desire to go back. However, they all wanted to get away from the disease-ridden Tunisian coast as soon as Gilly and Rodrigo were physically able.

The four comrades finally departed near the end of October, heading east, not having a particular destination in mind. They might join up with one of the existing crusader outposts, though by now even Gilly was disillusioned with crusading. Hearing of rich trade caravans in the area, the idea of returning to their old trade of thievery was appealing.

As they rode away from Tunisia, they had no idea that at the very moment of their departure, a fleet of ships was arriving, carrying Prince Edward and his contingent of English crusaders.

35

Standing at the rail of the ship, Beatrice had her first look at the coast of Africa, by far the most exotic land she'd encountered in all her months of travel. Leticia again had been right. Travel had been the best elixir for Beatrice's wounded spirit. The wonders she had thus far seen! And they were only now reaching their destination, where countless more wonders awaited.

Princess Eleanora came up beside Beatrice. Prince Edward's Spanish wife, Eleanora of Castile, was seven years older than Beatrice and, though she had already borne five children, was still quite comely. Taller than Beatrice, she still was far shy of the renowned height that had given her husband the nickname of Longshanks. Her richly dark hair was coiled into a chignon that was covered with a lace net.

"Here at last," the princess said in English oddly accented with mixed tones of Spanish and French, for her mother was French.

"But we are still quite far from the Holy Lands, are we not?" asked Beatrice.

"Yes, and Edward was never happy with this choice of destination. I do hope we get to Jerusalem eventually. It will hardly seem like a Crusade otherwise."

"Though it is now in the hands of the Saracens."

"If anyone can take it back, it will be my Edward."

Beatrice was touched by the light of devotion in Eleanora's eyes. What amazed her even more was that the prince was just as devoted, if not more so, to his wife. Beatrice hoped she could learn something of marriage from the couple, but thus far she had been too embarrassed to admit to the shortcomings of her own marriage. True, since departing England, Gareth had moderated his behavior somewhat. In the close quarters of ships and caravans, all others would have been privy to even a mild beating. While wife beating was a common practice in many households, it was not the kind of image Gareth wanted to present to his lord. Gareth was not blind to the remarkable relationship between the prince and his wife, and Beatrice thought perhaps there was some part of him that aspired to that kind of marriage as much as she did.

If Gareth did desire something more than he had, though, why had he made no move toward it? Or had he? She remembered their first shipboard dinner with Edward and Eleanora. Gareth had reached his arm around Beatrice, but she had tensed and shrugged it away. There had been other similar incidents. If he did move toward her, she inevitably moved away.

Was the marital discord her fault after all? Was he reaching out to her while she persisted at rejecting his overtures? Was she deserving of his abuse because she was unfaithful to him in her heart? Yet she could not help loving another. Gareth had practically forced her into marriage. He had never tried to win her heart but rather seemed more intent on only winning her obedience, and that by a heavy hand. If he had been older and more experienced and had the benefit of a father to guide him, things might have been different.

Or perhaps the problem was that he *had* had a father to guide him during his formative years—a man heartless enough to reject and scorn one of his sons.

She tried to think of Gareth being as much a victim as she and Philip. That line of thinking fell short, though, when she remembered that Philip had nearly as much contact with Ralph Aubernon as Gareth did, and yet he had turned into a kind, sensitive young man. Gareth could have chosen kindness over cruelty, but he hadn't.

Beatrice sighed. How she hated getting immersed in this convoluted thinking. Round and round her thoughts would go, never finding the end of it, never finding a solution.

"Are you troubled about something, Beatrice?" Eleanora asked.

Beatrice started. She had become so sunk into her thoughts that she had nearly forgotten the princess's presence. "No, Lady Eleanora, not really. I was just thinking of—" She faltered. She could not bring herself to reveal her confusion to this woman, a near stranger even though they had been companions for almost three months.

Eleanora reached over and laid her slim, soft hand over Beatrice's. "No matter how much time passes, we still think of our losses," she said, putting her own interpretation on Beatrice's unfinished sentence. "I still think of my two little ones gone to be with our Lord. Only girls, not of much account when you are trying to produce an heir, but I knew such joy at their births. Katherine, my firstborn, was two when she passed, and Joan only nine months. Old enough to make a place in my heart."

"My Edmond was three when he died." It seemed easier to talk of Edmond than of what really was troubling her, so she encouraged the conversation. "At least you have had other children to fill the void, my lady."

"Yes, it does help."

"Was it hard to leave them in England?"

"Very much so, but I knew without doubt that my place now was with my husband. You must understand that, for here you are, as well."

There it was, back to the crux of it. Perhaps this was a sign that she could take Eleanora into her confidence.

"I would be lying if I said I was here out of loyalty to my husband," Beatrice replied. "Part of me would have preferred a bit of a separation from him. . . ." She paused and gazed directly into the princess's dark eyes. "Not all can have the idyllic marriage that you enjoy, my lady."

"Alas, too few do!" Eleanora spoke earnestly, then added with a coy smile, "However, even our path is not always strewn with rose petals. We have our moments of discord. Somehow we manage to work them out."

"How do you do that?"

"Sometimes I simply don't speak to him for hours on end until it drives him so crazy he comes to me on bended knee to apologize." She giggled. "Sometimes I just shout at him—"

"Oh, Lady Eleanora, I have never heard you shout or even raise your voice!"

"Don't you know a woman can shout without raising her voice? That's when you speak through gritted teeth. Very effective." Eleanora laughed again. "Now, don't take me too seriously. I will say the shouting is probably better than the silence. Getting things into the open, I believe, is why Edward and I get on so well."

Beatrice wanted to ask if the prince ever hit Eleanora, but she simply could not. In reality she wondered if Eleanora could even conceive of the kind of discord that plagued Beatrice's marriage. Indeed, even Beatrice could scarce define it or its causes.

None of Edward's crusaders were pleased with the state of affairs they encountered in Tunis. News of King Louis's death came as a hard blow, but the events that followed were so infuriating they took the edge off the grief.

Edward was absolutely furious when he heard that Charles and the new king, styled Philip III, had made a truce with their infidel enemy.

"I feel as if I have been betrayed!" he lamented one evening shortly after landing. He and several of his closest knights had gathered for a meal apart from their French allies. Beatrice and the few other wives who traveled with the crusaders were also there. Edward's face was red, his eyes flashing. "This would not have happened had I arrived here sooner."

"That could not be helped, my lord," offered Gareth.

Beatrice wondered about that. Though it had taken a long time to raise money for the Crusade, thus delaying departure, Edward had also made several stops on the way to take care of business matters. Perhaps they could not be helped, but she did know that Louis had expected Edward to depart France with him instead of two months later.

"I will definitely not give my consent to the treaty!" Edward declared.

"My lord, have some wine," entreated Eleanora, lifting a goblet toward him.

Edward grasped the cup and took a long swig, dragging a sleeve across his lips before adding, "I have told Charles I will not accept any part of the emir's war indemnity. He had the nerve to imply that I was probably not entitled to a part anyway, since I was not here for the war."

"If you had let me, my lord, I would have called him to account for such a slight upon you," said Sir de Brampton.

"I would have, as well, my lord," put in Gareth.

Beatrice could tell he was disgruntled that he hadn't spoken up before de Brampton. Indeed, she would have liked to see either of them challenge the King of Sicily to a duel. But all the knights were restless. They had arrived at their grand Crusade only to find peace. They wanted to fight—infidels to be sure, although anyone else would do, even the French.

Perceptively Edward said, "Calm yourself, lads. We will fight our true enemies, but we must be patient. And though it try us sorely, we must stay our hand from the French. They are still our allies."

"I have heard Charles plans to return to Sicily soon and take Philip with him," said William de Valence, Edward's cousin.

"Yes, and I am afraid we will have to accompany them," Edward said. In response to unhappy noises from his men, he added quickly, "We have no choice. Though there is a truce, this land is still inhospitable to us. And the seas are too dangerous this time of year to take us safely to Palestine. We will winter in Sicily at Charles's invitation. Then in the spring we will continue our Crusade, but this time where it should have been in the first place, in the Holy Lands of our Lord."

This seemed to placate the knights.

Beatrice returned to her tent immediately after dinner. She hoped to have some time to speak with Leticia before Gareth returned. In their travels she and Gareth were forced to share a cabin on the ship and a tent now in this African desert. It had not brought them closer, but lately Beatrice had gained a new perspective on their marital problems. Seeing Eleanora with Edward had given her a picture of how a marriage could—should?—be. And she wondered more and more about her own culpability in their marital failures.

On entering the tent she remembered having sent Leticia with some other servants back to the ship to retrieve a few personal items left aboard. She would have liked to test her thoughts on her maid before trying them out on her husband, but did she really need Leticia's approval? It could only be the right thing to attempt to repair the rifts in her marriage.

In five years of marriage she had never really tried to talk to Gareth. She had always considered him the enemy. It was true, he had never treated her as more than chattel, but perhaps if she had tried harder . . .

When Gareth had approached her about marriage, she'd had few other choices. She could have accepted poverty and a bleak future for herself and her son, but she had *chosen* Gareth. Now she wondered if at the back of her mind she had believed that she would be able to wrap him around her will, much as she had every other man in her life. A smile threatened the corners of her lips. She had not exactly wrapped Philip around her finger—not when it had mattered. She recalled those times she had tried desperately to seduce him and he had withstood her. He had stood against her for *her* honor's sake, while she had cared only for her heart. Except for those most crucial times, he had always done her bidding. He had adored her, loved her.

A sudden stab of pain pierced her as a picture of him arose in her mind's eye. The dear, loving image that still came to her all too often, fine-featured except for the prominent nose, red hair that lent fire to his gentle mien. The way he had so often looked at her, very much like Edward's gaze upon his Eleanora. Ah, she and Philip could have had a marriage like that—

Stop! she told herself, harshly wrenching her mind from its futile fantasy.

Philip was dead, and such thoughts would only kill what little chance she had to make an amiable life for herself and the husband she did have.

She must try. She must!

As if summoned, Gareth strode into the tent and flung his cloak over the traveling chest.

"Curse that fool! No one can convince that man we are headed for doom," he declared with passion, though in the muted tone they had learned to adopt in these far from private quarters.

Normally Beatrice would have made as little response as possible to his casual comments, avoiding him in any way possible. But perhaps the first step in her new resolve should be simply to engage him in conversation.

"What do you mean, Gareth?"

"Returning to Sicily now will place us in a far worse position than if we pushed on to Palestine from here by land." He sat on a bench and bent to remove his boot.

Beatrice hurried to him and knelt before him. "Let me help you."

He gave her a perplexed look but thrust forth his foot, continuing to speak as she tugged the boot off. "If we winter in Sicily and then proceed by boat to Acre in the spring, we will arrive during the prime fighting time, but our horses will be in diminished condition from the trip. We would have to wait until they recover before we could fight, wasting even more time."

"How would the land route be better?" she asked as she pulled off the other boot.

"We could rest our horses here for a time, proceed to Outremer in the cool of the winter and, once in Acre, have time to rest again there and still engage the enemy in the early summer rather than the end of summer."

"Is not the land between here and Acre held by the Saracens?"

"Aye, and we would fight them as we came here to do. We have a force of a thousand men. Instead, we will grow soft and slow in Sicily for several months."

"It sounds like wise thinking, Gareth. I wish you could convince Edward." In truth she thought Gareth was being impetuous. She far more respected Edward's caution, but she was making a concerted effort to build up her husband rather than tear him down.

Again he peered at her narrowly. "You take my side, Beatrice? I can't remember the last time you did that." He rubbed his chin thoughtfully. "In truth, I can't remember the last time we spoke like this—with you listening like a wife should instead of trying to avoid me."

She hadn't realized he had noticed these things. Could he want a real marriage as much as she did?

"I want to do what is right," she said earnestly. "I don't enjoy fighting you all the time." She rose from where she knelt and drew a stool adjacent to the bench where Gareth sat. As much as she wished to make amends, she did not wish to do so on her knees before him.

"This quite shocks me," he said.

"Don't you wish to have a better marriage?"

"Better than what?"

"I don't know . . ." Thinking honesty might be a key element missing from their relationship, she added, "I have never had the benefit of watching another married couple in the depth that I have on this journey. Not all relationships are perfect. I have seen much tension between Sir Thomas de Clare and his wife, Elizabeth. In contrast, Lord and Lady de Brampton seem quite congenial. And Prince Edward and Eleanora are an exemplary example to all. I know 'tis only three couples besides us to judge, but watching them has opened my eyes." She took a breath. Her next words were difficult, much as they had to be said if she wished to make any headway in healing the wounds between them. "I see that I have treated our marriage more like a business proposition than a union—"

"Isn't that what marriage is—a business, the bringing together of estates? Marriage is about land."

"That is how they start," she replied patiently. "Surely politics determined Edward and Eleanora's union. By give and take, though, they were able to turn what had been thrust upon them into a clear union of love."

"Are you saying that you now love me?"

Beatrice tried to ignore the sneer in his tone as he spoke the word *love*.

"I must be honest, Gareth, and say I don't love you. However . . . in time . . . anything can happen."

He leaned back, crossing his arms, a superior look in his dark eyes. "Well! I could not be more shocked if Sultan Baibars came dancing in this tent dressed in a woman's frock."

"Gareth, c-could you . . . one day perhaps . . . love me?" She bit her lip. Never had words been harder for her to speak.

"Maybe if you gave me an heir."

"I have tried."

"Not hard enough. Your disobedience has made others question my virility. You have put me into a bad light. How can you speak of love when you continually flout me and our marriage by your deception?"

"I tell you, I want a babe as desperately as you—" She stopped as an unexpected sob escaped her lips. Tears spilled from her eyes.

She didn't expect the sudden slap, for he had not struck her at all in their travels. He glared at her and raised his hand again, but then the wind beating at the tent flap caught his attention, making him aware of their flimsy walls. He turned his open hand into a fist but made no move to strike her.

"You lie as skillfully as an infidel!" he hissed.

"N-no!" Tears flowed and she could not keep her voice steady. "Why do you h-hate me so, Gareth? Wh-what have I done to you?" She tried to gulp back her anguish. She began to see that he did not respect a compliant, deferential woman any more than he respected anything about her. Her only hope was to be strong. "Why, then, did you want to marry me? You could have had many other women with far more possessions to offer. Why me?"

"Simple," he sneered. "I wanted to possess you, and I do."

"Why?"

He looked at her for a very long moment, his lip slightly curled, his fist still held at his side. He wanted to hurt her, she could clearly tell that. There seemed only one reason, and she decided she had nothing to lose by venturing forth with it.

"Is it because you wanted everything that belonged to your brother?" she asked in a rush, then braced herself for that fist smashing into her face.

"Are you admitting, then, that you belonged to him, that you defiled yourself with him?" Amazingly, the fist did not move.

"I admit nothing of the kind! Yes, I cared for him, and he cared for me. There was nothing else. But you knew that, didn't you? And you couldn't rest until you had all that you perceived was his. Yet you won, so why the hatred?"

"You speak to me of love, yet you will never love me while you love him— yes, *still* love him." He tore open the laces of her bodice, grasped the chain she wore, and ripped it painfully from about her neck. He held it before her like an incrimination. "This brooch has the Hawken crest, yet it is not mine. You say it is a remembrance of your new loyalties, but I see the way you sometimes finger it, almost lovingly. Tell me it is not his. Tell me you do not still hold him in your heart."

She stood accused and had no ready defense. But she would be honest. "Gareth, had you given me just a little affection or kindness or gentleness, you might have dulled the memory of past love from my heart. Your brother is long gone, no doubt dead. It would not have taken much to turn my heart from a dead man to a living husband."

"A wanton, deceiving woman deserves no kindness."

"I wonder if you even know the meaning of the word *kindness.*" Tears of despair once more spilled from her eyes as she realized the truth. "I know now that we never had a marriage and can never hope to have one. It is not my fault, nor your brother's. It is you, Gareth! You have no understanding of a true marriage between a man and a woman. I did not love Lord Sardwick, and he fully realized that, yet he treated me with fondness and respect. Had we only had more time, our affection would have grown. But you are as unable to show kindness to a woman as you are able to sire a child!"

Then the fist came, striking her only once before he flung the brooch at her feet then grabbed his cloak and stormed from the tent.

36

Acre, Palestine
Summer 1272

A breeze dispelled some of the afternoon heat. It wafted over Beatrice as she sat by an open window gazing into the peaceful garden below. She found it hard to believe she had already been in Palestine more than a year. Even harder to believe was the relative peacefulness of the scene before her. They had arrived by ship last spring, sailing into a siege of the city by the sultan Baibars. Had it not been for Edward's army arriving when it did, one of the last strongholds of Christianity in Palestine might have been lost. But the new opposition made Baibars retreat, and Edward was welcomed as a hero by the residents of Acre.

Even after a year, however, this land still remained as foreign as at first. Beatrice doubted she would ever grow accustomed to the warmth of these southern regions of the world. The winter months in Sicily had been very like England in the summer, though perhaps a bit milder. But summer here in Outremer was downright oppressive. How did the people stand it for their entire lifetimes?

She thought especially of the Muslim women, wrapped head to toe in black, with veils over their faces so that only their eyes showed. They walked obediently a few paces behind their husbands, never seeming to complain—in public anyway. The wife of the merchant Bakr al-Qasim ibn Ayyub seemed more outspoken in her own home, as Beatrice had occasion to witness while she and the other wives of Edward's knights were lodging in their spacious villa. She'd noted the woman speaking in an animated fashion several times to her husband, though the language barrier prevented her from understanding the topic of the discussion.

Generally, the English women felt sorry for the Muslim women, observing that they were little more than slaves to their husbands. In conversations with other English wives, Beatrice would nod, as if she agreed. But was she any more free than the Muslim women? Lately, however, she had ceased to care about her freedom. After that pivotal conversation with Gareth in Tunis, she had sunk to her lowest depth of hopelessness since young Edmond's death. It was distressingly clear that no matter how hard she tried, her marriage would never be happy and only barely civil.

The only hint of passion in her life now was to be found in her desperate desire for a child. With a touch of envy she thought of Princess Eleanora, who at thirty years of age had given birth five times, though two babies had died in infancy. In Sicily, she had given birth to yet another child, but the undersized baby hadn't survived. Beatrice sympathized with the woman's grief, but she would give anything, even for a miscarriage, to know that the capability existed with her and her husband.

She was now all but convinced that her desire for a child would never be fulfilled, especially by Gareth. Nevertheless, she took Leticia's advice and willingly visited his bed when he bade her to come. Leticia said if she was more at ease, it might help her to conceive. Beatrice also used the herbal knowledge she'd acquired from Father Bavent to concoct potions and teas that were supposed to enhance fertility. She had discovered an apothecary in Acre, one the Templar healers used, and he had sold her a root from Cathay called ginseng that was reputed to aid fertility. She also bought a concoction of damiana, celery seeds, oats, licorice, and ginger that was supposed to aid a man, but Gareth refused to admit that he might have a problem and would take no herbs. She secretly sprinkled it on his food instead.

In her heart Beatrice knew Gareth simply did not have the seed for making a babe, and her thoughts more and more turned morbidly toward wishing for his death. Only then would she be free to find herself another husband, hopefully one more fertile. She knew these thoughts were evil, but she no longer cared. Sometimes in her most depraved moments she even pondered elaborate plans for doing away with him herself. She knew enough about herbs to know the most effective poisons. She thought of ways to slip them into his food and drink, as she did the fertility herbs.

But she never acted upon these ideas. Were thoughts enough to send her to hell? Maybe she should simply use the poison on herself.

"Lady Beatrice," Leticia said, entering the solar, "I've just received a message from Lady de Clare. She wishes your company on an excursion to the market."

"Please send her my regrets," Beatrice replied. Had the request come from Princess Eleanora, she would have been compelled to accept, but the princess was now homebound, due anytime with yet another child. "Tell her I have a bit of a headache." Beatrice was in no mood to socialize. Truth be told, she was never in that mood.

Leticia stared at her mistress for a long moment. Beatrice was lying upon a chaise, needlework lying in her lap.

"If that be the case, m'lady, I should make you a medicinal tea."

"Yes, perhaps so."

Leticia started to turn, then paused. "Lady Beatrice, it may be that some fresh air would be a better remedy. It is rare Prince Edward can spare enough soldiers to escort you to the marketplace. Would it not be a shame to miss the opportunity?"

"I don't know. . . ."

"It might do you good."

It had, in truth, been quite a while since she had ventured from the villa because Acre could be a dangerous place, especially now that hostilities appeared to be heating up between the Venetians and Genoese. In matter of fact, Edward, much to his consternation, had been spending a great deal of his time acting as a mediator between the two warring factions. He would have much preferred to battle infidels than factious Italian merchants. But these hostilities were no small matter. Each group had its own quarter in Acre, and the discord between them over the years had often led to wholesale destruction of property, making the streets unsafe for women, not to mention disrupting important trade.

"I have heard a new shipment of goods from the Far East has recently arrived," Leticia enticed.

Beatrice indulged a slight smile. "Is that so?" For Leticia's sake she tried to summon enthusiasm. "There might be some silk, do you suppose?"

"I would be almost certain. I could sew a new gown for you to wear at the next banquet."

Beatrice tried not to cringe at the thought of the endless banquets, often given by wealthy merchants trying to curry Edward's favor or by Arab chieftains with the same intent. Not only did she dread the socializing required but also that she must attend with Gareth and feign being a happy wife.

"When does Lady de Clare wish to depart?" Beatrice asked with a resigned sigh. Perhaps it was best to get out. When she was left to her own devices she was nearly overcome with morbid thoughts.

"Within the hour."

"I suppose . . ."

With a poor attempt to temper a triumphal grin, Leticia hurried to the clothing trunk and lifted the lid. "Your blue gown is freshly washed, my lady."

"That will be fine. And my gray linen cloak. Though it is too hot for a cloak, I would feel unclad outside without one, especially next to those poor Muslim women."

By the time she dressed she had mustered a modicum of enthusiasm for the shopping excursion. Lady Dyana de Brampton joined Beatrice and Elizabeth de Clare. They had an escort of six knights. Beatrice did enjoy the opportunity to ride, a pleasure that had seldom come during her travels. Of course the ladies were expected to ride sidesaddle, but Beatrice was pleased that she was the most accomplished equestrian of the women.

Acre was, of a certainty, one of the largest cities she had ever visited. It was the second largest in Palestine next to Jerusalem, with some twenty or thirty thousand souls. From the harbor, where they had first approached the city by ship months ago, it had appeared a lovely place—a pleasing mix of European and exotic Arab structures, such as the minarets of mosques. Since the Franks had occupied Acre, these mosques had been converted to churches, but their interesting form remained. Acre was one of the last Frankish strongholds in Palestine now, though Edward was determined to change that by winning back Jerusalem.

The surface beauty of the city was easy to forget when one attempted to traverse the crowded streets, from which a most displeasing odor permeated the air. Beatrice suddenly did not feel so sorry for the Muslim women with their veiled faces. The ladies held kerchiefs to their noses, though it hardly helped.

The silk market was crowded and bustling with activity, for a new shipment of silk had indeed arrived. The ladies picked out lengths they liked and let the knights do the haggling over prices with the merchants. Beatrice ended up buying more and spending far more than she had intended, with the thought of Gareth's consternation over her extravagance spurring her on. Gareth was reluctant to spend money, which galled her because the Sardwick holdings had brought substantial wealth to Hawken. Her saving grace was that her years of melancholy had made her lose interest in acquiring nice things.

When they returned to Bakr al-Qasim's house, Leticia immediately wanted to start on the new gown. Beatrice indulged her and patiently joined her in perusing the pattern supply to choose one. Then they surveyed the silk to find the one best suited to the pattern. Leticia draped the fabric around Beatrice, and they even giggled a bit when Leticia shaped one to resemble the outfit of one of the infidel dancers that entertained at banquets.

"Do you think I look like Salome of the seven veils?" Beatrice asked, holding a corner of the fabric over her face.

"I have never seen a Saracen with yellow hair!"

"You try it, then."

Gamely, Leticia took some silk, draped it around her, then began waving her arms and moving her hips in saucy undulation as they had seen the dancers do. Beatrice nearly doubled over with laughter. She had never seen her maid behave with such abandon. Surely she must be desperate to cheer her mistress.

A knock on the door brought the gaiety to a halt. Beatrice opened it to Sir Alain, one of Gareth's knights.

"My lady, there's been an attack!" The man was red faced and out of breath. Obviously he'd hurried over with the news.

Her first thought was that Gareth had been killed. She tried not to think beyond that, and she especially tried to ignore the small fluttering of relief she felt.

"Where?" she asked. "Are we in danger?"

"It was at the citadel, m'lady, and involved only the prince."

"What do you mean? Speak clearly, Sir Alain."

He was young and had only become a knight shortly before they had departed England. He took a breath and calmed himself, then said more steadily, "An assassin attacked Prince Edward. He lives but is gravely injured."

"Leticia, get my cloak," she said. "I must go now."

"There are physicians with the prince," Alain said.

"Then I must see to the princess."

"M'lady, this may only be the beginning. There could be other attacks. It may not be safe for you to be out. Lord Hawken would not—"

"Where is he? Does he know?"

"Yes, he knows. He was at the training field, but by now I am sure he has gone to the citadel."

Leticia brought the cloak, and Beatrice flung it over her shoulders. "Come, Sir Alain, we must hurry."

He argued no further and led the way to the stables, where his horse waited and where another was quickly saddled for Beatrice. The citadel, where traditionally the Frankish kings resided when they came to Acre, was by St. Anthony's Gate, a good two-furlong ride from where Beatrice was staying. Alain led them along several side streets in order to avoid the crush of the crowds on the main thoroughfares.

They were recognized and admitted to the citadel; then they quickly made their way to Edward's chamber. On the way Alain explained that Edward had been attacked by a messenger of the emir of Jaffa, whom he knew and had welcomed into his chamber. The messenger had been sent with a peace treaty.

"I thought Edward was opposed to a treaty," Beatrice said.

"With the sultan Baibars, yes. But the emir is no friend of Baibars, and no doubt Edward hoped for military support from Jaffa against Baibars."

"So the prince trusted the man, the messenger?"

"Yes, and thus Edward received him alone and unarmed. He thought the messenger was unarmed, as well. When the man drew a hidden dagger, Edward responded quickly, considering his surprise, but not before he was wounded. The two scuffled, and Edward killed the assassin with his own knife."

Just inside Edward's chamber a small group of concerned knights and servants was gathered. Beatrice elbowed her way through the group. She saw Gareth but ignored him as her gaze alighted upon Princess Eleanora, kneeling at Edward's side, weeping. She started toward the princess, but a low voice stopped her.

"Beatrice." Though Gareth's voice was soft, it held an edge that made her stop. She had not given much thought to her actions when she had hurried to the citadel, thinking only of the needs of the prince and princess. Now she began to doubt herself. Who was she to presume herself upon the royal couple? True, she had spoken often in a friendly manner to Eleanora, but was she considered a friend, to the extent of barging upon them at this terrible time?

She wavered, taking a quick look at Gareth, who wore a definite look of censure. Then another voice drew her attention.

"Beatrice!" It was Princess Eleanora. She lifted a beckoning hand toward Beatrice.

Without a glance back at her husband, Beatrice quickly acted upon her earlier instinct and the princess's gesture. She rushed forward.

"Your Highness, can I do anything?"

"Oh, Beatrice! I know not what to do," Eleanora lamented. "Just pray—and hold my hand."

Beatrice did both. She did not know how effective her prayers were these days with evil thoughts clouding her soul, but she didn't think it would hurt for her to try. As she silently prayed, she noted one of the physicians holding up a blood-stained dagger and carefully examining it.

"It is as I feared," he said. "The dagger was dipped in poison."

Edward groaned, speaking in a weak voice. "Can it be cured?"

Both physicians responded with grim looks that could only be interpreted in the negative. Beatrice saw the wound was only in the prince's arm. A thick bandage had been applied to stanch what little bleeding there appeared to be. Logic told Beatrice that bleeding might help cleanse the wound of the poison, but only that which clung to the surface. Much of the evil stuff had no doubt already penetrated into the man's system.

A shuddering sob escaped Eleanora's lips. "No!" she moaned. "This cannot be." She threw aside the quilt that covered her husband and bent toward the prince's wounded arm.

Horrified, Beatrice discerned the princess's intent and laid a restraining hand on her. "No, Princess—"

"I will not watch him die. I will do something!" She stripped away the bandage and lowered her lips to the wound. Beatrice had gained enough medical knowledge from Father Bavent to doubt that attempting to suck the poison out would help. For one thing the poison had probably been in the wound too long. But she also had another concern.

"Eleanora!" she said so urgently she forgot the formality of titles. "Think of your babe!"

A look of agonized helplessness etched Eleanora's countenance as she realized how her action might endanger her unborn child.

Not giving it another thought, Beatrice gently nudged aside the princess and did what the princess had intended. She set her lips to the wound and sucked at it, spitting blood, and she hoped poison, into a cloth the princess held for her. She still doubted it would help, but she understood Eleanora's desperation and knew that even a futile gesture was better than watching helplessly. Eleanora kissed Edward's cheek and spoke soothingly to him as he groaned at the pain caused by Beatrice's actions.

The two physicians watched with dubious expressions, but Eleanora said, "Thank you so much, Beatrice!"

"I hope it helps," she said.

"What else can be done?"

"I know of some herbs that might help."

"We should bleed His Highness," said one of the physicians.

Eleanora looked to Beatrice, who immediately felt the uncomfortable weight of responsibility. "I am no physician, Your Highness," Beatrice said. "My priest at home taught me a few things—"

"I trust you, Beatrice. Please stay with me. Offer what service you can." Even if Eleanora had not been wife of the heir to the throne of England, Beatrice could not have refused her look of helpless entreaty.

She did resist an urge to glance at Gareth before she spoke. "I am at your service, Your Highness."

Edward said, "If my wife trusts you, so do I." To the physicians he added, "Take Lady Hawken into your counsel." Then with a sigh he laid his head back on his pillow. Beatrice saw he was flushed and appeared fevered. Doubtless the poison was already taking lethal effect.

She wracked her brain, trying to think of all she knew of poisons and trying to remember if there were any medicines she had learned about that might offer an antidote.

"My lord," came Gareth's voice, "let us take a force of men to attack the emir."

"No, Gareth. There will be no retaliation," responded the prince. "We are too close to peace. And it may be the assassin was acting on his own or, more likely, as an agent of Baibars. It is more like something he would do. I believe the emir of Jaffa was sincere in his bid for peace." Edward's voice was weakening, his words breathless. "Leave me now, save for my wife and her lady."

37

Four days after Edward was wounded, Eleanora went into labor. The princess had been at her husband's side day and night, so it was no surprise the strain brought about her labor a few weeks earlier than expected. Beatrice, who was with the princess at the time her pains began, intended to stay with her.

"Beatrice, please stay with my husband," Eleanora implored. "He needs you more than I. Elizabeth and Dyana will attend me."

Reluctantly Beatrice promised to continue her vigil over the still-ailing prince. She was reluctant, because thus far she'd been unable to do much. The physicians resented her interference, and she really couldn't blame them. Who was she but a lady-in-waiting? She had not the training of court physicians. Her suggestions would have been brushed aside completely had not Eleanora been there to insist they try the poultices and herbs she recommended. With the princess now absent, Beatrice did not have the confidence to stand up to the doctors. Edward was too sick—half the time only semi-conscious—to speak up for her. Still, Beatrice did not leave him. She did little more than wipe his brow with a cool cloth. She prayed, as well, but like the treatments, that seemed to do little good.

At least Gareth did not trouble her. Although Edward had forbidden retaliation, fearing it would endanger the lives of pilgrims visiting the holy places, the security around the city was greatly increased and the fortifications strengthened, keeping Gareth busy and away from home for days on end. Besides, Gareth must know that her service to the prince would in the end reflect well upon him, so why should he interfere?

Finally the physicians gave up all hope for the prince. They were quite willing now to let the silly woman, who fancied herself an herbalist, have control in caring for the dying prince. Let his death be on her head. Beatrice was not willing to give up as easily as they had. She had lost far too many of those close to her, and in the last few days she had drawn quite close to the prince and princess. They had spent hours talking and praying together, mostly with Eleanora but also with Edward in his more lucid moments. She was not going to watch a friend die!

She had enlisted Sir Alain's help in searching out useful herbs. How excited she'd been when he found some fresh comfrey, though she had known it would be available in the Holy Land, for it was Crusaders who had brought it to England from this place. She'd made a poultice from the roots and leaves and had been applying it to the wound when she changed the bandage several times a day. But today as she lifted away the cloth, she saw the wound was not improving as she had hoped. Perhaps the lotion of sanicle and betony would help. She had given Edward several doses of juniper berry tea, which Father Bavent had told her he had once used to good effect on a lad smitten with a snakebite. She thought at least the systemic effect of the poison had been countered. It was the festering wound that presented the worst problem now.

By the end of the fifth day after the attack, the prince was still fevered and the wound no better. An idea occurred to her, but she feared it would be too drastic. If only Eleanora were here to offer her opinion and support, but the princess was in the midst of a prolonged ordeal of her own.

At Matins Beatrice made her decision, driven by fear that the prince would not make it through the rest of the night. She called the surgeon.

"You must cut away the putrefied flesh," she told him, mustering all the confidence she could.

"The pain of such a procedure could kill him, not to mention simply enlarging the festering area."

Edward stirred on his bed and spoke, his voice a mere rasp. "I will die ere morning. Do as she says. . . . My only hope. . . ."

Beatrice had been easing Edward's pain with doses of willow bark tea, but he would need something stronger now. She had nothing suitable in her small store of herbs and was about to send Alain back to the apothecary when the surgeon produced just what she was hoping for, syrup of poppy. It should help the prince through the painful procedure.

In England Beatrice had often been called upon to use her herbal skills on estate villeins and ailing townsfolk and thought she had a fairly strong stomach. But as the surgeon began cutting away at Edward's arm, she started feeling woozy. Yet she remembered her promise to Eleanora and refused to leave the prince's side. Choking back nausea, she helped the surgeon by stanching the flow of blood with a cloth and performing other necessary tasks. When it was over, she packed the wound with lavender to prevent new festering and then bandaged it.

She curled up on the cot she had placed near Edward's bed to wait. She quickly fell asleep and awoke only as a stab of sunshine shot through a crack in the heavy drapery over the window. She rose and stretched and then looked at her patient. He was asleep, but that didn't surprise her since she had given him two more doses of opium after the surgery. Was it her imagination or did he appear to be sleeping more peacefully than before? Her confidence was bolstered when one of the Hospitaler healers came and lent his approval to her efforts.

Leticia came in shortly afterward with a breakfast tray and news.

"M'lady, during the night Princess Eleanora gave birth to a healthy daughter!"

"And the princess is well, too?"

"Oh yes. Her joy is tempered only by her fear for her husband."

"I do think he is improved, Leticia." Beatrice reached over and laid a hand on Edward's forehead. It did feel cooler than even a few minutes ago.

She started when his hand suddenly covered hers. "Lady Beatrice, you are here," he said softly.

"I am, m'lord. You have my oath I will not leave you."

"Did I hear aright what your maid said? I have a daughter?"

"Yes, Your Highness. Congratulations!"

"Ah . . . I am pleased. I will go to my wife."

"Oh no, m'lord. You are not strong enough."

"I feel much better." His voice was still weak and his skin a bit flushed, but that could have been attributed to the opium.

"That is wonderful news, m'lord," she said. "Perhaps by Vespers you could venture a visit to your wife and daughter."

"I will do as you say, Beatrice. You have done well by me thus far." His hand slipped back to his side, and he closed his eyes.

"Are you in pain, m'lord?"

"A little."

"Shall I make another tonic for you?"

"No. It muddles my head, and I want it clear for later." He paused, letting out a fatigued sigh, then added, "I owe my life to you, Lady Beatrice. How can I repay you?"

"Only by living to a ripe old age."

"I will do that, but when we return to England, I will also reward you, so be considering what would make you happy."

Even the heir to the throne of England, nay even the king himself, could not give her that which would make her happy.

"Truly, I want nothing, my lord prince."

He smiled a little, closed his eyes once again, and slept.

Leticia grasped Beatrice's hand. "Mayhap the Lord God will reward your good deed by granting you the desire of your heart."

"Only He can," Beatrice said, a touch of hopelessness still clinging to her tone despite all the positive answers to prayer she'd had that day. She thought it likely God had healed the prince and safely delivered Eleanora's child for their sake, not for hers. That which was solely for herself she continued to doubt would be granted, not because of God but because of her own undeserving self.

Within two days the prince was sitting up in bed and eating heartily. He had made a brief visit to his wife and newborn child, whom they had named Joan of Acre. With the prince and princess on the road to health, Beatrice was released from her vigil. She returned to the merchant's house and, without the purpose given her these last few days, would have fallen into a deeper melancholy than before. But word spread through the community of Edward's army of what she had done to help the prince, and soon everyone with even the most minor physical complaint was coming to her. Often they sought her out before they did the physicians.

Of course Gareth disapproved of her new vocation. This did not surprise her. He would balk at anything that made her the least bit happy. She ceased having to worry about him, however, when he was called away with a detachment of knights to help bolster the fortifications of Nazareth, which Edward had captured shortly after his arrival in Palestine months ago.

For the first time since young Edmond's death, Beatrice found real purpose in her life. Her thoughts grew less morbid. Indeed, much of her time was now spent searching out herbs and remedies. With Gareth gone, she would often ride into the markets of Acre with Alain and two other knights Gareth had left to protect her. Once they even rode outside the walls of the city when she had heard of a place where hawthorn was in bloom. She already knew of this plant's most celebrated history, for it was believed that Christ's crown of thorns was made from the branches of hawthorn, its name, of course, referring to holy thorns. The apothecary, with whom she was becoming well acquainted, had told her of a use for this plant that was of particular interest to her. He said that women who drank a tea made of the flower would conceive a child within forty days. She supposed she would know in a month if this was true.

She was learning of other indigenous plants that had medicinal qualities, as well, such as fig and ginger, which were more abundant here than in England. She had also discovered spikenard, the oil of which was taken for headaches and melancholy. Beatrice found it especially fascinating that spikenard was the very herb that had been used by a woman in the Scriptures to anoint the feet of Christ. His disciples had rebuked the woman, but the Lord said to leave her alone, for she had done well.

It amazed Beatrice that after a year in the Holy Lands, she had not come into contact with any of the holy places except through her interest in herbs, and that was only through stories rather than the actual places. She wondered if she would depart this land having never laid eyes upon Jerusalem or Bethlehem. She had heard tales of miracles happening to some of the pilgrims at these places. Although she knew she was unworthy to experience such miracles herself, might not she become a better person just by visiting them?

She toyed with the idea of making her guards take her to Jerusalem, but they had already balked at taking her just a short distance outside the gates of Acre in search of her herbs. They would never disobey Gareth to the extent of taking her on a journey of several days, especially through land held by the Saracens.

Much to her surprise, it was Gareth himself who finally drew her out of Acre on her first extended journey. Alain came with news that shocked her, despite it having figured all too often in her most evil dreams.

"My lady, Lord Hawken has been wounded in Nazareth," he said.

It was a long moment before she could fully take it in and gauge her innermost reaction. Oddly, it wasn't joy. Perhaps she did despise him, and she might even have had thoughts of his demise. Still, he was her husband, and she did not want to be the kind of person who wished her husband dead.

"How badly, Sir Alain?"

"I know not, Lady Hawken, only that he was wounded in a small skirmish with infidels."

"He asked for me?" A tiny ember of hope flamed in her. Was it possible that he did care for her after all, calling for her in his time of need? It might be that she would not despise him so if he showed even a modicum of caring for her.

Alain merely shrugged that he did not know. So she called the messenger to her chamber.

"No, m'lady," said the knight, "he didn't ask for you in so many words, but we thought you might help him as you helped the prince."

"He didn't want me?"

"I'm sure he did not wish to endanger you by calling you to him. Though the road to Nazareth is controlled by crusaders, there are still bands of robbers terrorizing the way, not to mention Saracens, who don't recognize our control. In any case, he did allow us to fetch you."

"I see. What are his injuries?"

"An arrow that was likely poisoned entered his shoulder. He was still conscious when I left him several hours ago."

She gave a little shrug. She knew it was her duty as a wife to go, but she was sad that she felt no fear or worry for her husband—no emotion at all. When she thought of how distressed Eleanora had been over Edward's injury, guilt washed over her.

"Leticia, would you pack me some clothes while I get my satchel of herbs together?"

"Yes, m'lady. I will pack one for myself, as well."

She thought to have Leticia stay behind. Why place both of them in danger? She knew the maid would balk, though, and in truth, she did want the companionship. She wasn't sure what she would find in Nazareth. Perhaps a dead husband.

Since it was already late in the day when the messenger arrived, they had to wait until morning to leave. They departed before Prime and were well on their way as the sun rose and drenched the craggy mountainous road with light. The party consisted of Beatrice and her three usual guards, plus the knight who had been Gareth's messenger, and Leticia. Prince Edward, upon hearing of the attack, also sent along a handful of his knights as reinforcements, for Gareth had not been the only casualty in the attack.

Beatrice had heard so much about the danger of the roads that she nervously scanned the horizon for signs of peril, but Sir Alain assured her that their party was large enough to be a deterrent against molesters. Yet she thought the narrow, winding passes would be ideal for an ambush, and with surprise on their side, robbers might not need a large band to disrupt the crusaders.

"My lady, Templar Knights also regularly patrol these roads and have done so for a hundred years. Fear not," Alain added.

Beatrice saw no Templars—even they could not be everywhere at once—but they reached the town of Nazareth by midday unscathed. Beatrice's first thought upon seeing it in the distance was that if she wanted to experience a holy site, this place where the virgin Mary first heard from God that she would bear a child, the Savior, was certainly an important one. The Church of the Annunciation was built upon the supposed place where an angel had spoken to Mary.

Even more impressive was the knowledge that this was the town where Christ himself had lived for thirty years, where He played as a boy, where He studied the Scriptures, where He walked and lived and worked in His father's carpentry shop. Beatrice felt a little thrill course through her.

Despite its historical significance, the Nazareth that greeted her was a rather mean-appearing town—hardly even that, more a backwater village. A hundred years ago, under crusader rule, it had begun to thrive; churches were built, the population grew, and it had even become an important archdiocese. Since then it had been attacked and won and lost several times, until less than twenty years ago Saracens had overrun the town, butchered the inhabitants, and wrecked the churches. Now the town lay mostly in ruins except for a few of the whitewashed mud houses of the locals.

Beatrice remembered how Edward's army, including Gareth, had strutted about proudly over conquering the town last summer. She realized now the victory was only a moral one, for if it had not been Christ's home, it would have no political or economical value at all. But considering the dismal showing of Edward's Crusade, he'd best take his victories where he could.

As the party from Acre made its way to where the defenders were encamped in tents on the edges of the town, Beatrice saw why it was such a hard area to defend and hold. The town had no wall and thus was vulnerable to attack.

She was taken directly to Gareth's tent. He was lying upon a pallet, and as she drew close she saw he was quite pale, the contrast of his sickly flesh even more alarming framed as it was by his jet black hair, now lank and sweaty.

"Gareth, I am here," she said simply.

When he opened his eyes, there was a spark of surprise in them. "You didn't have to come."

"You are my husband. Of course I would come." She knelt down by the pallet. "They said you were wounded in the shoulder."

"The wound was not bad, but there was poison."

"Yes, I was told so."

With a grim half smile he said, "Will you suck out the poison as you did with the prince?"

"I am afraid that was only a gesture done to make the princess feel better. I doubt it helped much, and your poison has been in you far longer."

"Then I am doomed to die?" For the first time in her life she saw a hint of vulnerability in this man. She could almost feel sorry for him.

Almost. She still felt the sting of his cruelty toward her. And she could never forget how mercilessly he had used Philip.

"They say only the pure in heart die young," she said.

He laughed, though it was a rasp that disintegrated into a cough. When the coughing subsided, he said, "Then I shall live to a ripe old age."

"Can you turn a bit so I can look at your wound?" she asked, choosing not to continue with the previous direction of the conversation.

He obeyed her request, and she lifted the bandage to find an ugly festering wound. He was right about one thing. The wound itself would not have been serious if not for the poison. She made a poultice of a mixture of comfrey roots and leaves and packed the wound with it.

"Are you in much pain?" she asked.

"Some."

"I can give you something to help you rest."

He nodded. She saw that despite his careless attitude, he was in much distress from the pain of the festering wound and the heat of fever. She tried hard to muster sympathy for him.

She went to her satchel. She had several things that relieved pain. The surgeon had given a syrup of opium to Prince Edward. But she had something else that was effective in relieving pain and inducing sleep. Monkshood, or wolfsbane. It was extremely poisonous. She had feared using it internally on the prince because she was not confident of the proper dosage. Mixed with oil, it was an effective external rub for aches and pains. She lifted the small vial from her bag. Her hand trembled.

How easy it would be! Freedom lay in that vial. Perhaps even happiness. Though she was not certain of the proper dosage for healing, she had a fairly good idea of the amount it would take to kill. Could she ever be happy knowing she had committed murder? Even to someone so deserving?

"My lady—" Leticia's voice cut through Beatrice's thoughts like a knife of accusation.

With a startled gasp, Beatrice dropped the vial back into the bag. Her heart pounded against her chest like a gong.

"What!" she said sharply.

"I only wondered if you wanted some help. I have brought in our luggage."

"I . . . no . . . I am just going to prepare him a potion for pain."

"Is it serious, Beatrice?"

"As bad as the prince's wound. But we cured him, so I believe Lord Hawken will survive, as well." Beatrice filled a cup with water from a jug by Gareth's bed.

"If it is God's will," the maid said.

"That's just the kind of gift God would give me, isn't it?"

Leticia laid a comforting hand upon Beatrice's shoulder but remained silent. What could she say? What words of solace would be appropriate? Both women hated this man, yet they were not vindictive, evil souls. At least that was true of Leticia, and Beatrice was trying to convince herself of her own purity.

She gave Gareth a few drops of the opium, followed by a drink of water to wash down the bitter substance. Goodness, she didn't even have it in her to let him suffer a foul taste!

When Gareth had fallen asleep, Beatrice left the tent. When Alain made to follow her, she tried to wave him off.

"I wish to be alone," she explained.

"I will keep my distance. This village may appear sleepy and quiet, yet danger can spring up unawares."

"All right," she said with a shrug and a sigh.

Full of despair, she wandered into the village. The residents were going about their daily routines. It was close to Vespers for the few Christians left in the village, though since the major Saracen attack nine years ago that had annihilated the residents, there were only a handful who had returned. There were now more Muslims in residence, but they also had an evening prayer time.

In the center of the village was the one most constant fixture—the village well. Two women were filling jugs, so Beatrice waited a few paces away and watched. When they ambled away, she approached, smiling at the women as she passed them. She wished she could converse with them, but even if they were Christians, they were Arab and did not speak English.

She sat on the stone skirting around the well thinking that this was a good place to ponder her miserable life. Perhaps she should have gone to the ruin of the Church of the Annunciation, but though only the grotto still existed, she did not feel like being in or near a church. There might be a priest about, and she was not ready to make confession of the evil that lurked in her heart.

A crude well better suited her. She knew this was called Mary's Well. No doubt it had existed over a thousand years ago. Even the cruel Saracens respected the value of water too much to destroy a well in this dry region. She felt a little chill as she realized that the Holy Mother herself had doubtless come to this very place to draw water for her family. At that time, though, it hadn't been called "Mary's Well," for in those days Mary had been just another village girl and later, just one of the many women who used the water. Sitting there on the coarse stone, Beatrice had far more a sense of Mary, the simple young woman, than of Mary, the holy virgin. The woman who cooked and cleaned her poor cottage, tended her family. The rather common girl who one day was visited by an angel who transformed her life.

Beatrice ran her hand along the stone and felt a connection to that young woman. Of course Mary had to have been pure and godly to have been chosen to be the mother of Christ, but still, she was also a woman, and she must have been full of confusion and doubts about the miraculous thing that was about to happen to her. Surely God must have understood the virgin's confusion. Perhaps He also understood Beatrice's.

Yet God couldn't possibly understand murderous thoughts, could He? Could He forgive them?

Suddenly an astounding thought struck Beatrice. Just as Mary had come to this well, would not her firstborn son also have come here? Could Jesus have sat upon this very ledge and pondered life? Could He have reached over the edge with a pottery jug in hand to fetch water from the bucket for His mother?

"Oh my . . ." she breathed.

Many a pilgrim had returned to England from the Holy Lands telling of how they had walked in the footsteps of Christ. Now Beatrice was experiencing that very phenomenon. Could such an exercise truly have a miraculous significance?

Might she not see if it was so? She could ask forgiveness for her sins here and now. She could ask God to deliver her from her harsh existence by giving her a child, or by taking her husband—

No, God would not listen to a prayer like that. He said to pray for those who would despitefully use us and to love our enemies.

Tears sprang into her eyes, for she simply could not do those things. She could not pray for Gareth, except for his death. She certainly could not love him. Thus, she knew she was doomed to misery. She could sit where Jesus had sat, but she could not reach Him.

"I am so sorry," she murmured. "My heart is so black. I am not worthy to be in this holy place, to be in any way associated with the pure young woman who gave birth to the Savior."

She jumped up as if the old stone had suddenly turned to hot coals.

Yet even as she felt true remorse for her inability to reach out to God, she thought of the monkshood in her satchel. But now, for the first time, she contemplated using it on herself. It would be a mortal sin, yet was she not already damned because of her evil desires and thoughts?

Morbid thoughts continued to prey upon her for the next several days, though she did nothing about them. Instead, she tended her husband until he was well enough to travel back to Acre.

She would be glad when they finally departed Nazareth, the home of the Lord. She was not fit to be in such a place.

38

The tent of Sheik Ishaq ibn Talib was richly appointed. The chaise upon which he reclined was of red brocaded silk, as were the purple and yellow cushions positioned about for his guests. Tapestries hung upon the tent walls, and rugs of intricate design lay upon the floor. Bowls of fruit—figs, grapes, oranges, and pomegranates—sat on low tables. The sheik himself appeared to be an extension of the surroundings, garbed as he was in purple and yellow silk, with chains of gold about his neck and trim waist. A red kaffiyeh covered his hair, but his moustache and neatly trimmed beard were dark brown and oiled with a fragrant balm. He appeared to be in his middle years and was fit and handsome. His wealth certainly had not made him soft.

"I will pay two hundred of your English marks," the sheik said.

Philip fought back a grating sense of inferiority. This infidel need never know that he was a baseborn bastard, not even rightly a knight, though he had claimed that distinction. The closest he had ever come to nobility was in the castle of his father, but Hawken was far more of a military fortification than a palatial residence like this opulent tent.

Now was not the time to be thinking of Hawken and all the disappointments that name conjured. Here in the sheik's tent, Philip, or al-Rahib—the monk—as the locals called him, was a man to be reckoned with, perhaps even to be feared. He did not warrant the sobriquet "the monk" because he had a saintly nature, but rather because he had on a few occasions refused to accept the women offered by the Arabs with whom he dealt. He did not protest the title, because in the circles in which he now mixed, it was best not to use his given name.

All these thoughts scurried through his mind while his expression betrayed none of his inner turmoil, doubts, or fears.

"My lord sheik," Philip replied in an injured tone as Rodrigo interpreted, "when we spoke at Mishal's well two days ago, we talked about five hundred for the goods."

Philip made sure his gaze was as steely as the sheik's. The only difference between the two men lay in the color of the fire that sparked from their eyes—the sheik's were as black as obsidian; Philip's were as green as venom.

Except for the color of his eyes and the ruddy tan of his skin, Philip could have been an infidel himself. His long robe was of Arab style, though made of a coarse woolen cloth rather than silk, and his red hair was covered by a white kaffiyeh, now stained by the dust of travel and wear. Unlike most European men he wore a beard and moustache, though his was a bit more unkempt than the sheik's. This element more than anything gave away his true heritage, for no Arab had a beard so darkly red.

Nearly two years of life upon the Palestinian desert had changed him, outwardly at least. Not even his closest friends knew to what extent the lost bastard child still existed deep in his soul.

Sitting upon a brocade cushion, he gauged the man upon the chaise. How far could he be pushed before he signaled his guards to fall upon the so-called guests? Philip had dealt with the sheik before, and he had always been cool, even congenial at times. But Philip had learned that these infidels often used a smooth demeanor to cover a cruel, merciless nature. Philip wondered what Rodrigo thought as he sat beside him. Rodrigo spoke the language far better than Philip, for he'd had enough of a rudimentary knowledge of it from his mother back in Spain that he had picked it up easily. Philip used him as translator because his own awkward sentences were good only for trivial remarks. They had engaged in banal conversation for the last several minutes, and now the sheik was ready to get back to their bargaining.

"Forgive me, al-Rahib," said the sheik, "but when we spoke, I had not looked upon the goods."

"Do you say that I misrepresented them?" challenged Philip.

"Oh, you infidels take offense so easily."

Philip hid a smile over the Arab referring to *him* as an infidel, but that was exactly how these Muslims looked upon the Europeans. They were probably even more adamant about the apostasy of the Christian faith than a Benedictine priest was about the Muslim faith. It amused Philip that, though blood enemies, both factions were so much alike.

"We have done business before, Ishaq," Philip replied, "and I have always dealt fairly with you, have I not?"

The sheik gave a careless shrug. "I certainly do not impugn your character, al-Rahib. Perhaps I merely had higher expectations. I will admit the sampling of silks I saw are of extraordinary quality." He lifted a silver goblet to his lips and sipped the sweet pomegranate juice.

"I am happy you think so. I know you are a man of elegant tastes, and I would never insult you with inferior goods." Philip glanced at his own goblet of juice and knew he should drink some so as not to offend his host, but he had not acquired a taste for the stuff. He much preferred simple ale.

"The silks are indeed of a quality I would use to clothe my wives—not my favorite wife, of course."

"You would not use *extraordinary* silk for your favorite wife?" Philip asked dryly.

"I would use better than extraordinary for her. She has, after all, given me five sons. The others—" he shrugged—"yours would do for them."

Philip pretended to look wounded. It was part of the bargaining game at which he had learned the Arabs were masters. "Oh, my lord sheik, I know of a certainty that these are the very silks the great khan himself uses for his sons and daughters *and* his favorite wife. You will not find any of this quality in the marketplaces even in Jerusalem. The purveyor of these silks brings them from Cathay especially for me to offer to my most special customers." The statement was partly true. The silks did come from Cathay, and they were of good quality, but they had not been intended specially for Philip. He'd had quite a time prying them from the grasp of the infidel merchant who had been bringing them in a well-guarded caravan.

He hadn't particularly liked the idea of returning to the life of a brigand. Neither had his friends. To appease their slightly seared consciences they followed two strict rules: they robbed only infidels, reasoning that this helped the cause of the Crusaders by disrupting the enemy economy, and they would cease when they had enough money to finance their way to Cathay. The problem with the final rule was that Theo and Gilly still liked to drink and carouse away much of their cut. And another difficulty was that they had been the object of thievery themselves upon occasion, so their profits were slow in building.

"The khan is a barbarian," said the sheik. "Surely I would not wish to emulate him." The sheik paused and stroked his beard thoughtfully. "Why don't you bring in the silks, and I will look at them once again. I will call in my wife, as well."

The sheik clapped his hands, and a servant quickly appeared from behind a screen. The sheik spoke to him and he exited.

Philip was hesitant to bring in his wares, for once in the tent they would be that much harder to extract should the sheik decide he could as simply kill Philip and Rodrigo and keep them for himself without paying. As it was now, the goods were on packhorses on the edge of camp and being guarded by Theo and a few other men who had defected from the French army and joined Philip's band. To make the situation worse, both Philip and Rodrigo had been required to leave their swords with the sheik's guards outside the tent. Philip had his dagger hidden in his boot, and he knew Rodrigo kept a couple of knives secreted about his person, as well.

"Perhaps," Philip responded, "you would like to view them outside . . . ah . . . so you can see them by the light of the sun?"

"My women will be most likely to wear them inside, for as you know, they do not go out in public except in modest fashion." The sheik smiled. "Do not tell me that you distrust me, my friend!"

"I would never insult you so!"

"Yet you hesitate."

"Only because I want to present my wares in the best possible light." Philip grasped his goblet and drank deeply, as if to prove his conviviality.

"That will not be in any way a difficulty for me," said the sheik with an air of finality.

Philip told Rodrigo to fetch the silks but added in English, which the sheik only partially understood, that he should leave the other merchandise under guard of two men and bring Theo and the rest back with him. If the sheik did have treachery in mind, Philip wanted to give himself and his men, not to mention their belongings, half a chance of escape.

While he waited three women entered. Two, obviously slaves, were dressed in a revealing fashion with gauzy, colorful fabrics draped like swirls about their slim bodies. The other woman was no doubt the sheik's "favorite" wife, for her dress was more modest though clearly richer. The three bowed to the sheik and then took up positions slightly behind him.

More juice was served, and a short span of time passed before Rodrigo returned. He had the sheik's servants carrying the packages of silk, but when the tent flap opened, Philip saw Theo's hulking form outside along with a few of their other men. It gave Philip a sense of security to know Theo was close at hand. Though he may have abdicated leadership of the band to Philip, he was still a savvy and skilled warrior, not to mention extremely fearsome in his appearance alone.

The packages were spread out upon the rug and opened. The women scurried excitedly forward. The prospect of shopping for beautiful things seemed to make them shake off their reserve. With squeals of delight, they sorted through the fabrics, holding them up to one another and offering opinions about how they would look as various pieces of clothing.

Philip watched with smug satisfaction. Maybe it hadn't been such a bad idea to bring the goods into the tent, for the more the women grew attached to them, the more their worth would increase. And the sheik's favorite wife seemed as much, or even more, taken with the quality of the fabric as the others.

Just as Philip's confidence was building, the sheik gave a sharp clap of his hands.

"Enough of this, women!" he exclaimed. "Leave us!"

The chattering ceased instantly. Philip's confidence sank. A man who could control his wives like that was indeed to be feared. Nevertheless, even he must know his bargaining power had decreased with every female squeal.

"Women are such frivolous creatures," declared the sheik. "As insubstantial as your silk."

"But as fine and as beautiful," countered Philip.

"I will give you two hundred and fifty of your marks."

"I cannot part with this exquisite fabric for anything less than six hundred."

"What!" gasped the sheik. Philip noted how in that moment Sheik Ishaq realized his mistake in involving his wife in the proceedings.

Rodrigo also had a worried look on his face. For one who was half Saracen, he certainly hadn't inherited much of their inborn salesmanship. But Philip had enough for both. He could smell a profit and wasn't about to let it slip through his fingers. If he received enough for this sale, it could get him and his friends well on their way east—if they started before Theo squandered the money.

"Come now, Ishaq, you and I both know this merchandise is of the highest quality. A woman's discerning eye does not lie, eh?"

"This is robbery!" All pretense of Arab civility melted from the sheik's face. He was all business now. "I will continue to deal with you only because I enjoy pleasing my wife. I will give you three hundred marks, but not a pence more."

"You would be robbing me if I gave my wares for less than seven hundred marks."

Rodrigo gasped and said to Philip in English, "What are you doing? Are you mad?"

"Just translate," Philip replied coolly. "I know what I'm doing."

The sheik was of Rodrigo's mind. "Are you insane?" bellowed Ishaq when Rodrigo translated.

"I know what I have," Philip said. "I also know I can take these goods over to Sheik Bishr, and he will give me what I ask." He also knew Bishr was a bitter rival of Ishaq's. "But his wife is old and fat and would not do justice to these lovely fabrics as would your beautiful wife."

"I always knew you infidels were scurrilous barbarians!" the man spat.

Philip shrugged with a halfhearted smile. "I'll tell you what I will do, because I saw the light of joy in your wife's eyes when she looked upon these silks. I will let them go for a mere six hundred marks."

"That is magnanimous of you." The aplomb returned to the sheik's demeanor, though his tone was drenched with insincerity. The moment the man's hands moved, Philip knew he had pushed too far.

As the sheik clapped his hands, Philip had his dagger in his own hand and leaped at Ishaq. Faster than even the guards stationed within the tent could draw their swords, Philip had his knife poised at the sheik's throat.

The guards stopped in their tracks, but Philip could hear a commotion outside as, most likely, Theo and his other men were attempting to block the entry of more of the sheik's guards. In a moment, however, several burst through into the tent with Theo and his comrades close on their heels. During this time Rodrigo had already jumped one of the guards, slit his throat with one of his hidden daggers, and grabbed the man's sword to attack the other guards.

The sheik also was not sitting placidly by with a knife at his throat. When his men burst into the tent, Philip was momentarily distracted, and Ishaq seized that moment to wrench himself free of the threat of the dagger. But as he was drawing his sword, Philip lunged at him, slicing the man's arm and hurling him to the ground. They struggled together for several moments before Philip again overpowered the man.

"Call off your men!" Philip yelled, his dagger once more at his adversary's throat.

When the sheik hesitated, Philip punctured the skin. Ishaq gasped as blood trickled down the front of his shirt. It looked far worse than it was, but it proved that Philip had the will to kill.

"Cease!" cried the sheik.

It took a few moments as swords continued to clash—Theo was in the tent now fighting next to Rodrigo—before the sheik's order was heard. The guards reluctantly obeyed. There were far more of them than of the European barbarians, but odds of even a hundred to one would not prevent the loss of their lord if they persisted.

"Tell them to drop their swords," ordered Philip.

When this was communicated, swords immediately thudded to the tent floor.

"Rodrigo, gather up the silks," Philip said in French. "We will need to take them elsewhere to sell."

The look of consternation on the sheik's face indicated he understood more French than he had let on.

"So, Sheik Ishaq, does nine hundred marks seem a fair price to you after all?"

"Nine—?" Ishaq began with affront, then his entire demeanor changed drastically, and he burst into laughter. "You are almost as Arab as you look, al-Rahib! I will give you five hundred marks for your goods. I might have gone as high as six, but I see I have lost two good men today."

"We have one man dead outside," Theo said in French.

"My friend says we have lost a man, as well, so we are almost even on that count," said Philip. "I will agree to five hundred—and safe conduct to the border of your demesne."

"It shall be so."

"And, my lord Ishaq," Philip added, "a thousand apologies for staining your fine tunic." He lowered his knife as he spoke and tucked it into the sash around his waist, keeping it near at hand, for he wasn't certain the sheik's word could be trusted.

"My small wounds will be a reminder to me that I must never underestimate a white-skinned infidel." A servant had appeared and was already binding the wound with a cloth.

After receiving the sheik's coin, Philip, Theo, and Rodrigo cautiously exited the tent, followed by several of the sheik's guards sent to help unload the rest of the goods. Philip and Rodrigo retrieved their swords outside the tent and mounted their horses.

39

Philip remained alert long after crossing out of the sheik's territory. Of course, a man in his occupation never entirely stopped being vigilant.

Theo rode up beside him. "That was close."

"But successful, eh?" Philip replied carelessly.

Theo shrugged. It was obvious he had more to say but was reluctant, and when Philip made no attempt to draw more out of him, he fell silent. They rode that way for some time, climbing the mountain pass that led to their camp in the foothills of Mount Tabor in southern Galilee. They were within a league of the camp when a horseman approached from behind. Philip recognized the horse immediately; otherwise he would have swiftly fallen upon the rider, captured him, and been forced to kill him in order to keep their camp secret.

But it was Gilly. Philip had sent him on an errand a few days earlier and thus he had been absent from the meeting with Sheik Ishaq.

"This is fortuitous timing," the wiry knight said, wiping a gauntleted hand across his sweaty brow. Despite his small tough frame he seemed the most affected by the intense summer heat. Philip often poked at him by saying it was his age finally catching up to him. Gilly continued, "I debated whether to head to the sheik's camp to find you. Having no idea how long your business would take, though, I decided to return to our camp."

"Have you news?" Philip asked.

"Since we are so close to camp I'd rather give you my report while resting my aching haunches and quenching my thirst with a draught of water."

Though Philip was anxious, he did not persist. If it was bad news, Philip would rather hear it after some refreshment.

Their mountain camp was not as opulent as the sheik's, but it was comfortable, with several tents that contained rugs, mats for beds, chests for their belongings, and a good supply of cooking utensils and food. A nearby mountain stream provided ample water. It was occupied, at most times, by as many as fifteen men—Frenchmen who had defected the army to join Philip. All of these had fought with him at Tagliacozzo during the Italian campaign and were intensely loyal to him.

Philip went to the tent he shared with Rodrigo and immediately stripped off the mail he wore beneath his Arab robe. The weighty hauberk was like a millstone in this heat. After his robe was back in place, he removed his kaffiyeh and let his red hair fall free, its tangled and sweaty strands falling to his shoulders. The kaffiyeh served a practical purpose by concealing his most recognizable feature, but he didn't know how the Arabs tolerated the heavy, hot head covering.

Feeling more at ease, he went outside. Two men were stoking the fire while others were dressing several rabbits they had procured on their way from the sheik's camp. Philip poured water from a jug into an earthenware cup.

"I'll have some of that, too," said Gilly, approaching with a cup in hand. "I won't complain about the heat because I know what you'll say, but I will never know why God chose this cursed land above all others to call holy."

"Maybe that's exactly why He did choose it," offered Theo as he, too, came seeking a drink.

Philip sloshed water into their cups and then into his own. They drank deeply, and he quickly refilled them. He then said, "God must be splitting His sides with laughter watching all the fools fight like dogs over this pathetic bone of His."

"I should think you'd be in better spirits," Theo said, "now that you have a pocket full of coin."

"Five hundred marks won't go far among fourteen men." The fact that their number was reduced by one made him feel no better.

"You would have thought it was a king's ransom the way we nearly died for it—"

"All right, Theo!" Philip burst in. "You've had a bur in your side for some time now. What's eating at you? You may as well get it out."

"We might not have lost Marcel if we'd had Gilly with us—"

"I knew it!" spat Philip. "You've been grousing about that for days. But one man would not have made a difference today."

"Gilly is worth ten men."

"Please, Theo, isn't his head already too big for his shoulders?"

"What happened at the sheik's camp?" Gilly asked.

"Ishaq tried to renege on his earlier agreement," Philip replied.

Rodrigo, who had joined the group, added, "And he wasn't too happy when Philip kept raising the price."

"You pushed him too far?" Gilly knew too well Philip's risky methods.

"What does it matter?" Philip said defensively. "I got what I wanted in the end."

"It matters to Marcel," Theo said.

"I'm sorry about him. I truly am. But we had no guarantee the sheik would not have attacked us anyway. We were lucky to lose only one man."

"Thanks to Philip's quick reaction in capturing the sheik," Rodrigo added.

They drank their water in silence for several moments. Philip refilled the cups, then asked the question that was burning inside him. "Gilly, what news have you?"

It irritated him that Gilly glanced at Theo before he spoke.

"It is as you were told. They have been in Acre for a year."

So it was true. He'd known Edward had an army in Palestine, but he'd managed to ignore that and its implications. He simply would never have guessed that his brother would have been the type to go crusading. Three weeks ago he had run into a Jewish acquaintance of his from Acre who related a most fascinating tale of how Prince Edward had been nearly killed by an assassin, but one of his wife's ladies-in-waiting had saved him.

"Even the Arabs now look with awe upon the fair Lady Hawken. They call her Al-Mubarak, the blessed one."

"Lady Hawken!" Philip had gasped.

"Yes. She is quite famous now and more sought after for her healing skills than even the Hospitalers."

"She is here? In Acre?" Philip suddenly felt as if his world had tipped on end. In nine years she had never been physically closer to him than this. Dreams, of course, did not count, especially those dreams when he'd wake reaching out to grasp an image that seemed so real until his eyes opened.

"Several of the wives of Edward's closest comrades have traveled to Palestine with their husbands," the Jew had said.

Philip had been in the middle of some important transactions at the time and could not act on the news until a week ago, when he'd sent Gilly to verify the story. He still wasn't sure how, or *if*, he would respond. Now he just stared blankly ahead. What should he do? What could he do? Why should he do anything? She had betrayed him, and he despised her for it. Wasn't that reason enough to do something? If nothing else, wasn't it his right to finally take vengeance upon his brother? This was the first time in nine years he had the ability to do so.

"Actually," Gilly was saying, "they were in Acre. But shortly before I got there, Lord Hawken was called to Nazareth to help bolster the fortifications there. His wife joined him a few days later."

Divergent thoughts bombarded Philip's mind at once. The statement, "His wife joined him a few days later" pierced through him as if he had a right to be jealous over the apparent fact that she so hated being parted from her husband that she made the dangerous journey to Nazareth. Philip knew it was dangerous because he himself had always found the winding mountain road to be perfect for ambush.

Quickly, however, he realized something else. If he did want to seek revenge upon Gareth, it would have been almost impossible to breach the security of Acre. But Nazareth was another matter. The village was not walled, and it was poorly fortified even with the presence of Edward's troops.

He looked at Gilly. "Do you know how many men Edward has in Nazareth?"

"I would guess two or three hundred."

"What are you thinking, Worm?" asked Theo. "Isn't it enough that you've wasted Gilly on this fool's errand? Forget about Hawken before you regret it."

"Why should I forget?" retorted Philip. "I have a right to avenge the wrongs done to me. I had not the strength nor skill to do so before, but now I have both, as well as the opportunity. It must be fated."

"What of our rule not to attack crusaders?"

"This is different."

"I will ride with you, Philip," said Rodrigo. Then to Theo, "He does have a right to fight the man who robbed him of his honor."

"If every man here rode with him," Theo tried to reason, "and I am sure they all *would* ride with him through the gates of hell itself—he still would stand little chance of victory. Philip, listen to me. You have plenty of money now, enough for us to get well on our way to Cathay. Let's go now. I promise I will not drink it away."

"I cannot," said Philip.

"Is it as I always suspected, that you never truly intended to go to Cathay?" asked Theo.

"It is you who squandered all our money," Philip rejoined.

"If you would have made a stand, Gilly and I would not have done so. I think you let us."

"Why would I do that?"

"Maybe you knew that once you got to Cathay, you would never return. You would never have the opportunity to get your revenge upon Hawken. I think part of you wanted to go to the far end of the world and be forever free of the burden of hate upon you, but a stronger part refused to let go, refused to release you."

"That's not true!" Philip took the cup in his hand and threw it with such force against a rock that it shattered into a thousand shards. Spinning around he started to stride away but stopped. The truth of Theo's words struck him like a blow. They could have gotten to Cathay many times had he not stood passively by and let each chance slip away. Always, in the back of his mind so deep he barely knew it was there, lurked the indelible fact that he must one day return to England and avenge himself. He'd told himself that he would go to Cathay, find wealth, and return to England to flaunt it before his brother and his woman. But reason said Cathay was not the treasure trove it was made out to be. He would have doubtless spent his life there seeking elusive wealth.

He forced himself to turn back to face his friends. When he spoke, he ground the words out even though they were difficult. "Maybe you are right, Theo." With an apologetic glance toward Rodrigo, he went on. "I thought Cathay was what I wanted, but now I know what I truly want—in truth I don't *want* it, yet I have to do it. I have to face my brother. I'll never have a better opportunity than this."

"You'll have to move quickly, then," said Gilly. "Word is that Edward will make a treaty at last with Baibars. When that happens, which should be soon, the English will have to abandon Nazareth."

With pleading eyes Philip looked again at Theo. He needed his approval, his support. Philip knew better than anyone the value of a friend, and he wasn't certain he could sacrifice the best friend he'd ever had in order to taste revenge.

"Alas!" Theo said airily. "I was only trying to enlighten you as to both sides of the issue. I won't stand in your way, Worm. I will stand beside you, as I always have."

Philip managed a grateful smile even as he felt a lead weight in the pit of his stomach. Was he about to lead his friends to their deaths? Was vengeance really worth that?

But all he said was, "Thank you, Theo."

Gareth had healed nicely. His shoulder still gave him painful twinges when he moved it certain ways, but it was his left shoulder, so it did not much impede the use of his sword. Was he grateful to his wife for her aid? Dismally Beatrice had to shake her head to that inner question. Last night gave proof that he held her in the same contempt he had for years. The pain of the bruises he'd inflicted upon her still ached.

And what had caused his ire this time? Last night a caravan of supplies had arrived from Acre, including two casks of ale. The men had made a feast and had gotten quite drunk. Beatrice, the only noblewoman present, had been invited to join the men. She'd been very melancholy after realizing she was fated to spend the rest of her life in her present miserable straits. So she had imbibed a fair share of the ale, as well. In her giddy drunkenness she had joined in on the revelry, probably more than was seemly for a lady. One of the men produced a lute, and there had been dancing. She and Leticia, as the only English women, had joined in. It was all quite innocent fun. Naturally Gareth had been furious. He never liked to see Beatrice happy, but in such a scandalous fashion was even worse. He took his ire out on her when they were alone after the feast. He proved beyond doubt that his injured arm was well on the mend.

Now the day afterward, besides the painful bruises of Gareth's beating, Beatrice's head throbbed. Leticia had prepared a draught of willow bark tea last night, and as she sipped the brew, Beatrice had pondered recent events. One good thing had occurred. Along with the supplies, Edward had sent a message that he wanted Gareth to return to Acre. Negotiations were under-way with Baibars, and Edward wanted his close advisors present. Gareth couldn't be prouder to be included in this group. He would never admit that he had risen to this status largely because of his wife's service to the prince.

Gareth's return to Acre meant that Beatrice would also return. And there she would have the distraction of other women. Maybe Eleanora would allow her to assist in the care of her baby. She would also resume her duties as herbalist and healer. She didn't care what Gareth said or did; she would not let him prevent her from enjoying that pleasant diversion.

So it was with eager anticipation that she spent the afternoon packing her things for the journey. They would depart in the morning.

Nazareth was set in a basin of land, making it easy to observe from a height. Philip realized he didn't have enough men to attack the English camp, but he'd been watching it for three days now, hoping an opportunity would present itself. He also had hired some locals to act as spies.

He wondered how long he would wait. At the moment he could no more give up his quest than he could slit his own throat. He could barely take his eyes off the camp long enough to eat or sleep. He stood in the brush and tortured himself with wild imaginings of what Gareth and Beatrice might be doing down there.

Were they seated side by side in the shade of that fig tree, engaged in a pleasant husband and wife conversation? He was too far away to see details. Was that a man and woman down there now? Or were they within the tent, caressing each other with tender intimacy?

Such thoughts assailed him until he thought he would go insane with jealousy. Yet what right had he? After nine years he refused to believe he still loved her. Perhaps it was just that she was with *him*. He knew without question that the years apart had not quelled his hatred for his brother. He'd killed many men in all those years, both in battles and in fights. He had hated none of those men and had ended their lives as duty required or as self-preservation demanded. He knew he would no longer be squeamish to kill this, his blood enemy. He was no longer a tender eighteen-year-old.

Hearing rustling in the brush behind him, he drew his dagger and spun around. It was Rodrigo with one of the Nazarene locals.

"Philip," said Rodrigo, "this one brings valuable information. I've promised to give him two loaves of bread."

Philip knew these locals were so impoverished they would do anything for a scrap of food.

"That's fine," Philip replied. "What does he have to say?"

Rodrigo spoke a few moments with the man, then said, "This is the opportunity we have been waiting for! He says the prince in Acre has recalled his favored captain, the one they call Lord Hawken. He and a contingent of the army will return to Acre in the morning."

Philip nearly shook with excitement. "How many men will go with him?"

After another exchange with the Arab, Rodrigo said, "He thinks, by the look of the horses and supplies being readied, it can't be more than a score."

He wanted to ask if Lady Hawken would be accompanying him, but he didn't want to appear overly concerned about her. Besides, doubtless Gareth would not leave his loving wife behind.

"We can handle that many," he said.

"Easily," concurred Rodrigo.

"Pay the man—give him whatever he wants. Then we will leave this place and set up an ambush on the road to Acre."

Philip's heart raced. He rubbed his hands eagerly together. At long last, he would be avenged.

40

A trickle of sweat dripped down Philip's chest inside his mail hauberk. He could not remember being this nervous before an attack since that very first time in a Parisian forest.

Nerves were the kiss of death in any fight.

Yesterday he and his men had positioned themselves in an especially well-situated pass known as Wadi al-Haramiya, the vale of thieves. Though it was known for ambushes and the travelers would be on their guard, it was still a perfect spot for what Philip had in mind. He had three archers hidden in the crags above the road, while the rest of his men, eleven in number now with Marcel gone, were hidden just around a curve in the road, ready to spring upon the vanguard of the caravan the moment the archers began raining down their arrows. In the general mayhem, even if the English outnumbered Philip's force, he should be able to quickly overwhelm the enemy.

Then why was he so jittery?

Could it be that he well knew that nothing was certain in battle? That the smallest detail overlooked could prove a warrior's undoing? That losing one's concentration for even one moment could spell one's demise?

There had been times in the past when he'd had a bad feeling about an attack and, trusting his instincts, had called it off. He had such a feeling now, but he knew he would forge ahead regardless. His whole life, at least the last nine years, had been primed for this very moment. He could not turn back. Nevertheless he glanced at Theo, still loyally at his side. The big knight nodded, as if he understood Philip's turmoil.

Shading his eyes against the glaring morning sun, Philip glanced up into the cliffs above the road. He could not see Gilly, who was in charge of the archers, but he knew he was there with a full view of the road to the east. He would signal Philip when he first sighted the English caravan.

The men with Philip had dismounted and were having a spare meal of bread and dried fruit. No sense in unduly tiring themselves or their horses while waiting. There should be ample warning when the caravan was near. Even the men seated on rocks did not appear at ease. Tension could be felt even in the talk and occasional laughter. It was thus before any raid, for there was only one thing that was certain at such times—blood would be spilt this day. All of his men were French, so they were not squeamish about spilling English blood. But Philip was half English, and he felt no strong enmity toward them. He would rather face his brother in single-man combat without endangering others. Maybe he could work the attack in such a way as to take Gareth hostage. Would he be able to quickly pick him out from the other soldiers? He would be marked with Hawken equipage, but how much had he changed in nine years? Philip was certain that Gareth would not recognize him. Most likely he would think the attackers were Saracens, since Philip's men all dressed in Arab fashion.

Suddenly, out of the corner of his eye, Philip saw a flash of red in the cliffs. Gilly's signal.

Heart pounding, Philip mounted and signaled to his men to do the same. He wondered what it would be like to fight his brother. They were both seasoned warriors now. Did Gareth still drop his shield while concentrating on his sword? He would soon find out.

All the soldiers were more vigilant than ever, and they had picked up their pace as they traversed this particular stretch of road. Beatrice knew some parts of the road were more dangerous than others, and she thought this narrow, winding place could be treacherous. She scanned the hills but saw nothing worrisome. Yet she tapped her mount's rump with her crop so as to keep up. Alain was sticking particularly close to her and Leticia, the only women in the party.

Gareth was up ahead leading the caravan of about fifty men. Each one appeared ready to draw his sword at a moment's notice. She would be so happy to be out of these hills and even more so to be back in Acre. Was the rumor true? Was Edward about to make a treaty with Baibars? Would they soon be returning to England? Though she had nothing to look forward to there, she still was anxious to get back to familiar territory.

She heard the man scream before she realized an arrow had struck him; then followed a barrage of arrows. Alain and a half dozen men drew their swords as they circled her and Leticia. Beatrice's mount shied and skittered, but she managed to keep him in control.

The other men were scrambling in complete disorder to get to safety. Some began to race ahead, but before any had gone too far, several Saracens appeared before them as if magically springing from the rocks.

The clash of swords filled the air, along with the grunts and shouts of battle.

She expected to see more Saracens pour onto the road. Surely there must be more hiding somewhere. A few came riding down from the cliffs, obviously the archers joining the fight now that their arrows were no longer of use because the battling factions had met. Yet the archers had done significant damage, if nothing else by causing disarray among the English.

Gareth and his captains were shouting commands in an attempt to bring order to the scattered troops. Despite their earlier vigilance, they seemed to have been surprised by the attack. But it was more than mere surprise against them. Even Beatrice knew what savage and ruthless warriors the Saracens were.

Leticia's mount was also nervous, and finally the animal reared, throwing the maid to the ground.

"Leticia!" Beatrice cried. Without another thought, she jumped from her mount to aid her friend.

Alain yelled at her to stop, but before he could do more, one of the Saracens engaged him in battle. All the horses were moving dangerously around both women on the ground. Beatrice grasped Leticia in her arms and dragged her out of harm's way.

"Are you all right?" Beatrice asked when she thought they were safe.

"Y-yes. Just bruised a bit."

"Can you stand?"

Leticia nodded and, with her mistress's help, rose to her feet. They moved to the edge of the battle, hugging each other close, and watched in terror at the violence being wrought before them.

Philip's group had guessed the caravan would number only a score. There were twice that or more!

Inwardly Philip bemoaned his foolishness. Yet he knew he would have attacked the caravan even if he had known it would contain a hundred knights, or a thousand. This was his destiny. The only thing that would make the battle worthwhile would be if *she* saw him die and knew it was him—if she knew that he, too, could break his oath to her.

But why should he of all men be so fortunate? He would die, but it would mean nothing. Death was his only destiny. If only he hadn't dragged his friends with him.

The worst of it was that he could not even get close to Gareth. He saw him ahead wielding his sword with amazing expertise. Who was he fighting with? Then he saw it was Rodrigo. Good. The Spaniard was the best swordsman among them. If anyone could kill Gareth, it would be he, and though Philip wanted to have the honor, it was almost as satisfying that one of his closest friends should do it.

But was he to be robbed even of that satisfaction? Another English knight came up behind Rodrigo. The Spaniard spun to ward him off, and in that horrible instant Gareth swung his sword.

Rodrigo crumpled as his head toppled from his shoulders. The whole world seemed to stand still as Philip watched in utter horror. His knees felt weak, and his sword arm faltered. Only a deeply imbedded instinct made him raise his shield at the moment his own opponent's sword came crashing toward his head.

That same instinct kept him from surrendering altogether. How could he continue to live, knowing he had been the cause of his friend's death? He knew then that he could not let this massacre go on any longer. He and his paltry band were doomed. Surrender was out of the question, for they would be given no quarter. There must be another way to save the men that were left.

He saw that way as he ran his sword through his opponent, pivoted to take on another, and found none at hand. It was one of those moments in battle, a tiny pocket of reprieve, when one can take a breath and regroup. It was then, as he looked about for a new foe to battle, that he saw the two women huddled together on the edge of the battlefield.

He recognized her immediately. The hair like spun gold was unmistakable beneath the skewed wimple atop her head. She was with that maid of hers, from whom she was nearly inseparable. Her eyes were closed, but he would never forget the sparkling blue of them, and even beneath the smudges of travel and battle, he could tell her creamy skin had not changed. After all these years she was as stunningly beautiful as she had been that first day he had spied her racing her black mare carelessly over the meadows of Cassley.

Oh, Beatrice! he silently groaned. Every emotion he had ever felt for her crashed upon him, but still, after all those years, the strongest emotion of all was—no, it couldn't be love. He despised her! She meant nothing to him now except a means for escape.

He seized upon that moment of reprieve, racing to where she stood. Most of her guards were engaged in battle. He fought through the others until he could reach out for her, and he did just that, wrenching her from the arms of her maid and knocking the other woman to the ground as she tried to protect her mistress. Beatrice screamed and struggled as he pulled her up and slung her over the front of his saddle. Then he rode up the rocky path that led up into the cliffs, just far enough so that his voice would carry.

"Cease, if you value the woman's life!" he cried in French, knowing most of the English knights would understand him. He had wrapped a hank of her hair around his hand to keep her still while he held his dagger in his other hand poised over her.

He had to shout several times before he was finally heard over the din of battle.

Finally one of the knights wearing the Hawken crest pointed in Philip's direction. Gareth, who was close by, turned and looked. Philip recognized him immediately. He had changed no more than Beatrice had.

Immediately Gareth began shouting orders, and in moments the battle was over. Philip descended back to the road, and his men joined him. There were only seven left. One man who was seriously wounded was slumped upon his mount, barely hanging on. Seven were dead, including Rodrigo—no, he couldn't think of that. He still had to get the rest of them out of there alive. They would have to leave their dead behind.

"Don't follow us," Philip yelled, "for if we even smell pursuit, she is dead."

"How will we ransom her?" shouted Gareth.

"I'll let you know." Philip wheeled his mount around and galloped down the road in the direction from which the caravan had come.

His captive fought and struggled, and he knew he wouldn't get far like that, so when they were out of sight of the English, he paused, pulled a rope from his saddlebag, and trussed her up like a Christmas goose. He was not gentle as he yanked the knots tight, but it gave him less satisfaction than he'd thought it would. However he still had to contend with her voice.

"You won't get far, you dirty infidel!" she railed. "My husband will move heaven and earth to rescue me!"

Philip winced at the words. "Cease your chatter, woman, or I'll crack your head open." He continued to speak French, which he knew she understood a little. Obviously she did not recognize him, and for the moment, at least, he wanted to keep it that way.

"Oh, you are fearsome now, but by tomorrow you'll be dead!"

"Only a moment after you!" he growled.

He had not the heart to knock her unconscious as he had threatened, so he put up with her haranguing until she finally grew exhausted and fell silent. But far worse than her threats and imprecations was her nearness. Dear Beatrice, whom he had once loved—he refused to believe that he loved her still, though he had to stoutly deny the strong stirrings in his heart to do so. Beatrice, with whom he had ridden for so many sweet hours over the English countryside, to whom he had revealed his deepest feelings, and with whom he had dreamed of having a wonderful life was here, quite literally in his grasp.

Yet she belonged to another now, and he hated both of them more passionately than ever before.

PART FOUR

41

Mount Tabor
Summer 1272

At their camp after the disastrous defeat on the road from Nazareth, Philip went directly to his tent, removed a few of his personal belongings, then headed outside where the men were busy tending their horses and equipment. Despite the activity there was a heavy silence permeating the place. Seven men lost was a stunning blow to all.

Philip approached Gilly, who was guarding Beatrice. "Take her to my tent," he ordered. "Bind her and set a guard."

"Shall I feed her, too?" Gilly sneered. "Perhaps draw her a bath and wash her clothing?"

Philip replied only with a dangerous stare. Though Gilly knew Philip would not back that stare with action, at least not against a friend, he still obeyed, but not without a sour grunt of his own. He'd rearranged the cords binding Beatrice so she could walk, though she didn't do so passively.

"You'll pay for this," she warned. "I am a friend of Prince Edward himself. He'll hunt you down—"

"I know, I know," Philip cut in wearily. "He'll hunt us down like the dirty infidel dogs that we are." Saying no more, he turned his back on her and strode away.

He walked some distance to a lookout point in the craggy cliffs above the camp. Here they always set a guard. It had a commanding view of the west and south, from which intruders would most likely come. He felt confident that the camp was well hidden and they were safe. No one had breached it since they had first found it a year ago.

He needed to be alone awhile. Soon enough he would have to return, if for no other reason than to tend his horse, though likely one of the men would take care of it for him. He also should see to the wounded man, and he would have to make amends to all for the disastrous attack. But he couldn't face the men just yet.

Although he preferred being alone, he made no protest when he saw Theo approach.

Without even asking leave, the big man hunkered down on the ground by Philip. "It wasn't your fault, Worm," he said quietly.

"Tell that to Gaubert and Jevan and Rufus and Bran and Nouel and Robert and—" his voice caught, but he forced himself to say the last name—"and Rodrigo."

"Listen to me, Worm," said Theo. "Those men chose to ride with you. They knew the risks of battle."

Philip dropped his head into his hands and rubbed them over his face. He would have much preferred that Theo rail at him, as he had every right, because he had been opposed to the attack from the beginning. Philip could not bear the man's sympathy, his gentle tone.

"Theo, Rodrigo will never get to Cathay now," Philip groaned. "It's all he wanted."

"True, that was his dream, but he had another dream, too, and that was to die wielding his sword."

"It doesn't help. . . . It just doesn't help."

"We must grieve, Philip. God knows my heart is near to breaking. Rodrigo was a brother to me, as well. Don't you think I feel as responsible for his death as you?"

"You?"

"Had I been leading, Rodrigo would have done my bidding. We would never have made the attack. I say this not to heap recriminations upon you. Rather, because of my cowardice, leadership was forced upon you, and thus Rodrigo's loyalties shifted, as they should."

"You are no coward, and I was never fit to lead."

"That's not true, Worm. Though you were the youngest, you were always the most fit. And there is no sense in either of us bemoaning our ill fate. What happened today happened. We must accept it. This is no time to dwell on past mistakes. We must think ahead. We must make plans. There is the woman to think of now."

Lifting his head, Philip groaned. "That was perhaps the worst mistake of the day."

"Even I saw the necessity of it. Without taking her, we all would have died. Yet now we are stuck with her."

"Should I take her to Acre and leave her at the gates?" Philip asked.

"You would never get that close to the city and come away alive."

"I'm afraid I never thought beyond escaping the carnage today." Philip let out a frustrated breath. "Still, we could negotiate a ransom. That's what they will expect, and to do otherwise would only raise suspicions. I don't doubt that my brother would pay handsomely for her."

"Yes, that is probably the best course of action. I'll take a message to the English—"

"Not you, Theo!" Philip gasped, then to cover his distress over the thought of risking yet another friend, he added, "You stand out like a peacock among swallows. We must be more subtle. Let's give it some thought, plan it well." Better, he thought, than the fiasco today.

By now Beatrice realized her captors were not Saracens. Even worse, they were renegade Franks. They were more despicable than infidels or animals, for even animals would not turn on their own kind. As she sat in the dark tent, sweltering from the heat, she still could not believe she had been taken as a hostage. All this time in Palestine she'd been so sheltered and protected, and to be taken as they were leaving was impossible to believe.

Would she never see England again? If these men thought nothing of attacking their allies, why should they falter over slitting her throat? Her only chance was to convince them that she was worth something alive. She must make them believe that her husband cared enough to rescue her.

Did he?

Surely he would try, if only for the sake of show. Edward and Eleanora would insist upon it. They believed Edward owed his life to her and therefore would feel honor bound to do something. She must not give up hope.

Suddenly the tent flap opened and a stab of sunlight streamed in along with the wiry form of one of the outlaws. Though small, he looked fearsome, with tiny sharp eyes, a mean-looking scar over his right brow, and a frightening scowl on his face. At once her stomach knotted as she realized they could do worse to her than kill her.

Biting her lip to keep from screaming, she tried to scoot away from the man.

"Aw, don't worry, I'm not going to hurt you," he said in French. Elizabeth de Clare, who was French born, had been teaching Beatrice the language, so she was far more proficient at it now than she had been before. However, she understood it better than she could speak it.

"What do you want?" she asked in a trembling voice.

"I brought you water," he said.

She saw he was carrying an earthenware jug. "Thank you. It's very hot in here. Could I go out and get some fresh air?"

"It's hot out there, too. Drink the water. It will help."

Since her hands were tied, he held a cup to her lips. It was awkward and much spilled down her front. She coughed and sputtered.

"Can't you unbind my hands?" she pleaded. "My feet are bound, so I couldn't get far. Even if I tried, where could I run to in this barren land? I would die out there all alone."

He nodded his agreement but then shook his head. "We'll see what . . . ah . . . al-Rahib thinks."

"Who is that?"

"Him that took you, of course."

"He's an infidel?"

"That's enough questions. I'll bring you some food in a bit." He turned and exited the tent.

The man that captured her must be the leader, but how could he be an infidel with that ruddy beard? Maybe he was half infidel. It didn't matter. She hadn't gotten a very good look at him from the perspective of lying across his saddle. The brief look she did get told her he would have no qualms about raping her, killing her, and leaving her body out as fodder for the animals. Then she recalled how he had threatened to hit her over the head if she didn't quiet, but he never did. Had that been a show of mercy?

Well, she wasn't going to let that change her impression of the . . . jackal. No doubt he only wanted to keep her whole so as to get the most ransom for her.

It was dark outside when the flap opened again. This time a huge man came in. She'd noticed him already—it was hard not to notice him, big as he was. He looked no less fearsome than the others. A tangled brown beard covered his face, and a thick shock of wildly curly hair on his head was revealed now that he'd removed his kaffiyeh. Despite the scars of battle and the creases of life upon his face, there was, much to her surprise, a softness to his eyes.

When he knelt down beside her, she was not afraid.

"I'll remove these," he said and proceeded to loosen the cords that bound her hands. Oddly, his huge, clumsy hands were gentle as they worked to loosen the cords. "You can come out for some air and food if you want."

"Yes, I would like that." He then unbound her feet, and with his help, she stood unsteadily.

The air cooled considerably with the setting of the sun, and once outside, Beatrice shivered as the full impact hit her after being inside the stuffy tent.

"Warm yourself by the fire," the big man said. "I'll find you a blanket."

"Thank you." Beatrice looked around the camp and noted that most of the men were gathered around the fire eating. They were a somber group, which was no surprise considering their losses that day. For the first time she wondered about the English losses. She knew young Alain, her chief guard, had been killed, but how many others? Her husband had survived the attack, she knew, because her captor had shouted threatening words to him before riding off with her.

She sat down on the dirt before the fire. Some of the men looked her over, but for the most part they ignored her. In a few moments the big man returned with a blanket, and he placed it around her shoulders. She glanced up, unable to hide the surprise on her face. He merely shrugged and walked away. Someone else brought her a bowl of food, a stew of some sort, with a hunk of dry bread to sop it up.

As she ate she found herself looking around for the leader and found him sitting off by himself. He held a bowl of stew that he was hardly touching. Was he brooding? He should be after having led the failed attack. When he glanced up in her direction and saw that she was looking at him, he quickly turned his head away. Then the big man approached him. They spoke briefly, and the two of them went together to one of the tents. For the first time she noticed moaning sounds coming from there, and she remembered they had a wounded man. Setting aside her bowl—she wasn't hungry enough to care about finishing the unappealing stew—she started to rise. In a twinkling the wiry little man was at her side.

"What are you wanting?" he asked gruffly.

"I realize you have a wounded man," she replied, even as she questioned her behavior. Why should she care about the wounded thief? If he died, it would be one less for the English to fight when they rescued her. Yet she could not ignore the moans of pain that seemed to be getting louder. "I have some healing skills. Perhaps I could help."

"And why would you want to do that?"

"I would take pity even on a hurt dog if I found him in the street," she retorted.

He appeared taken aback by her plucky response. Saying nothing, he went to the tent where the leader and the big man had gone.

When he returned, he said, "Come with me, then."

A candle on a chest provided the only light in the tent. The wounded man lay on a pallet on the floor, and another man was kneeling beside him. The leader and the big man stood over him.

"Here she is," said the wiry man, who then quickly exited.

"Gilly says you can help him," the leader said.

Instantly she forgot about the wiry man's odd behavior as the leader drew her attention. For the briefest of moments there was a strange quality to his voice. Though she'd heard him speak before, this time his voice held a hint of helplessness and . . . something else. What was it? It was almost as if she'd heard it before, but that was impossible.

"I know something of healing," she said. "However, I don't have my herb kit. Let me look at the wound." She knelt down beside the injured man while another outlaw, kneeling on the opposite side, lifted the patient's tunic and removed a wad of cloth pressed into the wound. The cut in his side was quite deep. She could see some of the hipbone through a gash that was seriously inflamed and still bleeding, even hours after he'd received the cut. When she glanced up at the leader—al-Rahib?—his gaze was focused on her with such intensity it made her shiver.

Again he seemed shaken that he was caught staring at her. "It does not sicken you to look upon such a wound?" he asked.

"I have seen worse. Do your men have any herbs at all that I might use? Comfrey and lavender would be excellent. Even some ragwort—"

"I doubt it," he cut in impatiently. "Do something else," he ordered.

"I need something to work with," she replied just as shortly. "Did you expect me to wave a magic wand over him to heal him? Give him something for his pain, then. Have you no strong spirits? Surely a gang of thieves must have some mead or wine."

He bristled, but to the big man he said, "Theo, see what you can find. Simon has a fondness for smoking opium. See what he has."

"And find some clean cloth to use as a bandage. A lot of it," she added. "He will surely die if we don't stop the bleeding."

The man kneeling by the patient said, "Ph—"

"Guy," the big man called Theo cut in, "come with me. I have a task for you."

"I cannot leave him," the fellow protested. Beatrice saw for the first time that the man on his knees was young, only eighteen or nineteen by the look of his smooth beardless skin.

"This could save his life," said Theo. "Come now."

Reluctantly the young man rose. As he passed Beatrice she offered him a slight smile and said, "I will take care of him . . . Guy. Finding the things I need is the best thing you can do for him."

"He is my brother. Please don't let him die."

"I'll do my best for him."

Theo and Guy exited the tent, but from outside she heard Theo admonish the younger man. "You must call him only al-Rahib."

"But why? We have all used our proper names."

"He has his reasons. It is important. Now get your horse ready. You must ride to Acre to find the medicines she needs."

"No, Theo! I can't leave Juibert. I know I am just his little brother, but I am his only family. If he dies—"

"I think he will die for certain without the medicines, and with Juibert wounded, you are now our fastest rider. Besides, you know the way better than anyone. We cannot wait until daybreak. You must leave now in the dark. You can wait outside the gates until they open in the morning, get what we need, and then be back here by midday. It is best for you to go. You are young and won't arouse suspicions should they be on the lookout for us."

"I'll go, then," Guy agreed with great reluctance. Beatrice heard him walk away.

Theo entered the tent once again. "My lady," he said to Beatrice, "tell me exactly what things you need and where to find them in Acre."

"Go to the apothecary on Straight Street," she replied. "Tell him about the wound, that it is inflamed and the patient is fevered. He will know what to give you."

With a brief nod, Theo exited, and she was again alone with al-Rahib. Suddenly awkward with nothing to do but feel his presence and his gaze upon her, she began idly fussing about the patient, wiping his brow with an edge of the blanket covering him. He moaned and writhed upon his pallet.

"There, there," she murmured. When a man came with some cloth and a basin of cool water, she swabbed the wounded man's brow. The whole time she felt the leader's presence like the weight of a heavy cloak upon her shoulders. She tried to concentrate on the patient, but there was so little she could do for him.

Soon al-Rahib began to pace, and finally she could abide it no longer. "Sir," she said impatiently, "you can do nothing here. You may leave."

"I'll leave when I wish," he snarled.

She shrugged. "I don't care what you do. If you believe pacing in this tent will assuage your guilt for this man's wounds, then do so—"

"You know nothing of my guilt!"

"I know you are the leader of this gang and thus are responsible for what happened today. For this man's wound, for the dead—"

"You know nothing!" he shouted.

Juibert, the patient, cried out at the disturbing tone of al-Rahib's voice.

"Now you've woken him," she said.

"He was never asleep," al-Rahib said defensively. "You are now responsible for him, woman! If he dies—"

"Go ahead and kill me if he dies," she dared. "You were probably going to kill me anyway, you murderous dog!"

His venomous look could have leveled her like a battering ram. She gasped, fearing he might draw the dagger he wore tucked into his sash and do away with her then and there. Instead, he spun around and left the tent. Trembling, she tried to direct her attention back to the patient.

42

Outside the tent Philip gasped in air like a man who had been trapped in a dark, dank dungeon for years. He determined that he must stay away from her at all costs. She meant nothing to him, he told himself once again, yet he could not deny the stirring he felt inside when she was near.

How tenderly she had wiped Juibert's brow! It made Philip wish he were the one lying there with a lethal cut in his side. She seemed genuinely concerned for the man, a common thief and one of her abductors. Philip now saw that she had changed much from the girl he had known. He could see the effect of nine years upon her lovely countenance. Not necessarily an ill effect, more like the change in the patina of a fine sword with its use. It loses it shine, but somehow the nicks and marks of battle make it better.

The Beatrice he had known had been spoiled and headstrong, and there were still hints of this about her. It was tempered, though, by a confident maturity shown in the way she had known what to do for Juibert, in her very touch. Thinking of the sword scarred by battle made him wonder about her scars. The loss of her first husband, even if she hadn't loved him, must have been hard, if for no other reason than that he was the father of her child. And her own father? Philip well knew how beloved her father was to her. How great must her grief have been to lose him!

And what of her marriage to Gareth? Could it be loveless, as well? Jocelin had implied that it had been forced upon her, something to do with protecting her son. The Beatrice Philip had known could never have come to love a man like Gareth.

An oath is an oath, he tried to tell himself. Yet oddly, he could not make himself feel the same fury he'd felt when Jocelin had first imparted the news to him. He was older now, had experienced years of living in many gray areas of life. He knew better than anyone of the compromises one must make in order to survive. He'd done so many things he hated himself for, how could he judge her for being forced to break a youthful oath, not only for her survival but for her child's, as well?

Yet how could he forgive her? Every time he felt a weakening in the wall of his anger, he had only to picture her with Gareth, and the anger returned. Regardless of her feelings toward the man, they were still married; they still had been *together*. He knew Gareth well enough to know he would not leave a woman untouched, especially one of Beatrice's beauty. That she was here with him on Crusade must indicate an element of devotion.

Did they have children together? It must be so. And that would surely seal the bonds between them.

Round and round he went with such thoughts. One moment a tenderness would creep into his heart toward her, the next he'd imagine her and Gareth together, and a flood of fury would wash away the sentiment.

After a while Theo and Gilly approached. They both looked grave.

"Worm, you will drive yourself insane if you keep up this brooding," Theo said.

"The men are talking about going their own way," added Gilly.

"So much for going to their deaths with me," Philip said bitterly.

"Many did," Theo rebuked.

"Aye . . . they did, didn't they?" His throat knotted as he thought of Rodrigo and the others. With a kind of morbid resolve he added, "Tell the men I release them—"

"You owe them the courtesy of telling them yourself," Theo said.

"I can't face them like that," Philip admitted.

"Why don't you get some sleep," Gilly suggested with rare sincerity. "It will appear better by light of day. The woman says she will bide the night with Juibert, so the rest of us will divide ourselves between the remaining tents. Go to your tent and sleep."

For a moment Philip wondered if Gilly was serious. How would he find sleep amongst his inner turmoil? Yet it might be that his exhaustion was making the turmoil worse. He hoped everything would look better in the morning.

He rose and strode to his tent. There was room inside for the men who had been displaced from Juibert's tent, but Philip remained alone. The men would rather crowd into another tent than face him. Would they really leave him? Perhaps it was for the best. Their numbers were so decimated they could hardly be an effective force against even the weakest caravan. Would Gilly and Theo leave, as well?

His mind skittered in new directions as he lay upon his pallet. Must he now face life alone, as he had when he was a youth? He had come to value and depend upon his friends too much. He should have known it could not last. Suddenly he felt like the dejected bastard child that he was. Being near Beatrice must have brought out the pitiful side of him.

He tossed and turned, dozing a little, only to be awakened by a nightmare. The hard ground beneath his thin pallet was tolerable while he slept, but while he lay awake, it pressed upon his bones painfully. Finally he rose and left his tent to warm himself by the fire. He saw Beatrice seated before the fire at the same moment she saw him, and because he could not let her think he feared her, he boldly strode up to the fire. He was glad, though, that he'd been careful to replace his kaffiyeh.

They were alone. No one had posted a guard on her. She could not survive in the desert by herself, but still, she was a prisoner, and he wanted her to be treated as such.

He dropped a log on the glowing embers and thrust his hands over the flame that leaped up. He tried to pretend he barely noticed her, but he was as aware of her presence as his horse would have been of a bur in his saddle. Her eyes were focused on the flame as it licked up around the new log. Like a man twisting a knife in his own wound, he wondered what she would do if he revealed himself to her. She hated him now as the thief and kidnapper he was, but would that change if she learned he was the Philip de Tollard she had once loved, whom she had once been willing to offer her purity to?

"How is Juibert?" he asked, mostly to distract his mind from its pathetic course.

"The same," she said. "It became chilled in the tent, and I sought to warm myself."

"There is a brazier we can move inside the tent for warmth."

"No, the coolness is probably best for him in his fevered state."

A silence descended between them that felt natural. He remembered the long talks they'd had when he had chaperoned her on the many rides over the English countryside. To this day, there was no one who knew as much about him as she did—if she still remembered.

"I . . . I thank you for caring for him," said Philip. "You didn't have to."

"I don't mind. I like feeling useful."

"I would repay you somehow if I could," he found himself saying. "I would return you to your husband's loving arms if I could figure a way to do so without getting killed."

"Aye, you are in a precarious position."

He marveled that she did not seem afraid, but then, she had also been fearless when they were young.

"Why do you have an infidel name?" she asked.

"What?" He was taken aback. Did she wish to converse with him? He could not resist the temptation, to see where it would lead, to perhaps experience a taste of what they'd once had.

"You are not an infidel, yet you have taken one of their names."

With a shrug, he replied, "I deal mostly with Arabs, and I believe they respect me more if I blend into their ways. Maybe I am wrong. Maybe they laugh at me behind my back. But they dare to do so *only* behind my back, for they would not live long if they did it to my face."

"Aye, I understand you are a dangerous man." There was a hint of sarcasm in her tone. "What does al-Rahib mean?"

"The monk."

She looked surprised.

"I knew a monk once," he went on, "who was truly dangerous."

"A Muslim?"

"A Christian monk. I fought at his side for years, and he was a fearsome foe. I thanked his God that I never had to face him as an adversary. Because he had taken a vow of silence, I never learned what made him so angry."

"I also once knew an angry man. But he was not dangerous. He was gentle and dear, yet the anger seethed inside him. I myself never saw it explode."

"Maybe you had a way that soothed the savage beast."

She smiled, and he felt his heart nearly break.

"Was this man your husband?" he asked in a desperate attempt to cling to his fury.

"No."

"Someone you loved?"

"Why did you attack our party?" She apparently was not about to reveal too much of herself to a brigand. "Could you not see that we were a military expedition and had few riches among us?"

"I admit I was brash and foolish."

"Is it because you hate the English?"

"Only some English."

She looked up at him with such intensity that he was certain if it had been daylight, she would have been able to breach his pretense. He resisted the strong urge to turn away and was relieved when she bid him good-night and returned to Juibert's tent.

The next day he avoided her completely. Guy returned with the medicines, but Philip did not go to Juibert's tent. Instead he had Theo give him reports. He isolated himself upon the lookout, where twice more Theo urged him to talk to the men. Finally, two of the men, Reymund and Simon, came to him. They, along with Guy and Juibert, were all that was left of the French crusaders who had joined them a year ago.

Reymund seemed to be appointed spokesman. "Philip, we have been wondering what will become of our band. I know you have been suffering because of our losses and this is not a good time for such a discussion, but . . ." He glanced at his companion as if seeking help, but finding none, he forced himself to continue. "There are only seven of us left, six if Juibert dies. We vowed to follow you, Philip, as if you were our liege lord. We will not break our vow. Unless . . . surely you see we have not the numbers to be effective."

"Please, stop, Reymund," Philip said. "You need agonize over this no longer. I should have spoken sooner, but words failed me. Courage failed me." When Reymund started to protest, Philip raised a hand to stop him. "There are many kinds of courage, my friend. Give me a sword and an enemy to wield it upon, and I won't be stopped. But having the fortitude to tell my friends to leave . . ." He slowly shook his head. "It makes my nerve wither like a vine in a drought."

"You saved our lives, not only at Tagliacozzo but many other times since—"

"As you have mine."

"Still, we would not desert you."

"The time has come," Philip said solemnly. "I absolve you from your vow. You are knights, valiant and true. I have no doubt you can attach yourself to a legitimate lord either here or back in Europe. None of us were ever comfortable being brigands, so consider yourself fortunate you can leave this life behind you."

"What will you do, Philip?"

"I always wanted to go to Cathay. Mayhap I will do that yet."

"We will stay until the woman is ransomed," said Simon. "It may be we will have to fight the English again."

"No, I won't embroil you in this failure any further." Though he knew it was the right thing to do, the words were hard for him to utter. More than he could say, he wanted to keep on as things had been. Fleetingly, he thought he could recruit others to his band. The life he'd lived here in Palestine hadn't been entirely miserable, though dangerous and dishonest. And, though he'd often denied it, he had enjoyed his role of leadership. It had come naturally to him. It had never been the life he'd desired, but it had probably been better than he deserved. Now, by his word, he must end it all. Some inner sense made him know it was time, but still the pain it caused was deep, and new uncertainties were thrust upon him. He had no new life to step into, and he would probably be alone now.

Did he truly think it could have been otherwise? Hadn't he struck the death knell the moment he had captured Beatrice? He should have known all was doomed to change with that act.

He looked up at the two men standing with awkward uncertainty before him. "I ask only one thing of you. If Juibert dies, take Guy with you and set him on his way back to France."

"We will do this, m'lord," said Reymund.

Philip's brow creased. The men never addressed him with such a title. Given names were always used in a casual fashion. Yet he understood this was offered to honor him as their leader. He was deeply touched. He tried not to bemoan the fact that rightly he could have been their lord if life had not betrayed him.

The men left and Philip continued his vigil. He almost wished Gareth would find his hideout so they could do battle once and for all. Even as he perceived the desire, though, he knew it was selfish. He would not endanger his friends further. When Juibert's condition was stable, or when he died, and the men had gone, Philip would disguise himself and take Beatrice back to Acre. He hadn't thought it all out, for if he was seen with her, he would doubtless be a dead man. Perhaps he could get safely within a couple of miles of the city and then release her to find her own way back. Yet even close to the volatile city, it would be dangerous for her to be alone.

Well, somehow he would get rid of her, deliver her back to those she loved. If he died in the process, what did it matter? He had cheated death so many times that he'd probably lived too long anyway.

Several hours later Theo came to the lookout with the news that Juibert had died.

"The lady is very upset," he said.

"Because she now fears for her own life," Philip sneered, though halfheartedly because even he could not believe it of her.

"Nay," Theo replied wearily, "she is upset because a life has passed and she feels she failed him, though any who saw her tending him know she did all that was humanly possible. And"—he cast a censorious look at Philip—"despite her grief, she still has offered comfort and sympathy to poor Guy. She is a remarkable woman, this Beatrice of yours."

"That I never denied." Philip had known it from the first moment he'd seen her flying across that meadow upon her shining black horse. Why else had he fallen in love with her from that moment and sacrificed all for her and, even after years, still held feelings for her in his heart?

"The men will leave as soon as we bury Juibert," Theo said.

You and Gilly, as well? he wanted to ask but could not bring himself to appear so pathetic. He had told them they could go, although they had never made a formal vow to him.

"I will take the woman back to Acre immediately thereafter," said Philip.

"What are you saying? You will take her alone? You will ride right into Acre with the most sought after hostage in the area? Are you insane?"

"I can think of no other plan."

Theo rolled back his eyes and wagged his shaggy head. "I have heard that women make all men fools. Now I believe it."

"What else can I do?"

"Here is a plan if you are too dim-witted to think of something better. Take her to Ishaq's camp and let him barter with the English for her. It won't be the first time Ishaq has ransomed a hostage. The English will know, by the woman's word if nothing else, that Ishaq wasn't the one to abduct her, so there won't be reprisals. If they decide to hunt us down even after the woman is returned, let them. We have eluded better trackers than they."

Philip suddenly felt almost giddy at Theo's use of the words *us* and *we*. Was it too much to hope that his closest friends would not desert him? No matter how pathetic it was, unbidden emotion rose up in him. Tears burned inside his eyes, and he could barely speak.

He managed the query, "We, Theo?"

"What do you mean, Worm? Just because you released the others, you don't think you'll rid yourself so easily of me and Gilly, do you?"

"I . . . I did not know. You are free—"

"Bah! Who are you that you can set us free? We will come and go as we please."

"Gilly is of the same mind?"

With another roll of his eyes Theo replied in an exasperated tone, "Do you know nothing, Worm? After all these years can you not see that we are as brothers? Even Gilly considers you so, though he would never show it outright. You should know that. How many times must we save your life or ride with you into danger before you realize this bond we have? If you feel differently, then speak now and perhaps we will take our leave."

Philip now realized that all this time he had been so fearful of losing his friends, so sure he didn't deserve them, that he had never truly appreciated the bond that did exist between them. Of course, Rodrigo's death had begun to enlighten him, but it still had not fully sunk in. Now that Theo was mincing no words about it, he still found it almost too amazing to believe. Theo and Gilly were brothers, as he'd always dreamed of having!

"I don't feel differently," Philip finally said humbly.

"Good!"

Suddenly they felt awkward.

Brusquely, to cover up his emotion, Theo said, "How does my plan sound?"

"I like it. As long as Ishaq doesn't take it into his mind to keep Beatrice for himself or, worse, to sell her as a slave. She'd be worth her weight in gold in the slave market."

"While in Acre, Guy said he'd heard that Baibars is seeking peace negotiations with Edward. Ishaq is a second or third cousin of Baibars, so I doubt he would do anything to endanger the negotiations."

"Maybe it would work, then."

43

Digging a grave in the hard desert earth had been grueling, hot work, even shared with the other men. Almost immediately after Juibert had been properly laid to rest and Reymund, Simon, and Guy had departed, Philip went to be alone. He sat at the lookout for a time, soon growing aware that his clothing had grown stiff with dried sweat, and even he could barely stand his odor, so he headed to a pool a half a furlong away.

He stripped off his robe down to his braies, doused the clothing in the water, then laid everything on a rock to dry in the sun. But the one item he was most anxious to remove was his sweaty kaffiyeh. His head had been itching for two days because, with Beatrice in the camp, he had been especially careful not to remove it except to sleep. He probably had vermin in his hair along with the caked-on perspiration. Rinsing out the headgear, he laid it beside his clothes and then he eased himself into the pool. It was large for this dry land and came nearly to his waist. He dunked his head into the water and scrubbed at his hair, thinking nothing had ever felt better. He felt as if he were washing away the heavy gloom of the last few days, as well.

Unfortunately, the gloom was not as fleeting as the filth. The grief came quickly back to him with turmoil and bitterness.

Lifting himself from the pool, he sat on the edge to dry in the burning sun. He found himself wondering what would happen if Beatrice came upon the pool just then. Would seeing his red hair cause recognition to dawn upon her? It galled him that she had not yet recognized him. He'd known her immediately.

Could he have changed so drastically? He and Beatrice had been so close. How could a mere nine years blind her? Obviously he had not meant as much to her as he had thought.

Yet . . .

He glanced into the pool. The water had settled from his bath, and his reflection clearly stared back at him. There were several battle scars on his face that hadn't been there when he had known Beatrice—a nick on his forehead and one over his left brow that made a thin line where the hair never grew back. A deeper scar ran from the corner of his right eye down beneath his beard. Exposure to the desert sun had greatly darkened his skin and made permanent creases around his eyes where he'd squinted in the glare. It made him look older than his twenty-six years, but what truly shocked him about the face in the pool was that the real changes were not physical and had less to do with the creases around his eyes than with what lay *inside* the eyes. The eyes of an old man grimaced back at him, a man who had lived a lifetime of disappointments, failures, and losses. These were his eyes in only twenty-six years of life! They were eyes that held no laughter, no joy.

Had he truly become so dour?

He tried to form his lips into a smile, realizing even as he made the attempt how rarely he did smile or laugh. And as he did so now, he saw it did not touch his eyes. Mocking himself, he made a face at the reflection.

Threading his fingers through his beard, he wondered if it also added years to his appearance. Perhaps if he shaved it off, she would recognize him. Yet he reminded himself that it would not matter if she did. Even if she weren't married, how could they ever retrieve the past? It would be impossible. Even if they could, there was nothing to be done about the gulf of changes between them now.

With a disgusted grunt he lurched to his feet, turning his back on the cursed pool. His clothing was still a bit damp, but he flung on his undergarments and robe anyway, securing the kaffiyeh with the finality of a hangman knotting a noose around a condemned man's neck. It was time to get rid of the woman, to put aside his morbid, pathetic thoughts and move on to the next hurdle of his life, whatever that might be.

He was striding up the rise that led to the lookout when Gilly accosted him.

"There you are!" said Gilly. "There are riders approaching."

"What? Are you sure it isn't Reymund and the others returning?"

"Positive. They are about a league away, but even at that distance I can see the Plantagenet crest on Edward's banner. Come and see for yourself." Gilly turned and strode up the rise.

Philip followed him, and when he reached the place that gave the best vantage, he saw the riders. At least a score or more of them and definitely English. He thought he could make out a silver hawk in flight against a red background on the tunics of some, the Hawken crest.

"How did he find us?" Philip wondered aloud.

"They haven't found us. Not yet," Gilly said. "It may be simple luck on their part." He shrugged. "Mayhap Guy unwittingly led them here."

"But why wait a whole day before making a move?" Shielding his eyes with a hand, Philip peered across the distance. Beatrice had said her husband would move heaven and earth to rescue her, so great was his love. "At least Guy and the others left in the opposite direction, else they would have been killed."

"Yes, our friends are safe, but what about us?"

"Come, let us find Theo and decide what we should do."

They raced down the hill and back to camp. If the English knew the exact location of the hideout, they could be upon them in no time. *If* they knew. That was the debate among the three men as they discussed the possibilities. Theo did not think they could possibly know the exact location of the camp even if they did follow Guy, for they were moving slowly, as if tracking a prey. Perhaps they had learned of Guy's association with the kidnappers but too late to follow him directly. They might be following his trail, which would not be easy, because even in his haste Guy would have taken care to cover his tracks. Yet they had come this close. There must be one among them who knew what he was doing.

After a few minutes of discussion Philip said, "We haven't time to discuss this further. We must flee."

"And take the woman?" Gilly asked.

"We could leave her here for them to find," Theo suggested.

"No," said Philip. "We may yet need her for protection."

He saw his two friends exchange a covert look of skepticism. Regardless of what they thought, he was right. With their enemy closing in, they were going to have a difficult time eluding them. They needed a hostage as much now as they ever had.

"She'll slow us down," Gilly said. He looked ready to rebel.

"Philip is right," Theo agreed.

Philip blinked at the unexpected support.

Then Theo added, "I don't think we have a chance of getting away without her." He gave Gilly a stark look that silenced further protests.

Hurriedly they packed up any necessities they'd need; then Gilly went to the tent to get Beatrice. Philip had given Guy money to buy Juibert's horse for her, knowing they would need it sooner or later. But he wasn't sure he trusted her to ride alone. She was a good rider and could easily find a way to escape or, at the least, sabotage their flight. Yet he was reluctant to have her ride with him. He did not trust himself with her that close any more than he did her riding alone. Finally he decided upon an arrangement that would not put him in a suspicious light.

"Gilly, take the woman on your horse," he said, and when Gilly tried to protest, he added firmly, "You are both small. The weight will not slow you down."

"You won't get away," Beatrice said. "They are English knights, the best in the world!"

"We shall see," he responded, unable to come up with a more pithy retort. "And if you try to warn them—" He stopped short when a gleam in her eye indicated she hadn't considered making a verbal warning until he'd mentioned it. With a grunt, angry more at himself for giving her the idea than at her, he grabbed a spare sash from his saddlebag and strode toward her.

"When they see how you've treated me—" Her statement was cut off as he flung the sash around her mouth. She would have fought, but Gilly grabbed her hands. "Ow!" she cried as Philip cinched the gag tight.

"We have treated you like a princess, my lady!" Philip sneered, knotting the gag behind her head and giving it a final, not gentle, tug. "Tie her hands, Gilly."

Philip almost smiled as she sputtered and groused beneath the gag. But the whole incident was so reminiscent of their playful bickering back when they were together that the hint of a smile faded almost as quickly as it had come.

They mounted up and departed the camp they had occupied for a year. Theo led, with Gilly next, and Philip taking up the rear leading the spare horse. They covered their tracks as they went, which was more important than speed right now. When they were certain they could not be followed, they would make up time.

Philip decided they would keep to their earlier plan and take Beatrice to Ishaq's encampment. There was no reason not to do so unless Gareth's force caught up with them and a fight ensued. Then they would just fight it out, or rather be slaughtered, since the odds would be twenty or more to three. The idea of such a last stand appealed to Philip, for it would show Beatrice once and for all just what he thought of oaths. He'd make sure to rip off his kaffiyeh before he died so that both she and Gareth would know it was he. They probably wouldn't care, but it would still be a good way to die.

They traveled over steep, rocky terrain so treacherous in places they were forced to ride in single file and with great care. One misstep could send them plummeting over the cliff. But on this craggy trail he no longer had to worry about covering their tracks, for the rocks would reveal nothing to his pursuers.

It was well before midday when they'd been forced to flee the camp. They headed north and east, climbing higher into the mountains. Philip had been this way before. It was not the easiest approach to or from the camp, which made it the best escape route. He knew there was a pass that would eventually take them out of the mountains, and in order to reach it, they had a bit to climb yet. Since the path was rough and Philip was not very familiar with it, they could not travel after sunset, so they found a place to camp for the night, hoping they had shaken their pursuers.

Theo took first watch while the other two exhausted men rested. Philip wanted to keep Beatrice bound and gagged, knowing it would be easier to keep from falling prey to her charms that way, but Theo took pity on her and held to the argument that she knew she would die if she tried to make it on her own. Philip shrugged, threw down a blanket over the rocky ground, and tried to get some sleep before his watch.

Beatrice wrapped herself in her own blanket, but she could not sleep. She was more afraid now than she had been since her abduction, for she was convinced that these men had no intention of letting her go. They had been quite civil to her for a time, almost kind—the big man especially. Now she saw that it was just because she'd been nursing their comrade.

The flight today proved these brigands had ulterior motives; otherwise they would have left her behind at the hideout for Gareth to find. Instead they took her, claiming the need for protection. Whatever else they were, these man were seasoned knights who hardly needed a woman as a shield. The only conclusion she could draw was that they were not going to hold her for ransom at all. Wasn't she more trouble than she was worth? Now that the other men seemed to have deserted, there were fewer to guard her.

What could they have in mind if they didn't want a ransom? It did not seem they had a interest in ravishing her or murdering her. They had not so much as bruised her in the three days since they had taken her, though the leader had been overly rough when he bound her. If any in this band of robbers was going to harm her, he would have been the one. For the most part he had kept his distance.

A rock pressed against her shoulder. She turned over but another rock then poked her hip. Could they have chosen a more inhospitable camp?

Despite the discomfort, she managed to doze for a bit. Then she started awake. It suddenly came to her what the thieves' intention was. They were going to sell her as a slave. They must have a means to get more money for her in that manner than by ransom. Maybe they didn't believe her declarations of her value to the English.

God, what shall I do? she moaned silently. She had heard how infidels treated their slaves. She had even had a first-hand hint at a banquet given by al-Quasim, the merchant with whom she and Gareth had stayed in Acre. At the end of the meal and entertainment the man had paraded out a selection of his slave girls and offered them as "private" entertainment for Gareth and the other knights present. Beatrice did not doubt that Gareth had accepted the offer. When had he ever refused the charms of women who were not his wife?

Still, no matter how despicable Gareth was, the idea of becoming a slave to a barbaric infidel terrified her. She was certain they had ways that would make Gareth's cruelty seem tame. Lying awake, with rocks jabbing her body at every turn, her terror heightened as the darkness fed her imagination.

Finally she decided that dying lost and alone in the desert would be better than life as an Arab slave. She would run away now. Her foolish captors had not seen fit to bind her, and she might not have a better chance than this. The big thief and the one called al-Rahib were sound asleep, loud snores issuing from both, especially from the dangerous "monk." The strutting, arrogant miscreant lay only a stone's throw from her with his mouth ajar, emitting nasal rumblings like a decrepit old man. She almost laughed.

In the opposite direction, where the little thief was supposed to be standing guard, she saw him seated upon a rock, chin pressed against his chest, fast asleep. She wasn't surprised the men were so tired. They'd had a grueling trek that day and had none of her terror to keep them awake.

Quietly she pushed aside her blanket, which she would leave behind. If she lasted another night, she would be happy to sleep on the bare ground. She crept to where the horses were hobbled, pausing every so often to assure herself that her captors were still sleeping. Their snores continued.

The horses stirred a bit as she moved among them. Her heart racing, she murmured soothing words. She knew horses and they sensed her confidence.

The animals were still saddled, ready for a quick departure if it became necessary. She considered taking the other horses with her for a short distance and then setting them free so the thieves could not come after her. But she decided that might cause too much of a stir. Instead, she merely loosened their hobbles, leaving them free to wander off on their own. Taking a water-skin from one of the other horses, she grasped the reins of the spare horse and led him away.

The utter insanity of her actions suddenly struck her. The trail was treacherous enough in daylight and would be deadly in the dark. And what direction should she take? She had a good sense of direction in daytime, but without the sun to guide her, she was completely befuddled.

Well, she concluded, even if she spent the next forty years lost in the wilderness as the Israelites had done in this very country, she would be better off than in an infidel's slave harem.

She set off in the same direction they had taken to get there, at least as close to it as she could guess. By backtracking in that way, she deemed she had a better chance of meeting up with her rescuers. There was a half moon in the black star-studded sky to help light her way. And when she looked more closely, she saw a slight lightening of the sky in what she recognized to be the east. Now she had an idea of direction, but that also meant she had only a short time before her captors rose with daybreak and discovered her missing.

She kept going, realizing her escape would be futile, but after waiting three days for rescue, she had been passive long enough. If she got far enough away, she might have a chance to somehow signal Gareth and his men. They could not be far. There might be a flint in her horse's saddlebag she could use to build a signal fire. Even if the thieves caught her after that, the damage would be done.

That idea made her change her direction and choose a path that took her to higher ground. Maybe she should leave the horse behind and concentrate on the signal. Pausing, she opened the bags and riffled through them, looking for what she needed.

The suddenness of the hands grasping her from behind did not even allow her time to scream before one hand clamped over her mouth. She had not even heard a footfall break a twig.

"Well, m'lady," sneered the voice she recognized as al-Rahib's, "taking a late night stroll, are you?"

Struggling against his viselike hold, she could not answer except in garbled mumblings. She twisted her head back and forth. His hand moved a fraction, and it was enough for her teeth to slip over the fleshy part and bite down.

"Ow!" he yelled, loosening his grip enough for her to twist around and jerk up her knee to strike him between the legs. He yelped again, though the blow had not been enough to disable him. He did lose his hold on her, and twisting free of him, she started to run.

He dove at her, knocking her face down into the rocky ground. The pain of the fall momentarily took her breath away. A rock cut her chin.

"You treacherous beast!" she screamed when air finally filled her chest. But his crushing weight holding her down made further speech difficult.

"You have asked for this treatment," he retorted.

"L-let me g-go. I won't run. Truly." She tried to sound humble.

He laughed. "I rather like where I have you," he gloated.

"P-please! Don't—"

"Don't flatter yourself, m'lady. I don't have to force myself upon a woman to have her."

"I expect they call you Monk because no woman would have you!" she railed as he rolled off her. But before she could take advantage of the brief freedom, he had grasped her braid and wrapped it around his hand.

Laughter erupted from him once again. She had naught but words to attack him with, and they were useless if they only amused him. However, as she now faced him she saw in the dim moonlight that the laughter was merely sound emitting from his lips and was in no way amusement or mirth. His eyes remained as cold and hard as the emerald stone they resembled.

She fought against his hold, but the pain of her hair being nearly pulled from its roots forced her into submission.

Two things happened in the next moment that nearly robbed her of her breath once again. First, she noted that in their struggle, his kaffiyeh had been knocked from his head. Then, the first rays of morning sun shot over the top of the ridge and illuminated him from behind.

His hair was red; his eyes were green. It could be anyone, but it wasn't just anyone. She gasped.

44

Philip was no less shocked to see the look of recognition in her eyes. He'd been thinking of little else for days, but now that the moment had come, he didn't know what to say.

"I know I've grown hideous with the years," he said, trying to strike an indifferent note—and failing miserably—"but you look as if you are gazing upon Lucifer himself."

Mutely she shook her head. She continued to silently stare, and unlike when they were young, he could not fathom what she might be thinking.

Finally she said, "That's why you took me, then?"

"No, I took you to save us from being killed. I don't know why I attacked the caravan, but when I heard you and Gareth were among the party, I could not resist doing something."

"Are you really a thief?"

"Oh yes. A brigand, a scoundrel, a murderer, and now a kidnapper, as well."

"Philip de Tollard."

Hearing her speak his whole name struck him like a blow, yet her tone wasn't vindictive in any way. Rather it held a kind of compassion that seemed to encompass their entire short but momentous past.

He thought he'd try to conjure the same note by speaking her name.

"Beatrice Marlowe—" Stopping, he realized that was no longer her name. Bitterness once more welled up inside him. "Lady Hawken," he said through clenched jaw.

He had still been holding onto her hair, but touching her in such a manner was more than he could bear, so he dropped the braid.

"You no longer fear I will run?" she asked.

"I should have left you behind at the hideout yesterday."

"Why did you not?"

"I kept you for protection—"

"Ha! I doubt the dangerous al-Rahib needs the protection of a mere woman. You had other reasons."

"As I said before, don't flatter yourself." It was easy now to cling to his anger. He kept in front of his mind that she was, and always would be, Lady Hawken.

"When I knew you as only a common brigand, I thought your intent was to sell me as a slave. What did you think would happen, Philip?"

"I tell you I was forced into what I did by circumstances!" he yelled. Then he sucked in a breath to steady himself. She had recently commented that he had never vented his anger upon her, and he would not do so now, though his hands balled into fists at his sides.

A stirring of the brush made them both turn their heads. Theo and Gilly broke into the clearing where he and Beatrice stood. The sun was now fully risen and sending bright rays over the ridge.

"She tried to escape," Philip responded to their questioning gazes. "Bind her and gag her and throw her over the spare horse. We will leave immediately." He turned and stalked back to the camp to fetch his horse.

"I want something to eat first," Gilly groused.

"Eat in the saddle!" Philip called over his shoulder. "Move now!"

He didn't know if it was a tribute to his power of command or to his friend's loyalty, but there was no further argument and his orders were obeyed. He took no pleasure in the obedience. Nor would he take pleasure in seeing Beatrice flung over the saddle like a sack of wheat—not much anyway.

Gilly jogged off to find some rope. Theo gave Beatrice an apologetic look.

"Why do you let him order you about like that?" she demanded. "He is nobody, born a bastard with no claim to family, not even a true knight if he deceived you into thinking he was one."

"I know who he is," Theo said quietly.

"He has no right to order men."

"It is you, my lady, who do not know him."

"I knew him once," she said, her haughty tone tempered slightly. She wasn't sure why she was so angry except that this man, this al-Rahib, was not the Philip she had known and loved. All these years she had kept his memory in a small part of her heart, but it was the memory of the young, innocent, and dear lad she had known. She felt as if part of her were being torn from her with the stark reality of who Philip had become.

"I see your eyes are finally opened," said Theo.

"Yes, and what I see sickens me."

Just then Gilly returned with the rope. They tied her up and gagged her and slung her over the saddle, as Philip had ordered.

The brute! He had a nerve making them do this to her. What had she ever done to him? He had abducted *her*, held her prisoner, and finally brutally tackled her when she attempted escape.

Where had the gentle, kind, and honorable young man gone? When had the tender green eyes turned so hard and bitter? Her life had not been easy, but she knew her own eyes were not so sullen and malevolent. Jostling up and down on the back of the horse in the awkward position, her stomach churning, her head growing dizzy, she became more and more angry at him.

Only when she vomited, an especially vile thing with a gag around her mouth, did he relent and allow Theo to put her upright in the saddle, still bound and gagged. Oh, how she hated him! She would get her revenge on him somehow, someday!

They finally exited the mountains and came into a valley to the east. The trail became easier, but the heat of the sun remained relentless. Though they had covered her head with a cloth, it still ached from the heat, causing several dizzy spells. She made no complaint, though. She would not be the object of the man's pity, if he had a shred of such a decent emotion left in him.

They stopped at midday, and Theo helped her to dismount and recline by a rock, though he did not remove any of the cords that bound her. He did, however, take off the gag so she could eat the dried fruit and bread offered her.

"Where are we going?" she asked. "Not to Acre. I know that much."

"We are going to take you to a sheik associate of ours," Theo said. "He will arrange for your return to your people."

"Why must you do that? I don't want to be at the mercy of infidels."

"Because—"

"She doesn't need to know our business!" Philip cut in sharply. "You"—he glared at her—"keep quiet or I'll put the gag back on and let you starve!"

"You contemptible dog!" she spat back. "Maybe I *would* be better off with infidels."

He opened his mouth to retort, then spun around and strode to his horse. "Mount up! We've tarried too long."

"We are not finished with our meal, *Worm*," Theo said with great patience.

Beatrice thought it interesting how he emphasized the final word. Was it some kind of nickname? Or an epithet that would bring the men to blows? Perhaps she could use Theo's sympathy to her advantage.

But before she could consider this further Philip snapped at his comrade, "Shut up, Theo, and do as I say!"

With a sleek, agile movement surprising for a man of his size, Theo rounded on Philip, short sword drawn. "Don't push too far, Worm!"

Beatrice restrained a triumphant smile. The big man towered over Philip by a span at least and certainly outweighed him by a few stones. She held her breath, waiting for the men to come to blows, waiting to watch the big man crush the arrogant, malicious brigand she had once known as Philip.

As if by instinct Philip had his dagger in his hand and stepped toward Theo. His eyes sparked with fire. She remembered him once likening his anger to an erupting volcano, and though she had never seen him explode, she could tell he was close. Beatrice never thought she'd be so eager to see blood spilled.

Then, amazingly, he backed down, sheathed his dagger, and let his hands fall loosely at his sides.

"I'm sorry, Theo," he said. "I forgot myself. Finish your meal." He strode away into the brush, where she could no longer see him.

After he disappeared Theo glanced at Beatrice. "My lady, you are gloating."

"Should I not be pleased that my enemies are fighting amongst themselves?"

"Finish eating, my lady, and do not be so quick to judge matters on that which you see on the surface."

She popped a dried fig into her mouth and chewed thoughtfully, wondering what he had meant by that. He seemed to be defending Philip, whom he had only moments before threatened with his sword. She reminded herself once more that these were thieves and murderers and could not be trusted to be consistent.

Philip rolled his eyes when he saw Theo approach. He sensed that some kind of brotherly talk was forthcoming. Well, he deserved it. He'd been acting like a fool. He stayed where he was, hunched dejectedly upon a rock, and braced himself for it.

"Well?" he said, brow arched expectantly.

Theo squatted on the ground beside Philip's rock and still was almost on eye level with him. "You must make amends with the woman, Worm. We will reach Ishaq's camp tomorrow, and then the opportunity will be lost."

"Why should I?" Philip asked. "After I leave her with the sheik, I will never lay eyes on her again."

"I remember when I first met you," Theo said slowly, thoughtfully. "You were still a lad, and you had that fire of anger in you even then, but I clearly saw it was not who you were. You were still innocent of life despite all you had been through. You still saw good and hoped for good. You still *hoped*. Then the knight who had been your friend in England came, and he told you what Lady Beatrice had done."

"And you are surprised I changed after that?" Philip challenged.

"I suppose not, but I grieved to see it."

"Should I have remained a naive boy forever?"

Threading his fingers together, Theo tapped them against his lips. "I fear to anger you if I tell you what I think."

"It did not come to blows before, so I doubt it will now. Speak the truth, Theo. I need to hear it, for my mind is so muddled and confused at the moment that I fear it will burst apart."

"It is just this, Worm. A man who has been knocked about by life does not have to become a wall of hatred."

"Is that what I have become?" Philip couldn't help feeling defensive, though he'd asked for the truth.

"Look at you, Worm! You are so solid a fortress I cannot see even a crack where the stones have been fit together. I can see, because of the fondness I hold for you, but few others can."

"I don't see what is wrong with that," Philip reasoned. "The instinct to raise my shield in battle has saved my life many times. My fortress protects me."

"Yes, it keeps pain out, but it keeps everything else out, as well."

"Good. I am better off that way!" Philip replied smugly.

"Even if it causes you to raise your dagger against one of the only friends you have left?"

"You drew your sword first, Theo!"

"All right," he conceded. "But you know of what I speak. If you continue the way you are, you will crumble. Men are not meant to be fortresses."

"What has that to do with . . . the woman?"

"Everything, you dolt!" burst Theo, losing even his immense patience.

"What about my brother?"

"You may have to eventually forgive him, as well. But as I understand your past, he, at least, deserves your hatred. She does not." As Philip opened his mouth to protest, Theo added quickly, "Bah! Don't tell me about her breaking an oath. If she did it to survive, how can she be blamed? Would you have rather seen her dead? Is that what you call love?"

Philip wanted to cry "Yes!" Instead he said, "Tell me, Theo, you still have love in your heart for your Aletta, don't you?" When Theo nodded, Philip continued, "She will always be held dear to you, yes? It would not be so if you had parted from her in anger or if she had betrayed you. That's all I would have wanted for my memory of Beatrice. I know it is sinful to wish someone dead, but then, I am as sinful as they come, aren't I?"

"I am not one to judge that," Theo said. "And I don't think you truly wished her dead. Don't you see, Worm? If you forgive her, you will have a chance to recapture some of those fond memories that your hatred has blackened from your mind. And it may well prevent your own destruction. As I said, your brother deserves your hatred, but she does not. I have known her only a few days, and despite her oft sharp tongue, I have seen only a decent woman of fine substance. You saw how she cared for Juibert, not as a thief and her captor but as a man deserving tenderness. She embraced Guy in his grief and comforted him, not because it was in her mind to cajole her kidnappers, but rather because it needed to be done. If you think she would have lightly betrayed her oath to you, married your brother, even fallen in love with him, then by all means, truss her up and dump her at Ishaq's camp and forget about her."

Choked up by the images of Beatrice's nursing of Juibert and the other things Theo had spoken of, Philip was silent. He'd been trying hard not to think of this side of her, the true side.

"She always had a sharp tongue," he finally managed to say through his constricted throat. "I loved that about her. She never feared to say what she wished. She's become more compassionate and tender-hearted than I remember, but it was in her even then, else I would not have loved her as I did. I think what angers me most, Theo, is that she has not really changed, except for the good. I, on the other hand, have changed much, and all for ill. She would never be able to love me as I am."

"Is that what you want? For her to love you again?"

"Am I not more of a fool than you thought?"

"You love her still, don't you?"

"I never stopped loving her," he finally admitted. "The walls you spoke of were not because of hate. They were from the love burning inside me. I love her still—not an image from the past but the person she has become. How could I not?"

"Then you should speak to her."

"What? Shall I tell her I love and want her? Ask me to fall on my own sword instead! She will never return my love. She hates me, as well she should. And even if she had, by some miracle, an inkling of fondness for me, she is married."

"True, speaking words of love would be pointless," Theo said. "But what of forgiveness? You cannot continue to hold on to your hatred. You've said that you were born a bastard, alone and rejected as a youth. If you don't do something, you will die that way, as well."

45

Theo returned to the others. Beatrice arched her brow expectantly at him.

"No, my lady," said Theo in response to her unspoken question, "I did not kill him."

"He would have deserved it."

Gilly grunted as if he agreed.

"I am not in the habit of killing my friends, no matter how much they may deserve it." Theo shot a meaningful glance at Gilly. The little thief shrugged and took a large bite from the heel of bread he held.

"How long have you known him?" she asked.

"Several years. We found him in a Paris tavern getting a beating by a man he'd offended. He was too young and too foolish to know better than to pick a fight with a knight—"

"Two knights, if you recall," Gilly corrected. "We saved his hide, and I have wondered ever since the wisdom of such folly."

"How many times has he saved your skin since, Gilly?" Theo asked.

"Ah, well . . ." Gilly stuffed more bread into his mouth to avoid the question.

These men had known Philip almost since he had departed England, and Beatrice saw now there was a bond of loyalty between them. They must know

Philip better than anyone, especially better than she did. She and Philip had known each other only a few months. A few months! The reality of that shocked her, that something so brief could have had such a monumental effect. She had once believed with all her heart that he was her one true love. So certain she'd been that she had offered herself to him and never regretted doing so. To this day her only regret was that he had refused her, but she had loved him all the more for his deep sense of honor in so doing. If he were indeed her one true love, then why should it surprise her that she had never stopped thinking of him? Did she not still wear his brooch on a chain around her neck? She had repaired it after Gareth had ripped it from her, and she still wore it in defiance of her husband, though never at night when she knew he might come to her and see it. Even when thinking Philip must surely be dead, she could not let go of his memory, clinging to it as the sweetest time in her life.

Had she merely been trying to grasp at thin air? And now—? No, there was no now. There could not be. He despised her. And what of her own feelings? She was no longer a foolish girl who would allow past love to muddle her emotions. Yet for so many years she had yearned to find him again, knowing the truth of their love could not easily dissipate.

You are married, Beatrice, she reminded herself. Her heart suddenly skipped a beat as she realized if true love existed between her and Philip, nothing could stop her from taking hold of it.

To distract herself from this most unsettling revelation, she asked Theo, "Did he become a knight since then? You all fight with great skill."

"He didn't, not in the strictest sense. Even so, he has earned a knighthood many times over if not officially."

"You have been in many battles?"

"Yes."

"I'm surprised that he became a warrior—" she began.

"Why should that surprise you?" Philip said, striding into the camp. "Fighting was always the thing I did best."

"I remember you used to enjoy scholarship."

"Stupid, youthful fancy," he said with a shrug. "Fighting and killing suit me far better."

"Are we leaving?" Gilly cut in.

Beatrice thought he was trying to come to the rescue in his clumsy way, but she wasn't certain whom he thought he was rescuing.

"Shortly," said Philip, then he turned to Beatrice. "I would speak with you in private, my lady."

His tone was cool, but his eyes smoldered. She had never felt this afraid of him even when she thought him a brigand.

"You were in a hurry before," she said, a hint of desperation in her voice.

"Things have changed," he said sharply. "If you are afraid, then we can talk here in front of my friends. It matters not to me."

"W-where would we go?"

"Not far. They will be able to hear you scream should I attack you."

"Lead on," she replied in an amazingly steady tone considering the way her heart was pounding in her chest.

When they were several paces away and out of sight of Theo and Gilly, Philip paused and turned to face her. He did not speak for some time, and she did not push him, fearing more than ever what might come.

Finally he said in a tone far from contrite, "I have been told that I have behaved badly and that I should apologize."

"A forced apology is worse than none."

"True, but I agreed, and now that the moment has come, it isn't as easy as I thought it would be."

"Is it because you don't feel I deserve it?" Suddenly she swayed a little on her feet. The heat, the ordeal of the ride, and the emotional turmoil were having their effect.

"Please sit upon yon rock," he said. "This may take some time."

She did so gratefully, and he continued.

"You do deserve an apology for how I have treated you in the past few days. Your present malaise is proof of my most unchivalrous behavior. I ask that you accept my apology."

"I accept it."

He shifted back and forth upon his feet, and her heart clutched, for all at once she could see so clearly the Philip de Tollard she had known that she felt foolish for not recognizing him before.

"There's more," he said with resolve.

"Please, before you continue, would you care to sit? My neck—" She gasped as a memory assailed her.

He groaned at the same moment and closed his eyes as if he'd been stabbed by an enemy sword.

"Oh, Philip!" she said. "It breaks my heart that the memories I hold most dear must now be reviewed with such pain for us both. How is it that time has ravaged what once was so sweet?"

"How can you ask such a question? Do you think you could break your oath to me, marry my brother, then dance blithely on as if nothing happened?"

Then he added harshly, "And I don't care if your neck breaks! I realize now I cannot forgive you even if my ire does destroy me!"

Beatrice stared at him in shock. All these years he had hated her for breaking that oath! It had festered inside him like a poisonous wound. She should have realized it the moment she first saw him, but her marriage to Gareth was such a disaster, such a personal misery that she had long ago forgotten she'd even broken an oath. She certainly could not have guessed that Philip should have continued to hold her to it. Besides, she'd had no choice.

He seemed to guess what she was thinking. "You don't even believe you did anything wrong! But I suppose love for my brother blinded you to past commitments."

"Love!" she cried, unable to restrain her utter incredulity at such a term being applied to her miserable relationship with Gareth.

"Come now, only a devoted wife would follow her husband on Crusade."

Exhaling a groan, she shook her head with astonishment. But what astonished her more? That he believed she could love a man like Gareth or that it so deeply disturbed him that she loved him at all?

"Philip, you suffer under a deep misconception," she said.

"Will you tell me now how you were forced into marriage? How you nobly gave yourself to a man you despised in order to save your son's inheritance?" His tone dripped with sarcasm.

"You seem to know everything," she said coldly.

"Unless Sir Jocclin told me lies, I think I have a pretty good idea of what transpired. Will you call Jocelin a liar?"

"He would have no reason to lie to you."

A silence fell between them as her concordance seemed to momentarily rob the wind from his argument.

At length she said, "It would appear that my being forced into marriage has no bearing on how you perceive me."

"I had lost everything the day I left you," Philip said. "My future was bleak, and I did not expect to live beyond the morrow. All I had to cling to was your oath to me, that I could go to my grave knowing that though my brother had taken all from me, he would never have you."

"I'm sorry, Philip," she said humbly. "If it helps, I have regretted what I did every waking moment since—" Her voice broke as unexpected emotion welled up in her with the thought of her countless regrets. Tears spilled over the rims of her eyes and coursed down her cheeks. "My world had fallen apart around me," she explained, "and I felt trapped. Maybe if I had been older and wiser, maybe if I'd had more courage, I might have fled and found you. But I had not the slightest notion that you were even still alive. I made a mistake, Philip, but I have paid for it. Believe me, I have paid dearly for it."

He swallowed. She saw his jaw work spasmodically as he obviously fought back his own emotion. His eyes reflected pain. The fire was doused from them. She knew then that the Philip she had loved was not lost completely.

"What do you mean, you paid?" he forced.

"Don't make me tell you. I don't want your pity. Your hatred was better than that."

He dropped down on his knees before her. "Please tell me, Beatrice. I won't pity you. I well remember your pride. But you will leave tomorrow, and I don't want to go through the rest of my life hating you. I must know the truth. It is said that the truth sets one free. Maybe it will be so for both of us."

She thought of Gareth and knew she would never be free, yet she could help Philip find release from the past.

She knew telling was not enough. She would show him the marks of her marriage. When she began to lower the shoulders of her surcote, he grasped her hand.

"What are you doing?" he asked, a tremor in his voice.

She indulged a little smile, for she knew what he was thinking. "No, Philip, this is not like before, and even if it were, I have no virtue to offer you this time." With her chemise covering her modestly, she revealed her shoulder blade.

"I gave that to you," he said, "when I stopped you from escaping."

"No, Philip. Look closely."

He nodded. "I see now. I've had enough bruises to know this is an old one."

"Five days old," she corrected.

"How—?"

"Do you wonder, Philip?"

"Gareth?"

"He is quite adept at striking me where the bruises will not be visible." She replaced her surcote, then pushed back a strand of her hair, revealing an old scar on her jawline. "He wasn't so careful there." She let the hair fall back to cover the scar. "You think I came on Crusade with him out of devotion? He forced me to come because Edward and Eleanora wanted it. Well, he didn't have to force much. After my baby died, I—"

"Your child died?"

"Of fever. He was three years old. Leticia convinced me that going to the Holy Lands might be better than being all but imprisoned in Hawken with the dowager—"

"Lady Hawken—the former Lady Hawken? That old hag is still alive?"

"Careful how you speak of my dear mother-in-law!" Then she smiled. "Now you really pity me, don't you?"

"Oh, Beatrice! If only you'd gotten word to me! I would have returned—" He stopped, a look of apology in his eyes. "No more blame. I see now it is pointless. The truth is, once I was in France, it was years before I had the means to leave, but by then I'd spoken to Jocelin and made up my mind to hate you instead of rescuing you. What a fool I was!"

"Many were the nights I dreamed of your rescue."

"Truly?"

She reached inside her surcote. He'd been so intent on her bruise that he hadn't noted it before, but now she lifted out the chain and held the brooch in her hands. "I found it in the meadow that last time we parted. I have worn it ever since. I convinced Gareth that it was just a symbol of my connection to him and to Hawken."

"I am sorry to say I no longer have your brooch," he said. "In a fit of anger I threw it into a wood in France."

"I understand."

"But you truly kept mine, all these years?"

"Close to my heart."

His lip trembled, but he said nothing. Instead, he lifted the brooch into his hands, bowed over it, and kissed it tenderly.

She laid a trembling hand on his head.

"Are we fools, Philip?"

"Yes, we are fools."

"Will you still take me to the sheik's encampment?"

"I—"

He gazed up at her with an intensity that seemed to lay bare her heart and soul.

"I haven't thought about that."

"I don't want to go."

"What do you mean?"

Her heart was thudding, her head spinning, but it wasn't the heat this time that unsettled her. She was about to commit a mortal sin. How, though, could she do otherwise? Would even God expect her to return to the hell of her marriage when a miracle had brought her true love back into her life?

"I would stay with you, Philip. I would not lose you again."

She bent toward him, cupped his face in her hands, and drew him to her until their lips met.

"Thankfully," he murmured as he took her into his arms, "I have lost the cursed sense of honor that plagued my younger years."

He kissed her deeply, but it was different from when they were young. It held an edge of passion that could never have been there before, a passion borne of the knowledge that love was a fragile thing. Beatrice hoped, believed, that as with all healing, the places that had been broken and mended would become stronger than they ever were before.

46

G areth hated this cursed desert. How glad he'd been upon returning to Acre to report to Edward about the attack and refresh his men, to hear the news that Edward would make peace with Baibars. It meant an imminent departure from this deplorable land. What fools had ever called it *holy*?

Before leaving, though, Gareth had to make an attempt to find his wife. He'd been at it three days now with a score of men to aid the search. It had been quite fortuitous when they had identified one of the thieves in Acre visiting an apothecary. Instead of arresting him Gareth had decided to follow him to see if the fellow would lead them back to the brigand hideout and thence to Beatrice. But the man, though he appeared young, was adept at covering his tracks and he seemed to know the country well. They had lost him yesterday and were now combing the area to see if anything would turn up.

Gareth wondered how much longer to continue. What great loss would it be if he never found her? She'd been a thorn in his flesh since the beginning, never warming to him, far from obedient, and worst of all, apparently unable or unwilling to bear him an heir. The sense of victory in taking what he suspected had been his brother's had not lasted long.

Still, a pretense must be made; otherwise he would lose esteem in

Edward's eyes. Edward, and especially his wife, had been almost inconsolable when they had heard of Beatrice's abduction. The man would be king one day. Currying an alliance with him would be worth a few extra days spent in this miserable wilderness.

After scouring the Mount Tabor foothills for all of a day with no success, Gareth had turned the men southward. If the thieves were in the mountains, they probably would never be found, for hideouts were far too plenteous there and well disguised. It was likely, however, that the thieves might go to the south, where the slave markets were. They might believe their captive would fetch them more reward if they sold her than if they held her for ransom. Indeed, Gareth had pondered just how much he'd be willing to pay to get her back. The thieves might well make more in the slave market.

"My lord, look over there!" said Sir William de Cugey, Gareth's faithful vassal.

Gareth's gaze followed to where the man pointed. Down from the rise upon which they stood, there was an oasis, several trees, green brush no doubt surrounding a pool or creek. Though they were several furlongs away, he could make out horses grazing, riderless.

"Perhaps they have seen something," Gareth said. "Let's go question them, but with stealth, for these may be the very men we seek."

He ordered all but a few of his men to fan out and surround the oasis while dispatching archers to position themselves unseen in the brush. Then he and five others crept as close as they could to the place without detection. He saw three men bent over the pool, scooping up drinks of water into their hands. He immediately recognized the mount of the man they had followed from Acre. Could it be that he was not associated with the thieves at all? He'd been heading toward the mountains early yesterday, but now here he was quite a bit south of them. It was possible he had spent the night in the mountains and then come this far south, but why leave the safety of the hideout and the numbers that his brigand comrades represented?

"One of them is the man we followed from Acre," whispered William.

"Yes, I see that."

"And I recognize one of the other horses as also belonging to one of the thieves," added the knight.

"Are you sure?"

"I could not mistake it. I fought that man in the canyon."

"Then these are the men we seek, but not all of them, and certainly their captive is not among them. They may have separated from the main group for some reason."

Gareth signaled his men to draw closer. When the three thieves finally heard them, they drew their swords, but Gareth yelled, "There are archers trained upon you."

The three dropped their weapons, and Gareth sent a man to collect them while a couple of others grabbed the men, holding them fast.

"What is this all about?" protested one of the thieves, the older of the three.

"We are after brigands," Gareth said.

"We are but innocent pilgrims—"

"Bah!" Gareth spat. "I know who you are. You attacked my men four days past on the road from Nazareth, and you kidnapped my wife."

"You can see for yourself we have no woman—"

Gareth cracked the man across the face with the butt of his sword. "Start speaking the truth and I may not kill you. We recognize your horses, so give up the lies. Where is my wife?"

"We know nothing!" the man cried, blood spilling down his face.

"Bind them," Gareth ordered his men. "Then we shall see about finding the truth."

When the three thieves were bound and made to kneel upon the grass, Gareth looked them over and quickly decided to focus his attention on the youngest of the three. He looked like he would break quite easily.

"You!" Gareth said to the young man. "Tell me where the rest of your band is. Where have they taken my wife?"

"I-I d-don't know," said the lad, trembling.

"Tell me the truth if you value your life."

"I-I don't care for m-my life!" sputtered the boy.

Gareth nodded to Sir William. "See just how much he cares, William."

Wearing a pleased grin, William stepped forward and unleashed a torrent of blows upon the lad. After a few moments Gareth raised his hand, and William stopped.

"You three will hang for what you have done," said Gareth. "Not only for being brigands but for being traitorous dogs, turning on your own kind. But the worst of all your crimes is stealing a helpless woman from the arms of her family. That is the most vile of all crimes. If you have any humanity left, you will see she is returned to her loved ones, to her husband, her children." He directed these last words toward the young man, sensing him to be the most vulnerable to such sentimentality.

"Children?" said the lad. Gareth restrained a triumphant grin at seeing the man so readily take the bait. "I did not know she had children."

"And you have robbed them of her tender love!"

"No . . . no . . ."

"Guy, no!" implored the older thief. "Say nothing—" A blow to his face quieted him.

"No, Reymund!" cried Guy. "Taking her was wrong. She does not deserve this."

"You will betray *him* to save her?" said the one called Reymund.

Gareth decided to let the two debate the issue. They might unintentionally reveal information thereby.

"She cared for my brother," said Guy, "and you saw the way *he* looked at her. He would not hesitate to kill her if the mood struck him."

"You know that is not true."

"Still she deserves to be back with her family."

"He will see to that; you know it. Don't betray him!"

Gareth quickly stepped in, for he feared the older man might soon make a case for the man they spoke of, obviously their leader, the one who no doubt had taken Beatrice in the first place.

"Enough!" Gareth ordered. "I will give you one last chance, you scurrilous whelp. Tell me who took my wife and where they are or you will all perish here and now without benefit of trial."

"Guy, we are dead anyway," the older thief warned, but William throttled Reymund until he slumped over unconscious. When the third thief started to make protests, he, too, was beaten into silence.

"I swear on my father's grave," Gareth said to Guy, "if you help us to find my wife, I will spare your life."

"I do this not to spare my life," said Guy, "but because I take pity on her as she did upon my brother. Al-Rahib took her—"

"Al-Rahib?" questioned Gareth. "None of you are infidels, and I got a good enough look at my wife's abductor to know he was not one, either."

"No, he is a Frenchman like us."

"What is his true name?"

Reymund awoke in time to hear the brief exchange. He yelled, "Don't, Guy!"

"Will you spare the lives of my companions, as well?" Guy begged.

"Yes, I give you my word."

"The name I have known him by is Philip de Tollard."

Suddenly light-headed, Gareth stumbled back a step as if the ground were quaking beneath his feet. He managed a brief glance at his vassal, William, who appeared only a little less shocked at this revelation.

"That can't be . . ." Gareth muttered. Then to Guy, "You are sure?"

"I have known him thus for four years, when I first joined Charles of Anjou's army in Sicily."

Desperately pulling his wits back around him, Gareth asked, "Where is his hideout?"

"You would never find it on your own. I only can take you there."

Gareth had the three thieves mount upon their horses and had them bound firmly. The group traveled for the rest of the day back into the mountains, camped for the night, then continued all the next morning until they came to a clearing. The remains of a camp were evident—tents still stood, and cooking utensils and other items were scattered about, indicating the camp had been vacated in haste.

William examined the fire pit and judged it had been cold for many hours.

Gareth tried to get more information from the thieves, but it quickly became obvious that at this point they knew no more than Gareth did.

"Kill them," Gareth ordered, "then stake out their bodies so all who pass by know what becomes of traitorous dogs!"

Guy was silent in his shock and said nothing about Gareth's promise. The other two men, however, spat all manner of curses until six of Gareth's men fell upon the three with their swords.

Gareth paced some distance away from the carnage. He was not squeamish—death and blood had sickened him only once in his life, but after that time in his father's solar he'd sworn never to be so weak again. He might have actually enjoyed watching the thieves die if he hadn't needed some quiet in order to think about this incredible turn of events.

Philip was in Palestine! And he had Beatrice. Had the two met secretly and planned this whole abduction scheme? He wouldn't put it past them. Taking it one step further, he wondered if they had been in communication for the entire time since Philip had left England. Perhaps that was why she had come on Crusade so willingly.

Well, none of that mattered. All Gareth cared about now was that he find Philip, kill him once and for all, and take back Beatrice. Yesterday he had been willing to leave her in the hands of brigands and slave traders, but all had changed now. He would never let those two go off together in happy, romantic bliss. He would rend them apart, kill his brother, and . . . He wasn't sure if he'd let Beatrice live or not. He would have every right to kill her as an adulterous witch. But what a waste of such beauty.

He'd settle all that later. First, to find them.

He called the men together. "I plan to remain in Palestine until I find my wife and avenge her by killing her abductors. There will be a rich reward for every man who remains with me on the quest."

Along with a few of Edward's men, every Hawken knight with him, fifteen total, pledged himself to his liege lord's quest.

PART FIVE

47

Palestine
Fall 1272

C rossing the Judean wilderness was the most arduous of all Beatrice's travels. It spread before them like an invitation to a funeral, and sitting upon a dead man's mount did nothing to dispel Beatrice's morbid sensibilities. It had almost made her forget her utter bliss at being together with Philip again. Philip said they could have skirted this area; however, it not only would have added days to their journey to Jerusalem but would have brought them too near Crusader outposts.

"Philip, it has been two months since my abduction," she had told him before they had set out on this journey. "I am certain Gareth has given up by now. Especially since news has come that Edward has departed Palestine. Gareth would surely have gone with him."

It had been the news of Edward's departure that had induced Philip to leave the safety of the new hideout they had found in the Galilean hills. He'd done so because Beatrice had asked for this. The three men had been talking of heading east to Cathay, and Beatrice could not bear the fact that she had been in Outremer and not laid eyes on the most holy places. Philip tried to console her with the information that even King Louis had never seen Jerusalem on either of his Crusades. Nevertheless, she well knew that if they ever did get to Cathay, the chances of returning to the West were quite slim. Would it hurt to first visit Jerusalem?

Philip had given her a skeptical look when she tried to assure him about Gareth. "I wish I had your certainty," he said.

"I know *you* would never give up." She had smiled as she realized anew just what it meant to be truly loved by a man. "But I meant nothing to Gareth except as a spoil of war—his war with you. All he wanted from me was an heir, but that did not happen, so he is doubtless happy to be rid of me."

"My brother always was a fool." Philip gazed at her with such adoration it made her heart skip a beat. "If we make this trek it would be wise to keep from the coastal areas for a while."

At this Gilly made one of his meaningful grunts. Beatrice had not yet learned to interpret them all except to understand that they denoted displeasure, but Philip seemed to perceive the meaning and merely gave the man a sour look in response.

In his apparent role as perennial mediator, Theo said, "If you seek to follow the footsteps of Christ, my lady, the Judean wilderness should not be avoided. Here, John the Baptist 'cried in the wilderness' to proclaim the coming of Christ. And here, Christ himself was tempted by Satan. Look farther back, even before the time of Christ," he added, seeming to relish sharing his knowledge, "and you will see that here also is where King David, before he was king, hid out from Saul. You'll understand how two armies could camp nearly on top of each other in that broken land and not know of the other's presence."

"How do you know this?" Beatrice asked.

"Aye," put in Gilly, "even I didn't know that bit about David."

"I ask questions," Theo said smugly. "I listen, and thereby, I learn."

"I know someone with the same philosophy," Beatrice said. "You would like her." Thinking of her maid, however, sent a wave of homesickness over Beatrice. She knew Leticia must be suffering terrible grief over the loss of her mistress. How Beatrice wished she could get a message to her, but she had discussed this with Philip, and they had both concluded that it would be too risky.

Now, as Beatrice sat on her mount and took one last look at the barren region, she was glad their sojourn in this wilderness was drawing to an end. Theo had told her that the Hebrew word for this region was *Yeshimon,* meaning devastation. The land was dry, full of dusty ridges, jutting rocks, and blistered limestone. Often the rock and sand crumbled beneath their horses' hooves, causing them to slip and slide dangerously. Water was scarce. There were few wells, mostly cisterns of rainwater guarded selfishly by their Arab owners. Philip understood the infidel ways well enough to negotiate for some of the precious liquid to fill their waterskins, but in some places it was nearly half a day's ride between water places.

They had run out of water on the third day of their crossing with at least another two days to their destination of Jerusalem. Finally near sunset, all quite parched, they'd come to a cistern heavily guarded by its Arab proprietor. They were instructed to wait while the Arab lord and his people said their prayers, kneeling on the ground facing south toward their holy place, Mecca. After being allowed one drink, Theo and Gilly wandered off to see if they could hunt some meat for supper while Beatrice sat on a rock wall of a sheep-cote to wait. Philip paced in the dusty yard. He had seemed to grow more and more quiet as they drew nearer to Jerusalem.

"Philip, how much longer do we have in this desert?" she asked, longing to encourage him to speak, if only to make trivial conversation.

"Two days."

"I thank you again for allowing me to visit Jerusalem. I liked being in Galilee. There were many holy sites to see there, but to be where Christ suffered and died . . . I have been told there is nothing to equal it."

"I doubt that those people have seen much of the world, then," he countered.

Before she could respond the Arab lord came. It was just as well. She didn't want to debate such matters with Philip.

She watched quietly as he haggled with the lord over the price for using his water. Philip managed with the language well, but it helped that the Arab knew some French. Finally they agreed upon a price, and Philip doled out the coin. Then the Arab ordered his men to fill the waterskins Philip gave him.

She'd noticed in the time she'd been with Philip that he seemed to have great respect for the Saracen ways and for the heathen people. He dressed like them, talked like them, haggled with the best of them . . . did everything, it seemed, except prostrate himself on a prayer rug at sunrise and sunset facing Mecca. She didn't like that he had far sharper criticisms of Christians than of these Muslims.

They bided the final night of their journey in a village called Abu Ghosh, which was on the site of the ancient Emmaus. It was likely that on the very road they would take the next day into Jerusalem, some of Christ's disciples had met their Lord after His Resurrection. She was glad Philip had conceded to her desire to see some of the Holy Lands before they departed for the East.

The next day dawned warm and bright though it was October. She was excited as they approached St. Stephen's Gate in the northern wall of the city.

Theo explained it had been called Damascus Gate during the time of Christ, and much of this quarter of the city had been outside the walls, forming the infamous site of Golgotha. Now the Crusader-built wall encompassed it all, and the area had become the "Christian" quarter.

They passed through the dark gate tunnel into the city, and Beatrice felt bombarded with light and noise as they emerged into a large bustling market filled with the bleating of sheep and goats, the cries of men hawking their goods, and the voices of shoppers haggling over prices. She strained her neck to see everything. Clustered around the gate were houses made of pale stone, probably limestone, with flat roofs, seemingly piled on top of one another. There was a hospital and a chapel among the public buildings. Despite the present activity, this quarter was not as bustling as it no doubt once had been when crusaders held the city. The final expulsion of Christians in 1244 by the Khwarizmian Turks had ended crusader rule, it seemed once and for all. King Louis had failed twice to even get close to the Holy City, and Prince Edward had not even made the attempt.

Those last heathen conquerors had wrought much destruction in the city—destroyed churches, profaned holy places, and looted and burned the Church of the Holy Sepulcher. Only with the rise of Sultan Baibars in the last ten years was some restoration occurring. Christian pilgrims were once again permitted to visit the holy places, though Beatrice suspected this was mainly because of the coin their presence brought to the coffers of the city leaders.

"How I wish I could have beheld this place with the eyes of the first crusaders!" Beatrice exclaimed.

"You mean before they swooped down on the city and slaughtered all infidels in sight, with special attention paid to the Jews?" asked Philip dryly.

Beatrice arched a brow. Seldom since they had been together had she glimpsed this cynical side of Philip, though she knew it existed from their first encounters after her abduction. She had thought, and hoped, the joy of their reunion might have erased it from him.

"I'm sorry, Bea," he quickly continued. "Part of me is truly refreshed by your positive outlook. Yet . . ." He sighed. "Do not mind me, my love. As always, I am a fool."

"No, Philip," she said earnestly, "I want to know all that troubles you."

"Oh no, my lady, I don't think you want to know all that troubles my dark soul."

"I do not believe your soul is dark. You have been hurt and buffeted much by life, but there is good in the depths of your soul. I know that with all my heart."

"For your sake, I wish it to be true," he said. "If there is good in me, you bring it out." Wheeling his horse to the left, he said, "Come, let's find an inn so that we can rest a bit before exploring the city."

She followed him, as did Theo and Gilly, but she wondered why they needed to rest. They had only traveled a league or so since Abu Ghosh. She had a feeling he wasn't as anxious as she to visit "the way of the Cross." After all, he'd been in Palestine far longer than she and had not visited any holy sites. When she had first known him, his faith had been teetering on the edge of confusion. Now, she guessed, it was probably nonexistent. Yet who was she to talk to him about such matters, much less judge him? She knew her current path was condemned in the eyes of God, yet she would not veer from it. She tried to justify her actions by reminding God of all the grief in her life and of her husband's cruelty. Was she not entitled to some happiness? she oft appealed to God.

She knew not the answer to that question. The desire for happiness was not all that kept them together. And she had to admit that Philip's current dourness indicated he was not entirely happy about the situation. She had the feeling that if there had been any way to safely do so, he would have already taken her back to Acre. Not because he didn't love her and want her, but because, as much as he would deny it, she knew he struggled with that sense of honor he'd never been able to fully shake off.

Despite her own happiness, she, too, struggled with the choice she had made. But there was no easy way out. In her heart of hearts, she knew that Gareth was too vindictive to have given up the search for her, and if he had somehow learned that al-Rahib was Philip, then his zeal for the search would be tenfold. The danger aside, however, she had one reason, if there were no others, to cling to the present. Her monthly flux was late. Oh, there had been other times over the years when she had been thus deceived, experiencing a day or two of expectant joy only to be plunged into disappointment by the appearance of her "curse." For that reason she had said nothing to Philip.

Seated in the common room of the inn, Philip took a disinterested sip of ale. When the door opened, he tensed and looked about. Just a couple of strangers. He'd felt on edge from the moment he'd agreed to take Beatrice to Jerusalem. He wasn't sure of the reason for this. It couldn't be entirely because of Gareth.

He and Beatrice were finally free! They were together at last, and it was more amazing to him with each passing day.

Perhaps that was why he was so apprehensive. He simply could not believe he'd be allowed such happiness. He knew something must soon come and steal it from him. That's why he'd been so anxious to travel east. It seemed to him that the farther away they got from all that would tear them asunder—not only Gareth, but also the niggling sense of morality that he knew Beatrice could not easily escape—the better he could bear the whole situation. In Cathay there would be no churches, no holy shrines—Christian ones anyway—no Christians to pick away at their happiness. In Cathay they could hide from all their enemies.

Instead, here they were at the very citadel of Him whom Philip believed to be his most imposing adversary. But Beatrice was sacrificing so much for him that he could not refuse her this simple boon.

Theo and Gilly strode toward him. "Where is Lady Beatrice?" Theo asked as he slipped onto the bench opposite Philip. Gilly fetched earthenware jars of ale, then sat next to Theo.

"She is in her room freshening up," said Philip. "I have ordered us a mid-day meal before we tour the city."

"Good. I'm starved," Theo said.

"How long do you plan to stay here?" Gilly asked after taking a long, noisy drink from his cup. "Even dressed as we are in infidel clothes, I feel exposed. The local people know we are not mere pilgrims. They don't like knights, even renegade ones such as we, roaming about their city."

"Knights come here on pilgrimage," argued Philip.

"Regardless, I do not feel safe." Gilly drained his cup. "I don't know why we had to come here in the first place. We will have to backtrack nearly fifty leagues now, and we risk again squandering our money away."

"I am sick of your constant complaining, Gilly!" snapped Philip.

"Well, you are the one always moaning about losing our coin just when we have enough to travel east."

"We're here now, so accept it." Philip finished his ale and rose, grabbing his friend's empty cup before striding to where the innkeeper kept his cask. He had the cups refilled and returned to his seat, setting down Gilly's cup with enough force that the liquid slopped over the rim.

"Wonderful!" Gilly groused. "Throw more money into the cesspool!"

"I'll throw it in your face if you don't watch out!"

"Try it!"

As if by instinct they both stopped and glanced toward Theo, quietly sipping his ale.

"Why look at me?" Theo said smugly. "I am content to let you both at each other's throats once and for all. You've been prodding each other for weeks, and I am tired of interceding."

Shrugging, Philip plopped back down on the bench, though he made no apology to Gilly, who also had none for him. Philip didn't know why all the old tensions between them had resurfaced. He suspected it had something to do with Beatrice, but he hadn't wanted to ferret out the truth.

He did feel, however, that some concession must be made. "I had reservations, as well, about this journey," he said, making an attempt to appease his friend. "I want to be on our way east, too. But . . ." It was still hard to admit he was allowing a woman to dictate his decisions.

"Gilly," Theo said, "you have never had a woman—that is, never *loved* a woman. You don't understand how a man is driven to please her in every way he can."

"Every way except the one she most desires," Gilly said.

"What do you mean by that?" demanded Philip.

"Forget it. I misspoke."

"No," challenged Philip. "You have been piqued about something ever since Beatrice joined us. Let's get it out in the open before we kill each other."

"You will not like what I have to say."

"I seldom do."

"Beatrice is a lady," Gilly said tensely, "not a common trollop, yet you have made her one."

Anger flared in Philip as quickly and lethally as Greek fire. He jumped up, tilting up the table, making the cups tumble to the floor, ale spilling everywhere. Reaching across the table he grabbed the front of Gilly's surcote and fairly lifted him off the bench.

"Stop it!" yelled Theo, no longer a smug spectator. He knew when his fiery friend had been pushed to his limit.

The innkeeper also rushed forward. "Please! This is a respectable establishment!"

For a brief moment Philip was sure this was the moment he would commit murder. But maybe there was indeed a force more powerful than his fury, for he found, almost as if by some impulse outside himself, his hand loosening its grip on the fabric of Gilly's clothing. Gilly flopped back into his seat.

"It is all right," Philip tried to assure the worried innkeeper, though his voice shook and he was panting like a man still about to attack.

"If you hadn't come with a lady I would surely throw you out into the street," the innkeeper warned.

"There will be no further disturbance," Philip said, forcing calm into his voice as he resumed his seat.

Though Gilly glowered at Philip, he managed to say, "I deserved that."

"No, I did." Philip looked around for his ale, then realized he'd knocked it all on the floor. His throat was as parched as if he'd been in the desert for a year. "I have loved her for so long," he said finally. These were his friends, his brothers. He could not afford to alienate them. "She came to me willingly, Gilly. How could I turn her away? I suppose we are both damned now."

"I think," said Theo with understanding, "that Gilly's words sprang from the fact that he has grown fond of Lady Beatrice and doesn't want to see her hurt. Is that not so, Gilly?"

"That is it," Gilly said sincerely. "Would that I could speak as eloquently as you, Theo."

"Theo has become quite a poet in his old age," Philip said, trying to defuse the tension with humor. But he could not forget the truth that had been spoken by his friends. "We will leave this place in the morning and head east," he said with serious resolve. "I know we will find peace in Cathay."

Theo and Gilly both nodded, but he could tell they were merely appeasing him. Theo would no doubt tell him that peace came only from within. Because Philip believed that was an impossibility for him, he tried to convince himself that it could be found elsewhere. Certainly he'd known little real peace since finding Beatrice. Some happiness, yes, for he'd have to be made of stone not to feel joy with her. But not a moment passed that he did not struggle over the very matters Gilly mentioned. He hadn't seriously thought about spawning a bastard child in years, hadn't even cared. Until now. How could he ever face such a child knowing he'd had a choice to prevent such a horrible fate befalling him? How could he face Beatrice if he forced her to endure the grief and heartache that had surely killed his own mother?

Many times in the last weeks he'd come to the brink of taking her back to Acre. But crossing into Crusader lands was as good as a death sentence for him and his friends. Moreover, he could not trust what Gareth might do to Beatrice.

Or were these mere excuses?

Just then Beatrice came into the common room. She was dressed in a surcote of pale yellow over a kirtle of creamy white, a chain of linked gold rings around her waist. Her spun gold hair was caught up in a crispine, a net of silken thread studded with jewels. He'd learned about women's clothing when they had gone into Tiberius in Galilee for supplies for this very journey. They'd happened upon a bazaar where they had discovered some European apparel for sale. Beatrice had been in dire need of clothing, having only the dress in which she had been abducted and a couple of Arab garments they had bartered for from a passing caravan. He'd sensed Gilly's disapproval even then when he had spent a few marks on several beautiful gowns. But Philip could give Beatrice so little, especially what she most desired—wedding vows—that he tried to indulge her in other ways.

This was the first time he'd seen her in her new finery. Seeing her thus garbed took his breath away but also caused a stab of pain. She was indeed a lady, deserving of all the finery there was. He told himself again that once they were in Cathay, he would find for her a palace and silken gowns and shoes made of crystal.

He smiled at her to hide his inner turmoil. "You look like an angel," he breathed as he took her hand and guided her onto the bench beside him. Having her so close never failed to excite him. The joy it gave him was so great he wondered that his paltry flesh could contain it.

48

The Church of the Holy Sepulcher was the holiest shrine in all of Christendom. Though it was only a building, and in poor condition at that, Beatrice would have had to be made of stone herself not to feel a thrill as she stood in the very center, turned slightly to the west, and gazed into the empty tomb of Christ. It was only speculation that this was indeed Christ's tomb, but it very possibly could be so.

Toward the east was the high altar, but they had arrived too late in the day to view the daily reenactment of the Resurrection.

"This place has been destroyed and restored so many times," muttered Philip, "that it makes you wonder."

"Wonder about what?" she asked, trying to be patient. He had suggested that he take care of some business matters while she toured the church, but she wanted him to accompany her. Now his scornful attitude was starting to bother her.

"I don't know. Couldn't God protect it better? I mean if it is such an important site."

"God doesn't protect us from our own choices."

"Ah yes. His way out."

"Philip—" biting her lip, she went on more evenly—"if you have things you'd rather be doing, perhaps it would be best if we met later. I should like to attend Mass while I am here."

"I don't mean to ruin it for you. I'm sorry."

She touched his hand and smiled. "I understand how you feel, how you blame God for your misfortunes. I wish it could be different."

"And I wish I believed enough to blame God," Philip admitted. "For your sake, if for nothing else, I wish I could come into a place like this and feel the presence of God."

"Truly, Philip?"

"It will never happen, so why offer myself up for another disappointment, eh?"

"Go and take care of your business," she said.

"You won't be mad?"

"Of course not."

"Then I will return later with a basket of food," he said with an attempt at enthusiasm, "and we will go outside the city walls to the Kidron Valley and have a picnic, as we used to in England."

"That would be wonderful!" she said, matching his enthusiasm.

Despite the prospect of a picnic, she watched him go with a touch of sadness. He was trying so hard to be happy, yet it was obvious that the marks of the past were too deeply embedded in him to simply disappear. She'd so hoped that coming to this most holy place would touch him, would work in those festering marks like a soothing balm of comfrey. She'd hoped that she could nurse his unseen wounds, as she had so many physical wounds of others. Was it true that those you loved most were the hardest to heal?

Physician, heal thyself. . . .

The words came so clearly to her mind that she gasped and glanced about to see if someone had actually spoken them to her. But they had indeed just come from her own thoughts. She'd heard Father Bavent speak them when he had been laid up with a touch of rheumatism and she had visited him. He made the observation when she told him how bad she felt because she did not know how to help him. It was early in her training in the use of herbs.

She knew this phrase coming to her now had to do with more than physical matters. Perhaps if she cleansed her own heart, that might somehow influence Philip. She had no idea how or why God would use such a weak vessel as herself, but as precarious as her own faith was, she at least had held on to it. Despite her shortcomings, she still loved God. She had that if nothing else to give to Philip.

A priest entered the large vaulted chapel area where she stood.

"Greetings, my daughter," he said. "I saw you and your husband enter our sanctuary." He looked around. "Where is your husband?"

"He's not my—" She could not bring herself to admit Philip was not her husband even if it did not need to indicate their actual relationship. "He had to leave, Father, to take care of some business matters."

"Ah, that is too bad. I would have said Mass for you both."

"Could you . . . say it just for me?"

"Of course, my child. We do not often have women of your obvious quality here these days. It would be a pleasure."

"Perhaps with the new peace treaty more pilgrims will come," she offered.

"We shall see. Would you care to look about more before we begin the service?" He lifted an arm and gestured toward the south side of the chapel. "Through that door the stairs lead to the cistern where St. Helena discovered the remnants of the True Cross."

"May I see the place?"

"Unfortunately no, for the stair is in disrepair and too dangerous at the moment. Also in the south wall were the tombs of the crusader kings, but when the Khwarizmian Turks overran the city, they destroyed the tombs and scattered the bones of the kings."

"That is too bad," she said. "I am thankful I could come here now, for who knows what might be left even in a few years."

"Nothing lasts forever, my child." After a thoughtful pause, the priest added, "Faith cannot be built of stones and mortar. It must be a matter for our hearts and souls."

"Yes." It was so much easier to understand tangible things like stones. That was why she had so desired to come to this place. She had hoped the building itself would bring her closer to God.

"Also in the south wall, above the tombs of the kings, is Calvary," said the priest.

"Golgotha," breathed Beatrice. Some of her sense of awe, though, was broken by the fact that it was all stone and mortar, not a desolate mount impaled by three crosses.

"Now, my lady, if you will wait at the altar," said the priest, "I will retrieve my vestments so I can serve you Communion after you've made your confession."

The priest disappeared through one of the doors by the altar, and Beatrice moved to the rail. Almost by sheer instinct she quickly found herself on her knees, for who could stand so boldly before God's altar? As she bowed humbly, she suddenly felt as if she were desecrating this place more vilely than the Khwarizmian had. How could she come before God; how could she take Communion with her life steeped in sin?

"Oh, God! I want and I need your forgiveness for what I have done. I do not want to bear a child in such sin, and yet . . . I don't know if I am strong enough to truly repent. I know what you would ask of me, and I know what is the right thing to do. But how can I leave him now that I have finally found him? You know as well as I that it would destroy him." Tears sprang to her eyes, and though her prayer was silent, her throat clogged with pain. "God, my spirit is willing, but my flesh is weak. I need you to be strong for me, because I cannot do this alone."

Several leagues southeast of Jerusalem lay the lush oasis of Ain Feshka on the Dead Sea coast, lush in comparison with the rest of Judea. On the east side of Jerusalem some of the effects of the oasis were present, but the olive groves, fig trees, date palms, and hawthorns clinging to the slopes of the Kidron Valley and Mount of Olives were too few to actually call the place lush. In October, after a dry summer, it was an especially parched and colorless area. It was, however, outside the city and offered open air for riding. Philip knew Beatrice still loved to ride, though she'd told him how Gareth had kept her homebound much of the time.

He wanted to give her everything his brother had withheld from her. He wanted her to know such love and devotion that she would never even think of leaving him.

But Gilly was right, for despite all his desires, he could not give her what he knew she wanted most. He hadn't even been able to give her a pleasant day touring the holy sites! He could not help that he grew as dour as an old crone and as nervous as a goose on Christmas when he was near a church. The last time he had been in one was when he had sought sanctuary at St. Bartholomew's in England.

Beatrice said she understood. But even *he* didn't truly understand. How could he let his soul be damned? He knew men who had come on Crusade, risking and often sacrificing their very lives in order to save their souls by heeding the call of God. Of course, they thought killing infidels was God's will and the way to salvation. Philip's apostasy spared his believing that untruth. Questioning and doubting might not be such a terrible thing after all. He had gone much further than that, though, hadn't he? He had abandoned belief itself.

Yet he was not content with this state of his soul. No matter how much he tried, he wasn't an evil reprobate, not at his core. If there was a way not to be outside God's fold, he would seek it. He'd been on the outside of society all his life. To be accepted at last . . .

He looked over at Beatrice. She had been quiet since her visit to the church. Sunk in his own thoughts, he'd not pressed her for conversation. But his thoughts were becoming too oppressive even for him. Given a few more moments, he'd be on his knees or acting out some such spiritual foolishness. He was not, and never had been, in God's fold for a reason. He simply didn't fit in. The condition of his birth had marked him too deeply.

"It's a pity we don't have time to ride over to Ain Feshka," he said, desperate for something, anything, to deliver him from his thoughts. "I'd like the change of some green."

"I thought nothing could grow in the Dead Sea," she said.

"*In* the sea," he replied, "but there is an oasis near it. Who knows the ways of nature?"

"How far is it?"

"A day's easy ride."

"Need we be in such a hurry to leave this region?" she asked. "What would a few days hurt? Isn't the Dead Sea to the east, and isn't that the direction you wish to travel?"

"The Dead Sea and the oasis aren't directly to the east. And it wouldn't be the road we need. I plan to travel by roads I know for as far as we can. Thus, we must head north through Galilee, though this time we will pass through the wilderness to the east and keep closer to the Jordan Valley. After that we go to Damascus, which is where all the roads from the Far East converge. From there we will easily find the way to Baghdad and Persia, and then . . . well, finally a bit farther east of there we will find Cathay."

"Do you know how to get to Cathay, Philip?"

"I have an idea," he replied just a bit defensively. "I've spoken to men who have come here on caravans from Cathay. We will find it." Suddenly he reined his mount as they came to a cluster of olive trees that provided a little shade. "I'm hungry. Here is a good place to eat."

He laid out a blanket on the ground where there were some weeds pushing through the cracked earth. It should make the ground soft enough. He took his saddlebag, in which earlier he'd placed figs and goat cheese and good brown bread he'd bought. The food was good, but she ate of it quietly, thoughtfully.

"I promised Theo and Gilly," he said as if the earlier conversation had only that moment occurred. "If we don't leave in the morning, I am sure we will lose the money we've saved for the journey."

She nodded silently.

"Don't be angry with me," he implored.

She blinked, seeming surprised by his tone. "Philip, I'm not angry."

"You've been quiet since we left the city. I feared I offended you, if not just now then because I didn't remain with you at the church."

"Please believe me, it isn't that." She nibbled at her cheese. "It was quite moving being there, being so close to the place Christ suffered and died."

"I'm glad for you." And he truly meant it. He didn't begrudge her her faith. Perhaps he was envious of it.

"Are you?"

"I applaud you, Beatrice. I feel we must grasp happiness wherever we may find it. I have found my happiness in you. I'm glad I didn't turn you away yet again. You are my faith, dear Beatrice."

"Don't say that, Philip. It is on the verge of blasphemy."

"I take it back, then. I merely wanted some way to let you know how much you mean to me. To the depth of my heart, I thank you for what you have given me these past weeks."

She took his hand in hers, and if any single action made him feel more unworthy of her, it was this. Her hand was white and smooth, her fingers as delicate as the finest silk. Such a stark contrast to his dark, callused paw, scarred from battle like the rest of his body and toughened by the sun. He wanted to clutch his hand back, but she wished to comfort him and had no idea it was having the opposite effect. He had not the heart to tell her.

Instead, he leaped to a new topic of conversation. "Do you realize Mount of Olives is the name of that hill yonder?"

"I wondered if it was. Christ spent much time there. The Garden of Gethsemane must be nearby, as well."

"Would you like to go there?" he asked, though it was the last place on earth he wished to go. "There are churches and monasteries to mark the places."

She studied him for a moment, and he knew she could read his thoughts as clearly as if he'd spoken.

"No," she said. "It is late. We will barely get back to the city before the sun sets."

"I would take you," he insisted, as if to make up for all he could not give her.

"I know, Philip." She gave his hand a squeeze and let it go. "You have given me so much, my love." When he opened his mouth to protest, she laid one of her pale, slim fingers against his lips. "You have given me more than I dared even hope for. You have given me what I have always wanted and feared I would never have." She seemed about to say more, then a sad smile curved her lips before she fell silent.

"I'm glad of that," he said simply.

"We best return to the city before they begin their infidel prayers and we are shut out." She rose from the blanket and, like a chivalrous knight, reached her hand down to help him up!

She smiled in the playful way that he remembered from years ago when they were young. He grinned back as he rose. He was happy enough right now to last a lifetime, to make up even for losing his soul.

49

They departed Jerusalem at first light, leaving once again from St. Stephen's Gate. From here they would take the road north and east to Jericho, a much-traveled pilgrim route, for it led to the Jordan river and the place where Christ had been baptized. Beatrice should be thrilled that she'd have the opportunity to see more sacred places. Instead, she felt tense, as though she were fleeing something rather than anticipating more wonders. How naive of her to have wanted to visit holy places when she was so impure and weak! She should have known that when faced with the choice between God and her fleshly desires, she'd be too cowardly to make the right choice.

How many times since they had shared a meal at the foot of the Mount of Olives had she tried to tell Philip that she must return to England and her duty to her husband? Tried and failed.

He now stared intently ahead of him as if he also was having similar thoughts. His jaw was set, his eyes, squinting against the sun, were determined and hard. She knew now why she had not insisted that he take her to the Mount of Olives or to the Garden of Gethsemane. She feared that if Philip's heart ever did truly change toward God, he would be stronger than she in doing what was right. He'd always had a core of honor in him, and she knew it was still there, though he tried to hide it beneath a hard and cynical veneer.

The road they now traversed was almost as treacherous as any they had traveled thus far. Stretches of it were steep and tortuous, and possible danger lurked beyond every turn.

"This is the very road Christ was thinking of," said Theo, "when He told the parable of the Good Samaritan. Even then, robbers found this road especially conducive for preying upon travelers."

Beatrice looked about nervously.

"Theo, you dolt!" exclaimed Gilly. "You are frightening Lady Beatrice with such nonsense. My lady, we have the Templars now to patrol this road and keep it safe."

"How long will it take to get to Jericho?" Beatrice asked, trying to keep her voice steady.

"About two days," answered Theo, "because it is . . . uh . . . a difficult road." Pausing, he added humbly, "I am sorry if my words before unsettled you, my lady. I only thought that you might be interested in hearing of the historical significance of this land."

"I am, Theo. It means much to me to know of the relation of these places to the Scriptural stories the priests tell. I would that you not hold back on my account. I do not frighten easily."

Theo smiled, appearing pleased to have been vindicated. She pretended she didn't see the smug glance he shot in Gilly's direction.

This road had fallen into decline in the last hundred years, and Beatrice doubted that Templars still patrolled it. But she had three strong knights to protect her, so she determined not to worry. There were not many travelers these days, not as there must have been during the peak of crusader rule. Perhaps that meant not as many robbers, as well.

That was the least of her worries, wasn't it? If she decided to stay with Philip, she would have to tell him that she carried his child. That which should be joyous news was steeped in confusion. How would he react? Did she expect him to embrace with joy the news of expectant fatherhood? Wasn't this more like his most dreaded nightmare coming true?

They negotiated a long, steep descent called Wadi al-Haud. The horses slipped frequently over the loose stones and dry earth. Philip called a halt at the monastery St. Euthymius. It was a stout structure, for even the monasteries on this road were fortified. Only a few hardy monks remained in residence, and they welcomed the tired and thirsty travelers to refill their waterskins at the cistern and rest. It was too early to bide the night here, but Theo assured her there would be a place down the road.

While she sat upon a stone wall nibbling at a meal of dried fruit and bread, Theo and Gilly went off to check out the area—in truth she thought they were more restless than tired. Since the horses needed to rest, the men went off on foot. Philip paced about the yard, and she had a feeling that he would have joined his friends had he not felt he should remain with her. She knew it wasn't that he disdained her company, but there was great tension between them, and she believed it was her fault. She must speak to him, but before she could raise her courage to do so, he came and sat on the wall beside her.

"What happened in Jerusalem?" he asked. "You've been different ever since we left there."

She was taken aback by his words, seeming, as they did, to come out of nowhere. His perceptiveness also surprised her.

"Nothing," she heard herself respond. Then she silently cursed herself for squandering another opportunity.

"You are not going to leave me, are you?" he asked with brutal bluntness.

She'd always loved, and hated, that about him—his dear honest soul would be the death of them. "What would make you think that?" she asked, still skirting the issue.

"You would not be the first person changed by standing upon Golgotha."

"Is that why you refused to spend any time touring the church with me?"

"Yes," he replied like a challenge.

"You don't want to be changed by God?"

"I don't want anything to change. What I have at this moment is perfect. Why would I want it to change?" But the sharp defensiveness of his tone negated his words.

Sucking in a breath, she knew it was time. "Philip, I am with child."

He stared, and blinked, and stared, but beyond the surface surprise, she could not read whether that look indicated joy or pain.

Finally, in an even, still unreadable voice, he asked, "Is it mine?"

The words could not have crushed her more. "Of course."

"I am not completely ignorant of these matters," he said. "You were with . . . your husband less than three months ago. It could be—"

"Philip, it is our child, yours and mine. I am certain."

He was silent.

Theo and Gilly returned then, and there was not another opportunity for her and Philip to resume their conversation. In any event, neither made any attempt to do so. They mounted their horses.

The descent became steeper now. The road had once been paved, probably by the Romans eons ago, but now what remained was broken and treacherous, making the going slow and intense. Theo said they were passing through Wadi al-Qilt. Then the road began to climb. Many names had been applied to the region they now passed through, such as the Red Ascent or the Ascent of Blood. Given the stories of robbers and of a pilgrim aided by a good Samaritan, Beatrice thought the name had as much to do with the blood spilt here over the ages as it did with the prominent red streaks in the limestone ridges.

They traveled quite a distance before they saw on a hill the Templar Fortress of the Red Cistern, which was the largest fortification built by the Templars. The others, strung out along the road, were mere towers or lookouts. The fortress was vacant now, another indication that Gilly's faith in the protection of the Templars was unfounded. Near this was a khan, or a shelter. Here pilgrims would camp for the night before continuing on the worst stretch of the road that lay ahead. Since it was near sunset they thought it best to stop here.

Beatrice was exhausted, despite the fact that she'd been carried by her horse the entire way. But the sun had burned down on her, seeming to pound on her head, giving her a terrible headache. Yet even more oppressive than the sun had been Philip's silence. She tried to console herself that his silence was as much from vigilance as from anything else, for it was not a path on which to allow one's attention to wander. She had imagined dark, sinister shapes behind every rock.

There was enough water in the cistern to give the animals a drink, but the humans had to content themselves with their waterskins. Theo said they had more than enough to get them to Jericho. Beatrice drank sparingly, though she wished she could pour the entire contents of the skin over her throbbing head.

"My lady," said Theo, "you would be interested to know that this khan is said to sit upon the site of the Inn of the Good Samaritan, where, in Jesus' story, He brought the injured traveler to be cared for."

"How I wish it were still an inn," she said, "with beds and hot food and even ale!"

As if in an attempt to grant her wish, Theo and Gilly went off to see if they could find some game. Although Beatrice could not imagine any wild creatures surviving in this barren land, an hour later they returned with a brace of rabbits. Philip had—in silence—built a fire, so when the game had been skinned and cleaned, it was roasted over the flame.

Beatrice burned her fingers on the meat when it was done, but she had come to appreciate the taste of game freshly roasted, eaten out-of-doors. Years ago Philip had rejected her appeal to join him in his fugitive life, saying it was not the life for a lady. Now here she was, eating under the stars, sleeping on the hard earth, riding over vast wild areas day in and day out. She hardly ever complained; moreover she had no inclination to do so. She missed none of the so-called comforts of a lady. Could she have adapted so readily nine years ago? She'd been young and spoiled. She couldn't imagine the Beatrice of so long ago eating with her fingers. But now any life seemed better to her than life with Gareth.

No wonder her courage failed her when she thought about returning to that miserable existence.

Philip maintained his silence through the meal. He took the first watch that night. She could not sleep, the tension between them weighing heavily upon her. Whether she returned to England or remained with him, they must heal the rift her words had caused. Rising from her blanket and pulling her cloak tightly around her—when the sun went down these lands turned quite cold—she went to where he sat on a rock gazing into the night.

"Philip," she said quietly, so as not to startle him. He did not turn. She slipped onto the rock beside him, forcing him to move in order to make room for her.

He gave her a sour look. "You must always have your way, mustn't you?"

"Do you think I became with child on purpose? To force you to keep me with you?"

"It sounds as if you feared I would send you back," he countered. Pausing, he turned to face her, the first time since Jerusalem that he had really looked at her. "I would be a fool to send you away," he said earnestly.

"I never feared it."

"Then why do I feel of late that you are so distant from me?"

She smiled. "I feel the same of you."

"Beatrice, you have given me back my life!" he declared. "I would sooner fall on my own sword than send you back. Indeed, death would be better than losing you again."

"Don't say that!"

"I would merely set your mind at ease about my faithfulness."

"I never doubted your faithfulness." I am sorry, God, she silently agonized, but I cannot do this to him! Neither can I do it to myself, sacrificing the sweetest love a woman can know for the doom that awaits me in England.

"I am happy about the child," he murmured, as if he were afraid to admit it. "I am sorry I cannot make you my wife."

"We won't think of that," she said. "In Cathay no one will know otherwise. We will be married in our hearts."

Wrapping his arms around her, he kissed her fiercely, then held her close for the rest of the night.

Gareth had not been idle in the time since his wife's abduction. He had sent spies throughout the country seeking information about the red-haired renegade crusader, and he had learned that his bastard half brother had not changed over the years except to become an even more iniquitous character. Since coming to Outremer two years earlier, de Tollard had become a high-wayman, mostly, it was said, attacking infidels, though Gareth highly doubted he so limited himself. Until the failed attack on Gareth's company, Philip was known to ride with, and lead, more than a dozen renegade Frenchmen like himself. The attack had decimated his numbers, sending him, no doubt, into deeper hiding than before.

Only one with the determination of a spurned husband would be able to find him, and Gareth was drawing close. His spies had tracked Philip to Gal-ilee, though they could not discover his hiding place in the hills. Then, feeling the trail was growing warm, they had sent a message to Gareth in Acre—his headquarters for the search—and told him he might wish to come and ques-tion these people for himself.

Thus Gareth dogged Philip's trail through several Galilean villages. He had learned that al-Rahib, the monk, as he was known by the infidels, was moving in a smaller company now. He'd been seen in Tiberius with two men who, Gareth was certain by their descriptions, had been involved in the attack on the road from Nazareth. One of his companions was a sharp-tongued wiry little man, and the other was huge and bearlike, hardly one to keep around if you wished to be invisible. Gareth knew this miserable gang of three were the ones he sought because with them also was a woman who matched Beatrice's description.

What galled him most about the information was that his wife was hardly behaving like a captive. De Tollard was spending money lavishly upon her, Gareth had been told, and she was at his side, smiling and willing. They had departed Tiberius only a week ago and were heading south, not back toward the hills.

In the squalid village of Bethshan or, as the Crusaders called it, Beisan, he found his best lead. A party fitting the description of Philip and his com-panions had come to that town to buy supplies, outfitting themselves for a journey to Jerusalem.

"The little one drank too freely of my ale on his last night here," said the local innkeeper. "He said they were headed to Jerusalem, and he was not too pleased about it. He said it was in the opposite direction of where they should be going."

"Where was that?" Gareth asked.

"He did not say."

"When did they leave here?"

The man scratched his bald pate. "Let me see. . . . I had made a new batch of ale. . . . Was it before or after?" He thought for a moment. "Ah, I am sure it was the new batch the fellow had because he'd commented on how good and strong it was. That's no doubt why it so loosened his tongue. That was . . . hmm . . ."

"When was it?" Gareth demanded. He felt close to his prey, and his patience was growing as thin as the man's hair.

"Three days . . . or was it four—no, it was three days ago, I am certain."

Deciding he'd get nothing more accurate from the dullard, Gareth spun on his heel and strode outside. This was as close to his brother as he'd been since the attack. Philip had only a three- or four-day lead! Moreover, he had no idea he was being dogged by such a relentless pursuer. Philip had kept in careful hiding for a time, but now it was obvious he felt safe to parade around with his very identifiable friends. He had no idea that Gareth knew the identity of his wife's abductor. Philip had to believe Gareth had given up the search and returned to England with Edward or shortly thereafter.

Though Philip would be taking no more than the usual travel precautions, Gareth was no fool. He knew Philip was an experienced warrior, a canny highwayman, so his *usual* precautions would be far superior to those of most men. Still, if Gareth and his men rode hard, they could shrink that lead considerably. Perhaps they could even overtake him. At the least they could be in Jerusalem waiting for him.

He ordered his men to supply themselves for a hard march through the wilderness. He was down to a mere ten men now. A month ago he'd lost three in an attack by brigands, while two more had contracted fever and were laid up in Acre. Edward had offered some of his own men to aid the search, but Gareth had reasoned that with fewer men he'd be able to travel faster. And he'd certainly need no more against three enemies.

Three days later he and his men approached St. Stephen's Gate of the Holy City. Gareth had never been to Jerusalem, but he had no time for awe or sentimentality.

He came close to being barred from the city, for his men hardly looked like pilgrims. All except he and Sir William were forced to tarry outside the walls. In order to prove he had come as a pilgrim he was forced to make the motions of visiting the Church of the Holy Sepulcher. He gritted his teeth the entire time he was there, and after having benefited little from exposure to the sacred site, he left as soon as he was sure he wasn't being watched.

He went to the inn where most pilgrims stayed, and he discovered his brother had been there only the night before!

The innkeeper had no trouble identifying Philip and his companions.

"The devil with the red hair nearly caused a row," he said. "With his own friends at that! He was a vicious one, I'll say. I'd not want to be on his bad side."

They had left Jerusalem that morning! Philip was only hours ahead of Gareth now.

The innkeeper could not say where they were going, but more questioning of the gatekeepers revealed they had departed the city by way of the St. Stephen's Gate, heading east along the road to Jericho. Again, they had taken no pains to disguise themselves or their intentions. Though it was midday, Gareth was confident he'd catch up to them now. They were traveling with a woman and doubtless in no hurry.

He collected his men at the gate, and they rode as hard as they dared upon the perilous road.

50

Philip woke the next morning in the hour before dawn, refreshed. A cool breeze brushed his face. He knew that soon the sun would blaze down upon them, but now in the cool of the morning he could not imagine life being better. It had been days since he'd slept so well. He was finally certain that Beatrice truly loved him. She was willing to sacrifice all for him! He tried to ignore the part of him that was unsettled at this thought, the part that knew he was a knave to allow her to do so.

After breaking their fast with a cold meal, they rode for about a league before they were forced to pause because Beatrice's horse became lame.

"Do you remember when we first met?" Beatrice asked as Philip examined the animal's offending hoof.

"It is seared upon my heart as one the most joyful days of my life!" he exclaimed with a grin.

"You did not seem so joyful when you took me to task for my ill treatment of Raven," she said playfully.

"There," he said, removing the pebble with the tip of his dagger. "As then, my lady, this was merely a surface injury. And my ire at that time was only to mask the way my heart had begun pounding with one look at you."

"Riders!" yelled Gilly, who had been vigilantly scanning the country for any sign of trouble.

Philip lowered the hoof he'd just fixed and strode up beside Gilly, who was standing upon a rise in the road. Theo joined them, as did Beatrice.

"They are knights," said Theo.

With relief Beatrice said, "At least they are not robbers."

"They ride with great purpose," put in Gilly.

Philip peered hard into the distance. Indeed, the riders were closing the distance quickly. He judged there were no more than a dozen of them, perhaps fewer. With the new peace in the region, knights were allowed more freedom, but these hardly appeared to be pilgrims. Then the sun behind Philip glinted off one of the shields. His heart nearly stopped.

"Gilly, take Beatrice up to yon tower!" Philip ordered, pointing about a furlong up the ridge to a Templar tower. When Gilly seemed about to argue, Philip added, "You can move quickest, and you are the best archer. As soon as the riders are within range, you must give Theo and me cover."

"Philip, are they robbers?" Beatrice asked.

"No, my love. Their shields bear the Hawken crest."

Though he read fear in her eyes, she spoke bravely. "They want me. Let me go and there will be no bloodshed."

"Do you think they will suffer any of us to live?" he asked harshly. Then he added more gently, "Please, Beatrice, I beg you! Go!"

She mounted her horse, and he watched as she rode off with Gilly. Philip had given his stash of arrows to Gilly, for he himself had never been much of an archer and had kept the bow only for hunting. Theo had given Gilly a handful of arrows, as well, keeping a few should an opportunity arise to use them. The ridge was steep and a difficult climb for the animals, but Gilly and Beatrice would make it to safety long before he and Theo engaged the enemy.

"I count ten," Theo said. "Do you think your brother is among them?"

"He is." Philip could not specifically identify Gareth from that distance, but he knew he was there. Beatrice had underestimated the man, but Philip felt certain his brother's tenacity came from a thirst for vengeance rather than from a longing for his wife. He also knew that somehow Gareth had discovered the identity of his wife's abductor, and that surely would have spurred his determination to find them.

Philip and Theo mounted and drew their swords. They were already clad in their mail. They would not travel this treacherous road otherwise. Philip considered seeking a more defensible position, but against ten knights there was hardly a defense possible. He and Theo would die there, and then Gareth would kill Gilly and take Beatrice, likely killing her, too. Nevertheless, there was no point in surrender. Gareth would certainly give them no quarter.

Hope sparked in him despite himself as Gilly's rain of arrows fell upon Gareth's men. Three fell in the first round. Theo got off a round, as well, felling one more.

"The odds are better, eh, Worm?" he said, grinning.

"Yes. Now it will take longer for us to die."

"Always spoiling the mood! Shall we go meet them, then?"

"Why not?" Philip said lightly. If he could pray, he would ask only that he be given the boon of facing his brother. If he could kill Gareth before he died, then there might be a chance for Beatrice.

By the time their swords clashed, Gilly had knocked out one more Hawken knight. He and Theo had tackled worse odds and survived.

Philip was easily able to pick Gareth out from the bunch. Always conscious of his position, he wore a tunic of a different color from the rest. The others wore red tunics with a silver hawk, while Gareth's was white with a red circle on the front and the silver hawk within that. Like a target, Philip thought grimly as he charged to meet his mortal enemy.

Gareth was now a seasoned warrior, though according to Beatrice he'd fought only in a few minor skirmishes with Saracens. Philip had far more experience in every kind of warfare and called it all to his aid now as he confronted two opponents. He concentrated on keeping them both in front of him. If one managed to flank him, the fight would be over. He wondered if Gilly would dare take a shot now that he and Theo were in close quarters with the enemy. It might be worth the risk. Concentrating on his own battle, he tried not to think of Theo engaging the other three.

They fought thus for several minutes. He feared he would tire ere getting a chance to make a decisive move. His sword arm was starting to feel like a lead weight. Gareth nicked the fabric of Philip's tunic when he let his shield drop. He knew Gareth was grinning beneath his helm.

"You still do not match me, bastard!" Gareth taunted him.

"Always too confident for your own good, brother!" Philip said the word *brother* as if spitting bile from his mouth. Then he lunged and sliced Gareth's arm as if to prove his estimation of the man.

After getting only the one successful blow, Philip had to retreat because Gareth's comrade was making a move toward his left flank. As he made the sudden move, his horse stumbled over a deep crack in the ancient paving stones. Dropping his shield, Philip seized the reins to steady the animal, but it was too late. The horse went down. Philip was ready for the fall and rolled clear.

Scrambling to his feet, he heard the hiss of an arrow, quickly followed by a thud as it struck its target. The arrow struck Gareth's horse, and it went down. Would Gareth fall clear of the animal or be crushed by its weight? Philip held his breath for several heartbeats. Gareth's spur caught in the stirrup, and he could not cleanly roll away, though he cleared most of the beast's weight.

Philip's attention was drawn away by the other knight, still on his horse and now charging him. Philip dodged and escaped the sword. An arrow flew but missed the knight. From the corner of his eye, Philip saw Gareth furiously trying to free himself from the stirrup.

The other knight made a second attack. Philip swung his sword and in a single motion sliced off the man's leg while gouging a deep wound in the horse's flank. Philip felt more pity for the horse than for the man screaming in agony as he and his injured horse crashed to the ground.

Philip turned to assist Theo, now facing only two knights. All three were unhorsed. One of the knights had a slice in his arm and could barely hold up his sword. As Philip killed him, he saw over the knight's shoulder three men racing up the road on foot. Apparently they had received only minor wounds from Gilly's arrows, or only their mounts had fallen. In a few moments the odds would swing back into Gareth's favor.

"Theo!" Philip yelled, jerking his head toward the new arrivals.

He did not see that Gareth had freed himself and lurched to his feet. Philip turned as Gareth's sword sliced toward him, piercing his mail and burying itself deep into his side. Gasping with shock and pain, he still managed to swing his own sword. Weakened by the wound, he only managed to knock his brother off his feet with a blow to the arm.

Suddenly Theo appeared upon his horse, and reaching down his strong arm, he grasped Philip up, dragging him across the front of his saddle. In the same fluid motion, he reined his mount around and raced up the ridge toward the tower.

Gilly and Beatrice had only moments before arrived there. The structure was built more as a lookout than a fortification, though it had stout walls for defense. It could house a dozen knights and their mounts; thus Philip and his companions and their three remaining mounts fit easily inside.

"He's hurt," Theo said, dismounting and gently lowering Philip to the ground.

"What are they doing out there?" Philip asked as he tried to rise to see for himself.

"Lie still," Beatrice said, nudging him back to the ground. "Let me look at your wound."

"They are regrouping," Gilly said. He was peering down the ridge from one of the arrow slits in the wall. "There are five of them now. I'm afraid my arrows were not as true as they should have been."

"You did well, Gilly—" Philip said, but his words were cut off by more blinding pain as he tried again to see for himself. After a few moments he added, "We could not have survived without you, my friend."

Beatrice had gone to fetch her herb pouch from her saddlebag. When she returned, she knelt down and tenderly kissed Philip's forehead. "I must remove your tunic and mail," she said. "It will hurt."

He nodded. "I'm sorry . . . I did not kill Gareth."

"Hush, my love. It will be all right."

Then she began lifting away his clothing. Jagged edges of mail were embedded into his wound, and when she pried them away, the pain was so great he passed out. When he came to, he judged he'd only been out a few moments. Theo was beside him, and he and Beatrice were talking in low tones, unaware that he was awake.

"What will happen now?" Beatrice asked.

"They will wait us out, my lady," Theo said. "We have no water except what is left in our skins, a day's worth if we are careful. Gilly has no more arrows, and I have only a handful, but our enemies are out of range from here."

"We have been in worse fixes than this," Gilly said, still keeping watch at the arrow slit.

"Theo," rasped Philip, "take me to the wall. I can hold them off . . . while you three slip out the back. . . ."

"We leave together or not at all, Worm," Theo declared.

Philip licked his lips. They felt more parched than if he'd been in the desert for days without water. Even so, when Beatrice lifted a cup of water to his lips, he shook his head. "Not yet." Then he said to Theo, "I won't leave this place—"

"No!" cried Beatrice.

He grasped her hand weakly in his. "I have seen enough battle wounds to know when one is mortal. What is important now is for you to get away . . . with our child." His breath gave out, and it took a long, painful moment for him to catch it again.

"I won't let you die—" A sob cut through her words and she, too, had trouble getting her breath.

She tore away the hem of her chemise and packed the cloth into his wound to stanch the bleeding. He saw tears pour from her eyes as she worked. He wanted to hold her and comfort her. He wanted to tell her that he didn't mind dying knowing that part of him would live on in their child. He wanted to say so much, but his strength to even speak was ebbing quickly.

"Theo," she said, "I have not the skill to properly treat him. But those monks down the road where we rested yesterday—they would know what to do, wouldn't they?"

"Yes, they may have a healer among them," said Theo. "But—" He glanced toward the tower wall.

With as much vigor as he could muster, Philip said, "Tell her, Theo. I haven't got enough time for that. You must escape. I can . . . hold them off—" He tried to lift himself, but mocking his own words, he fell back helplessly.

"Theo," she said, "when the bleeding stops, pack the wound with this." She held out a small leather pouch.

"But, Lady Beatrice, you will do a much better job nursing him than I—"

"I must go, Theo—"

"No, Beatrice!" Philip groaned.

"It is the only way to end this," she insisted. "I must return to my husband. I think we both knew it had to eventually come to that. I never had the courage before, but now there is no choice. It is God's will."

"Curse God!" spat Philip, and his words were immediately followed by a terrible racking cough, so painful he knew it was he, not God, being cursed.

"I know you don't mean that," she whispered.

"Gareth will kill you," Philip implored, sputtering between coughs.

"I don't think so. Do you think he wants the world to know his wife betrayed him? That has always been his greatest weakness—caring what others think."

"I am so sorry . . ." Philip moaned.

"This way I will live; our child will live. That's all that matters now."

Philip was silent, trying to take it all in. He did not have the faith in Gareth that Beatrice seemed to have, even in his weakness. He wouldn't put it past Gareth to kill the child once he found out about it. Unless . . .

"I know I can't stop you," Philip said. "But—" He took a shuddering breath, each word an agony. "If you do this, then . . . you must find a way to make Gareth think the child is his. Having Gareth for a father would be better than growing up as I did."

"Philip!"

"You know *that* is the only way." Philip was glad he was about to die because it would have tormented him his whole life knowing his child would have such a father. At least the child would live and inherit Hawken. There would be some small triumph in that.

"I will do it," she promised. "And I ask of you an oath in return. If you must die, then I beg that you die in peace, Philip. Do not curse God, but embrace Him so that in the end you will know the peace that has eluded you all your life."

"That will make you happy?"

"Don't do it for me. Do it for yourself. God will know what is in your heart. Do it because if there is a small chance that we might see the kingdom of heaven, despite all our sins we will one day be together."

"All right—" Pain forced him into silence.

She bent and kissed his lips, then rose.

"Take your horse, my lady," Theo said.

"No, you will need the horses to get him to the monastery with all speed."

Philip tried to watch her go, but his eyes kept drooping shut. He heard Theo and Gilly bid her farewell and was certain she hugged both of them. He knew they were fashioning a flag of truce because he heard them talk as they did so. Gilly had ripped the sleeve from his tunic and they tied it to one of Theo's arrows.

"I love you, Beatrice," Philip called, even though his voice was barely audible. She knew anyway, just as he knew she loved him, else she would not have made such a sacrifice.

A long time passed in silence, and finally he could stand it no longer. "Is she there yet?"

"Yes," said Gilly. "They are talking. She must convince him to take her."

"I knew it!" Philip groaned. He scrabbled about on the ground again. Pain nearly blinding him, he managed to heave himself up onto his hands and knees. "Give me a bow! A bow!" he yelled.

"What are you talking about?" Gilly said. "Theo, he's out of his head."

"No-I'm-not!" Philip desperately bit each word out. The ground was undulating beneath him, and he knew he could not last long. "If he hurts her, I will kill him."

"You can barely lift yourself, much less a bow," Theo said. "Gilly will do it. He's the best shot."

"Don't miss," Philip said resignedly, falling back to the ground. Vaguely he remembered that Gareth and his men had been out of range. He must indeed be out of his head. Yet somehow he would have vengeance if Beatrice was harmed.

"You've said your brother is a fool," Gilly said. "Now I know the truth of it. Or Lady Beatrice is more cunning than I ever gave her credit for. Hawken has come up the ridge to meet her. He's in range now. Why don't I just pick him off for the fun of it?"

"No," Philip managed, reason finally penetrating his befuddled mind. "If something happens to Gareth, his men could turn around and kill her for spite."

"Ah, there they go, walking down the ridge," Gilly said with disappointment. "He's helping her onto his mount."

"I wonder what she said to convince him," Theo mused.

"It matters not as long as she is safe," said Philip.

"A flag of truce," Gareth said, striding up the ridge to meet her.

"They let me go," Beatrice said, "in return for their lives."

"What makes them think I want you?" Gareth sneered.

"You stayed in Palestine to rescue me, did you not?"

"Or to kill you!" He reached her, and she judged they were both within arrow range now. She knew Gilly or Theo would kill him if anything happened to her.

"Why, Gareth? Do you think I wanted to be abducted?"

"Put aside the guileless words, Beatrice. I know it was my brother who took you."

Those words were a blow. Her stomach lurched. But that also reminded her of what this was all about, of what mattered. Philip was right. Gareth must never know about the child.

"Yes, that is true," she said coolly. Desperation seemed to turn her blood into ice. "Amazing, isn't it, that he happened to be in Palestine at the same time we were? When he heard you were here he could not miss the chance to kill you. Taking me was only a side benefit, or as he quickly found out, a liability."

"I am to believe this all happened by mere chance? That the two of you didn't somehow concoct this entire farce?"

She laughed. "Gareth, you are jesting! You think I went willingly with him?"

"Why did he keep you, then?"

"To torment you, of course! I tried to make him believe that you cared for me and would rescue me and kill him."

"I spoke to people who saw you together. They did not think you were being coerced."

They had been careless, lost so in their happiness they had forgotten the danger they were in. But she made herself keep up the ruse. It was her only hope. "I had to seem willing in order to survive. Those men are brutes, Gareth, Philip de Tollard the worst of the lot. He is a violent, ruthless man. He beat me worse than . . . well, worse than I ever knew before I finally submitted. The bruises are only recently healed. Believe me, he is not the same man we knew in England."

"You never tried to escape?"

"I did once, but he proved how easily subdued I could be. After that, it was impossible. He watched me like a hawk."

Gareth said nothing for a short time as he considered this, then he asked the question she most dreaded. "Did he have his way with you?"

She, however, was prepared for it. She laughed again. "Do you know what the Saracens call him? Al-Rahib. It means 'the monk.'"

"I have heard this."

"Well, it is true. That is, it is true he does not like *women*."

"What!"

"It embarrasses me to even speak of it, Gareth." She tried to appear properly mortified at encroaching upon such an indelicate subject. "I will just say I saw things that made my toes curl."

"I find it hard to believe."

She parried with what she thought was her best bit of evidence. "Did he ever do anything in his youth to make you think otherwise?" She well remembered that Philip's fear of producing a bastard like himself had made him shy away from women when he was young. "I've tried to tell you he never touched me back in England. Now I know why."

Gareth rubbed his chin. "It could be so," he finally admitted.

She knew then she had convinced him. "Gareth, I know I don't deserve it, but I beg you to take me back. This dreadful experience has made me appreciate our marriage. I would come back to you in peace."

"In peace?"

"Yes." Despite her resolve, the words still nearly choked her. "I would be the submissive, caring wife I know now I should be. I would willingly perform all my duties toward you."

"All?"

"Yes, all."

"Then I accept you," he said without warmth, more as if sealing a business contract. "First, though, I must kill my brother." She didn't know what she had expected. But she hadn't expected those words.

"Gareth, don't!" she exclaimed, nearly spoiling her previous ruse. Quickly she added, "They have arrows trained upon us. If you make a move toward them, they will use them. Besides, Philip is mortally wounded. He said you inflicted the wound."

"Yes, I did."

"He was near death when I left. It is possible he is already dead. Let's just go, please, before one of us gets killed. We have a chance at a new life. Let us not throw it away. Let God's justice prevail rather than having your brother's blood on your hands."

He glanced up toward the tower. Following his line of sight, she saw through the arrow slit that an arrow was indeed knocked and ready to fire.

"As you wish, Beatrice. Perhaps this will be an end to violence."

He took her elbow in his hand to help her with the descent. She tried to find some tenderness in that touch, but all she felt was heat and the sweat from his palm.

B eatrice sat by the window of her solar gazing down on the garden below, her herb garden. Though a few plants had survived the winter, the annuals were all dry dead stems. Now was the time to plow and fertilize and sow seeds, but there would be no garden this year. Even if she weren't so great with child, she had not been allowed to leave the castle since her arrival there last winter.

She had faithfully kept up her end of her bargain with Gareth. She had done such a good job of it she was certain he believed the child she carried was truly his. For one thing, she admitted to him that she had indeed in the past sabotaged her ability to conceive by taking an herbal concoction—she was vague about what it was because, in truth, she knew of no herb for such a vile deed. It only mattered that he believed her, and that was mostly because he *wanted* to believe. He desired more than anything to have an heir.

It might have been easier for him to put her aside and wed another woman. Heaven knew he could have concocted countless reasons the Church would have accepted for an annulment. But the only thing more important to him than fathering an heir was the esteem in which his lord, Edward, held him. And Edward was now king of England. His father, Henry, had died last year while Edward was en route to England from Palestine.

Gareth well knew that King Edward and his queen, Eleanora, held

Beatrice in far greater esteem than they did him. If he labeled her an adulterer and divorced her, it would shock the royal couple and certainly expel Beatrice from their favor, but it would not raise Gareth any further in their favor. Only with Beatrice at his side could he remain in the close counsel of the new king.

Rather than accept the state of things and live in peace, Gareth chose otherwise. Beatrice now knew that Gareth would never change. He was a vindictive, hateful man. Instead of honoring Beatrice for the way she helped him curry the king's favor, he punished her. His beatings continued despite her condition. Once, early in her pregnancy, she nearly lost the baby when she went into premature labor after a particularly nasty beating. Thanks to Leticia physically interceding and taking a few blows herself, Gareth was stopped in time. Beatrice had to take to her bed for a month, and the child was saved.

Dear Leticia! She knew everything, though Beatrice had been reluctant to divulge who the babe's real father was. She had feared that would be the final insult to her pious maid. But when she finally did learn the truth, Leticia understood and wept with Beatrice over the loss of Philip.

"I believe your heart is pure, my lady," she had said. "And God knows your heart, as well. You have honestly repented. That is what matters."

"I truly have, Leticia. And I am trying to do what is right now." Rubbing a bruised arm, she added, "Gareth does not make it easy."

"God never promised that doing right would be easy."

"Aye, 'tis so," Beatrice said. "And I don't mind that it is hard—not really. God has truly been good to me despite all I have done. He has given me the gift of this child when He didn't have to give me anything."

"God does not give us gifts because we deserve them, my lady. Does not the Scripture say that when we were sinners, Christ died for us? I have heard so from the priest. I only hope that before Philip de Tollard died, he was able to grasp hold of this greatest gift. I pray for his immortal soul every day."

"That is good." Beatrice smiled. "Because I am sure he is not dead and therefore needs our prayers more than ever."

"But, Beatrice, you described his wound to me, that it was beyond your skills to heal—"

"I would know if he was dead," she said firmly.

She had come to accept that there would always be a deep connection between her and Philip; perhaps it even could be termed a spiritual bond. The child was an important link to that bond, yet it went beyond that, for the bond had never diminished, even after their nine-year separation.

Gareth, however, seemed the least of her problems after she finally came face-to-face with Clarise Aubernon, the old dowager. While Gareth had been in the Holy Lands, Clarise had gone north to spend time with a sister. When there, she had become quite ill.

Unfortunately, she had not died.

Beatrice had done her share of penance for that thought—for each time she had thought it, actually. But even God must realize that the woman was a scourge upon the world!

Clarise had been beside herself that she had been unable to be at Hawken to welcome her son home, but Gareth had gone north to visit with her for a month. Thankfully, Beatrice's condition saved her from making the journey. Finally the dowager had become well enough to travel, and she had arrived at Hawken a month ago.

Much to Beatrice's disappointment, the woman looked in the pink of health. The two women quickly fell back into their old roles as adversaries. However, the dowager increased the intensity of her vehemence during their first private conversation.

"My son told me of your . . . ah . . . adventures in Outremer," Clarise said. She had come to Beatrice's solar, where Beatrice spent most of her time now, fearing that too much activity would bring back the problems Gareth's beating had caused earlier.

"It was quite an ordeal," Beatrice said. She reclined on the chaise while the dowager took a chair provided by Leticia, who was immediately afterward ordered by the dowager to leave the room.

"Don't think you can get away with that drivel with me, my dear," the woman said in her usual icy tone when they were alone.

"Whatever do you mean?" But Beatrice knew it would be impossible to fool this woman with her ruse.

"I know the whelp in your womb is not my son's."

"You know nothing!" Beatrice retorted. Not a soul in England knew except Leticia, and Beatrice knew her maid would take the secret with her to her grave. The dowager was only speculating.

"For seven years you could conceive nothing," sneered the woman, "then after two months cavorting about with that bastard de Tollard, you make peace with my son, and miracle of miracles, you are suddenly with child? And, please, don't pawn off upon me that hogwash about taking herbs to prevent yourself from conceiving. I know how those concoctions work. Along with removing the fetus, they make the mother grievously ill, often mortally so. You have never been that ill."

Beatrice tried to get in a word, but Clarise barged on.

"Next, when you birth the little whelp, I suppose you will try to convince us that it is two months early?"

Beatrice felt the blood drain from her face. That was exactly her plan. She had wondered the entire time about the irony of having to tell so many lies in order to do God's will. But what else could she do?

"I see I am right," Clarise said smugly.

"You can prove nothing." Beatrice tried to grasp the edge of the cliff she knew she was approaching. "Gareth has accepted the child as his. He even sent a message to King Edward in France, telling him not only of my safe return to England but also of the blessed event to come. The king has agreed to be the babe's godfather. Will you ruin your son by revealing your *suspicions?*"

Clarise was silent, and for a brief instant Beatrice thought she had won. She had put up a strong offense—or was it a defense?—against the old dowager and was victorious.

But her elation lasted only a moment.

"You are right," the dowager said. "Too much rides upon your good favor with the king. You have not won, though! Mark my words, I will not have your little bastard, especially the son of that misbegotten devil de Tollard, inherit Hawken. Do you understand? *It will not happen.*"

The child stirred within Beatrice as if trembling at the lethal quality of the woman's words. Beatrice's heart skipped a beat, but she managed to say with a hint of pluck, "You'll have to deal with Gareth regarding that."

"My son will do what I say." Clarise rose and strode to the chamber door, where she stopped and added, "If it is a girl, I may suffer the whelp to live. But a boy shall not draw a second breath."

It utterly shocked Beatrice that one could be so evil. "You would not commit murder. You would hang."

"Oh, you poor deluded thing! Do you think anyone would know? It would be simply another poor infant to die in childbirth."

Her lips twitched into what Beatrice supposed was a grin, although a poor imitation of one.

"Be careful, my dear, or the mother may die in childbirth, as well. All would grieve for your loss, and your husband's place at Court would not suffer. Hmm . . . I don't even need to wait for your confinement, do I? You best watch what you eat. You just never know of what I am capable."

Had Beatrice not been reclining, she was certain she would have collapsed the moment the woman exited. As it was, the room spun and bile rose in her throat.

Leticia found Beatrice unconscious a few moments later.

When her mistress came to and told Leticia what had happened, there was no question in the maid's mind what must be done. She had to get her mistress out of the castle as soon as possible. She went to the stables, saddled two horses, and hid them in a back stall. But when she returned to Beatrice's solar to help her pack, she found two Hawken knights stationed at the door.

"What is the meaning of this?" she asked haughtily.

"A threat has been made against Lady Hawken's life," said one of the knights.

Leticia blinked. What was the old woman's game? "By whom?" she asked.

"I know not. I was ordered to guard the lady's solar and allow no one in or out under pain of death—my death, if you please."

"Good. I am glad my mistress is well protected." Leticia stepped toward the door, but the knights moved to block her.

"As I said, miss, we are to allow no one admittance except the dowager and Lord Hawken."

"I am her maid. I must tend her."

"The dowager said if you were to seek admittance, I was to send you to her."

With a sinking heart, Leticia went to the dowager's chamber, where she was told she was no longer in the employ of Hawken and must leave the premises immediately. She had until Vespers, which were nearly upon them, to pack her belongings and leave. Leticia begged to be able to bid her mistress good-bye, but she was refused. She was also told that should she attempt a rescue or even hint to anyone that Beatrice was being held against her will, Lady Hawken's life would be forfeited.

Leticia went to the village, where she had several friends. She was welcomed to stay in the home of the Cubbins, the miller and his wife. When asked what had happened at the castle she told the tale the dowager had instructed her to tell: she was accused of stealing one of the dowager's brooches, but because of her years of faithful service, the lord would release her from her duties rather than put any of them through the public embarrassment of a trial.

Idonea Cubbin did not believe for a moment that her old friend Leticia was capable of stealing. Unable to ferret the truth from Leticia, though, she welcomed her and said no more.

Leticia spent her days after that trying to think of some way to free her mistress. She did much of this thinking at St. Bartholomew's, on her knees.

As was the dowager's wish, Beatrice now lived in fear. For the first two days she hardly ate for fear of poison, but she had to give the child sustenance, so she plotted a plan whereby she required her guards to taste her food. She convinced them that it was their duty to protect her. She would have been inconsolable if either of them were to die, but they didn't. The dowager was far more devious than that.

Even Clarise was taken aback by a surprise visit by the king and queen. They stopped for one night on their way to London from France. They were, in fact, just returning to England from the Crusade, having tarried in France, visiting their fiefdoms and paying a state visit to the newly crowned King Philip.

Beatrice had to be given the appearance of freedom during this time, though she knew her every move was watched except for one brief half hour.

When the queen of England approached the guards at Beatrice's solar, they could hardly refuse her.

"Your Majesty, how kind of you to come see me," said Beatrice, offering Eleanora a seat on the chaise.

"You sit there, Beatrice," said the queen. "I well know how it feels to be six months with child." Since it was actually closer to eight for Beatrice, she appreciated the chaise all that much more. "Sit and put your feet up," Eleanora continued. "Indeed, you look quite pale and thin. I was told about the threats made against you. Who could be so vile?"

"We know not, my lady, though it may be a loved one of someone I treated who did not survive." This was the story Clarise had put forth, and Beatrice was compelled to promote it.

"You mustn't let it get you down." Eleanora pulled her chair close to the chaise that Beatrice now occupied. "It appears you are well protected."

"I am." How tempted Beatrice was to tell the queen everything! She was tired of all the lies. But Clarise would find a way to twist the truth to her advantage. She would make Eleanora believe Beatrice had lost her mind or something equally awful. However, she felt certain this meeting alone with Eleanora was not a mere chance.

Beatrice had been praying with great intensity since that confrontation with the dowager. She was trying to place her fate in God's hands. The dowager thought Beatrice was totally alone and powerless, not knowing that Beatrice's faith had grown greatly of late. She was not alone, for no matter how that cruel woman tried to isolate her, she could not keep God out.

"If the king knew who was making these threats," said Eleanora, "he would deal with the matter."

"We don't know, though, and I do not want any innocents to suffer."

"Do not forget, Edward still owes you a debt. He has not forgotten how you saved his life in Outremer."

Beatrice had not forgotten either. In Outremer she'd had no interest in seeking the king's boon. But she'd had a strong and persistent thought lately, one she had tried without success to wipe from her mind. She fantasized about Philip coming to rescue her. Oh, it was a foolish fancy, yet she believed that only he could do it, should God choose to use him, of course. If he lived, though, Philip was banned from the country.

Suddenly Beatrice knew what the greater purpose was of this unexpected visit with the queen.

"My lady, I never thought I would take advantage of the king's offer," said Beatrice, "but perhaps there is a favor I could ask. May I tell you, and will you judge if it is worthy to be presented to the king?"

"Yes, Beatrice, you may tell me."

"What if there was a man accused of serious crimes and exiled from the country—"

"What crimes?"

"Murder, Your Majesty. I hasten to add that he was falsely accused. Yet to return to this country would mean he'd be under penalty of death."

"This is a man of your acquaintance?" Eleanora leaned forward. "A relative, mayhap?"

Suddenly Beatrice realized how foolish she was. Philip was dead, and even if he lived, she must never see him again. Whyever would God use him to rescue her? He who had joined her in terrible sin? But only he would have the will to stand against the evil of Clarise and Gareth in order to save their child. Even if Beatrice told the truth to Eleanora, the pious queen would never be free to support an adulteress no matter how repentant she was.

"Beatrice, do go on," prompted the queen.

"No, it is silliness."

"Were you thinking that upon your request, the king might pardon this . . . ah . . . cousin of yours?"

"He is not a cousin." Beatrice had to be at least that honest. "He is a friend. But it was foolish of me to even think such a thing."

"You say he is innocent."

"I would stake my very life on it."

"Mayhap I will speak to the king. He will not abide such injustice. What is the man's name so that His Highness can look into the matter?"

Oh, what a mess that would be if the king started asking questions about Philip! It would be very soon afterward that Beatrice would suffer a fatal "accident."

"I am sorry to bother you about such a foolish matter," Beatrice said. "It was of no consequence, really. A silly fancy, as I said. I was merely reading a story, and I didn't like what the king in the story did, so I wondered what a real king would do. You see I made the whole thing up. I am so sorry." Now the dowager would have no trouble at all convincing the queen that Beatrice was insane.

Eleanora peered at her intently. Then she said lightly, "Women in your condition do have many silly fancies, don't they?"

They talked about other matters for a time, and then Eleanora left. The king and queen departed Hawken the next day before Beatrice rose from her sleep, so she did not see them again for a long time.

However, that night before she went to bed, she asked God to forgive her for her foolish indiscretion.

"God, though I try not to, I still love him. I need him; I want him. It is definitely for the best that he can't return to England. I fear I would run to him again. I am that weak. But, dear Lord, I beg you to do something, send someone to rescue me. I cannot live like this much longer!"

52

P hilip did not die that day in the Templar tower, but it was a long time
before he was grateful he had survived.

Slowly he healed from his wound at the St. Euthymius Monastery, though
he was not a model patient. Half the time he so wished he were dead that he
rebelled against the monks' treatment. The other half he was just confused,
wanting to grasp something better but afraid to do so. His friends, at one
point, had tried to confront him with the oath he'd made to Beatrice.

"Even she realized God would know my heart in the matter," he had
argued.

"She wanted you to have peace," countered Theo.

"In death."

"Bah!" threw in Gilly. "Now that you live by God's grace, you would spit
in His face? You are the most factious, miserable, damnable—"

"Ahem!" interjected the monk, Brother Elias, who had cared for Philip and
seldom had left his side since he had been carried there, more dead than
alive.

"Well, brother," said Gilly in a defensive but calmer tone, "would you have
him ruin all your work by slitting his own throat?"

"I am not going to kill myself," Philip insisted, still argumentative because
he had to convince himself as much as them.

"Not by your own hand," said Theo. "But do you eat?"

"I'm not hungry."

"Do you take the tonic Brother Elias prepares for you?"

"It tastes like cow dung."

"When have you ever tasted cow dung?" Gilly challenged.

"Your stew would qualify!"

"Why, you—"

"Please, good sirs," Brother Elias interrupted quietly. "I see I was mistaken in thinking your friends might help lift your spirits."

"So that's why they have suddenly appeared," Philip said. "I thought when you left here a week ago, I'd seen the last of you. I thought you'd be long gone to Cathay by now."

"That was your dream," said Theo, "not ours. We only left when we knew you would heal because, well—pardon me, Brother—we are not the kind of men who fit readily into the life of a monastery. We have been waiting in Jerusalem these last few weeks."

"Waiting for what?"

"For you, you dolt!" burst in Gilly. "Waiting for you to heal and move on. Do you think we'd abandon you?"

"You should have moved on," said Philip in an apologetic tone. He didn't want them to think he was entirely ungrateful. "Surely you can see I am no fit companion."

"What does that mean?" asked Theo.

"Nothing."

He'd been fully prepared to make his peace with God and die. Of a truth, he'd done just that, as he'd promised Beatrice, though he now would not admit it to his friends or to the monks. In a way he felt that once again God had not kept His part of the bargain, and he wanted no public admission until he sorted out what it had really meant. A deathbed confession? Or something that transcended that?

He went on, "Look, Brother Elias says my wound continues to fester. I may yet die. I can no longer hold you to any oaths of loyalty."

"I am afraid it is not so easy to rid yourself of friends," said Theo.

Out of the corner of his eye, Philip saw the monk smile.

"I see that." Suddenly overcome with fatigue, Philip lay back on his bed and closed his eyes.

What could a man do with such friends? It was very hard to keep saying he'd been abandoned and rejected all his life when, in truth, for the last nine years he'd been given companions more faithful, more loyal, than many men could claim.

Quietly he murmured, "I did make my peace with God." Opening his eye a crack, he saw the monk's brow arch and the looks of astonishment on his friends' faces. "I thought Beatrice could have been right, that it might be my only chance for true peace. I had never been able to find it in any other way. However, when I was not dead the next morning, I wondered what would happen next. Maybe I expected too much." He looked at the monk. "Brother, should there not have been . . . I don't know, some flash of heavenly light? A vision, perhaps? A quaking of the earth? All I felt instead was the deep heaviness of my grief. I felt no joy, no peace. Only grief and emptiness. Is that all God has to offer me? I know I am only a miserable bastard, but could He not just once give me a good gift?"

"You have had no good gifts from God, my son?"

Philip felt foolish as he looked at his friends. He felt as if the gently spoken question was an admonition. "Somehow I have always had eyes only for the bad things," he admitted.

"It is the way of men, I am afraid."

"Brother Elias, how do I get peace, then?"

"By surrendering to God."

"I already did that. At least I thought I had. I did what I had heard priests say I should do. I confessed my sins and repented. But still no peace."

"Look deeper, Philip," said Brother Elias, "beyond your grief and loss. Peace is not a substitute for these things. In truth, you cannot truly know peace unless you know grief and loss. And don't expect that it will make these things vanish, either."

"Then what good is it?"

"When you have it, you will know the answer to that question."

"I think you are speaking in riddles."

"If you believe that, then your search is over. But if you think there might be truth to what I say, then your search begins. It is up to you."

"More riddles," groused Philip. He closed his eyes again. He was so tired. He felt like a man who was running his heart out but getting nowhere. The only thing he knew for certain was that he didn't want the search to end. He had nothing else left. Yes, he had friends, but even they could not fill the huge empty place inside him.

That's when he had decided to stay at St. Euthymius. He bid Theo and Gilly good-bye, assuring them that he would be all right. He was searching for something now instead of running away. Brother Elias called him a seeker and implied that was a good thing.

Now he had been at the monastery six months, and he had finally found his peace. As Elias had warned, or promised, he still ached inside when he thought about Beatrice and the child he would never see nor be able to claim. Beside the grief, though, there was something like a small light, a candle burning next to the dark place. He could explain it no better than that. He might wander in the darkness for a time, but he knew the candle flame would always be there to welcome him back. No matter what adversity he might encounter, the flame was always there to greet him. For the first time in his life he was neither alone nor rejected.

Of course this new peace of his had not yet been tested, for there was nothing more conducive to tranquillity than life in a monastery. His mail, his sword, his father's dagger were neatly packed away. Brother Elias had hinted on one or two occasions that he ought to begin thinking of disposing of these things. He could not, especially the dagger. He didn't think the weapons themselves were evil. He had known many good and pious men who were warriors. Whether he would again become a warrior he did not know. He wasn't a true knight; moreover he had never aspired to be a knight except as it would elevate his social position. Fighting had always come naturally to him—perhaps it had come far too naturally.

Was the life of a monk for him? Despite the tranquillity of the monastery, it was a rigorous, at times even grueling, existence. Up at midnight for prayers only to be awaked again for more prayers at Laudes, and finally to rise for the day with the sun at Prime. More prayer vigils through the day and usually two Masses, sometimes three, were interrupted by work in the vineyard or in the kitchens or scrubbing the halls. Hands simply were never idle.

The abbot of St. Euthymius had spoken to Philip several times about taking his vows. But this was an Orthodox monastery, and Philip considered himself a Latin Christian, since that was his upbringing. The abbot, however, would have been quite happy to convert a Latin to Orthodoxy.

It was neither the work nor the ideology that kept him from taking that most monumental step. Six months ago he had barely even believed in God. He certainly hadn't had a congenial relationship with Him. Was he ready to completely devote his life to the service of God? Or was he merely taking the easy path? He was safe here, but was that a proper reason for taking the vows?

He put the question to God on many occasions and never got past his unsettled feeling inside. Though Brother Elias would have been thrilled to have Philip as a true brother in Christ, even Elias had to admit it would be a mistake to proceed on this spiritual path without being completely sure.

One day Philip was in the vineyard, hoe in hand, breaking up a hard patch of earth so some vines could be transplanted from an area where the abbot wanted to build a new work shed. He was enjoying working the soil and began to wonder if the life of a farmer was after all his true calling. On the other hand, last week when he had been assigned to the kitchen, he had considered becoming a baker.

"Will I never find my proper place in this life?" he muttered. Then he smiled and thought of Brother Elias's more positive way to phrase it. "I am a seeker! Some day, perhaps, I'll be a finder!" But he thought he would never be arrogant enough to ever actually finish seeking.

"They've got him talking to himself, Theo! We are too late" came a voice a few paces away.

Spinning around, Philip grinned as he beheld his friends. His grin quickly faded as he noted the grim look on Theo's face.

"What else are we too late for?" the big man asked, eying Philip in his mud brown habit, with deep sleeves pulled back to allow freedom for handling the hoe.

His friend must not have noted that, though his beard was shaved, his red hair was merely tied back at the nape of his neck, not tonsured. Philip knew what Theo was thinking. Instead of quickly reassuring him, he set his tool against a stout vine, steepled his hands together in an attitude of prayer, and humbly bowed his head. "Peace to you, good sirs. I welcome you in the name of the Lord." It was not entirely an act with which to tease his friends. This was how the monks had taught him to receive outsiders.

"Please, Worm, don't tell me . . . You haven't . . . Are we . . ." Theo stammered.

Philip smiled. "Not yet."

Relief washed over Theo's face, and then it tensed with concern again. "Not yet?"

"Theo, it was you who encouraged me back to my faith."

"To make your peace with God, not to—" Theo swallowed and tried again. "I am sorry. It is only a shock to see you thus."

"I've been happy here, my friends."

"That's good, then," offered Gilly. He seemed far less shocked over the change in Philip.

"Let's go inside out of the heat," said Philip. He stepped between the two and put an arm around each. "I am pleased to see you. Have you been to Cathay, or perhaps only Persia? To France and back again?"

"We never left Palestine," Gilly said.

"Truly?"

"We hired on as mercenaries in King Hugh's army," Gilly explained. "It is easy duty—patrolling the roads for pilgrims, a skirmish or two with brigands."

They reached the main building, turned down a long cloister, and finally came to the refectory. It was too early for the midday meal, and the rule was strict against serving food at other times. Philip thought the greatest drawback to the monastic life was the spare meals served. When he regained his health and his appetite, he found he was always hungry. Brother Elias said the lean diet was to build godly character. Philip thought it was because the monastery was not as wealthy as it had once been in the height of crusader rule a hundred years ago.

Philip did manage to purloin a cup of beer for him and his guests. They sat at one of the long trestle tables.

"Tell me, what brings you this way?" Philip asked. "I know the king's rule does not extend this far south."

"No, it doesn't," said Theo. "Would it surprise you that much if we came merely for a social visit? It has been many months since we saw you last."

"I'm glad you've come," said Philip. "My friends are the only things I have missed during my stay here."

Gilly made one of his grunting noises, then said, "Theo, are you going to tell him why we have come?"

"Can we not socialize a bit first?" Theo retorted.

"We nearly broke our necks getting here in haste. Now you wish to drink beer and chat about the weather!"

Theo stared at his cup for a long moment. Finally he mumbled, "It's probably foolishness."

"I will tell him if you don't," Gilly threatened, then he went on without giving Theo a chance to do that very thing. "Lady Beatrice is in danger, and we must go to England to rescue her!"

Philip listened with a calm that surprised even him. Months ago he'd had to deal with his fear for Beatrice's safety. His greatest lesson from his time in the monastery was to learn to put her fate into God's hand.

"We always knew Gareth posed a danger to her," he said quietly. "But she was fairly certain he cared enough for his social position not to . . . harm her."

"This is different," Theo said.

"Theo had a dream," Gilly explained.

Giving Gilly a sour look, Theo added, "That is why I now feel so foolish. It was only a dream—"

"You told me it was so real you awoke in a cold sweat, gripping your sword and panting as if you'd actually done battle," cut in Gilly.

"Tell me this dream," said Philip, still in a quiet, calm tone. When Theo seemed reluctant, Philip added, "I have been around spiritual matters for months now. The monks have been known to have dreams and visions. I will not think you crazy, if that's what you fear."

"All right, but as I said, it was only a dream. Lady Beatrice was tied to a stake, as one might do to a heretic. Instead of flames at her feet, there were swarms of snakes—poisonous vipers! And she was holding a babe in her arms."

"The child is not due to come for another month or more," Philip said.

"I don't know about that. All I know is that she held an infant and was crying out for help. Other than the child, she was all alone—not even a crowd of spectators there to watch her die." Theo swallowed as he said the word *die*.

Philip knew his friends had grown fond of Beatrice, but only now did he realize that they cared almost as deeply for her as he did himself.

"She cried and screamed. No one came until Gilly and I galloped to the edge of this great snake pit and tried to get to her. We hacked and hacked at the snakes, but they never diminished in number."

"That's when she cried out your name," Gilly said, seeming to relish this part of the account. " 'Philip, please come!' she cried." He paused and glanced at Theo, who nodded for him to tell the rest. "Over and over she called your name, but you did not come, and we could not get to her."

"What happened then?" Philip's mouth had gone dry, and his serenity was slipping.

"I awoke," Theo said, "with sword in hand. As I said, I felt as if I'd truly been in a battle. Only by God's grace did I not hack off some innocent comrade's head in my sleep."

"Likely it would have been my head," said Gilly, "since I was on the pallet next to yours."

"Do you believe the dream was from God?" asked Philip.

"He did at first," answered Gilly. "That's why we deserted our post and hastened here."

"Halfway here my senses returned," said Theo. "I realized God would never send a dream to a reprobate like me."

"Yet still you came."

"We were bored with garrison life," Theo said, "and we were past due a visit with you." His explanation was not very convincing. He sat back, picked up his cup, and drained off half its contents before he finally admitted it. "I lie. Though I have no idea why such a dream would come to me, I have no doubt of the truth of the dream."

"Truth?" probed Philip. "Do you believe these things actually happened?" Though it was completely farfetched, he could not help a shudder at the very idea.

"It was a dream," Theo replied. "And as dreams do, it made little sense. Sometimes the infant had your face, but a moment later it had the cracked and chipped countenance of the Christ child on an ancient relief. Once, my face was on Gilly's body. At times our swords became snakes. The true part was the sense of danger, of impending doom."

"When did you have the dream?" Philip asked.

"A week ago. As I said, we came here as quickly as we could."

"Have you had the dream before?"

"That is what is odd about it. I have worried about Beatrice since she left us, but never before have I had such a dream. Why now, Philip?"

"I don't know," Philip murmured, feeling the old ache of grief rise up in him.

"She's in trouble," Gilly declared.

"She has always been in trouble," countered Philip.

"She is alone," said Theo.

Philip knew that Gareth had the ability to cut her off from friends and any who might be sympathetic toward her. He'd done it to some extent before. He could easily hold her prisoner in the castle. But why? How could that be to his advantage? What danger could she be in beyond his periodic beatings? It angered Philip to think of his brother striking Beatrice, yet no one in his right mind would storm a castle to rescue her. Not that he hadn't thought of doing it. He took some comfort in knowing that he had given her up into God's care.

"She has God," said Philip.

"And what if God would use you as the instrument to save her?" demanded Gilly.

Philip rubbed his hands over his face, feeling his tranquillity cracking and chipping away like old mortar. "Why would God send me back there, where almost certainly I would lack the strength not to sin again?"

"Because," said Theo, "only you have the will for such a perilous quest. Do you think it a coincidence that I have had this dream only as her time of confinement draws near? I think the danger has multiplied the closer the time comes to the child's birth."

"Why?"

"What if Gareth knows in his heart the babe is not his? What if he cannot accept it, hard as he has tried? What do you think he'd do then?"

"Oh, dear God!" groaned Philip.

"We still have time to get to England," said Gilly. "That is no coincidence!"

Philip asked his friends if they could leave him alone for a time, and then he went to the chapel. On his knees at the altar, he asked God for confirmation of this astounding dream. When nothing came, again no heavenly light, no shaking of the earth, not even a "still, small voice in his heart," he simply prayed for wisdom.

He remembered something Brother Elias had recently read from the Holy Scriptures. "Trust in the Lord with all thine heart and lean not unto thine own understanding. In all thy ways acknowledge him, and he shall direct thy paths."

Several hours passed before he left the chapel. His friends had grown worried, but he assured them that it was nothing for a monk to spend a few hours on one's knees. He had known one who had lain prostrate at the altar for two days seeking God's wisdom. He didn't mention that man had been himself.

"Do you know, then, what you will do?" asked Theo. He'd worn an uncomfortable look when Philip had said "it was nothing for a monk." He was still worried that Philip was ready to take vows. But Philip knew that he would not.

He replied, "I only know to walk and see where God leads."

He went to his tiny cell, still in the guest quarters. Theo and Gilly followed. There, Philip opened a small chest at the foot of his bed. With a sense of purpose he did not understand yet felt he must obey, he took out his mail, his sword, and his dagger. Nevertheless, when he slipped out of his coarse brown habit, he felt as if he were peeling away a layer of skin. The peace of the monastery would be a part of him that he would always miss, but he knew now he was not destined to hide there forever.

53

Beatrice found that it had been different when she chose to spend her days in her solar than it was now, being forced there as a virtual prisoner. Of course the biggest difference was that then she'd had Leticia. Now she was so alone. Add to her fear sheer boredom, and her misery was quite complete.

Her meals were brought to the guards, and one of them carried the tray into her room after tasting the food. But there were other mundane chores that needed to be dealt with—the linens aired, the chamber pot emptied, water for bathing changed, laundry. These were tasks previously handled by Leticia. And, though Beatrice was surely capable of carrying out these tasks herself, she decided to act the helpless noblewoman just to see how the dowager would solve the problem. She was surprised at the solution. On the fourth day of her captivity, the old manservant John came to the room carrying a pail of water he'd drawn from the cistern that served that floor of the keep.

"For you to bathe, my lady," he said. "I shall return when you are finished to take away your laundry and tidy up." He was very awkward. He was not accustomed to being a lady's maid.

Beatrice thanked him, and when he left, she used the water and a cloth to clean herself. She supposed it would be too much to hope for a bath in the big wooden tub. She had just tied the silk cord of the voluminous skirt she wore to cover her huge girth when there was a knock on the door. John entered when she gave him leave. He did his chores quietly and finished, seemingly as quickly as he could.

He came three days later to do the same. Although he was her husband's servant, Beatrice knew John was really the dowager's lackey. She sent him on all manner of errands and had him do unsavory tasks, such as dismiss unsatisfactory servants or dump the imprisoned lady's chamber pot. But he had always been kind to Beatrice. He was a soft-spoken man with impeccable manners. He was also rather ancient, having been with the family for at least thirty years. He had been the old lord's servant. Beatrice thought she'd heard that John had even gone on Crusade with the old Lord Hawken.

She knew John couldn't be trusted, but when he came next she was so desperate for diversion that she tried to engage him in conversation as he did his work.

"John, I heard you went to Outremer with the old lord. Is it true?"

"Aye, my lady."

"It's a fascinating country, isn't it?"

"I was happy to return home to England," he said as he swept under the bed. "I do not much like foreigners."

"But you were the foreigner, not the Saracens."

Pausing in his task, he knit his brow together while he considered her words. "Aye, I suppose you are right. But they have odd, unnatural ways."

"Was there nothing you liked over there?"

"Hmm, the fruit was nice. I'd never had an orange before." Gradually he seemed to lose some of his initial tension at being engaged in conversation by the lady of the house. "And you, my lady, what are your views of the place?"

"It was hot and dry and had so little greenery, unlike England." She sat down on the chaise, hoping the conversation would last awhile. "I did think the Saracens had odd ways, but did you know they consider *us* infidels?"

John sputtered. "How dare them!"

Beatrice smiled, then thought of a far more interesting question. "John, what was the old lord like?"

"Surely your husband speaks of him to you."

"Never. And when I have asked, he offers no response."

"Then mayhap I should say nothing, either."

"It would be a sad thing, John, for the man to be forgotten."

Finished with his sweeping, John began straightening the bed linens. He was silent for a few moments, then said, "I will never forget him. He was a courageous knight, a skilled warrior. I was proud to serve him. It's too bad—"

He stopped and returned his attention to fluffing a pillow.

"What is too bad, John?"

"Nothing, my lady." He set down the pillow. "There, that is the last of it. Is there anything else I can do for you, Lady Hawken, before I take my leave?"

She wanted to press him about the old lord, but she didn't want him to carry back to the dowager that she was trying to get information about the man.

"No, John. Thank you very much."

"I am at your service, my lady." Before he opened the door, he added, "I am sorry that you must be . . . ah . . . shut up like this, my lady."

"That is kind of you, John. Perhaps we will talk again when you return."

They did. He was not the most erudite of conversationalists, but he helped ease Beatrice's boredom. After two weeks of her captivity, he came one day, did his chores as usual, then came and stood very close to where she was reposed upon the chaise.

He spoke in an even more quiet tone than was his habit. "My lady, I have a daughter in the village. I go there periodically to visit her and my grandchildren. While there this past Sunday, I met a mutual acquaintance."

Beatrice creased her brow, perplexed. Surely they knew many villagers in common.

John reached his hand into his tunic and pulled out a parchment. "It was difficult for her to find the means to write this because such materials are not common among the villagers. Therefore, she cannot write often."

Beatrice hardly needed to ask whom it was from, since she recognized the hand in which the message had been written. She wanted to ask John many questions, but she could tell he was reluctant to speak so openly. He constantly looked over his shoulder to make sure the door was closed.

Clasping the letter to her chest, she breathed a heartfelt thanks.

John turned to leave. "The dowager does not own all of me, my lady."

Near tears, she nodded.

"Burn it as soon as you read it."

When she was alone she opened it and read:

> My lady, first be assured I am well, and I pray the same is true of you. Though I trust the bearer of this letter, I will not put in writing exactly where I am. There's no sense in publishing it abroad, though it may be no secret, in any case. I know not what I can do for you, but I pray about it daily. I fear to tell any of your plight because of certain threats. I know there is a way, and I will find it soon. In the meantime, do not despair. God is with you, and He will deliver you.
>
> All my love, L.

"Thank you, God!" Beatrice murmured.

How hard it was to put that precious missive to the flame, but she made herself do it. She didn't need the parchment to remind her that she wasn't as alone as she sometimes felt.

"Please, God! Help Leticia find a way to rescue me soon! It will be only weeks before my baby comes. Heavenly Father, please save us!"

Leticia felt the press of time, and with it the weight of helplessness. Soon the month of May flew by, and it came time for the shearing of the sheep. Leticia judged, by her best calculations, that Beatrice's babe would be due around the day of the Feast of the Nativity of St. John the Baptist or Midsummer Eve. That was now three weeks off.

Leticia had tried and tried to come up with a rescue plan. She thought she might take the risk of telling Father Bavent the story. He was fond of Beatrice and might have some ideas. He would also be constrained by the seal of confession to keep her revelation to himself. She was shocked when she made up her mind to go to St. Bartholomew's one day and found him gone, a new priest in his place. Apparently he'd been reassigned to a parish in Winchelsea and had gone immediately because of some pressing need. Leticia thought this most suspicious. She was certain the dowager's hand was in it. The woman was removing any possible allies Beatrice might have.

At least old John was proving useful. He hated what was being done to Lady Beatrice, and Leticia was certain he knew more than he admitted. He was the dowager's lackey, and the woman most likely trusted him enough to speak freely around him. But did the dowager realize how much the man hated her? He was only loyal to her because she held something over his head. What it was, Leticia never discovered.

Leticia was not satisfied being able to get the occasional message to Beatrice and to receive them, though it was comforting. There had to be something more she could do.

One evening at dusk, early in June, Leticia was returning home with a pail of water fetched at the village well. She reached the porch of the miller's house and, upon turning, saw a stranger approach. The miller's house was on the edge of the village with the woods behind it. It had proved to be a good place for Leticia to bide in relative seclusion. The stranger had come from the direction of the woods, and that alone struck fear into the woman, because thieves and brigands came from the woods. This man was huge, taller than any door lintels in the huts. He was not fat, being more like a towering oak than a barrel. He was dressed in a simple tunic of drab gray wool with a mail hauberk beneath. A sword was strapped at his side, and he led a horse that was not the finest beast but certainly a knight's destrier. His brown hair was curly and unkempt, and unlike many Englishmen, he wore a full beard. He looked fearsome, and though no one was about at this hour, she doubted any who saw him would have questioned him or stood in his path, as they would with any other stranger.

He came right to the miller's yard! Leticia nearly dropped the pail of water. She looked frantically about but knew she was alone. Will Cubbin was working late at the mill. Idonea and the children were down the lane visiting Will's sick mother. This stranger had chosen his time to approach wisely if he had mischief in mind.

The maid reminded herself that she had been to foreign lands! She had seen real Saracens! Oh, she had not come as close to them as her mistress, but she was not some sheltered woman to quake at the sight of a fell knight, even one such as this.

Sucking in a breath, she said, "M-may I h-help you?" Her voice cracked over the words.

"I look for a woman name Leticia," he said in poor but understandable English. His accent was French, Leticia thought. "I am told she be here, yes?"

His broken, uncouth manner of speaking seemed to take the edge off his fearsomeness, and it gave Leticia courage. "I am she." In her desire to appear brave she forgot that her presence here was somewhat of a secret and it might not be wise to blurt to a stranger who she was, but it was too late for that now.

"My name is Theobald LeFauve," he said.

"Pleased to make your acquaintance, good sir." Not knowing what else to say, she repeated, "May I help you?"

"I think we may help each other, eh?"

Though she didn't know what that meant, she welcomed him into the miller's house when he asked to speak privately with her. It was unseemly to be alone inside with a man such as this, and surely unwise, but she had a feeling he would not have taken no for a response. He tied his horse to a post and followed her.

He had to duck his head inside the house, but he moved with a certain grace surprising for a man his size, and he behaved politely. He sat at the trestle table, almost dwarfing the table that was large enough to seat all the Cubbin family and her.

"May I offer you a cup of water, or milk perhaps? We have some fresh."

She stood uncomfortably. Having been a servant all her life, she would never have dreamed to take her ease at table with a knight. At least she thought he was a knight and not a robber. By now a robber would have already murdered her and taken what little of value the Cubbins possessed. She reminded herself that he had asked specifically for her.

"No thank you, miss. Please sit. I have urgent matters to discuss with you."

"How do you know me?" Leticia asked, still nervously standing, although her curiosity was overcoming some of her fear.

"A fair lady spoke of you when I knew her in Outremer."

Her heart pattered quickly for a moment. She recalled now some of the things Beatrice had told her of her adventures after being abducted in Palestine. She'd been with Philip, of course, and there had been two other companions. A sharp-tongued small man and a man nearly as big as a tree with a tender spirit and gentle heart to match. Gilly and Theo!

"Good sir, is Philip de Tollard in England?"

"He is, miss."

The effect that news had on Leticia surprised her. Long ago she'd had a very high opinion of de Tollard because he had behaved honorably toward her mistress despite the fact that Beatrice had practically thrown herself at the young man. Leticia well knew how hard it was to resist Beatrice's demands, especially years ago when she had been young and spoiled. Lately, however, Leticia's estimation of the man should have plummeted, for he had in the end succumbed to temptation and despoiled Lady Beatrice. He should have shielded them both from sin, though Leticia understood that what had happened between Philip and Beatrice had not been a one-sided affair. Nevertheless, she should be annoyed at the man if not outraged.

But when she heard he was here, perhaps in the very wood by the village, her hope soared. She knew in the depths of her being that Philip dearly loved Beatrice and would move heaven and earth to save her.

She smiled at the big knight. "This is good news indeed. My lady has told me what a skilled knight de Tollard has become, and she says his companions match or better his prowess."

Beneath all the hair on the man's face she saw a smile twitch.

With total earnestness Theobald LeFauve said, "What skills we have are hers, Leticia. We three are pledged to sacrificing our very lives to save her."

"We will pray it doesn't come to that."

"I have never rescued a damsel in distress, so I plan for the first time to be successful."

"I like you, Sir Theobald."

"And I like you, miss," he replied sincerely. "The lady has spoken of her faithful maid, as well. I have a feeling we will work well together."

"But what shall we do? I have racked my mind and come up with nothing. I fear to tell anyone of Lady Beatrice's plight. Her husband's mother says if any learn of it, harm will come to my lady."

"Is not Lady Beatrice in good favor with the king?" asked Theo. "She once mentioned something about nursing him after the attempt on his life."

"I'm sure she was too modest. She saved the king's life, and no mistake. But if the king knew about her present circumstance what could he do? It might even go against her if he discovered she'd been unfaithful to her husband. It could come down to her word against Lord Hawken's. And regardless of the scoundrel Hawken is, he is, and has been for years, a faithful vassal of Edward's. The king would have no choice but to support Lord Hawken, even if his sympathies leaned toward Beatrice. The lord has enough power and influence to start another civil war should the king turn against him. The country has only just begun to heal from the last one. The king would avoid such a threat at all costs."

"Yes, that solution seemed too easy," said Theo with a sigh. "As we are only three men, storming the castle is out of the question. Some clandestine escape perhaps—"

"She is well guarded. One servant has been able to get messages back and forth, but at great risk. I've thought about bribing some guards, but Lord Hawken won't let that happen again, as when de Tollard escaped. The men on guard now are fiercely loyal to their lord. He's made sure of that."

"We have no money to make bribes anyway. Is there no one in the country who will stand up for her?"

"Not against Hawken. Only . . ."

When she hesitated, he prompted her. "What, Leticia?"

"It is too farfetched."

"I am afraid that at this point we have naught but the farfetched to aid us. Tell me what you are thinking."

"Years ago after the rebellion, the Cassley lands were forfeited because of Lord Cassley's support of the rebels. Lord Cassley, as you may not know, was Beatrice's father. Lord Hawken got control of the estate, but every Cassley knight refused to pledge his loyalty to Hawken." Theo leaned forward, his eyes glinting with interest. Leticia went on, "To a man, they chose self-imposed exile rather than join their liege lord's sworn enemy."

"What became of them?" Theo breathed the question with the awe of a man who suspects a treasure is close at hand.

"I have heard they are in Wales, in the service of Llewellyn, who of late has not been on friendly terms with King Edward."

"How many?"

"Only seven or so remained after the rebellion. Cassley was never a wealthy estate."

Theo laughed. "Oh, my dear woman, do you know what wonders we could do with seven knights!" He tried to temper his excitement with reason. "Would they aid Lady Beatrice?"

"Never were knights more loyal to their lord or his family!" Leticia declared proudly. She certainly felt as loyal to her old lord. "Chief among them was Sir Roland Leyburn. He would have happily led the Cassley knights in an attack upon Hawken eight years ago when Lady Beatrice was forced into the marriage to Hawken, but she forbade it. They would have been slaughtered, and there had already been too much bloodshed. They would help her now if they could be found."

"We will find them."

"But, Sir Theobald, what would prevent a slaughter now? Hawken still has three times that number of knights."

"Three to one? Is that all?" He grinned and rubbed his hands together. "I would call that a stroll down the lane."

Leticia looked at this man with wonder. She believed indeed that he alone might be worth ten men. Perhaps the small one and Philip de Tollard would take up the rest of the slack.

———

Two days later when John came for his regular cleaning, he had another parchment for Beatrice. She opened it, and in Leticia's hand were only three words.

He is here.

Joy surged through her. Even the babe in her womb seemed to leap for joy. Beatrice patted her swollen stomach. "Yes, my sweet little one, your father has come to rescue us!"

54

It was a cold and wet evening in the wood bordering the Hawken lands. Philip was exhausted. He'd just returned from a grueling hundred-league trek into the heart of Wales. He'd covered that round trip in six days, pushing himself and his horse past limits he'd not even imagined he had. His poor horse had been half dead when he had finally arrived, but fortunately he'd been able to exchange it for another mount at his destination, Llewellyn's stronghold. It took another day to round up the former Cassley knights. There were only five remaining, for two had died in the years since their exile. But all were willing to join him once he'd convinced him of who he was and of Beatrice's peril.

Among them was a stalwart man, Sir Roland Leyburn, who vaguely remembered Philip from his stint as groom at Cassley, though he might not have recognized Philip except that he'd shaved his beard at the monastery as an act of humility. That, with his red hair, helped his cause. And Sir Roland also knew of the events surrounding the death of Ralph Aubernon, the old lord. He knew Philip was a bitter enemy of the present Lord Hawken, and that was enough for Roland, who had nursed his own bitterness against the lord for eight long years. Roland might be grayer than Philip remembered, but he hadn't been idle in Wales, training vigorously and keeping fit.

When Philip arrived at the hidden camp in the woods, there was much jubilance. Gilly and Theo had been waiting impatiently for days, having remained behind so that Philip could travel all that much faster. They had fretted and worried that Philip might meet some catastrophe or return empty-handed. When Leticia heard Philip had returned, she came quickly so that she, too, could greet the Cassley men.

Now the planning began.

"With only eight men, we must use subtlety," stated Philip.

"There will be nine, if you please, my lord," put in Leticia.

Philip tried not to recoil at her persistent use of a title in referring to him, but he'd given up trying to correct her.

"That is, eight men and one woman," she added. "I will be going with you."

"That is out of the question," Theo said firmly.

"There will be much fighting," said Philip.

"Which is exactly why I must come. Who knows what condition my lady will be in? Someone must care for her while you men kill each other."

Philip had to concede the logic in that. Theo leaned toward him and whispered, "That is some woman, aye?"

"I can hear you, Sir Theobald," said Leticia.

"And do you mind a compliment?" Theo countered.

"Nay. I like them, truth be told." She smiled at Theo, and Philip could actually see a bit of pink rise in the skin above the big knight's beard.

"Please!" put in Gilly. "I care not if the woman comes or stays behind, but we need no distractions on this mission."

"He's right," said Philip, and both Theo and Gilly registered surprise at this rare event of Philip actually agreeing with Gilly.

"Don't worry about that," Theo gruffly assured. "Now, let's be planning. Will we use the old Trojan tactic?"

"I doubt there would be any way we could disguise you, my friend, and sneak you into the castle," said Philip. "Besides, who would we open the gates to since we have no army waiting outside? I propose we scale the wall by rope at night. In my day the north tower was always inadequately guarded. I see not why it should be any different today, for it backs upon a treacherous slope that is a deterrent against attack. Leticia, can your man inside the castle tell us if this is still so?"

"He might," she replied. "I wish I had paid attention to such things."

After plotting out as many other details of their plan as they could, Philip stretched out upon the ground, wrapped in his cloak, to attempt to sleep. The steady drizzle and the wet earth did not bother him as much as the anticipation of what lay ahead. Though every muscle in his body screamed with fatigue and he knew he must rest, he could not find sleep. He thought of everything that could go wrong. He thought of dying at the gates of Hawken knowing he'd failed to rescue Beatrice and their child. When he did snatch a few moments of sleep, he dreamed of wading through a sea of snakes toward the stake where Beatrice and the babe were held captive. He fought and fought to reach her but always failed.

Bleary-eyed, he faced the dawn. The rescue would be that very night. It would be the last without a moon for another month.

———————

Beatrice woke with a start shortly before dawn. She listened, thinking a noise had disturbed her sleep, but heard nothing save the usual night sounds of the castle. A short time later she realized what had awakened her. A pain shot through her abdomen.

"No!" she moaned.

Long moments passed before another pain assailed her. It couldn't be time! Philip was here. He was going to rescue her. The babe could not come now!

She remembered with her first babe she'd had some pains a good week before the birth. This must be what she was experiencing again, for the baby wasn't due for at least another week.

She rose from her bed and went to the window, where she sat on the ledge to watch dawn light the sky. Somewhere out there Philip was waiting for the right moment to come for her. She could not impede the rescue by being in the middle of labor. And she could not have the babe before he came. She might hide her early labor from the dowager for some time, but eventually the woman would know. And then she would come and murder the child.

Beatrice had waited for days for another parchment, but none had come. John said the dowager had heard that a stranger had been spotted in the village, and she suspected it might be an ally of Beatrice's. Could she possibly suspect that it was Philip and his friends? Beatrice had no doubt that Theo and Gilly were with Philip, and any one of these men would be hard-pressed to remain unidentified for long. Gareth would certainly recognize Theo and Gilly from a description. He had fought them on two occasions.

For the last two days John had been unable to leave the castle to exchange messages. He would try again today.

Around midday the pains stopped, and Beatrice breathed a sigh of relief.

Feeling her confidence return, she determined that if the child did come now, she would hide it from the dowager. She had heard of Bedouin women who birthed their babies without midwives in the desert. Remembering her screams with her first child, though, she realized how impossible it would be for her to deliver a babe in secret, yet she convinced herself she could do it. She would not scream. She could be brave; she could be strong for the life of her child.

When her supper was brought to her, the guard was none the wiser. But she could not eat. Then a terrible thing happened—she felt water flow down her legs. She knew then her labor could not be stopped.

"Why now, God?" she cried, collapsing in despair upon her bed.

Still, she determined to be brave. She took a thick satin cord from the drapery and bit down upon it when a pain came. She managed thus for some time, but as the sun sank in the western sky, a pain, harder than any previous ones, took her unawares, and she cried out.

The guard opened the door. "My lady, did you call?"

"No," she said, trying to make her voice sound normal, but the word trembled from her mouth.

"Are you all right?"

"Yes." Then another pain struck, and she could not prevent a yelp from escaping her lips.

"Is it your time?"

"No!" she screamed.

He didn't believe her. She knew what he would do after he shut her door. Frantically she scrambled from her bed even as another pain hit and doubled her over. She didn't know what to do or where to go, but her every instinct urged her to flee.

She was lying on the floor several minutes later when the door opened again and the dowager rushed in with a midwife at her heels.

"So it is time," said Clarise. She grasped one of Beatrice's arms while the midwife took the other, and they lifted her to the bed.

"No, just early labor," Beatrice said. Her lips were trembling so she could barely get the words out.

"I see the puddle on the floor," said the dowager. "It won't be long now."

"What do you want from me?" Beatrice pleaded. "I'll do anything . . . anything you ask, but please don't hurt my baby."

Ignoring her, the dowager said to the midwife, "Keep me informed. I want to know immediately when hard labor starts."

Beatrice was trapped. Maybe God was finally punishing her for her sin.

The night was deep and dark, and Philip well knew that at times like this darkness was a strong ally. There were eight rescuers crouched at the foot of the north tower of Hawken Castle. The ninth, one of the Cassley knights, waited in the wood about a half furlong away with the horses. If all went as planned, the rescuers would exit the castle by the main gate, where their horses would be waiting.

Now they had only to wait until the night was deep and the castle was soundly asleep. John had managed late that afternoon to bring them some good news. First he assured them that the north tower was indeed still neglected because it was deemed an unlikely place for attack, not that there had been much threat of any attack for the last eight years since the rebellion. There might be some extra alertness because of Beatrice's situation, but no doubt the lord of the castle was confident he had cut her off from all aid. The other piece of news was that the garrison of household knights was only about fifteen. Gareth had not yet been able to replace those knights lost in Outremer. Also, Gareth was in residence.

Philip had lost two prime opportunities to kill his brother in Palestine. Now he would likely be presented with another. But Philip no longer had a taste for blood. All he wanted was to get Beatrice to safety. He planned to take her to the priory to have her baby—their baby—and then she could live out her days there if she wished. He knew he could not have her. That was not why he had come to England. Nor had he come to England to kill his brother. Gareth would live and continue to be Beatrice's husband even if she remained always at the convent. Though she would never be free, she would be safe.

Theo came up beside him. "That's a long climb," he said, gazing up at the wall.

"Forty ells, if I remember aright."

"It is easier going down than up," Theo commented dryly. He had heard about Philip's escape descending this very wall almost ten years ago.

"Look—" Philip pointed. "There's the rope John secured for us. I feared he would not have time. I remember John from the old days. He seemed a sniveling, ingratiating sort, all but groveling before Lady Hawken, though he was my father's servant. I didn't like him much. I suppose I was wrong about him."

"People do change, don't they?"

Philip smiled. "It is possible." He looked around and saw they stood apart from the others. "One person who hasn't changed one hair is the good maid Leticia. Then, as now, a stalwart woman, and not hard to look upon, either, eh, Theo?"

"I hadn't noticed," Theo mumbled, obviously abashed. "I've been too intent on our mission."

"I could have sworn I saw you look in her direction at least ten times today."

Theo shrugged, apparently unable to form a riposte for the truth. "You choose an odd time to take an interest in my . . . ah . . . social situation."

"Perhaps I'd like to see one of us live, as in the troubadours' songs, happy for ever after."

Theo laid a hand on Philip's shoulder. "Ah, Worm. Life takes odd turns, does it not? But don't forget, we are hardly close to the 'ever after,' or the 'hereafter,' for that matter. Happiness may still come to you. You are young yet."

"I feel dreadfully old sometimes. But why do I complain? I have peace, contentment, even a certain joy. Happiness isn't necessary—" He stopped. He knew the words were drivel and would never convince Theo.

"Listen, Worm. Lord Hawken may die tonight; then your Beatrice would be free."

"Theo, I implore you, do not kill Gareth!" Philip said urgently. "Unless it is in defense of your life or another's. I will not have her that way. I have already pledged to God that I will not kill him, even to save my own life."

"That's foolishness!" Theo exclaimed, almost too loudly for comfort. He forced his tone lower. "There will be a deadly battle inside. You cannot give away your life like that."

"I must do this."

"Will you give everyone that order?"

"I will tell Gilly, because I think you both would be tempted, as I surely would be, to eliminate this obstacle to my happiness. Gareth's death in this manner would not make me happy. As for the others"—he looked over his shoulder at the Cassley knights—"I place them and their actions in God's hands."

In the distance they heard the faint sound of St. Bartholomew's bells chiming Matins. The hour had come.

55

Beatrice counted the long labor a blessing.

"It may be breech," the midwife said grimly.

That would mean death to mother and child. If the babe was going to die, Beatrice did not care to live, either. She could not bear to lose another child.

The midwife made her lie in various positions, hoping to change the child's presentation. It was torture for Beatrice, but she obeyed, for she had not the will to keeping fighting it. The babe would come. She could do nothing about it.

At long last she felt a fluttering in her stomach. The child had moved. The pains began with a relentless tattoo.

All but two had ascended the rope. Leticia was climbing now, with Theo still on the ground. He'd insisted on going last since he was the biggest. If the rope did not hold his weight, it would mean only one lost. Also, he wanted to be on the ground in case Leticia slipped so as to catch her or break her fall. As feared, she was having difficulty with the climb.

Roland, with two men holding him, leaned over the wall as far as he dared, reaching down a hand to grasp her as soon as she was within reach. Philip watched with held breath, at the same time keeping an eye upon the battlement. He saw the Hawken knight approach. Philip drew his sword, but

Gilly had seen the man first and leaped toward him, dagger in hand. Before the man could register a sound, his throat was slit.

Philip groaned inwardly. It had begun. By rights these were his knights, and now he must kill them. He vowed then and there that after this night he would put away his sword forever.

Finally Leticia was pulled over the rampart. Theo scrambled up easily, the stout rope holding his weight. The party of invaders stealthily and quickly made their way down the tower stairs. Philip estimated there would be two guards on the gate, two at the keep's main doors, and two more guarding Beatrice's door. That left eight asleep in the Great Hall. This was the household contingent. Also on guard would be a dozen or more knights upon the ramparts and towers, but even if an alarm was sounded, they would not leave their posts not knowing whether an assault was coming from outside.

Keeping to the shadows, they crossed the yard to the keep. While the others hid out of sight below, Theo ascended the keep stairs. It was a short but perilous journey because the steps were designed so that any who climbed them would have his sword arm against the wall and thus be impeded. But he didn't plan to use his sword.

"Halt!" ordered the guard.

There was only one outside, probably a couple more inside.

"Who are you? How did—?"

Gilly, having climbed the wood framing at the back of the stairs, seized the guard and held his dagger to the man's throat.

"Order them to open the doors," Theo said.

"Never! You'll have to kill me firs—" Gilly's dagger slipped between the man's ribs just as he was taking a breath to shout a warning.

Gilly and Theo, with their thick French accents, could not believably disguise their voices to give the order themselves, so one of the Cassley men climbed the steps.

"Unbar the door!" he cried in a voice amazingly like the dead guard's. "There is trouble outside."

Movement could be heard inside the keep. Men were being roused even as the bar grated. Philip's men hurried up the stairs and rushed in the moment the door opened. Philip saw Gilly slip the bar back in place to slow any reinforcements that might come. An instant later swords clashed.

"Push!" cried the midwife.

Through the tears that drenched her eyes, Beatrice saw the dowager standing at the midwife's shoulder. A large tub of water had been wheeled into the room. She knew it was not to be used for bathing the newborn, but she could not keep from pushing her baby into the evil world that awaited.

The lusty infant cries were a mockery of the inhospitable welcome awaiting it.

"A boy," announced the midwife.

"A pity," said the dowager.

Sounds filtered up to the chamber. Shouts, metal clanging. Philip was here. Beatrice had to buy time. But the dowager recognized the significance of the sounds, as well.

"So rescue has come," said Clarise, reaching out her hands for the child.

"Please!" cried Beatrice. "Don't . . . don't let my baby die in sin. G-give him last rites, I beg you!"

The midwife looked at the mistress. She was no doubt being well rewarded for her evil assistance, but was any reward worth sending an innocent infant into the depths of hell?

"It will only take a moment, my lady," the midwife said in a shaky voice.

"We only have a moment. Go ahead. Even a misbegotten whelp deserves that much."

The midwife held the child. In circumstances where a baby was not expected to live long enough to allow a priest to be called, a midwife had a dispensation to carry out the rite herself.

"In the name of the Father, the Son, and the Holy Spirit," said the midwife as she ran her thumb across the child's forehead in the shape of a cross. The babe bellowed again, as if insisting he was far from ready for last rites.

"May I hold him just once?" begged Beatrice. Was that footsteps on the stairs?

"Enough of this foolishness!" bellowed the dowager, growing anxious as the sounds below grew more intense. She grabbed the babe from the midwife's arms.

Philip could not believe his ears. Was that the cry of an infant? Of his son?

But he could give it no further thought, seeing Lord Hawken himself racing down the inner stairs, mail hastily donned, sword drawn. Philip was at the foot of the stair, already fighting two men at once. He'd been trying to clear a path so that Leticia, who was nearby, could get up the stair and reach Beatrice's chamber.

Theo appeared and engaged one of Philip's opponents. Philip had a moment to jump back a couple of steps as Gareth leaped over the side, halfway down, into the melee. He'd have done better to have continued all the way to the foot of the stair and block ascent. Philip's main concern was to clear a path to the stairs. Taking his time, stepping back and to the side gradually so that his opponents did not suspect his intent, he edged them away.

"Theo," Philip said with a quick jerk of his head toward Leticia. They had fought with each other long enough to need no more than that to communicate their wishes.

Theo quickly ran his blade through his opponent as if he'd needed but Philip's signal to quickly dispatch the man. He then raced toward the stairs. Gareth realized his mistake too late. Theo grabbed Leticia's hand, and they ran up the stairs. But two guards still stood at the solar door. They had been faithful to their assigned duty and had not joined the battle below. No doubt Gareth had made sure of that before he had descended the stair.

Philip was still parrying blow for blow with his brother. He'd seriously wounded the other man who was stretched out on the floor. "Gareth," he said as he dodged his brother's sword, "you can stop the killing now. Give me Beatrice."

"You'll never have her, bastard! She will always be my wife!"

"I don't want her that way. I only want her safe. I know what you plan to do to the baby. Don't do this unholy thing!" Philip begged.

"You have no right to judge what is holy," panted Gareth. "You ravished my wife. Now you will pay with the life of your bastard spawn."

"I deserve to die for my sins, but not the innocent babe!"

"No more talk!" Gareth swung his sword.

The blade thudded hard against Philip's mail at his side in the same place where Gareth had, less than a year ago, inflicted an almost mortal wound. The blow shuddered through Philip, and because the place was still tender, it nearly took his breath away. For an instant he lowered his guard, but instead of taking advantage of Philip's momentary vulnerability, Gareth took the opportunity to move closer to the stairs.

A quick glance assured Philip that Theo and Leticia had made it to the top. The sounds above indicated Theo had engaged the two guards.

Leticia inched toward the chamber door. Although Theo was fighting mightily against both guards, he had not been able to clear them completely from the door. She tried to keep calm, but from inside the room she could hear the cries of an infant. The babe had come. Was the dowager there? She must be.

One of the guards sliced Theo's arm with his blade. Blood spurted. Leticia gasped. She realized she felt a bit more fear for the big French knight than she did for the other invaders. She knew the heroic fool had said he would give his life to save Lady Beatrice, but she prayed mightily that God would spare him. The big bear of a man stirred emotions in her she had not felt since her beloved Allan had died.

Suddenly one of the guards stumbled back toward her. Almost without thought, she drew the dagger Theo had given her when they left the wood. Before she touched him, though, he crumpled at her feet. She wouldn't have had the strength to penetrate his mail anyway. The door was now clear, and Theo was fighting the remaining guard several paces away.

Leticia laid her hand on the latch and flung it open. She was greeted with what could have been a Satanic ritual, though, of course, she'd never actually seen one. It seemed like something drawn from stories of the ancient Druids.

The old dowager held the babe in her hands poised over a basin of water.

Leticia stopped dead, fearing any sudden move might spell the end for the baby.

"My lady dowager," Leticia said, trying to still the tremor in her voice while at the same time forcing respect to her tone. "Don't do this thing. There are witnesses now. You will be tried and executed."

"Do you think I care?" sneered the old woman. "All that matters is that de Tollard's whelp will never have Hawken."

"We could make an agreement that it would never happen," reasoned Leticia. Glancing toward the bed, she saw that Beatrice was lying quite still, unconscious or—no, she could not be dead!

"That is not good enough." The woman's arms lowered.

At that moment Theo burst into the room like a raging bull. He charged and collided with the dowager. The basin of water overturned with a crash, a flood of water hitting the floor. The midwife ducked out of the way and, crouching upon the floor, whimpered.

As Theo and the dowager tumbled to the floor, Leticia leaped forward and caught the babe as it slipped from the old woman's grasp.

Several Hawken knights lay sprawled upon the floor of the great hall. Two or three Cassley men were dead or wounded, as well. Gilly was fighting with one arm, the other spurting blood at the wrist. His hand was gone.

Somehow Philip and Gareth were fighting in an isolated corner. Philip had not wanted it to come to this, brother against brother. A fight surely to the death. He heard the cries of his child upstairs—blessed cries! It meant the babe was still alive. Philip found it harder to uphold his oath to God about giving his life rather than killing Gareth. He desperately desired to be a father to his child, to give to the babe what he had never had, even if he could not be a husband to the mother. He could have it all with one sure stroke of his blade. He could see Gareth was weakening. He had never been the swordsman Philip had become.

One stroke and Philip could have what he rightly deserved. One sure stroke!

Then Gareth stumbled over a fallen candlestick. He kept his feet but lowered his guard. The warrior's instinct made Philip instantly take advantage of his opponent's weak moment. He swung his blade, clipped Gareth's hand, and his brother's sword flew to the floor even as he crumpled to one knee.

Something other than a knight's instinct stayed Philip's hand from inflicting the deathblow he was poised to do. At the last moment he drew back so the tip of his blade rested upon his brother's throat.

"It's over, Gareth. Call off what remains of your men."

"Not while I live!" Gareth cried with contempt. Only Gareth could have a sword pointed at his throat and still feel contempt for the victor. "Kill me or admit defeat," Gareth taunted.

Philip lowered his sword. In an instant Gareth pulled his short sword from its scabbard. As Gareth lunged toward his brother, Philip let his broadsword slip from his fingers. The weapon thudded into the rushes, and he knew he would be true to his oath.

A shout rang out just over his shoulder.

"For Cassley!" came the cry. Before Philip could think, react, or even blink, Sir Roland had leaped toward them, his blade flying in a lethal arc.

That quickly, Gareth was dead. Sir Roland stood over his body, panting, gasping, full of blood lust.

"For my lord," the old knight growled.

Philip turned away and vomited. He'd seen much death in his life, but that wasn't what sickened him now. Gareth was his brother. Half of their blood came from the same source—from a father whose love neither of them had been able to win.

56

A ssured that the battle was over, Philip raced up the stairs, taking two at a time. He paused at the top, realizing he knew not which was Beatrice's chamber. Quickly, however, he spied a door gaping open and ran toward it.

In the room he first saw Leticia seated on the edge of the bed, holding the babe. Philip's eyes immediately shot to the occupant of the bed. Beatrice lay there so still. His heart clutched inside him.

"She is not—?" he gasped. He could not even voice the final, awful word.

"No," said Leticia. "She fainted."

He looked closer and saw the gentle rise and fall of her chest. Leaning over the bed, he brushed away a damp strand of her hair. Her eyes opened.

"You are here," she breathed.

"I am."

"We have a son."

"Thank you for keeping him safe," Philip said.

"It was Leticia and Theo . . ." Her eyes fluttered shut. "I am so tired."

"Rest then, my love. And know that the boy is now Lord of Hawken."

From a corner of the room there came a shuddering cry. Philip turned and saw Theo holding the dowager captive, his arms around the struggling old woman.

"I am sorry about your son, my lady," said Philip to her with quiet sincerity. She only spat in his direction.

"Philip, my friend," said Theo, "can you find some cord that I may use to bind this one? I can bear no more of her clawing."

Philip did as he was bid and gently but securely bound the dowager's hands. "I wonder what will become of her," Philip mused.

"The old shrew deserves to be hanged," hissed Leticia in a rare high dudgeon.

"No murder has been done here today," Philip said.

"You murdered my son!" accused the dowager.

"I did not," Philip said. "He died as a knight protecting his fief. It was not by my hand, nor did my father die by my hand. But you know that, don't you, my lady? Regardless, it is over now. As soon as the king gives his counsel, I feel certain you will be allowed to go free, to a convent of your choice, where you may live out your days in service to God."

To Theo, he added, "Take her to her chamber and lock her within. It is not good for the child to be exposed to such venom."

After Theo had removed the dowager, Philip returned his attention to the mother and child.

"Would you like to hold him, my lord?" asked Leticia.

"I am clumsy," Philip replied, quaking for the first time that day. "I will harm him."

"You will never harm our child," said Beatrice. "Take him in your arms as your father never held you. Take him; love him."

Philip held out his arms, and Leticia placed a tiny bundle in them. He wept as he looked down into the sweet face. He thought he'd known what love was with Beatrice, but this was inexplicable. Beatrice he'd known and desired for years; he'd only that instant looked upon this little life. Such love and pride swelled his heart that he could not fully fathom it. He would die for this child. He would live for this child!

He smiled as he noted a small tuft of auburn on the boy's head. "Ah, my poor son, you have my red hair! I hope you have some of my good attributes to make up for it. And all of your mother's!"

"I have not thought of a name," said Beatrice.

"I would have a name that has not been known in either of our families," said Philip. "Something entirely new as a symbol of the new hope and the new lives that lie before us. But his surname should be my father's—Aubernon. He has rightly come by it."

"As have you, Philip."

"Perhaps, but I will not take the title. I would that it pass directly to . . . young Hugh. I have been blessed far beyond what I have ever dreamed and could not wish for more."

"Hugh . . ." she said thoughtfully. "I like it. How did you choose it?"

"I had a friend named Hugh. He once gave me some very good advice. If only I'd heeded it sooner." He thought of Pippin's last words and still did not understand why they had been directed at him, but he was certain the ex-monk had been given some final heavenly insight in his last moments. Philip murmured, " 'Seek ye first the kingdom of God, and all these things shall be added unto you.' "

He grasped Beatrice's hand and said, "By my oath, I pledge to you and to God that I will spend my life doing just that, seeking Him."

"Philip," Beatrice said, smiling through her fatigue, "let us have done with oaths. Let it be enough that we both simply do our best to serve our Lord, for we know better than any that we are only human and can fail so easily. Yet we also know of the great mercy of God."

"Ah, my Beatrice! So lovely, so wise!" Philip smiled, also, this time the joy not only reaching into his eyes but lighting them, as well.

EPILOGUE

P hilip and Beatrice attended a wedding a month later but not their own. Though Philip did not want his child to live as a bastard any longer than necessary, he desired all the questions regarding the recent events at Hawken and those of nine years ago to be sorted out by the king before he wed.

The wedding was for Theo and Leticia. They married at St. Bartholomew's in a huge festive celebration, with all the village, all the household staff at Cassley, and most at Hawken in attendance. Many of the Hawken people chose to stay on even after the death of their lord and the departure of his mother. Indeed, many were thrilled to work under the new master of Hawken and his parents. His mother they already knew to be a kind and generous lady, and the lad's father was quickly showing himself to be fair and honorable.

Philip and Gilly stood up for the groom. Gilly's wound was on the mend, and thanks to Beatrice's skillful treatment, he avoided losing his whole arm. His skills were still superior to many two-handed knights, and he proved an able instructor to the young squires that came to Hawken for training. But he had little other opportunity to use his battle prowess because the Hawken lands knew many years of peace.

The old dowager was sent to a convent to live out her days in the north of England near where she had been born. She died two years later, still bitter and unrepentant for her deeds. The sisters at the convent had to do much penance for their lack of sorrow at her passing.

It was not for several months that the king and queen were finally made aware of the entire story of these events. Upon the servant John's testimony regarding the death of the old Lord Hawken, the king bestowed upon Philip a full pardon and would have given him his rightful title except that Philip still refused it.

"Well," said Edward, "I can't have the father of one of my most powerful lords have no honor at all." He thought for a moment, then impulsively said, "Kneel, Philip." Philip obeyed. Edward drew his sword and touched the flat of the blade to each of Philip's shoulders. "By God's grace I dub thee knight, Sir Philip Aubernon."

Philip smiled a secret smile at Beatrice, who stood near. He knew without doubt he already had all the honor he desired and more than he deserved. He was even more completely aware of that when, on Christmas Day in the year of our Lord 1273, he finally wed Beatrice. The infant lord bawled through the whole ceremony, but to Philip's ears it was music fit for a Mass. It reminded him that by God's grace his child would not be a bastard. He would know, his whole life, the embrace of a loving family.